The Fate
A Tale Of Stirring Times

by

G. P. R. James

The Fate
A Tale Of Stirring Times
by G. P. R. James

Copyright © 2024

All Rights reserved.

ISBN: 978-93-61420-61-0

Published by

DOUBLE 9 BOOKS

2/13-B, Ansari Road
Daryaganj, New Delhi – 110002
info@double9books.com
www.double9books.com
Tel. 011-40042856

This book is under public domain

ABOUT THE AUTHOR

George Payne Rainsford James, a London-born novelist and historian, was born on August 9, 1799, and died on June 9, 1860. He served as the British Consul for a long time in a number of locations across the continent and in the United States. During the final years of William IV's reign, he was the honorary British Historiographer Royal. In 1799, George Payne Rainsford James was born in London's Hanover Square on St. George Street. His father was a doctor who had been in the navy and had fought alongside Benedict Arnold in the Battle of Groton Heights in America during the Revolutionary War. James went to the Putney school run by Reverend William Carmalt. He became passionate in learning new languages, such as Arabic, Persian, Greek, and Latin. When he was younger, he also studied medicine, but his preferences took him in a different way. His father, who had served in the navy himself, opposed his desire to enlist, which ultimately led to him being able to enlist in the army. James was injured in a minor battle after the Battle of Waterloo and remained in the army for a brief period of time during the Hundred Days as a lieutenant.

CONTENTS

PREFACE

Change of scene I believe to be as invigorating to the mind as change of air is to the body, refreshing the weary and exhausted powers, and affording a stimulus which prompts to activity of thought. To a writer of fiction, especially, the change may be necessary, not only on account of the benefits to be derived by his own mind from the invigorating effects of a new atmosphere, but also on account of the fresh thoughts suggested by the different circumstances in which he is placed.

We are curiously-constructed creatures, not unlike the mere brute creation in many of our propensities; and the old adage, that "custom is a second nature," is quite as applicable to the mind as to the body. If we ride a horse along a road to which he is accustomed, he will generally make a little struggle to stop at a house where his master has been in the habit of calling, or to turn up a by-lane through which he has frequently gone. The mind, too, especially of an author, has its houses of call and by-lanes in plenty; and, so long as it is in familiar scenes, it will have a strong hankering for its accustomed roads and pleasant halting-places. Every object around us is a sort of bough from which we gather our ideas; and it is very well, now and then, to pluck the apples of another garden, of a flavor different from our own.

Whether I have in any degree benefited by the change from one side of the Atlantic to the other--a change much greater when morally than when physically considered--it is not for me to say; but I trust that, at all events, the work which is to follow these pages will not show that I have in any degree or in any way suffered from my visit to and residence in America. I have written it with interest in the characters portrayed and the events detailed; and I humbly desire--without even venturing to hope--that I may succeed in communicating some portion of the same interest to my readers.

A good deal of laudatory matter has been written upon the landscape-painting propensities of the author; and one reviewer, writing in Blackwood's Magazine, has comprehended and pointed out what has always been one of that author's especial objects in describing mere scenes of inanimate nature. In the following pages I have indulged very little in descriptions of this kind; but here, as every where else, I have ever endeavored to treat the picture of any particular place or scene with a reference to man's heart, or mind, or fate--his thoughts, his feelings, his destiny--and to bring forth, as it were, the latent sympathies between human and mere material nature. There is, to my mind, a likeness (a shadowing forth--a symbolism) in all the infinite variations which we see around us in the external world, to the changeful ideas, sensations, sentiments--as infinite and as varied--of the world of human life; and I can not think that the scenes I have visited, or the sights that I have seen, in this portion of the earth--the richness, the beauty, the grandeur, the sublimity--can have been without influence upon myself; can have left the pages of nature here a sealed book to one who has studied their bright, mysterious characters so diligently in other lands.

Nay, more, I have met with much, in social life, well calculated to expand the heart, as well as to elevate the mind, which I should be ungrateful not to mention--kindness, hospitality, friendship, where I had no claim, and enlightened intercourse with powerful minds, in which I expected much, and found much more.

Sweet and ineffaceable impressions, ye can not have served to deaden the feelings or to obscure the intellect!

I will rest, then, in hope that this work, the first which I have commenced and completed in America, may not be worse than its many literary brethren, and merely pray that it may be better. Let the critics say, Amen!

G. P. R. James.

Stockbridge, Massachusetts, 30th July, 1851.

CHAPTER I

There is no mistake more common among historians, no mistake more mischievous, than to take for granted, without deduction, all the statements of the satirists and splenetics of past-by ages as to the manners and customs of their own times, and of the people with whom they mingled. There are half a dozen, at least, of the pleasant little passions of human nature which lead men, especially men of letters, to decry their companions, their friends, and their neighbors--nay, even their countrymen and their country. To say nothing of "envy, hatred, malice, and all uncharitableness"--sins common enough to be wisely prayed against--pride, vanity, and levity point the pen, direct the words, or furnish forth a little drop of gall to every man who is giving an account of the times in which he lives and the country in which he dwells, for those who are living or to live at a distance of space or time from himself. It is pleasant to place our own brightness on a dark back-ground; and the all but universal propensity of mankind to caricature derives an extraordinary zest in its exercise, when, by rendering others around us contemptible or odious, we can bring out our own characters in bolder relief. But there are other, perhaps even meaner motives still, which induce men frequently to portray their own times in broad and distorted sketches. The faculty of admiration is a very rare one; the faculty of just appreciation a rarer one still; but every one loves to laugh; every one feels himself elevated by the contemplation of absurdities in others. There is a vain fondness for the grotesque lurking in the bosoms of most men; and a consciousness that sly or even gross satire, and delicate or coarse caricature, are the best means of giving pleasure to the great mass of mankind, is probably one reason why we find such depreciatory exaggeration in the writings of all those who have given pictures of their own times. The letters of Petrarch, the statements of Hollingshed, the pictures of Hogarth, the romances of Smollett and Fielding, all furnish, it is true, certain sketches of their own times from which we can derive some valuable information, but so distorted by passion, by prejudice, by a satirical spirit, or a love of the ridiculous, that the portrait can be no more relied upon, in its details, than Bunbury's caricature of a Cantab for the general appearance of Cambridge scholars.

To give such pictures is mischievous in itself; but I can not help thinking that for an historian to follow them without allowance is more mischievous still. If there be a deviation on either side--though any deviation should be avoided, if possible--surely it would be better for every moral object to paint the past more bright rather than more foul, as the past alone contains the just objects of imitation, though we may emulate contemporary virtue or aspire to ideal perfection in the future.

Truth--plain, simple truth, with such reflections upon the verities of the past as may tend to benefit mankind in the present and the future, forms all that the historian can desire; but he might as well hope to draw truth from the pages of the satirists of any age, as a future portrait painter might represent Lord John Russell or Lord Brougham from the caricatures in Punch, where a certain likeness is kept up, but every peculiarity is exaggerated with the grossest extravagance.

I enter my caveat against the picture given of the state of England in the year 1685 by Mr. Macaulay, in his great and fanciful historical work, and especially against that part of it which refers to the English country gentlemen of those times, and to the English country clergy. That such men did exist as those from which he has drawn his statement, there can be no doubt; that they did exist in a greater proportion than at present, there can be no doubt either; but that the great mass were such as he has represented, may be very safely denied. Pickwicks, and Tupmans, and Winkles are full of truth; but society is not made up of these; and the reign of Victoria would appear very ill in history if, by misfortune, it should have for its future historian one inclined to paint the state of England in 1850 from similar sources to those which have been pressed into the service of Mr. Macaulay.

Nor does his reasoning afford any support to his statements; for, when important elements are left out of calculation, the result can never be admitted. Thus, when he says, "A country gentleman who witnessed the revolution was probably in receipt of about a fourth part of the rent which his acres now yield to his posterity. He was, therefore, as compared with his posterity, a poor man, and was generally under the necessity of residing with little interruption on his estate." The historian forgets to state what was the comparative value of money at the period he speaks of, and therefore can not draw as a fair inference from the amount of rent, that the country gentleman of those days was condemned by poverty to perpetual seclusion in the country, which is, in fact, what he attempts to show. The tastes, the habits of a country gentleman of that period kept him probably more in the country; but it was not poverty. Even in the eighteenth century, we find gentlemen of an estate producing two thousand pounds a year keeping a pack of hounds without burdening their property, and every true picture of country life which has descended to us shows that the country gentlemen in general lived more at their ease than the same class in the present day, and were as numerous in proportion to the population. If their enjoyments were not so refined, it was because the age was not so refined; and though the picture of Squire Alworthy may be a pleasing exaggeration on the one hand, that of Squire Western is an unpleasant caricature on the other, while the truth lay between, and a multitude of country gentlemen existed of a very fair degree of polish, without all the refined virtues of the one or the brutal coarseness of the other.

CHAPTER II

On the borders of Lincolnshire stood an old building, which had preserved the name given to it more than two centuries before, though the purpose which had given significance and propriety to that name had passed away. It was a long, tall edifice of stone, somewhat like the body of a church, and, as if to give it more resemblance still to a religious edifice, another building had been added to the end of the first, a story higher, and having some resemblance to a tower. This additional part was built of brick; but moss and lichen had reduced both stone and brick to very nearly one color; for though, when viewed nearer, a variety of hues were to be discovered in the cryptogamous vegetation which covered the walls, at a distance the general tint was a brownish gray. The windows in the longer portion of the building were placed in pointed arches, somewhat rudely and carelessly decorated; those in the taller and newer portion were, on the contrary, generally square, with a stone label above them, though some had that flattened arch peculiarly characteristic of the worst Tudor architecture. The whole building was not very large, and it was clear, at first sight, that the long portion was devoted to barns, stables, cart-houses, &c., while the other was separated for human habitation. At the distance of some sixty or seventy yards from the house, a long triple row of old elms topped a high bank, affording nesting-place for innumerable rooks; and a little, clear stream, not unconscious of trout, ran babbling along, mixing its melody with the music of the birds. A stone wall, breast high, and in some decay, encircled the whole, with two large uncouth posts ornamented with fragments of urns, giving entrance, unimpeded by any gate between them, to any one who might wish to approach the front door of the dwelling-house. There probably had been a gate there once, for some iron work on the posts seemed to show that they had been intended to support something; but if so, the gate had long been gone--made into pikes in the civil war for aught I know.

The scene around this old house, when viewed from the top of the bank, was desolate enough. A wide, fenny piece of uninclosed land stretched out far toward the north and east, only interrupted at the distance of some three miles by an undulating rise of woodland. But, nevertheless, the coloring was often fine, especially on autumnal evenings, when the moor assumed a solemn, intense blue tint, and the pools and distant river gleamed like rubies in the rich light of the setting sun.

On the other side, behind the house, the country had a more cheerful look, with some well-cultivated fields sloping up, as the land rose to the west, and many a knoll and gentle wave, and scattered trees, with a thicker wood beyond, while sweeping away southward were hedgerows and a hamlet here and there, the tower of a village church, and the chimneys of a distant manor-house.

Such was the aspect of the building and the scene around it; and now let us say a word of its history and its name.

In former years, when Plantagenet was the royal name of England, when popes were powerful in the land, and it was sinful to eat beef on Friday, among the best fed and best taught people of the country were the abbots and priors of the various monasteries, who somehow, notwithstanding vigil, prayer, and fasting--nay, even occasionally vows of voluntary poverty--got fat, prosperous, and wealthy. Large domains had these good men, and productive fields, besides tithes and dues of various sorts, which were usually paid in kind. As the abbot, and the abbot's bailiff, and other officers made their little profit upon the sale of such commodities as they did not consume; and as, in a benevolent and Christian spirit, they took good heed to have plentiful stores laid up to aid the people in time of scarcity, it was requisite that they should be provided with barns and garners to preserve the fruits of the earth which they received. These barns were called granges, and very often had a small farm attached to them. The masonry of the edifice was generally solid, and the style of the architecture in some degree ecclesiastical. When the grange was built near the abbey, it usually stood by itself, without any dwelling-house attached; but when it was at a distance, on one of the abbey farms, as was frequently the case, a good mansion for grieve or farmer was often added by the care of the monks; and a farmer who had pretty daughters, or brewed good beer, generally contrived to get very comfortably accommodated.

The house I have been describing was still called The Grange, and such as I have stated had been its original destination. The long building had been the real grange or barn of a neighboring abbey; the taller building had been added afterward for the convenience of the abbot's bailiff. When the monasteries were suppressed by the arch plunderer Henry VIII., we all know how many and how great were those who shared in the pickings of the defunct fowl of Rome. The Grange and the farm attached to it fell to the lot of a nobleman in the neighborhood, together with much other valuable property. He bestowed it upon a younger son; and from that younger son it had descended in unbroken line to its present possessor. The fortunes of the house had varied considerably; some had proved gamblers, some had been soldiers, some had been profuse, some penurious, some had even made love matches, and now the farm, and the house, and the family were all in a state not very prosperous, not very disastrous, somewhere between decay and preservation. It was lucky, indeed, that the owner thereof had but one son, for, had he been blessed with as many babes as a curate, there might have been some danger of a dearth in the pantry. As it was, he could afford comforts--an occasional bottle even of claret. Punch was a frequent accessory to digestion, and good sound ale, which would have done honor to any Cambridge audit, was never wanting for a friend or a poor man.

The owner of that house, however, was a man of a peculiar disposition, which prevented him from enjoying as much as he might have done the favorable position in which fate had placed him. I do not mean to say that he was of a discontented mood, nor that he was precisely a melancholy man. He was whimsical, somewhat cynical, and certain it is he had always the art, though a good and kind man at heart, of discovering the bad or ridiculous side of every thing. He was a learned man withal, and could often fit an occasion with a quaint quotation, often twisted considerably from its just application, but always serving his own purpose very well. He had passed a long time at the University, and gained odd habits and some distinction. He had then suddenly married a very beautiful woman of good family and small fortune. For her sake he determined to exert himself, to strive with the crowd for honors and distinctions, to place her in the same position in which his ancestors and hers had stood. For this purpose he went to the bar, around which he had been indolently buzzing for some time previous. He was engaged in one cause: circumstances favored him; the senior counsel was taken ill; the weight, the responsibility fell upon the junior, but with them the opportunity. He made a brilliant speech, a powerful argument, carried the court and jury along with him, and saved his client from fine and imprisonment.

Then came the heaviest blow of his life. His wife died and left him with one infant. The law was thrown up; the object of ambition was gone; all his old habits returned, more wrinkled and stiff than ever. He retired to his small property at The Grange; and there he had lived ever since, cultivating his acres and his oddities. But let us venture within the old walls, and see the proprietor in his glory.

Mark the knocker as you pass, reader--that great truncheon of iron, I mean, suspended by a ring surrounded by a marvelously cut plate of steel, with a large boss at the lower part, just beneath the obtuse end of the hammer. The door, too, is worth a look, with oak enough in it to build a modern house. Then we come to a low passage, none of the widest, and diminished in space by two chairs with tall backs, each back having round rods or bars joining the two sides together, ornamented with round, movable pieces of wood, which may be rattled from side to side, and resemble exactly those upon the curious machine with which in popular schools we teach the infant mind to count, now that we have discarded nature's original numeration table furnished by our own ten fingers. Between the chairs, in order not to leave space for intruders to pass too readily, is a suit of complete armor, somewhat rusty, while on the other side are three cuirasses and three steel caps, with sundry pikes, swords, and gauntlets, arranged with some taste and garnished with much dust and many cobwebs.

Now, take care! There is a step--not up, but down; for the floor is made to accommodate the ground, not the ground leveled to accommodate the floor. Then this small door on the left hand, with sundry names and capital letters carved in it with a penknife, to prove the universality of idle habits in all ages and countries, leads into the room where we would be.

But, ere we enter, let us take a glance around.

Seated at a small table, near a fire, with one foot resting on the massive carved brass dog's head which ornaments the end of the andiron, at the imminent risk of burning the slipper, and with the other drawn up under his chair--which, by-the-way, was as tall and stiff-backed as a corporal of dragoons, and would have been a most uncomfortable seat had it not been well cushioned and partially covered with Genoa velvet--sat a gentleman of perhaps five-and-fifty years of age. He wore his own gray hair, though wigs were even then beginning to domineer over the crown, and the somewhat slovenly easiness of his whole apparel forbade the supposition that he would have ever consented to embarrass his cranium with a load of horsehair only fitted to stew the brains of the wearer into an unintellectual mass of jelly. He had upon his back a brocade dressing-gown, which might have been handsome at some former epoch--say twenty years before;

but which, though not actually dirty, was faded, and though not actually ragged, was patched. He wore stockings of gray thread, and breeches of a chocolate color, and by some antipathy between the waistband thereof and the fawn-colored silk waistcoat above, a large portion of that part of his shirt which covered the pit of his stomach was exposed to view; but then that shirt was of the very finest and cleanest linen. Every man has somewhere a point of coxcombry about him, and fine linen was his weak spot. The ruffles and the cravat were of lawn, and white as snow.

On the table before him was a large candle, shedding its light upon an open book; and ever and anon, as he read, he raised one finger and rubbed a spot a little above the temple, which, by long labor of the same kind, he had contrived to render quite bald.

The room was by no means a large one, and the ceiling was of black oak, which rendered its appearance even smaller than the reality; but the greater part of three sides was covered with book-cases, and an immense number of curious and antiquated pieces of furniture encumbered the floor. The chairs were of all sizes and all descriptions then in use; the tables were as numerous and as various as the chairs. The latter, moreover, were loaded with large glass tankards, curious specimens of Delftware--some exceedingly coarse in material and coloring, but remarkable in device or ornament--richly-covered wooden-bound books, strange daggers, and fragments of goldsmith's work, with one or two pieces of China and enamel of great value, besides coins and small pictures inestimable in the eyes of an antiquary. The large center-table was tolerably clear, for supper-time was approaching, and on it he took his frugal evening meal, although he had a dining-room on the other side of the passage, furnished with the most remarkable simplicity, and paved with hard flag-stones. It was enough for him, however, to be disturbed once a day; and he visited what was called the eating hall no oftener.

This elderly gentleman, however, was not the only tenant of the room. On the other side, as far as he could get from the fire--for the evening, though in early spring, was by no means cold--sat the son of the master of the house, a young man of about one-and-twenty years of age. The father might have been pronounced a good-looking man, had he taken any care of his personal appearance; but the son had inherited his mother's beauty, with a more manly character; and although youth was still very evident, though the mustache was scant and downy, and the face fair and unwrinkled, there was a good deal of thoughtful decision about the eyes, and a world of resolute firmness about the mouth and chin.

He, too, was reading; and sometimes the book beneath his eyes excited a smile, sometimes engaged his attention deeply, but more frequently his mind seemed to wander from the page. He would fall into deep fits of thought; he would play with a knife which lay beside him; but, more often still, he raised his eyes, and fixed them anxiously, thoughtfully upon his father's face. It seemed as if there was something working in his mind to which he wished to give utterance, and it was not long before he spoke; but let us reserve what followed for another chapter. It affected too much the fate and the immediate course of the personages before us to be treated briefly at the end of a mere descriptive passage.

CHAPTER III

The father looked up from his book, and closed it with a slap, saying, "'Et tamen alter, si fecisset idem, caderet sub judice morum.' It is a bad book, and if another had written it he would have been put in the stocks or whipped at the cart's tail. But this man will get fame, and honor, and wealth by it; not that I am affected by the 'tristitia de bonis alienis.' Each man should rejoice when he sees a worthy neighbor successful, even if he may detect some flaw or fault in his performances, for envy is the basest and most destructive of passions. 'Nulla pestis humano generi pluris stetit;' but when one sees a man of some ability direct all his efforts to produce that which can only work evil to his fellow-creatures, gild vice, decorate folly, and corroborate falsehood, and yet be lauded and rewarded, it does excite anger, and produces a sad conviction of the unworthiness of our kind."

This was not a very auspicious commencement of the conversation to which the young man was looking with some anxiety for an opening to propound certain schemes and purposes of his own. Nevertheless, it was some satisfaction to him that his father had left off reading, for that was an occupation not to be interrupted; and he hastened to make a reply, in hopes that some turn would afford the opportunity he desired.

"Bad books are sometimes very useful, I think, sir," he said, with a good-humored smile.

"Ever in paradoxes, Ralph!" said his father "how may they be useful, boy?"

"By giving better men than their authors occasion to refute them," replied Ralph; "not that I mean to say"--he continued, knowing the peculiar argumentative character of his father's mind--"that the mere refutation would be sufficient, for that would leave matters just where they were before" (his father waved his hand), "but because, in the act of refutation, a thousand new arguments would be drawn forth in favor of truth and right, which might not occur to the multitude if no controversy ever elicited them."

"You have not put your case as strongly as you might have done, Ralph," replied his father; "complete refutation would not absolutely leave matters exactly where they were before. It is with a truth, with a principle, as with a sword-blade: its strength can not be fully known till it is tried. True, the strength, whatever it is, remains the same, but to those who have to use it, the trial adds confidence. It is not of half as much importance to be armed with a good sword as to have one and know that it is good from having proved it. The abstract truth of any proposition remains the same, whether it be assailed and defended or not; but the question before us involves another element, namely, the effect of the assault and defense upon the minds of men; and therefore, as you say, books assailing truth may sometimes be useful by calling forth a complete vindication of the truth. But the man who writes them is equally culpable; for even were we to admit that he might desire to establish truth more firmly by calling forth a strong defense, he would fall into the offense of promulgating falsehood with the knowledge that it was false, and truth refuses to be served by deceit."

He paused for the moment, and his son carefully abstained from furnishing new matter for subtle arguments, well knowing that his father had no mercy upon hobby-horses.

At length the old gentleman laid his hand, smilingly, upon the tome, saying, "I do not suppose that you intend to refute this work, Ralph: first, because I imagine that you do not know what it is, and, next, because I have remarked any thing but a vaulting ambition in you, my dear boy; indeed, perhaps too little. Now,

'Ambire semper stulta confidentia est,
Ambire nunquam deses arrogantia est,'

as has been said, in not the sweetest Latin that ever flowed--"

"Your pardon, dear father," replied Ralph, "I am very ambitious; not, indeed, of refuting the book of any author, living or dead; that I leave to you, in every way fitted for the task, if falsehood be the opponent. But anxious am I--most anxious, 'ambire palmam,' on the great stage of human life. To speak straightforwardly, I have been thinking for some time of asking your permission to go forth and try my fortune on a wider stage. I think I have not done ill at Cambridge" (the father nodded his head approvingly); "but yet none of the paths which a collegiate life opens to a man have temptations for me, and I would fain see whether I can not carve out one for myself."

"What, at the court?" asked the father, shaking his head; "Ralph, Ralph, you forget the means, and know not half the expenses which a court life requires even before the slightest advantage can be gained. With the rich and the courtly, only the rich and the courtly find favor. 'Sus sui, canis cani, bos bovi, et asinus asino, pulcherrimus videtur.'"

"Oh no!" cried Ralph, "no courtly life for me, sir. Some powerful friends I may need, but those I know you can procure me; for not only they who are connected with you by blood, but they also who have had the stronger bond of personal friendship with you in former years, will assuredly value your recommendation too highly to slight your son. As to means, the small sum I receive from my college, and a part of what you were kind enough to allow me there, will be ample."

His father shook his head with a somewhat doubtful air, and asked, "But if you should fail, Ralph?"

"I can but return here," said the young man, "and matters will be just where they were before."

"You are fond of that phrase, Ralph," replied his father, "but you are mistaken--all are mistaken who use it; nothing that has passed through any change is ever the same as it was before. There is always something gained or something lost. It will be so with you; and who shall say, in all the various complexities of circumstance and character, of accident and conduct, which life in the great world implies, how the balance may incline when you visit this old dwelling again."

He fell into deep thought after uttering the last words, and his son would not disturb his revery; for the ice was broken, the first announcement made, and he was very certain of gaining his point in the end. Oh how eagerly did the youth long for the attainment of that point! What was it that attracted him so strongly? No truant disposition; no idle weariness of the spot where his ancestors had dwelt; no gilded dreams of sport and pleasure; no overcolored picture of the world's brightness. But it offered him hope; one small spark of that sacred fire, the extinction of which is death. He felt within him strong energies; he had proved somewhat severely his own abilities; he had a great purpose before him, a strong passion to lead him, and all he wanted was hope and opportunity. He dared not tell his father all that was in his heart, for there is a cold mist about age in which the flame of hope will hardly burn; and if prescience were equal to experience, youth would never struggle on so far and overcome so much, for want of sunshine on the way.

The father sat gazing thoughtfully into the fire; the son remained with his head leaning on his hand, till both started at a sharp rap upon the door of the house from the heavy iron knocker which I have mentioned.

There was, indeed, no need of starting, for both knew they were to have a visitor that night, to taste a bowl of punch and chat over the affairs of the country round. But they had been so deeply involved in personal feelings that they had forgotten the flight of time, and the guest was upon them ere either was aware that the usual hour of his visit on a Wednesday night was actually come.

The father buttoned up a portion of his waist coat, and drew on again a slipper which, under the pressure of cogitation, he had kicked off his foot. The son put straight several of the chairs, which somehow or another had got into a state of confusion; and in the mean while was heard a sound, such as might have proceeded from a seal new caught scrambling about in the bottom of a boat, but which, in reality, was caused by the movement through the passage of a short, fin-legged maid-servant, eager to open the door without delay to his reverence the parson, of whose weekly visitation she had been more mindful than her master. Hardly two minutes elapsed after the stroke upon the outer door when that of the little library opened, and not one visitor, but two, presented themselves, and both bedecked with cassocks.

I can not but regret the rubbing of the face off the coin wherever I see it in society. I love local color; I love class costume, though not class interests, however they may be disguised. Every profession, every calling, honorably exercised, is honorable, and there is nothing so vain as the vanity, nothing so pitiful as the pride which would conceal any external indication of a position we have no right to be ashamed of occupying. The Norman peasant girl, in love with her immemorial white cap, would feel herself degraded were you to dress her head up in hat and feathers. The New Haven fish-wife has an honest pride in her yellow petticoat. The doctor in former times could still be known by red roquelaur and gold-headed cane; the divine by the garments of his order. The soldier aped not the civilian, nor the civilian the soldier; each ship carried its own colors, and could be known by those that sailed by it. I see not those inconveniences of the system, which have produced a change in our day. However, in the times of which I write, each parson could be known by his clerical garments; and both the two gentlemen who now entered were evidently churchmen, though very different both in appearance and demeanor from each other.

The first was a fat, rosy personage, in a bran new cassock, glossy and black as a raven's wing. In personal appearance he was no mean representative of the old friar, wanting, however, the shaven crown and the bare feet. The glance he gave around the room had just such a degree of strangeness in it as might imply that he was not a frequent visitor there, though not altogether unknown.

The second was an older man, perhaps sixty years of age, tall, pale, and thin, with garments well worn, yet whole and decent. His hands, though they not unfrequently held the spade in his own garden, were peculiarly fine and delicate, and his face had seemingly been very handsome in early life.

Now, from the time of the suppression of monasteries and the reformation of the Church of England under Henry VIII. (if reformation that movement could be called which took place under the wife-slayer) to the present day, some five or six complete revolutions have occurred in the state and character of the clergy of Great Britain. Those are now living who remember one or two. By a very natural reaction, the fishing, and shooting, and hunting parson of the early part of the nineteenth century, the man unmindful of all outward observances, and very little careful of even the more solemn duties of his calling, has given place either to the man of forms and ceremonies, of surplices and genuflexions, of crosses and candlesticks, or to the eager, laborious, anxious evangelical minister, ever visiting the sick, attending to the school, or frightening the wicked with vivid pictures of damnation, and diversifying labors, almost too much in themselves for any one man, with missionary meetings, propagation of the Gospel societies, and tract and Bible distribution. The parson Trulliber (I know not if I spell the name aright, as I have no books with me), the parson Adams, the Vicar of Wakefield--although each certainly very much overdrawn, if we consider them as representatives of a class--give us some idea of the various phases of the clerical state in the last century; and innumerable memoirs, histories, and essays show the real condition of the clergy in the end of the seventeenth and beginning of the eighteenth centuries. At none of these periods, be it however remembered, was there not among the clergy of the day an infinite difference, in manners, character, and condition, between different individuals, according to circumstances. The man placed at a distance from refined society, in some remote country parish, was apt to lose the more polished manners acquired at college. This was especially the case where, as sometimes happened, the shameful smallness of the stipend compelled the parish priest or curate to eke out the means of subsistence by hard manual labor. But even then it was not always the case; and hands that have held the plow or dug the glebe have often, washed and clean, during the evening hours, penned words of fire, which have not only found their way to the hearts of men, kindling a flame of pure religion in the breast, but have lighted the writer himself on the road to high preferment.

Again, the chaplain of the lord or great landed proprietor, depending upon his patron for advancement in the Church, and sometimes even for his dinner, was often inclined to be subservient and lickspittle, to undertake degrading and sometimes shameless offices, to forget the dignity of his calling and the dignity of man. But this was merely occasionally; and occasionally, also, you would find a chaplain as stern and harsh as the most fierce reformer, keeping the whole household in awe, and even reproving the faults of his lord himself. These, however, were the extremes, and the general course lay between. There you would find the domestic priest, plodding on quietly in his duties, doing as much good as a not very zealous character could accomplish, bearing the crosses of his situation meekly, and looking forward to a better and a freer day when the long-expected living should be bestowed.

All the coarse caricature daubing in the world can not alter the lines of the picture left to us by the authentic records of those days, and, though it may make the idle smile and the ignorant applaud, yet it will not deceive those who are really conversant with the manners and customs of other times.

Two clergymen of the seventeenth century are now before us, reader, but they belong to neither extreme, and the difference between them, though very great, only serves to show that even the middle ground admitted of much variety. The first who entered advanced, after a momentary look around him, directly toward the master of the house, and took him by the hand with kindly warmth.

"Mr. Woodhall," he said, with the slightest possible touch on an Irish accent, "I am delighted to see you again. It is full six months since we last met, for I stayed behind my lord, being obliged to remain in London on account of having to go to Dublin about some little affairs of my own; my dear aunt having at length thought fit to take her departure for the realms of bliss, when, faith, I thought she had put off the journey altogether. She left me--God bless her!--a neat little comfortable income of two hundred pounds English, a large China bowl, and a pair of Tangier slippers. Heaven reward her, as I am sure it should, for she never troubled it till she could not help it."

"I am glad to see you back, Mr. M'Feely," replied the master of the house; "you have been much wanted to bless the venison up at the hall."

"Oh, the currant-jelly does that mighty well without me," replied the chaplain. "Mr. Ralph, I am right glad to see you. Alma Mater abandoned, I hear. Done with the old lady, eh? Well, it must be so with all fathers and mothers. Children will quit them, must quit them; and there is no use of going cackling about like a hen after a brood of young ducklings when first she sees them take to the water. Every animal knows its own element, and will find it sooner or later. My poor mother, rest her soul, was sadly afraid that I might fall into the errors of popery, and yield to the seductions of the scarlet woman; but, faith, I had no turn for vows of celibacy, and so I came over to England to be out of harm's way. No, no, wedlock is an honorable estate--especially when there is another estate to back it; and as to being married to the Church, upon my soul and conscience I never yet saw the church, be it stone or wood, that I would like to marry any how."

While this part of the worthy gentleman's discourse was going on, addressed to the son, the father had been welcoming his other guest, the parson of the parish.

"Good evening, doctor, give you good evening," he said; "you have caught me here, the lean and slippered pantaloon; but, good faith, Ralph and I were so earnest in talk that I forgot how time went. Nevertheless, 'tis well as it is. Conversation never walks so much at ease as when slipshod; and we will scant ceremony to-night. Come, lay aside your periwig, and we will have a bowl of punch anon."

We will pass over the brewing of the punch and the conversation which sweetened it, whether that conversation turned upon the decline of lemons, which the chaplain declared were not half as juicy as when he was a boy, or upon the enormous price of sugar, which the good parson mourned over sincerely. After the two first ladlefuls had passed round, however, other more important topics were started; rumors from London, tales from France, an epigram, a court ball, a passage of Lucan, and a newly-discovered method of solving some very puzzled questions connected with conic sections were all mentioned and discussed.

Ralph Woodhall had no interest in any of these things. Of some he was ignorant, of some he was tired; and at length he rose, saying he would go out and take a walk for half an hour.

"To study the stars, Ralph?" said his father.

"Nay, to write a sonnet to the pale-faced moon," replied his son, laughing, and away he went.

"The boy has lost his wits," said the Irish clergyman, "to leave such a bowl as this, and such edifying conversation for a green lane and a moonbeam. He must be melancholic."

"Indeed, he has been somewhat heavy and thoughtful of late," said the father, "but he always loved these rural walks, visere sæpè amnes nitidas."

"But not by darkness," replied the parson; "he was never a night-walker."

"The lad's in love," exclaimed the Irishman; "that is the plain truth, as sure as my name is M'Feely. You never see a lad of about twenty get moping and walking by moonlight, looking into babbling brooks, or sitting with his hat off under an elm-tree, but you may be sure that he is infected with that sauntering, heigh-ho, lamentable idleness, love, rightly called a passion, if passion means suffering, and as rightly called a madness or a disease by some doctors, whether the seat thereof be in the liver, or the midriff, or the brain, or the heart."

"Hold, hold, doctor," exclaimed Mr. Woodhall; "pray make some distinctions. There are various kinds of love: some honest, noble, ennobling, others base, evil, and degrading. To say nothing of divine love, holy love, and all kinds and descriptions of honest affection, even the love of man for woman is often too pleasing and blessing to be called a disease. It may perhaps be termed a sort of mental titillation, which, when not extravagant or in excess, is agreeable and even salutary. Many Eastern nations take the greatest delight in being gently tickled; the Chinese enjoy having the soles of their feet titillated either with the finger or a feather, and yet we know that, carried to excess, the tickling of the feet has produced convulsion and death. All depends upon moderation: every excess is evil, on whichever side it be committed: nay, I hold that an excess of abstinence is more sinful than an excess of indulgence, for the one is a despising of God's good gifts, while the other is merely a superfluous enjoyment of them. I can not but think that the saint who stood on a pillar, and the anchorites of the Thebaid, were not only great fools, but blasphemous fools; for, if they did not convey by speech, they signified by action, a foul and false imputation upon the character of the Deity, for which they deserved to be burned--if ever any men did merit such a fate."

"But if your son be in love, who is the person with whom he is in love?" asked the parson. "There is no one in the parish for whom I think it at all likely that he should conceive such a passion."

"He is not in love at all," replied the father; "the truth is, my reverend friend, he has conceived a strong desire to go forth and seek his fortune in the world, and we were speaking of that very subject when you came in. I had neither consented nor prohibited; and probably, doubt--the most painful of all modes or conditions of the mind--has made him wander forth to-night."

"The boy's in love!" grumbled Mr. M'Feely, authoritatively; "the boy's in love! But as to sending him forth to seek his fortune, that is the very best thing that can be done for him. It is the best remedy for love in the world. He'll puff and sigh like an angry cub for the first fortnight. Then he'll find there is something else to be done in life than sigh. Then he'll struggle on, all for the loved one's sake! Then he'll forget the loved one in the struggle. Then he'll find she has forgotten him, and he'll console himself by saying,

'There are more fish in the sea.' Bless your soul, Mr. Woodhall, when I left Ireland, with what I could scrape together, to study at your University of Oxford here, I was dying for love of no less than nine of the prettiest girls in all the north of Ireland. Not one of them didn't swear she would die a maid for my sake; and yet you see I'm a bachelor over forty, and they are all matrons--some of them grandmothers, I fancy."

"What do you say to it, my worthy friend Barry?" asked Mr. Woodhall, addressing the parson. "I do not like to part with my son so soon after his return from college; I do not like to throw a lad like that upon the wide world without any decided prospect before him. Yet if it be for his good, I will cast away parental fondness and parental anxiety, and let him go."

"You will let him go in the end, Woodhall, whatever you determine now," replied the clergyman, with a look of kindly meaning, "and it is better to do that graciously which you will do eventually. Besides, I think you will do right. The most important part of education is the education of the world. Those who keep their children back from this till they are themselves gone, leave them to receive the hard instruction, without any one at hand to render it more easy. You have given Ralph every preparation. His mind and his heart have been cultivated highly. Let him go to receive the lessons of experience, while you are still here to give aid in case of need."

"Well, he shall go," said Mr. Woodhall, with a sigh; "I have still some friends left in the great world who will lend a helping hand, and to them he shall have letters."

"I have but one," said Mr. Barry, "but he is a good and faithful one; and Ralph must know him."

"Bless your soul, I will get him twenty letters from my lord in a jiffy," exclaimed Dr. M'Feely; "the lad is a great favorite of his, and I have nothing to do but to write them, and my lord will sign and address them."

Thus was it determined that Ralph Woodhall should go forth to try the world.

CHAPTER IV

I mentioned the stream--surely I mentioned the stream. Oh dear, yes, I certainly did, although, in the hurry of telling a story, one is sometimes apt to forget small particulars. But I know I informed the reader, in describing The Grange, that there was a small, pleasant stream, not unconscious of trout, which wandered past the back of the old house, and then, as if it had a peculiar affection for the place, made a graceful turn round one of the sides, serving for a fence--even if there had not been a dilapidated old wall there for that purpose.

It was a very beautiful little river, for it deserved a grander name than rivulet, seeing that it was at that spot some twelve or fourteen feet broad; and although the country to the north and east was flat, yet a number of little hills and eminences, and a general sloping tendency of the country to the south and west, from which it descended, had contrived to give it a rapid and hurried motion, which was accelerated by several miniature cascades and rapids. There were trees growing by its side, too, and often overhanging it, canopying its glistening waters with interlacing boughs, and green, shimmering foliage. Sometimes they swept afar, leaving broad, open meadows, where the angler might throw his fly with fearless sweep of arm; but sometimes they crept close to the bank, so close that their great brown rounded roots would obtrude from the rugged bank, mingling with the mossy turf and oozy rock, and curl down into the stream with many a twist and many an aperture, affording fit concealment for the hole of the water-rat or otter.

On the left-hand bank, however, whether along green meadow or among the dim, shadowy trees, close to the margin of the stream, and following all its turns and windings, ran a broad, dry, well-kept path; and as beautiful and pleasant a walk it furnished for any one who loved quiet musing, or was studious of the tranquil face of nature, as could well be found in the wide world. The very bounding, rush, garrulous boyhood of the stream, as it rushed on, struggling with the rocks and impediments in its way, overleaping some difficulties, rushing round other obstacles, and still, in spite of all, making its way onward, might furnish fancies to a poet and thoughts to a philosopher. Then the view over some of the open fields, often, indeed, broken with hedgerows, and often dotted with church spire, and cottage, and farmhouse, but not unfrequently extending for miles and miles away over blue fen and dusky moor, had something wide and expansive in it, which seemed to open the heart and make the breast heave more freely; and where the trees fringed the stream, the eye could still wander far, for there was no thick wood, but a mere belt of planting without undergrowth, leaving smooth banks and grassy slopes between the old trunks and stems, over which the sight might range along tracks of sunshine, and often catch a glimpse through the green avenues of a far-extending distance beyond.

Oh! the homilies of nature, how they pour into the heart of those who will hear them lessons of peace, tranquillity, and love, which might well reform this harsh and jarring world if man would but study there. The characters which man's hand traces, even if spared by the wearing course of time, whether written on parchment or graved upon the rock, pass from comprehension--become a riddle or a mystery. The learned scrutinize, the bold or the wise interpret; but the interpretation is denied, and the dead man's tongue becomes a matter of dispute and contention to the living. But the wisdom of the page ever open before our eyes is written in the universal language, and man has but to look and read to find himself wiser, better, greater from the permitted commune with a spirit above his own.

It was a fair and pleasant walk that path beside the stream--pleasant in the early morning, when dew was upon the grass and flowers, and the slant rays peeped under the green branches as if the first glance of the day at the new world were timid and doubtful; pleasant at noon, when the green boughs afforded shade, and the brief walk across the meadow rendered the shade more grateful, and the fresh air from the ever-moving stream more sweet; pleasant at evening, when the rosy light tinctured leaf and moss, and blade of grass, and painted the old trunks of trees, and sprinkled the foam with rubies. Pleasant also was it, most pleasant, when the yellow moon was hanging high in air, and her beams, weaving themselves with the shadowy branches, spread the way with a net-work of black and silver. Then how the stream would seem to dance, and gambol, and leap up, as if to meet the looks of the Queen of Night; and how every little cascade and rapid would sport with the shower of diamonds that fell upon it from on high!

Along that path, under the moonbeam, Ralph Woodhall took his way, with slow and thoughtful pace, while the next step in his future course was under discussion in his father's house. He paused at the first meadow and looked up to the broad moon, and then moved on again, sometimes gazing at the stream and drawing dreamy images from its flashing waters, sometimes fixing his eyes upon the path and giving up his whole mind to commune with his own thoughts. They were somewhat sad and dark--at least the ground-work was so; but still a gleam of hope stole through, and checkered with brightness the gloom of the untried future. Onward he went for about half a mile. There the stream approached the little village, yet it came not too near; but, sweeping past the foot of the little rise on which it stood, left a single field dotted with one clump of trees between its bank and the first house. Ralph paused there and looked up at the church, and strange fancies passed through his mind. They were like those embodied in Schiller's song of the Bell, full of association, partly sad, partly joyful. Oh! how many a scene, and himself an actor in them, all passed pageant-like before his eyes during the brief moment that he spent there--all life's great epochs--all their emblems--the cradle--the bridal ring--the coffin.

He walked on musing. He came to a low wall, with a stile of hewn stone and thick trees beyond; and passing over, he followed the path, still running by the side of the stream. Through the trees the moonlight could be seen resting upon the open, waving ground, with many a dell and glade, and here and there a deer lifting up its antlered head at the sound of a footfall. Presently another sort of light gleamed between the branches, but more directly on his path--a redder, less placid beam; and shortly after, a tall, irregular house was seen upon a terrace, to the foot of which the path approached very close, with a bright blaze coming forth from three casements on the lower story, while a ray or two shone out of the lattices above.

The young man took a few steps aside to a spot where the trees approached nearest to the house, but remained under their shade, and gazed up at one particular casement with a look intent but sorrowful. What might be his thoughts and feelings at that moment? What might they not be? The ringing sound of merry laughter came from the fully-lighted windows below. There were men there carousing jovially, but their merriment had no music for his ear. Did he envy them? Oh no! Perhaps he might think how strangely Fate shaped men's lots; perhaps he might ask why he, in whose veins flowed the same blood as in some of those rejoicing there within, who was conscious of as high a mind, as bold and true a heart, should be placed in comparative poverty, should be looked upon as in an inferior position, because his father's great-grandfather, about a couple of centuries before, had chanced, without his own consent, to be born a younger son. Yet he envied them not; he coveted not aught that they possessed; nay, of all within those walls, longed for but one thing; but for that how he did long! He could not obtain it; and yet the only bar was the lack of that which those revelers possessed. That thought added to the objects of desire; but their wealth, their rank, their station were only coveted as means--means to the great end and objects of all his heart's desire.

Thoughts came in crowds; but still he fixed his eyes upon the lattice. A shadow crossed it, and he said to himself, "She knows not I am gazing here." Then, again, he said, with some bitterness, "If she did, what would she care?" but the next moment added, "yet I wrong her; she would care-- she would grieve--perhaps she would come forth to cheer me--at all events, to bid me farewell. Would I could let her know."

He was taking a step forward with some unfixed purpose in his mind, when a small door at the side of the building, not far from the bright casements, emitted a momentary light, which was instantly obscured again. The next instant a figure--a woman's figure, passed along the terrace, crossing the blaze from the hall, and Ralph advanced a step or two; but he retreated as rapidly, for the figure turned suddenly from the sound of the revelry, descended the steps of the terrace, and approached the very path by which he had come.

Oh how his heart beat at that moment; hers, perhaps, might have throbbed wildly had she known who was near. But it was quite still, though somewhat busy, and she took her way on, paused for an instant to look up at the sky where the moonbeams vailed the stars, and then entered the path beneath the overhanging boughs. Ralph Woodhall took a step forward; it fell upon some of the withered leaves of the last year, and the sound startled her. She stopped suddenly; and, fearful that she would turn and fly, he pronounced her name.

"Margaret," he said, "Margaret, be not afraid; it is Ralph. I am glad you have come out, for they seem merry-making at the hall, and I did not like to go in, though I longed to see you."

Margaret gave him her hand; and whose heart was beating then?

"They are making a terrible noise," she replied; "more than usual, I think, though perhaps it may be that my head aches, and that makes their mirth sound louder than at other times. I fancied that the cool air would do me good, and therefore came out to stroll along by the stream."

"I will guard you on your walk, Margaret," replied Ralph; "it may be the last time I can do so for a long time to come."

"The last time!" said the young girl--for she could not be more than seventeen or eighteen; "you are not going to leave us, Ralph!"

"Yes, indeed, for a time, dear Margaret," he replied; "I am going away into the wide world to seek my fortune--at least I have asked my father's leave to do so."

"Fortune!" said Margaret; in a musing tone, walking on slowly along the path; "what can there be in fortune, that makes men sacrifice so much to seek it?"

"Nothing in itself," replied Ralph, "but every thing as a means--to me, at least, every thing."

"I see not why it should be more to you than to others," answered Margaret; "why is it?"

"I will tell you in an instant," replied her companion; "here I am hardly at home from college, when I wish to go away again, to part from my father, and you, and all my friends. That is what you would say, I know, dear Margaret. But if I stay at home, content with the little that Fate has given me, without an effort to make it more, or to win honor, and station, and renown, there must come a bitterer parting still; I must see the one I love best in all the world leave me for another home, not only deny me her presence, but deny me her thoughts, bestow heart and hand upon another, and be to me almost as a stranger."

Margaret trembled, but answered nothing, and Ralph went on: "Shall I wait tamely, Margaret, and, without an effort, see all this come rapidly; or shall I, with a strong heart, battle with Fortune, and try to conquer her for the hope of her I love?"

"Oh, yes; go, go!" cried the girl, eagerly.

"I may not succeed, perhaps," continued Ralph; "all my efforts may fail--it is very likely. I may have to endure the same pang, to undergo the same loss, notwithstanding the utmost exertions--that is in God's hand; but, at all events, I shall have one consolation--I shall have striven, I shall have labored, I shall have done my part; and you, Margaret, you will think better of me; you will remember me and my disappointments with sorrow; you will pity, if you must not love me."

"I shall always love you, Ralph," she replied, in perfect simplicity; but then suddenly stopped, adding, with a deep sigh, "I speak foolishly, I fear; but you will not misunderstand me."

"Margaret," he said, in a tone of deep feeling, "Margaret, we must fully understand each other. I love you, Margaret; I shall always love you; I shall never love any but you. Yet hear me, dear girl, and do not tremble so," he continued, drawing her arm within his; "I seek to bind you by no tie to one in whose dark fortunes it needs the eye of eager love to see one spark or hope. I ask of you no promise to be mine, for I know right well that in my present state it were well-nigh madness for either you or me to dream of such a far-off bliss. I have that madness, Margaret, for I still dare to hope; but I would not have you share it, lest my own bitter disappointment should be doubled by breaking your heart too. It is well for me to go, and leave you free to act as your own heart may dictate or circumstances may impel; it is well for me to go, and to seek with the energy which only love can give for all those bright jewels of the world which are but too estimable in the eyes of those in whose hands your destiny must lie. So long as you are Margaret Woodhall, hope will live, exertion will continue, and strength will be given me to struggle on; but should I ever hear of you by another name, the light of life will have gone out, and, as my father has done, I will sit down to fade in darkness."

"What shall I do? what shall I say?" murmured Margaret, as if speaking to herself. "Oh, Ralph, if I could add to your hopes, if I could strengthen your efforts, how gladly would I do it; but my fate is in the hands of others. I have no right to promise any thing. And yet a promise might strengthen me myself; it might give me vigor to resist, should resistance be needful. Still, my father has been very kind to me and to you. Ought we, Ralph--ought we to do or say any thing that he would blame and condemn?"

"No--oh no," answered Ralph Woodhall, firmly; "I ask it not, Margaret. I only ask, let me still hope. Keep your heart and hand for me as long as may be, and though it may seem wild, rash, insane to dream that in a few short years I may accomplish enough to lessen the disparity between your state and mine, yet, so long as the beacon burns before me, I will go on, let the road be ever so rough and perilous. These are strange and stirring times, Margaret; changes come suddenly and often; all men are struggling; let me struggle too; and if Margaret will but bid me hope, my heart shall never fail."

Margaret laid her fair hand upon his, and, looking up in his face, replied, "Hope, Ralph! hope--hope all--hope always. I too will hope, and struggle likewise."

As she spoke the moonlight poured through the branches on her fair face and lighted her beautiful eyes. The look and the words were too much to be resisted. Ralph bent his head over her, and their lips met.

"Hark!" said Ralph, after a moment's trembling pause, "I hear footsteps coming up the path. Let us turn back toward the hall."

"Yes, yes, let us turn back," said Margaret, unclasping his arms from around her, yet gently, kindly; and then, as if she would not leave him wholly comfortless, she added, in a low voice, as they walked onward, "there is at least one thing I may promise, Ralph, I will not plight my faith to another; I will not yield to any entreaty--nay, or command--till I have given you notice, and allowed time sufficient for you to come and deliver me from that which would be a thousand-fold worse than death, if deliver me you can. But now let us be calm, for I hear the steps coming quick behind us."

When those steps were nearer still, Margaret was more calm than her lover, for such is woman's nature. Perhaps he had been less deeply moved than she had been--he could not be more; but the stronger spirit, like the deeper water, when once in motion, remains longer agitated.

"Ah ha! Mister Ralph," said the voice of Doctor M'Feely behind them a moment after, "upon my life and soul, this is my country's way of taking a solitary ramble. You go out to walk alone with a companion, eh? Why, fair Miss Margaret, does my lord know of your night roaming?"

"Quite well," replied Margaret, with very little sign of emotion; "I often walk through the park in the moonlight, doctor, but do not often have such good luck as to-night in meeting Ralph to keep me company. Ralph loves books better than the moon, I fancy."

"He loves a pretty face wherever he can find it, I fancy, be it the moon's or not," replied the chaplain.

"As to my solitary ramble, doctor," said Ralph, "I believed, when I set out, it would be solitary enough; but I can not say it has been less unpleasant for not being so."

"Ay, devil doubt you," said M'Feely to himself; "but moonlight walks are pretty dangerous things, as I know to my cost; there was the widow Macarthy--but no matter for that. The moon is considered a cold planet, but, on my faith, I think she has a greater knack of scorching than any sun I ever saw."

All this was uttered in an under tone, so that no distinct sense was conveyed to the two by whose side he now walked. It was evident, however, that his suspicions were excited, and Ralph, somewhat impetuous in disposition, and ever ready to confront a danger, asked boldly, "What are you talking to yourself about, doctor?"

"Oh, nothing at all, but some of the queer freaks of nature, my boy," replied the other; and Margaret interposed, saying, "Ralph has been telling me of a queer freak of his, doctor. He says he is going to travel, and leave us all here in this dull place. He has not been home from college a month, and is weary of us already. Can not you persuade him to stay a little, if but for civility's sake?"

"By my conscience, but that is the last thing I shall do," replied Doctor M'Feely; "it is the best thing for him to go and see the world, and may be just as well for other people too. No, no, I have promised the old gentleman to get my lord, your father, to give him letters to all the great folks he knows, who may help him on in life, and the sooner they are given the better."

"Well, I do not know what I shall do when he is gone," said Margaret, following unconsciously a policy almost instinctive in woman's heart, and showing a portion in order to conceal the whole; "I shall have no one to talk to but you, doctor, and no one to draw me out of the river if I fall in, as Ralph did when I was a little girl, for you would never wet your cassock for my sake."

"Wouldn't I, though, darling?" cried the jolly priest; "I can help you at a pinch, and will, depend upon it; and as to conversation, mine will do you a world more good than that of any young scape-grace in the land. But now, as to asking my lord about these letters, can it be done to-night? is he in a fit state to be talked to, Mistress Margaret? There was an array of bottles on the table when I left, and the Bordeaux was none of the worst."

"Fit to be talked to!" cried Margaret; "fy, doctor, to be sure he is. Would you have me tell papa that you think he gets tipsy every night?"

"No, no! For Heaven's sake not such a word, or there goes the living!" cried Doctor M'Feely. "Oh, you little fox, so you have turned the tables upon me! Well, you shall see how discreet I can be, and you be discreet also, and don't say a word. We'll keep one another's counsel; and mind, my darling, when you have an opportunity, speak a good word for me about the living. I have been ten years in the house--ever since you were a little thing not up to my knee--and not a benefice has been offered me but that horrid marshy hole of Agueborough cum Flushing-gap, where I should have had to read prayers to yellow-bellied frogs, and preach to the seamews. I shall never be a bishop at this rate, and I am resolved to comfort my arms in lawn if it be possible. But now we are coming near. You trot up to your own room, Mistress Margaret, and I and Ralph will go in; then the old lord will never be a bit the wiser as to your moonlight rambles."

"On the contrary, I shall go straight in," said Margaret, boldly, "that is to say, if all these drunken sots are gone, and will ask my father for the letters for Ralph myself. You are altogether mistaken, my reverend friend, if you suppose that I care about my father knowing where I have been, or that I met Ralph accidentally. Only take care not to put any wrong construction upon my walk, doctor," she added, in a warning tone; "for the plain truth, I fear not."

When they reached the house, however, it was found that the party in the Hall had not yet broken up, and the sounds that issued forth warned Margaret that it was no scene for her to appear in. Doctor M'Feely judged, also, that his presence would not be acceptable, and the three parted at the door. It can not be said that Ralph's fingers did not press more warmly on Margaret's hand than on that of the chaplain as he bade them severally adieu.

CHAPTER V

It was too much for the warmth of those lovers' hearts to part in the cold, frozen solitude of even the little world around them. The many makes a solitude for the few. No prison walls are harder, sterner; no fetters more rigid, more binding; no penitentiary cell more silent, more solitary, than the wall of hard human faces, than the fetters of conventional forms, than the dull, hemming in, unresponsive circle of an unsympathizing crowd for hearts that feel together, and would speak to the ears that can comprehend.

They could not bear it; they risked all for the sake of pouring out the thoughts of each bosom to the other; and on one bright morning, the day before Ralph's departure over the brown heaths and moors--Heaven knows how they found the opportunity; they hardly knew themselves: it was the impulse of the moment--fortune favored; the skies winked at the lovers' wish, and there they were. No eye, it would seem, perceived their going forth; none whom they knew met them in the lonely lane; and once in the wild commons, they were but a speck upon the wide extent.

They heard the cry of dogs afar. They saw hounds and mounted horsemen sweep over the distant hill. They felt little alarm; for so broad was the expanse, that it would have required long calculations to discover how many chances there were to one that the hunt would not come within seeing distance of themselves. Sometimes they walked on together; sometimes they sat side by side on the dry sandy bank. Margaret's hand rested in Ralph's, and their eyes looked into each others'.

"You will not forget me, Margaret, among all the gay, and proud, and high who throng your father's dwelling?"

"Can I forget myself, Ralph, and all the memories of which my existence is made up? But will you not forget me? You are going forth from me into a giddy world, where all is new and untried to you; where thousands of sights, and feelings, and hopes, and passions, and efforts, and changes, may well wipe away Margaret's image from your heart."

"Do you believe it, Margaret? Do you think that in aught I meet with I shall ever forget for one moment the object of my going forth? What will be to me all that the world can give or show--what haughty grandeur--what supple flattery--what upstart wealth--what official insolence--what eager, hasty business--what cunning policy and low cabal--what lordly halls and crowded courts, and glittering gems, and eager strife, without the hope, the one bright leading hope, which, like the mariner's star, may lead me away but to guide me surely home again? Oh no, these things form but the waves of a sea through which my bark must steer; but if they once break in, then I am wrecked indeed. Would, dear Margaret, while I am gone, that you could see every thought and feeling of my heart--behold, as in a glass, every act in which I am engaged."

Margaret mused. "Would we could both know the future," she said, "at least as far as our own fate is concerned; would we could see how all this will end. They tell me there is a man lives yonder, down by those few scattered houses on the moor, who can read horoscopes, and tell by various means the destiny of those who will consult him freely. What think you, Ralph," she asked, with a laugh and a blush; "shall we go and ask him our fate? What if he were to say you would prove untrue, and love some fair lady of the court, and forget Margaret? Are you afraid to inquire?"

"Not in the least," he replied; "for I should give no weight to his words, Margaret, whatever he said. The stars tell us of God's might, and every thing throughout nature of his love and bounty; but man's fate is a sealed book, which no stars, nor aught else in the great creation, can aid us in reading. Had the Almighty ever designed that the destiny even of the next coming hour should be known to us, he would have given us clear means of learning it; for the same Being who has taught us all that is necessary for us to know for our conduct here below, and for our salvation hereafter, would not have left us ignorant of any thing that could be beneficial to us to comprehend in our after destiny. However, I have no fear, so let us go."

It may be a question whether Ralph really felt the full amount of skepticism in regard to arts, which obtained almost universal credence in those days, which he assumed. Reason is a fine thing; but alas for poor human nature! reason but too often fails to convince. There would seem to be intuitive convictions, against which argument the most logical fails to operate. Ralph had a thousand times pondered and discussed with himself all the points of superstition that affected the age in which he lived. He had proved to his own satisfaction that the calculations of the astrologer, and all the terrors of supernatural visitants, were either impostures or dreams--to his own satisfaction, I have said, but not to his own conviction, and the two are very distinct. However, he did not suffer the lingering feelings of unwilling belief, in that which his reason rejected, ever to affect him in his conduct, and he again expressed his willingness to go.

Margaret, on the other hand, had never argued the question with herself at all. Not that she gave full credence to all the wilder and grosser superstitions of the day; for a mind naturally strong and bright had guarded her against much, though not against all. She had heard with horror and indignation of the trial, condemnation, and execution of some unfortunate persons for witchcraft not very long before the period of which I speak; but yet, when we remember that Sir Thomas Brown himself, the great reformer of "vulgar errors," could not free his mind entirely from the superstitions of his day, it was not to be expected that a young girl of Margaret's age should be entirely devoid of them.

She went on, then, with her lover, with more faith in the experiment they were about to make, and of course with more eagerness also; but, at the same time, her fears and agitation were naturally greater likewise, and before they had taken a hundred steps she almost regretted having made the proposal. Curiosity, however, was stronger than apprehension-- perhaps I might say, hope was stronger; for undoubtedly one great motive of the inquiry she was about to make was to strengthen her own heart in the coming hours of trial by the assurances of after happiness which she fondly trusted to receive.

The scene around as they advanced, and the way that they took, were well calculated to impress the mind with that feeling of awe which was a good preparation for that which was to follow. The base of all superstition is awe at the thought of some great unknown thing, and whatever tends to impress the mind with grand and solemn fancies naturally aids in that direction. I never saw the cause of superstitious fears, so universal in the mind of man, clearly and rightly reasoned but once, and that was in the work of an American writer less generally known, at least in England, than he ought to be. He makes one of his characters speak as follows: "Fear is not cowardice. You may encounter unmoved the greatest danger that can threaten you, as death in any shape, and yet be frightened at a trifle merely because its exact magnitude is unknown to you. And this convinces me that there is something somewhere in the universe more terrible than death, or any ill that we know of, or whence comes this all-pervading instinct of fear, which begins in the cradle, and follows us to the grave? There is some undeveloped cause of fear somewhere, some terrible evil which the imaginations of men have not been able to find a shape for."

Any thing that strikes the mind and produces sensations of awe, even of sublimity or grandeur, has a powerful effect in rousing up all that is superstitious in our nature, and the scene through which the two wandered on was well calculated to have that effect. I know nothing more solemn and impressive than a wide, far-extended, uncultivated moor upon a dim day, when no bright gleams of sunshine diversify the expanse with catches of golden light, when the sky above is all gray, and the eye rests upon nothing but long lines of brown and purple heath, like a broad, desolate ocean spreading every where around. Such was the scene which presented itself to the eyes of Ralph and Margaret ere they had gone a quarter of a mile. The undulations of the ground had by that time hidden the plowed fields and meadows around. The Grange, the hedgerows, and tall trees were no longer seen; the church, and the village, and her father's hall were shut out from sight, and the only part to be discovered of the higher country to the south and west was a dark, greenish-black line of hill covered with somber wood. The small, scattered houses toward which they wended their way, and which were to be seen distinctly when they stood upon the upland, were now lost to the view; and not a trace of man's habitation or his industrious hand greeted the eye to relieve the prospect from its air of utter desolation. Even the path--if path it could be called--which they followed to arrive at their object, showed none of the rich coloring which could relieve the general somber tints of the view; but, formed of the dark gray sand of a peaty soil, harmonized well with, but enlivened not at all, the black and swampy ground that lay on either side. Here and there a pool lay glistening upon the moor, but the effect was not cheerful, for it reflected nothing but the gray sky above; and round the edge, where the grass and heath had rotted under the action of the water, the dark tangled roots and dull brown moss, ragged and tufted, gave a more dreary look to the ground.

The distance was greater than Margaret had supposed; for the cottagers, who were, in reality, intruders on another man's land, had taken care to build at some distance from the cultivated ground, not, indeed, in the hope of escaping observation, but in order to render it not worth while to dispossess them. The solitary man, too, who had established himself at no great distance from them, was not inclined to court the proximity of the gay general world, and he had planted his dwelling even some four or five hundred yards further in the moor than the cottagers themselves.

Thus the walk was nearly two miles in length, and the ever-recurring sameness of the view--its vastness--its desolation--sunk more and more heavily upon Margaret's spirits as she and her lover walked slowly on over the numerous slopes of ground, where the prospect was only varied by a different arrangement of the same monotonous materials and hues; and she literally trembled as she approached the lonely dwelling, where, she more than half believed, her future fate might be made known to her.

The house itself was a sad and solemn looking one; not a mere clay hovel, like those which had been passed before, but a tall dwelling of rough stone, with a perpendicular row of four windows, and two low and narrow doors. It had evidently been built a long time, for moss and lichen clung about it, and a thick stem of ivy rose at one corner, and sent out its matted foliage of dark green over the greater part of two sides of the building. It might have been a tower, erected in times of trouble for watching the fens; and if a lodge in a garden of cucumbers afforded to a Hebrew a good image of desolation, an Englishman could conceive no habitation much more gloomy and dreary than a solitary stone house in the midst of the marshes of Lincolnshire. In one respect it had the advantage over the little hamlet situated near. It was placed upon the top of the highest elevation of the low grounds, probably for the purpose of descrying afar off any object that moved across the fens. It was on a little mound, rising about some twenty feet above the general level of the moor, and, consequently, the situation was drier and more secure than could have been found any where else in the neighborhood. But still it looked damp, and cold, and miserable enough.

At the door which the two young people approached hung a large bell, and laying his hand upon the pulley, Ralph drew it sharply down. It gave forth a dull, melancholy sound, which made Margaret start. No one appeared, however, at the door, although they waited for several minutes in expectation. At the end of that time Ralph rang again, but still no one appeared, and at length he lifted the latch and opened the door. As he did so, he saw the foot of a tall stone stair-case before him, and at the same moment a loud, deep voice called from above, "Come up!"

When the young man turned toward Margaret, he saw that her blooming cheek had become very pale, and that she was evidently much agitated.

"Shall we go on, dearest Margaret?" he said, taking her hand tenderly in his.

"Oh yes, yes, let us go on now," replied Margaret, in a low voice; "perhaps if I had known I should be so frightened I might not have asked this, but I will not turn back now."

"There is no occasion for alarm, dear girl," rejoined Ralph; "I will go first; but let me have your hand, Margaret;" and thus, hand in hand, they ascended the long stair-case, while the voice from above repeated, in a tone of command, the words "Come up!"

They passed two doors, one at the top of the first, and one at the top of the second flight of steps; but Ralph judged that the voice sounded from a place higher up still, and went on. The stair-case was very dark, only illuminated by a narrow loop-hole here and there; but in the middle of the third flight a brighter light began to shine upon the steps, and Margaret detained her lover for a moment to recover breath and courage, saying, "Stay a moment, Ralph. Let me stop my heart from beating so;" then, after a short pause, she added, "Now let us go on; I am ready."

CHAPTER VI

At the top of the stairs there was an open door, from which what light there was in the sky streamed out upon the landing-place, upon the old oaken bannister which guarded the descent, and upon one half of the flight of steps to the floor below. This light was so bright, so clear, compared with that upon the common, especially when separated from it by the darkness of the stair-case, that Margaret and Ralph both thought for a moment that the clouds had cleared away, and that the sunshine was streaming through some window that they could not see. Such is the common effect of mounting to a high point when the atmosphere is very thick; but these two young people had never experienced it before, and they were surprised when they found, on looking up, that, through what they termed a window in the roof--in other words, a sky-light--the sky appeared as gray and clouded as ever. Now these sky-lights are supposed by many to have been unknown at the period I speak of, and the vanity of modern discovery leads men to believe that many things are new inventions which were as well known to our ancestors as to ourselves. It is the general introduction of comforts and conveniences that is slow; the discovery of them is often made centuries before they are applied.

There was a regular sky-light, with a small portion giving light to the top steps, while the larger part served to illumine the room beyond, the door of which was open.

The interior of the room was visible entirely to the eyes of Margaret and Ralph as they ascended, and very different was it from that of the learned Doctor Sidrophel, as described by Butler. It was nearly destitute of furniture. There were two chairs and one table, formed of old hard oak, upon which stood a telescope, pointing toward the sky-light I have mentioned. Beside it lay a number of mathematical instruments, and an enormous number of pieces of paper, or card, on which were inscribed an infinite quantity of lines and figures, only understood by the initiated. There were no stuffed beasts in the room, no skin of alligator or large lizard; but upon a board at the side were inscribed with a piece of chalk innumerable inscriptions and strange figures, which Margaret did not at all comprehend. Near the table--the only table which was to be seen--stood the master of the house, dressed in long black garments, with boots of yellow morocco leather. In short, his whole dress was singular, and at once denoted the profession of an astrologer. It was not gaudy, nor in bad taste. It seemed not as if he thought to proclaim his pretensions, but merely adopted a peculiar garb for his own convenience. His figure and appearance were impressive. He was a tall, powerful man of more than six feet in height, and unbowed by the weight of years, although many must have rolled over that tall, smooth brow, and the bald crown above. The hair on the temples and back of the head was as white as driven snow; but the eyebrows were still black as night, and but few wrinkles appeared in the soft, smooth skin, which was as fair and soft as that of any lady in the land.

At the moment when the lovers approached the door of the room, he was looking anxiously at some papers in his hand, and he seemed wholly engrossed by the subject of the moment. He moved not from the position in which he stood, but simply repeated once or twice the words "Come up!" and it was not until Margaret and Ralph had been some moments in the room that he moved his eyes to ascertain who were his visitors. At length he fixed a keen and eager glance upon them, and asked, in no very gentle tone, "What brings you here, young people? Come you to seek information of the past, or the present, or the future? I can tell you either, and will tell you; for I know you too well to fancy that it is some lost spoon, or strayed sheep, or any idle nothing of village life which brings you here, as so many are brought, to inquire of the *wise man*, whom they only think wise because he is different from themselves in their own foolishness."

He spoke in a somewhat sneering manner, and Ralph answered in a calm but bold one, "We have heard, sir," he said, "that you have studied deeply sciences of which we know nothing, and that you are capable of giving us information, or at least believe so, regarding our future fate. But you seem to know who and what we are already, and now we desire to hear, not what may be judged or fancied from the probabilities of our existing situation, but rather that which is indicated by science and calculation."

"You are a scholar, sir," said the astrologer, looking at him from head to foot, "and doubtless hold in contempt the things which other ages venerated. It is the mood of young scholars; but it matters not. I do know you both well. I know you from the cradle until now. The past, the present, and the future, as it regards you, are all before me. I knew when you would come here, and that was why I told you to come up, though I am not willing to be interrupted in my studies at this hour. Now, Ralph Woodhall, what would you that I should tell you? and you, Mistress Margaret, what is it you desire of me? Would you fair dreams and specious promises, visions of bright and golden happiness, love and enjoyment, long life, and a good old age? You will have none such from me. Do you wish to hear the truth, or do you not? Are you bold enough, fearless enough, to look upon the future with an unwinking eye, and shape your course accordingly?"

"I am," replied Margaret, in a firmer tone than might have been expected from her previous agitation; "it is for that I come. Say, Ralph, is it not better that we should know what is in store for us, than go on in doubt and uncertainty?"

Ralph was silent. There was something so impressive in the old man's mariner, a strong conviction, so clear in his own mind, that some belief was compelled; and yet the youth did not wish to acknowledge that he placed any reliance on the other's pretended science. The pride of argument and reason was against it; and he paused so long that the other went on with a somewhat angry frown.

"You are incredulous," he said, "or would seem so. Happily for you, belief or unbelief can not affect in any degree the immutable decree of Fate. Now mark me. I need not the day and hour of your birth. I know them both right well, and I will tell you broadly that which is coming. To you, lady, in the first place, let me say the little I have to say. Be true; be cautious; persevere! Strive not in any degree to resist what seems impending over you. Yield to it, without a pledge; but keep your troth pure and unsullied at the last, and you shall still be happy."

"But not without him," exclaimed Margaret, laying her hand upon Ralph's arm, and looking up in the old man's face eagerly, "not without him, or it can not be true happiness."

The cloud passed away from the old man's brow, and he looked at her with a smile the most sweet and benignant. "Truth will always make happiness," he said; "without truth there can be none. You know how you are plighted to each other. Be true to each other, and you shall be happy; but it will not be without sorrow, and trial, and difficulty. Now to you, young gentleman, I will speak. You are full of vain hopes and expectations; love makes you ambitious; and I tell you that you shall see one bright prospect fade away after another, and hopes extinguished as soon as they are born. You shall struggle on against hope, and meet with disappointment after disappointment. This is your course. Lo, I have told you!"

He paused for a moment, gazing fixedly upon the countenance of Ralph Woodhall, and then added, in a lower tone, "But persevere; be true, and be happy in the end. In the moment when you least expect it--by the means you least foresaw--your fate shall be worked out, and your success accomplished. But hark! there are others coming who must not find you here. Get you into this other room; keep you as still as death, and wait till they are gone."

Thus saying, he opened a door in the wainscot, disclosing a small chamber, utterly without furniture, and with one little window looking out upon the moor. There was a sound of horses' feet, and people speaking below; and the moment after the great bell rang, scaring Margaret and her lover into their place of concealment with very hurried steps. The voice of the old man was then heard, calling from the top of the stairs, in his loud, sonorous tones, "Come up!" and the instant after, another tongue was heard, shouting, "Where the fiend are you? Do you hide yourself in the attic? Truth they say lies in a well, and wisdom, it seems, at the top of the house."

"Wisdom and truth are not so far separate," said the old man, speaking rather to himself than to the other.

At the same moment, Margaret, who had been leaning on Ralph's arm, took a step forward, and shot a heavy bolt that was upon the door into the staple; and then, raising her beautiful lips toward her lover's ear till the sweet breath fanned his cheek, she whispered, "It is the voice of Robert Woodhall, your cousin and mine, Ralph, though nearer akin to you than to me."

"Little akin in kindness," replied the other, in the same low tone; "I have not seen him for seven or eight years, so I may well forget his voice. His haughty, imperious mother treated me so ill, and abused me so much when last I was at the castle, that I will never go again."

Margaret laid her finger on her lips, terrified lest their retreat should be disclosed by any sound; for steps were now heard coming fast up the stairs, and there seemed to be more than one visitor approaching. The next instant a voice sounded in the neighboring room, which both Margaret and Ralph knew well, for it was that of her own brother; and though it was more civil in its tone than that of the first who spoke, there was a great deal of that rough levity in the words, which was much affected by the young and dashing nobility of the day.

"Good-morning to you, Moraber," he said; "I have brought my cousin here, Lord Coldenham's son; or, rather, as I should say, Lord Coldenham's brother. We want to see which way the hunt has taken. I tell him you are a wise man, and he says to me nay, for that no wise man would live in this moor."

"Fools might be made judges of wise men, and yet not much hanging done in the land," replied the person he called Moraber; "not for want of folly enough in the judges, but for want of wise men to be judged."

"Come, Master Moraber, or whatever is your name," said the voice of Robert Woodhall, "show us a trick of your art. What in the fiend's name is this you have got on the table?"

"Something that you can not understand," replied the other; "an instrument that makes me see things that you can not see. What are you holding out your hands for? Do you suppose that I practice chiromancy? or do you come hither for the purpose of insult? If so, beware of your neck; for that window is high, and you may have a speedy path to the bottom."

"No, I don't come to insult you," replied the voice of the other, in somewhat craven tones; "how the devil should I know how you tell people's fortunes?"

"If you want palmistry, go to the Egyptians; I deal not with such trash. The luminous influences which rule the destinies of mankind, and which have been read with truth and certainty, from the days of the Chaldean sages down to this present hour, are the letters of the book I study. If you wish to know any thing that they may say regarding your fate, put your questions and I will answer them; for I have the horoscope of every man, above the rank of a churl, within fifty miles of this place."

"I don't know well what to ask," replied the voice of Robert Woodhall; and there seemed to be a whispered consultation between him and his young companion. "Yes, yes, ask him that," said the voice of Margaret's brother.

"Well, then," said Robert Woodhall, aloud, "tell me, if you can, in all these choppings and changes of the times, what shall become of the two kindred houses of Coldenham and Woodhall?"

"They shall be reunited," said the old man, at once and decidedly, "and that before four years are over."

"Ay! How is that to be?" said the voice of Robert Woodhall, seemingly puzzled by the reply; and then, after a moment's pause, he added, "I suppose you mean that I shall marry my fair cousin Maggy."

Margaret's hand pressed tight on Ralph Woodhall's arm, and her beautiful eyes fixed straining upon the door, as if she hoped that their earnest gaze might reach the face of the old man, and read upon it the answer ere it was uttered. The next moment, however, she heard him reply, "I did not say so. I tell you what is to be, not how it is to be."

"Well, then, tell me," exclaimed Robert Woodhall, in a more serious tone, "shall I marry my cousin Margaret?"

"You shall go to the altar with her," replied the old man; but, ere he could end the sentence, her brother Henry exclaimed, "You must have changed your manners, and your morals too, Robby, before then, or I tell you fairly I would stop it, even if it were at the altar step."

"It is not for you to stop it, young man," said the other deep-toned voice; and then, suddenly breaking away from the subject, the old man exclaimed, "There! if you desire to know which way the hunt has gone, lo! there it goes over the fens hard by, and, if they take not good heed, many a horse, and perhaps some men, will leave their lives there."

"There it goes," cried Robert Woodhall; "come, Hal, come! Do not let us stand wrangling and befooling ourselves here; let us to horse and after them;" and the next instant was heard the sound of the two young men's steps running rapidly down the stairs.

In the mean time, Margaret leaned her forehead upon Ralph Woodhall's shoulder and wept; and, after a brief pause, the old man endeavored to open the door from the other side.

Ralph drew back the bolt, but there were two sad faces which met Moraber's eyes; for both the lovers had read his words in one sense, and both, if the truth must be told, put some faith in them.

"Why weeping?" said the old man, gazing kindly at Margaret.

"You told me," said the beautiful girl, "to be true, and I should be happy. How can I be either true or happy if I am to wed that man--a man whom I abhor, a man who frightens me?"

The old man smiled. "It shall all be as I have said," he replied, "though you can not see the how or the when. If the book of fate, dear lady, could be laid open before your eyes, it would appear to you only full of darkness and contradictions, unless you could perceive all the myriads of fine links and intricate threads which unite event and event together. These I myself can not see, and much that my art discloses seems contradictory to me as well as yourself. Nevertheless, that it *shall be* I know; and if you find that my words come not true, and all seeming contradictions melt away, I give you both leave to call me liar and fool, and if I be still living, pluck me by the beard in the public street. Nay, more, in compassion for your weakness, and your partial want of faith, you may, when you find events seemingly going contrary to my prediction, come to me, send to me, write to me in your dread and apprehension, and I will give you renewed assurance, and, perhaps, clear information. Be not afraid, dear lady; have faith, and it shall go well."

Margaret shook her head and sighed, and the old man, turning to her lover, asked, in a low tone, "When do you go forth?"

"In two or three days," replied Ralph; "but how did you know I was going forth?"

The old man smiled. "I should be little worth consulting," he replied, "if I knew not so trifling a thing as that. In two or three days! You must take a long ride before that. You must go to a place you have not seen for years, and to people that you love not. To-morrow morning early, instead of hanging about the nest of this sweet bird, mount your horse and ride away to Coldenham Castle; see the proud old lady, see her eldest son. She will receive you ill, and treat you with neglect, perhaps contempt. But laugh at it, Ralph Woodhall, laugh at it; and mark every thing that you see in every chamber that you enter--every chair, and table, and decoration, and piece of tapestry. You shall be better than she is some day, and have rooms as fine, and ornaments as gorgeous. If the woman is very fierce, just say to her, calmly, that she has not done you justice, and that the day will come when she must think better of you."

"But I love not to go near her," replied Ralph; "she is hateful to me in many respects--a bold, harsh, bad woman; and, moreover, I see not the use in visiting one whose only intercourse with my father or myself led to total estrangement between him and his lordly cousin, and to my mortification and injury."

"Go!" said the old man, in a tone of authority. "Go! as I have told you; let her not say that you slunk out of your native county without venturing to see your nearest relations. Perchance she may offer to advance your views."

"Then I would spurn her offers with contempt," replied Ralph.

"What!" cried the other, laying his finger lightly upon Margaret's hand, which rested on the table; "what! with this in view?"

"Margaret could never wish me to do a mean and base thing," answered Ralph, "even for the greatest happiness that Heaven could bestow."

"Go, at all events," repeated the other, with a look not altogether dissatisfied; "refuse or accept her good offices as you will; but go! and now mark me further, youth: you will need a servant with you on your wanderings. I know where you will find one who will suit you."

"Alas! good sir," replied Ralph, "I have no means to indulge in such attendance. I can neither afford to pay a servant or to feed him."

"Did I not say that I knew one who would suit you?" asked the other, "and when I said that I meant that he would suit you in all respects. The one

I speak of will have payment of a certain kind, but not from you, and as to the rest, he will find means to feed himself; you must take him with you, for he may be needful. Now remark: as, on your return homeward from the castle, you pass through the village of Coldenham, you will see a low white house, six doors beyond the church; you will know it by the beams of the frame-work shining in lozenges through the whitewash, and by the gables being turned to the road; stop at the door, and ask for Gaunt Stilling: a lad will come out to you, and you have but to say to him, Moraber says you are to be at Halling's corner at such an hour of such a day, in order to go through the world with me; and if you are punctual to the time you tell him, you will find him at the place to the moment of the appointed time. Ask him no questions, indulge no vain curiosity, and he will serve you well and faithfully. Nay, more, he will, in case of need, be able to communicate quickly with me, should I not be here when you need counsel and assistance."

Ralph mused a moment, and then, looking up frankly, answered, "This is all strange enough, but I will do as you desire. I hear all the people round say that you are a good and kind man; that you cure them of their ailments, relieve them in their need, and often, by your timely help, turn the trembling scale of fortune in favor of the good and the industrious. You would not do aught, I am sure, to raise hopes that are vain, or to thwart efforts that are honest."

"I would not," replied the old man, solemnly, "but I would do the reverse. And now it is time for both of you to speed home. The hunt will soon be over. Do you know the way by the black lane?"

Ralph answered that he did; and saying "Take that, it is the safest," the old man led Margaret to the top of the stairs.

CHAPTER VII

In a large and handsome room; in a splendid building of ancient date--one of the few which, either in consequence of the political or religious opinions of the owners, escaped ruin during the civil wars--situated upon a gentle eminence on the confines of Nottingham and Lincolnshire, with green turf sloping away to a wood of old trees, to have wandered among which would have rejoiced the heart of Evelyn, sat a lady considerably past the prime of life, yet with all the fire of youth in her jet black eyes. She was not very tall, and yet there was something commanding in her figure and her carriage which gave a beholder the idea of greater height than she really possessed. The figure, indeed, had suffered little from the ravages of time; and although youthful grace might be gone--the supple, easy undulation of unstiffened muscles--all the native dignity remained, rendered harsher but not less remarkable by a certain degree of rigidity.

No one could deny that the features of the face were handsome, but yet they did not possess that outline which is generally pleasing, and there was something peculiarly repulsive in the expression--perhaps it might be its unfeminineness (to coin a word); to this the general cast of the features lent themselves greatly, now that the plump roundness of early life had departed. The nose was aquiline, and strongly marked, though beautifully cut; the eyebrows were thick, and still quite dark; the eyes, as I have said, were black as jet, but no small twinkling orbs, as is very frequently the case with very black eyes. On the contrary, they were large and oval. The chin had probably been very beautiful, though somewhat prominent, but now it had that tendency to turn up which age generally gives to this feature when the nose is aquiline. The hair, as white as silver, was turned back from the forehead, just suffering two or three little snowy curls to escape above the temples. Her dress was gorgeous, and even at that hour--it was before noon--she wore a number of costly jewels.

To look upon her, one felt that there was a person of a strong will and powerful intellect, but no one could imagine that any of the tender weaknesses of woman's heart had ever found place in that bosom.

She had before her, at the moment I have chosen to present her to the reader, a number of papers--stewards' accounts, household books, statements of building expenses, and estimates; but with these she seemed to have done, for though her jeweled fingers rested upon them, her head was lifted, and her eyes turned toward the casement, though the sun was shining through it fiercely; and on her face there was a look of stern desolation--of melancholy, not gentle, but hard, which might well picture disappointed expectation from those worldly goods, which always, in the words of the poet, "turn to ashes on the lips."

As she thus sat, a servant entered and approached quietly within a respectful distance, and then stood waiting for her notice. For a moment she pursued her revery, whatever was its subject; but then, seeming to become by degrees conscious of the man's presence, she slightly turned her head and inclined her ear. Well versed in all her ways, the man immediately announced his errand, saying, "Mr. Ralph Woodhall, my lady, is below, and desires admittance to you."

"Who? who?" cried the lady, almost starting from her chair, while her face grew alternately white and red, and her eye flashed with angry brightness.

"Mr. Ralph Woodhall, the gentleman said," replied the servant.

"Let the beggar's son ride off!" said his mistress, fiercely; "he shall not-- no, he shall not--yet stay--give him admittance, but not at once--not at once; keep him five minutes or so, then bring him in."

The servant bowed low and retired, not at all surprised by bursts of strong feeling, to which he was apparently well accustomed.

As soon as he was gone, the lady rose and walked up and down the room. "Ralph Woodhall," she said aloud, "Ralph Woodhall! what can bring him here at the end of seven or eight years? I thought I had freed this house of him and his miserable inert father--come to beg, perhaps. Well, no matter, they can do no great harm, now that my good lord is dead; or perhaps--but no, that can not be--Ralph Woodhall. But hark! they are coming;" and she resumed her seat, smoothing her brow, and affecting to look quickly over the papers before her.

The next instant young Ralph Woodhall was ushered into the room, and his name pompously announced; but the lady took no notice, and still turned over the papers, comparing one page with another. Ralph was well dressed, and the glow of youth and exercise were upon as fine and manly a face as eye could look upon. He observed at once the studied negligence of his reception, and his first impulse was to turn upon his heel and quit the room; but he thought that by so doing he would give the proud woman the advantage, and, doubting not that it was her intention to keep him standing like a dependant till she chose to notice him, he advanced, with wonderful tranquillity of air, and seated himself in one of the green velvet chairs exactly opposite to her, throwing himself back, and letting his eye run quietly over the decorations of the room.

Her eye was instantly upon him, and a bright red glow came into her cheek. "Young man," she said, after a moment or two of bitter silence, "nobody seats himself in my presence till he is asked to do so. You are unmannerly."

"Pardon me, Lady Coldenham," replied the young man, boldly, "I seat myself in the presence of any one but my king, and the more readily where I see there are not manners enough to prevent my doing so unasked." The lady gazed at him for an instant with flashing eyes; but then something seemed to give a turn to her motions, and she burst into a laugh, crying, "This is too good! you are a scholar, I think, young man. Pray, under what professor did you study manners?"

"Under one, madam, who taught me that riches are not superior to gentle blood," replied Ralph; "that rank is to be respected only where it is combined with higher qualities, and that high station should meet with reverence when it is ornamented with courtesy, but not otherwise, except from fools and sycophants."

"By the book!" said the lady, "by the book! marvelous well remembered and recited; and now what brings you here, Sir Scholar? To what do I owe your polite attention? You come not here without cause--without motive, I suppose."

"I have been over-persuaded, Lady Coldenham," replied the young man, "to ride over, before I set out upon a somewhat long excursion, in order to make a formal call at the house of my father's cousin's widow, the only title by which you can be known to me--the only title which justifies or gives occasion for my visiting you."

Instead of a violent burst of passion, which he certainly expected, Lady Coldenham sat perfectly silent, leaned her head upon her hand, and repeated to herself once or twice the words "The only title!" She recovered herself soon, however, and replied, with a knitted brow, fiery eye, and stern bitterness of tone, "You are an insolent coxcomb--you always were."

The old man's words recurred to Ralph's mind at that moment, and he replied, as he had been prompted, though not with perfect accuracy, "Lady Coldenham," he said, "you have not done justice to me and mine, but the time will come when you must do us justice. I came not here to quarrel with you, or to bandy angry words, but with some hope that time might have made a change in you, or, at all events, might have banished bitter memories. I find it is not so, and therefore I will take my leave."

Thus saying, he rose, and was about to depart, but the lady exclaimed vehemently, "Sit down! I wish to speak with you."

He did as she desired, and for several minutes the old lady remained in thought, apparently struggling with some strong emotions in her own breast. At length she raised her eyes, which had been fixed vacantly on the table, and said, with a quivering lip, "You are bold and harsh, young man; but that I can forgive; I am not timid or tender myself. We are about to part for long, perhaps forever. Tell me, what can I do for you? If I can do aught, I will. That I owe to the memory of others."

"You can do nothing for me, madam, that I will accept," the young man replied; "a man must be base indeed to receive favors from one who grants them unwillingly. Happily, I need nothing, and certainly I would accept nothing at your hands even if I did. I am glad, however, that you have made the offer, as it suffers us to part with less angry words upon our lips than passed before. I thank you for your offer, and now will take my leave."

Thus saying, he arose and left the room, where the lady remained musing without uttering a word. On descending to the hall, he was met, in crossing it, by a young gentleman gayly attired, the eldest son of Lady Coldenham, and the actual possessor of the family title and estates. He might be two or three-and-twenty of age; but such had been the dominion exercised by Lady Coldenham over her husband during his life, that he had left, on dying, immense and unusual control over his whole property to his widow, besides a large jointure. Whispers, indeed, had gone abroad that the death-bed of the old lord had presented a painful and unsatisfactory scene, not only because he had died without faith and hope, but because the domineering spirit of his wife had been exercised, at that last fearful moment, with more violence and eagerness than even during his lifetime; and that she had watched his bedside night and day, not with the purpose of soothing and consoling, but, as the servants judged, from her never suffering him to be alone for a moment with any one, for the purpose of keeping him her slave to the last.

The young man looked for a moment at Ralph Woodhall as a stranger, but then suddenly recollecting him, he held out his hand frankly, saying, "Ah, Ralph, how is it we never see you now? Why, your face had well-nigh passed from my recollection, it is so long since you were here."

"When last I was here, my lord," answered Ralph, "I had no great encouragement to come back again."

"Oh, you mean my mother's conduct," answered the young lord; "you should never mind her. She bullies every one. She always did; and if every one she maltreats were to fly from her, she would have no companions but the family portraits. Come along with me; I have a famous mew of hawks to show you, which I have had trained after the fashion of the olden time."

Ralph, however, pleaded want of time, and, after a few minutes more spent in kindly conversation, the two young men separated; it must be owned, with some regret upon Ralph's part at least. Lord Coldenham had been the only one of the family who had shown him any kindness in his younger days. He knew him to be like what his father had been, placable, good-humored, and generous, full of honorable impulses, though too easily governed, and he could well have made him a friend, perhaps to the advantage of the young lord himself.

At the great door he found his horse fastened to a ring, the servants, who always take their tone from the leading spirit of the house, having judged it not worth their while to take the beast into the stable, or to hold him till its master descended. Ralph tried to banish all angry feelings, but a deep and indignant sense of ill treatment remained which he could not master; and, mounting without delay, he rode off toward the village, which lay at the distance of about two miles. His beast was weary and wanted food, so that his first care was to seek out the little public house, which he remembered well. He there gave the horse into the charge of the hostler, and then set out for the house which had been indicated to him as the place where he would find a servant. As he strolled along through the village, he could not help remarking the increased appearance of decay which was manifest in all the houses, the buildings, and the little gardens. Though never very prosperous, Coldenham, when last he saw it, had appeared at least neat and comfortable; but now the broken thatches, covered, but not concealed, by houseleek; the windows patched, or very often without glass; the railings and fences dilapidated, and insufficient to keep out the pigs and cattle, and the gardens half cultivated and full of weeds, presented a sad change. The only building which had remained much as he had seen it was the old church, standing upon a piece of ground raised a good deal above the road, with its grave-yard surrounded with a low stone wall. Ralph paused for a moment, and gazed up at the tall, thin, graceful spire, which he remembered having contemplated often in former years, wondering how it had been built to such a height. All was as he had seen it then. The tooth of time had fed upon it largely in years long past, crumbling down the rich cut ornaments, corbels, and gargoyles; but, as if the destroying monster could sometimes weary of his diet, there was no appearance of his having touched the building since Ralph stood before it last. Nor had any thing been done to improve it; the same green, mossy look, which had been given to the stone by the damp air sweeping through the fens, was still there; and one of the coping stones of the little cemetery wall which had fallen off, and which he had often seen lying within the fence, was lying there still unreplaced.

The door was open, and, walking through the cemetery, the young man went in. The tombs of his ancestors were there, and he wished to take another look at them before he went afar. Walking up the aisle, he soon stood before the spot where stood the monument of Sir Robert Woodhall, who was considered the founder of the family. A gorgeous monument it was, richly carved and ornamented; and the gratitude of. the old knight's posterity had recorded, upon a tablet on one side, the numerous virtues, real or imaginary, of the dead: how he had fought for his sovereign in the field; how he had aided him with his wisdom in the council; and how he had left two sons, both of whom he had lived to see become peers of the realm. Then came the tombs of the two sons, Robert, Lord Coldenham, and Ralph, Lord Woodhall; and then the tombs of two more, another Robert, the grandfather of his own father and of the late Lord Coldenham, and another Ralph, the progenitor of the present Lord Woodhall. They were all Roberts and Ralphs, with the exception of here and there a Henry, like a graft upon an old stock. Every one has felt the eternally-speaking moral of old monuments; the comment they are ever reading upon the vanity of all the struggles, passions, and hopes of earth--upon the vanity of vanities, ambition. I will not, therefore, dwell upon it, except as it affected the young man who there stood and gazed. He might feel that he came there with overeager expectations, with strong desires and aspirations after worldly greatness--after things which, whether as a means or an end, are but as a part of that great strife which ends in emptiness. There lay around him, gathered into one small space not a dozen yards square, a multitude of his own kin, who had struggled, and toiled, and hoped, and desired like himself; who had even succeeded, and had yet inherited nothing, for all their pains, but six feet of earth and that piece of moldering marble; while the very deeds which had gained them luster and renown their hopes, fears, and exertions, occupied but a point far less in the vast waste of time than their grave upon the surface of the earth. Feeling sad and reproved, he was turning away, when a voice near him said, "Would not the best epitaph of all be, 'He lived and died?' It is all that can be said with certainty of any man."

On looking round, Ralph perceived standing near him and looking over his shoulder an elderly man in the dress of a peasant well to do. He had put off his shoes and laid down his hat somewhere about the church, and by these indications Ralph concluded rightly that he was the sexton. He asked him whether it was so, however, and the old man replied, "Yea, truly, I am the sexton."

"You were not here when I was last in Coldenham," said Ralph; "what has become of Harrison, who was sexton here before you?"

The old man pointed with his finger to the pavement, saying, "Down there--he is as good as a lord now, and occupies just as much room. When he died, I was sent for by the old lady; for I come from a distance out of Dorsetshire, her own county."

"Then of course you are a great friend of hers," replied Ralph.

"Nay, why should you think so?" asked the old man.

"Because she put you in this good office," said Ralph.

"That is no reason," replied the sexton; "gifts do not always come from favor, nor fortune either. I take what I get, and am thankful. I ask not whence it comes, nor why. I can not be the friend of a great lady nor the friend of a proud lady. Good office call you it? Marry! the dead often do good to the living, and so it is with me; but the living do no good to the dead, and so in one sense the office is not a good one. It is like that of the hangman, who is said to do the last offices to a culprit; but mine go beyond his, and are the only true last offices; for I give back to the earth what the earth gave to the light, and there is no hand between mine and eternity."

The conversation had a somber hue, and Ralph sought to turn it, saying, "It seems to me that the village is much decayed since I last saw it. The people do not seem so comfortable--so much at ease, as when I was here before."

"How should they be so?" asked the sexton. "The many are always more or less dependent upon the few; and in a country village of this land, they derive their prosperity from the great folks near them. Mind, young master, I speak of prosperity--not alone of wealth--of the happiness that cheers labor, of the protection which prompts it, of the example which leads in the right way, and of the generosity which rewards those who follow it. How would you have the people prosperous here, with no one of wealth and station near them but an old woman all pride and diamonds, whose only object is to maintain her state and her two sons; and their only bounties are the riding over our fields and gardens, and the debauching of our wives and daughters? Marry! well may the fences go to decay, the thatch go to decay, and the roof-tree fall in. There is a good receipt for rendering a place desolate, and these people have found it."

"I fear so, my good man," replied Ralph; "but you speak freely dangerous things."

"I fear not, master," replied the old man, with a quiet smile; "although, to say truth, I might not speak such things if you were not a traveling stranger in the place."

"I am nearer akin to those you mention than you are aware of," replied Ralph, turning toward the door; "but be not afraid, I will not betray you, for I think much as you do."

"I am not the least afraid," replied the sexton, following him slowly, and taking up his shoes and hat as he went; "I shall do very well, whatever is said of me."

Ralph walked on, and took the little path branching to the right from the church porch, which led in the direction of the house that Moraber had described. It was at no great distance beyond, so that you could see it from the little gate of the church-yard; and Ralph was surprised, as he advanced through the old elms that shaded the little graves, at the neatness and air of comfort which the dwelling presented. It was larger and more roomy, too, than most of the other houses near; for the doctor and the lawyer had not yet sprung up in every village in the land, and the parsonage was the only good-looking edifice in Coldenham, except the church.

Before the door, on a little patch of green which separated it from the road, stood a fine old oak greatly decayed in the heart, but having a bench underneath its shattered branches, where the cool air might be enjoyed of a summer's evening; and pausing for a moment beside the tree, the young gentleman looked up at the dwelling with some doubts as to whether he was right or not.

The persevering old sexton was upon him the next moment, asking, in his ordinary quaint tone, "Seek you any one there, young gentleman?"

"Yes, I do," replied Ralph, "if I am right in the house. I am seeking a young man named Stilling."

"An old man named Stilling is talking to you," replied the sexton; "but what is the Christian name of the man you seek?"

"Gaunt Stilling, I was told to ask for," replied Ralph. "Are you his father?"

"So it is supposed," replied the old man, "but he is not within. Will you come in and wait till he returns?"

"I must needs see him," replied Ralph, thoughtfully; and at the same moment the old man opened the door which led into the house. As he did so, a female figure with a beautiful face, of which Ralph had but one glance, passed quickly across the passage, giving a look round, and then disappearing instantly.

The young man made no remark, but he thought he saw traces of tears upon the bright face that glanced by him. The sexton's countenance fell a little, but he bated not his courtesy to the stranger, leading him into a neat sanded parlor, and pressing him to take some refreshment. With his own hands he brought in some cheese and bread, and excellent butter, and then went out and fetched a foaming brown jug of good strong ale.

"Homely fare for a young gentleman of the house of Woodhall," he said; and he continued to talk and moralize for some ten minutes, while Ralph, to say the truth, enjoyed his viands amazingly. At the end of that time the young man began to reply and ask questions in return; but their further conversation was interrupted by the dashing up of a splendid horse to the door. To Ralph's surprise, the old sexton started up from his seat, ran to the outer door, and turned the key in it. Then, after looking at it for a moment with a grim smile, he returned to the little parlor, saying to himself, "Nay, nay, not so."

He had hardly seated himself when a hand was laid upon the latch of the outer door, and some one pushed hard. The lock, however, barred all entrance, and the visitor knocked once or twice, saying, "Kate! Kate, let me in!"

"Thou wilt soon have some one to deal with thee," said the old man, in a low tone; and a moment after another horse was heard coming quickly along the road, and then followed the sound of angry voices.

"Get home with you!" cried one; "I warned you before; and be you lord's son or beggar's son, if I see you within a hundred yards of that house, I will give you such a hiding as will take some of the rankness out of you."

"Insolent scoundrel!" replied another voice, in the tones of which Ralph thought he recognized those of Robert Woodhall; "I have a great mind to send my sword through you, and if it were not for Kate's sake, I would. But you shall be punished for your insolence notwithstanding Lady Coldenham will soon send you and your old puritanical father packing back to Dorsetshire."

"As for your sword," replied the other, in a scornful tone, "you dare not draw it out of its sheath, and if you did, I would break it over your back. As for your mother, you had better go and ask her what she will do before you announce it. I have seen her since you have, and proud as she is, she will not back you in your rascality. Get you gone speedily, for my fingers itch to seize you by the throat and grind your face into the mud. But you are a coward as well as a scoundrel, and not worth punishing. You have done harm enough already, and you shall do no more harm here."

After these words there was a momentary pause, sufficient for any one to have mounted on horseback, and then the prancing of a horse's feet, while Robert Woodhall's voice uttered some words, apparently of a very offensive nature; for, although Ralph could not hear them distinctly, they were followed by a loud and angry exclamation from the other person, who added, "If you boast truly, I will have the best blood in your heart."

Some one then cantered away from the house, and the old sexton rose and unlocked the door, giving admission to a youth of three or four-and-twenty years of age, whose form at first sight appeared so lithe and spare as to be fitted only for great agility, but which, when examined with a more careful eye, showed all the indications of great strength in the sinewy muscles and exact proportions. His face was heated, and he entered the room with a hurried step, but stopped short on perceiving a stranger.

"Calm thyself, calm thyself," said his father; "thou art too hot and rash, my son. Hast thou said to the old woman what I told thee?"

The son nodded his assent, and the father added, "Not a word more or less."

"Not a word!" replied the son.

"Then he will come here no more," said the father; "but yet, as it is impossible to put bridles upon young men bred up in luxury and vice, it were well to follow the course we have determined, and we must set about it quickly. Here is a gentleman, my son, who has come hither asking for thee. Hear what it is he seeks."

"What is it you would with me, sir?" asked the young man, in a civil tone.

"I have but a message to give you," replied Ralph; "Moraber says that you are to be at Halling's corner at nine o'clock of the morning on Thursday next, to go through the world with me."

"That gives but two clear days," exclaimed the young man, looking at his father; "it can not be."

"Yes, yes, it can," cried the old man, eagerly; "you must not deny him, boy."

"But I will not have her stay here," replied the younger Stilling; "come what will, that shall not be."

"I will go with her myself," replied the old man; "you can remain here till Thursday morning; by that time I shall be on my way back, and at home by Friday night. He shall come, sir, he shall come. Tell our friend that he will not fail."

"If you mean by that the person calling himself Moraber," replied Ralph, "I shall not see him again before I depart; but doubtless he will know of your son's compliance with his wishes."

"Oh yes, he will not fail to know," answered the sexton; "but why do you say 'calling himself Moraber?' Think you that is not his real name?"

"That is clearly a foreign name," replied the young gentleman, "and his tongue bespeaks the Englishman."

"Oh! he knows many things that you little dream of," answered the old man, "and can speak in one tongue as well as in another; however, my son shall be with you at the time and place."

"I would fain know first whom I am going with," said Gaunt Stilling

"My name is Ralph Woodhall," replied the young gentleman, "the son of Mr. Woodhall of The Grange."

The other paused and mused for a moment or two, after which he said, "Well, sir, I will go with you; I have heard you spoken well of--the only one of your name."

"Nay, nay," replied Ralph, "my cousin Henry, Lord Woodhall's son, is surely an exception to your censure."

"He is well enough," replied the other; "not so bad as the worst, nor so good as the best; but he may pass among young blades for a phœnix, perhaps."

"Well, but his sister Margaret," said Ralph, the color slightly deepening in his cheek, "surely you have no ill word to say of her."

"Oh ho! sits the wind so?" cried Gaunt Stilling, with a laugh; but the moment after he added, in a grave and earnest tone, "No, sir, I have no word to say against her; she is ever named as a good and sweet young lady, gentle to every one, kind and generous to the poor. She is very beautiful, too; that I can testify, for I once saw her. He who wins her will be a rich man, for she is a treasure. However, sir, I will be at the place appointed on Thursday morning, and ready to serve you to the best of my power, and all the more willingly because you are hated by those whom I hate. It is a good sign to have such men's enmity."

After this engagement Ralph waited no longer, but taking leave of the old sexton and his son, and thanking the former for his hospitality, he returned for his horse to the little alehouse, mounted, and rode away.

CHAPTER VIII

Happily for Ralph Woodhall, the morning was bright and beautiful: I say happily, because, although as far as his own person was concerned, he would have little cared had the rain poured down as it has never poured since the days of Noah, yet the sparkling brilliancy of the morning cheered his spirits, and lightened the weight of parting with those he loved. It is curious how much there is in association, and how a sort of latent, diffusible superstition mingles with all associations, especially those connected with the weather. "Happy is the bride that the sun shines upon; happy is the dead that the rain rains upon," is an old proverb. The day is said to "frown" upon an enterprise; and who is there that, undertaking any thing in which great interests are involved, sees a gloomy and menacing sky over his head, and does not thence draw evil auguries?

The morning was bright and smiling when Ralph Woodhall set out upon his journey. All nature appeared to rejoice; the fresh green trees, the sparkling river, even the dark brown moor seemed to revel in the sunshine; the light air waved the branches, and carried now and then a small floating shadow from a hardly-seen cloud over the bosom of the landscape, bringing out the brightness with stronger effect. The moment was one which Ralph had dreaded. The parting had been very different before: first, because the tenderer ties which bound him to that spot had not been so strong; and, secondly, because, on every former occasion, there had been a fixed limit to his proposed absence. He had gone to the university for his term, and knew or hoped that, when it was ended, he should return. But now all was vague and misty. Months, years, the better part of life itself, might wane before he saw his father's house again; and then the long, long absence from his Margaret! It was in vain that he reasoned with himself--that he argued that departure afforded the only chance of winning her; that to linger on there, spending hours which should be devoted to active exertion in the storm-foretelling calm of temporary happiness, was only to insure bitter disappointment, and to render that disappointment ten times more bitter. It was all in vain. He had looked forward to the moment of parting with dread; but, as I have said, the brightness and the light, and the sparkling of the scene, gave preponderance to hope against fear. It seemed a happy omen to him; it seemed to promise the smile of Heaven upon his endeavors, the sunshine of success to light his way.

Early in the morning, with the first light, he had risen from his bed, and made his final arrangements for departure. All that he intended to take absolutely with him had been packed into two large leathern bags, commonly used by travelers in those days, which strapped to the back of the saddle. A large trunk-mail stood filled with a variety of little articles that he prized, books, gifts from friends, some curious relics of olden times, and all the fine apparel that he possessed, to go by one of those innumerable carriers who at that time traversed the country in every direction, following often paths peculiar to themselves, and at one time, when the plague was raging in the land, actually tracking out new roads, or changing small by-lanes into high-ways, in order to avoid infected places.

When he was dressed and ready, he descended quietly to his father's room, and opened the door with a gentle hand, for Mr. Woodhall was never a very early riser, and Ralph fancied that he might be still asleep. He found him, however, lying reading in his bed, and, after taking a brief parting, not without its tenderness and depth of feeling, however few the words might be, the young man retired. When he was near the door, however, old Mr. Woodhall exclaimed, "Ralph! Ralph!" and added, when his son turned toward him, "you have not forgotten your Cicero, I hope; you said you would put him in your saddle-bags; he is a good companion, Ralph." His son assured him that Cicero had not been forgotten, and then departed.

The next parting was a silent one, but not less full of emotion. There was a little rise in the ground upon the road which he traveled, whence the whole of one side of the mansion of Woodhall was visible to the wanderer's eye. The house was indeed so near that small ornaments of stone-work could be easily distinguished across the stream, and at one of the windows, which, by one means or another, he had learned to know better than any of the rest, there was a fair face gazing out upon the road. Ralph paused for an instant, and waved his hand; a hand was waved in return, and then Margaret retreated hastily from the open window, and he thought he could see her kneel down at the foot of the bed, as if to pray or weep.

"I will win her or die," said Ralph to himself, and that last interview armed him, perhaps, more than all else, to struggle with the difficulties before him. There is nothing in the world so invigorating to the wrestler, man, in his combat with the world, as a strong passion and a strong resolution.

From that spot he rode on rapidly, gaining the high country by degrees, sometimes sweeping over a bare hill side, sometimes passing along under a bank from which stretched forth a canopy of trees. At the distance of about four miles there was a small hamlet, from which the inhabitants of the cottages had principally gone forth to their early labors in the field; but one old woman, withered and blear, with such a face as would easily have made a witch in any land not more than fifty years before, was sitting spinning at one of the doors. As the young traveler came up she raised her eyes, and said aloud, "Ay, those ride fast who ride to ill."

Ralph heard the words, and, somewhat more impressible that morning than usual, he checked his horse and turned to the old crone: "Why say you so, mother?" he asked; "I have never done you any ill, but good, and to your son's family too."

"Ay, it does not matter, Master Ralph," replied the old woman, shaking her head; "what I said is true, notwithstanding;" and she repeated it.

"Do you mean to say I am riding to do ill or to suffer ill?" asked the young man.

"Ay, to suffer more than you know of," replied the woman.

"Then I do not thank you for telling me so," said Ralph, half angrily; and, turning his horse, he rode away at the same quick pace as before. For an instant or two the old woman's words made some impression on his mind; but then hope and expectation bounded up again. He looked to the bright blue heaven, and the glorious sun, and the sparkling landscape, and unconsciously giving a wave of his hand toward it, he exclaimed, "I go with no evil purpose; I will do no base deed; and the God who made all these, who rolls the stars aloft, and brightens the skies above, and sends rain to fertilize, and sunshine to vivify, will guide, provide for, and protect me also."

The distance to Halling's Corner, where he was to meet his new servant, was considerable, but when he reached the spot no one was to be seen. It was a place where two roads crossed, and Ralph looked up and down each of them. No one was in sight; and, taking out one of the cumbrous watches of the day, the young man found that, by dint of riding fast, he had arrived nearly half an hour before the time appointed. There was nothing for it but patience, and, dismounting, he loosened the girths, and walked the horse up and down. At the end of about twenty minutes, while he was a few yards distant from the corner, he heard the voice of some one singing a common country air of the time; and when he could see down the other road, he perceived another horseman coming quietly up at a jog-trot. Rightly concluding that it was his new man, Gaunt Stilling, he waved his hand for him to make haste, and proceeded to refix his saddle The other, however, did not hurry his pace in the least; and when he reached the spot, Ralph told him, somewhat impatiently, that he had been waiting half an hour.

Stilling smiled good-humoredly, and replied, "Well, sir, you are now master, and I am man, and it is bad for the master to wait upon the man; but I have heard that, in point of punctuality, it is as bad to be too soon as too late. It wants just five minutes of the hour, if I judge the time right."

"No harm can happen from being a little too soon," replied Ralph.

"Sometimes, sir," answered Gaunt Stilling; "many a man has got his bones broken for being half an hour too soon; as, for instance, If a man appoints another to help him in a fray, and gets to his enemy half an hour before his friend, he will have time to take a mighty good drubbing for his lack of punctuality."

"True, true," answered Ralph; "punctuality is, I believe, the best rule, after all, and punctuality admits of no deviations. My horse carried me somewhat more speedily than usual."

"More's the pity, sir," replied Stilling, "for his pace will not be so good, nor his strength so enduring as if he had come slower. Take a horse out coolly--bring him in cool, is a good maxim in my part of the country. But here is a letter I have to give you."

Ralph took it and looked at the superscription, which imported, "To his grace the Duke of Norfolk, greeting. These by the hands of Ralph Woodhall, Esquire, a gentleman of mark."

"Who gave you this for me?" asked the young gentleman.

"I know not, sir," answered Stilling; "it was left at our house."

"I have another letter for the duke," said Ralph, thoughtfully; "who can this be from?"

"Two are always better than one," replied his companion; "one may hit the nail that another misses."

"If so, it is fortunate," rejoined the young gentleman, "for I am going straight to the duke's house in Norwich, judging that he might best forward my views."

"I fancied that you would wing your flight thither, sir," said the other, "as soon as I saw that letter."

"Why so?" demanded Ralph, "if you know not from whom this came?"

"Because I judged that no one would send you a letter for a place to which they did not know you were going," was Stilling's reply; and with it Ralph was obliged to be content, for it was very clear that if the man did really know more, he was in no mood for telling it. One question, however, he did ask, after they had mounted and were on their way: "Do you know, Stilling," he said, "whether this letter is or is not from old Lady Coldenham? My conduct in regard to it will be decided by your answer: for if it be from her, I will not present it: not that I fear the nature of its contents, for she can say naught truly against me, but because I will receive no favor at her hands, from reasons of my own."

"Would that all others had such reasons, or had attended to them," replied the servant, in a somewhat bitter tone; but then, suddenly changing his manner, he added, "the contents you can easily see, sir, for the letter is unsealed; but I am certain it is not from the dame at the castle, as I know her hand-shrift right well."

"I shall certainly not open it," answered Ralph, as they rode on; "I hold that the man who opens a letter intrusted to his care, and reads the contents, whatever be his excuse, must feel himself a base and degraded being forever--worse, far worse than an eaves-dropping spy; for the latter has nothing trusted to his honor, the other every thing."

"What, sir, if the letter is left open for the purpose!" inquired the other.

"Ay, under any circumstances," answered Ralph; "we can not widen the line between honorable and dishonorable dealing. Unless I am clearly told that a letter is intended for my reading, nothing should induce me to read it."

"Did all men hold so," answered Gaunt Stilling, "many a famous general would have been defeated, many a famous army beaten, many a great victory lost."

"Not so," replied Ralph; "when I am at war, any property I can take from my enemy is mine, and his secrets against myself above all; but for opening any other letter except those intercepted from an enemy, there is no excuse. No man can tell what may be in them; no one can tell that secrets, which the writer would not have published for the world, and not at all affecting those to whose sense of honor they are confided, may not lie hid within that little fold of paper. Oh! how we ought to blush, if, venturing upon such an act on any pretense, we were to find within that which no man of honor ought ever to have seen. No, no, Stilling, I will never look into a letter intrusted to we, let the consequences to myself be what they may."

"I don't suppose the consequences could well be bad," replied Stilling, "for I suppose that no one would give you an open letter containing abuse of yourself, unless, indeed, they knew your prejudices about such things; so you can put the letter by, and give it to the duke in all safety, I believe."

"I have another letter for the duke," replied Ralph, "which I shall deliver first, as I know who it comes from."

Ralph somewhat quickened his pace, but Gaunt Stilling, though exceedingly respectful, seemed to have a will of his own, and not to be at all inclined to over-hurry the beast that bore him. He lingered behind, then, and the conversation consequently dropped. At the end of about a mile and a half, however, Ralph, who had ridden on for about three or four hundred yards, and might well be supposed by any observer to have no connection with the young man who followed, had his ear attracted by some sound behind him, and, turning round his head, beheld his new servant off his horse, and undergoing the very unpleasant process of being well cudgeled by three stout men. It was a woody part of the country, properly suited for an ambush, somewhat like the scenes which the famous Dutch painter chose for his attacks by banditti. To save him as much as possible from the infliction which he was undergoing, Ralph returned at full speed; and as Stilling was struggling with all his might, which was not little, and had nearly mastered one of his opponents, although the others were beating him all the time, his master's coming to his help turned the strife in his favor. An immediate inclination to flight displayed itself on the part of his assailants; but Ralph contrived to get a thrust at one of them with his sword-blade ere he ran away, and, at all events, drew blood; while Stilling, taking advantage of the assistance afforded, pummeled the one on whom he had principally fixed his attention in no very gentle manner before he let him go.

The men, who speedily disappeared in the wood, were disguised with handkerchiefs tied round and partly over their faces; but Stilling seemed either to know them, or to have very little curiosity; for when his master asked him in one breath whether he was hurt, and if he knew the men who had attacked him, or their object, he replied, very briefly, that he was not hurt, and as to the men, that he knew all about them, and what brought them there. He showed, in short, so little disposition to be communicative, that Ralph resolved to ask no further questions, but only bidding him follow more closely, hurried on at a quicker pace than ever, and soon after reached a better-beaten and more-traveled road.

CHAPTER IX

There is in the fine old town of Norwich, I believe, even to the present day, the remains of a whilom inn, which once stood not far from the River Wansum. Now nothing remains of it but a gable or two, transmuted to purposes very much below the dignity of receiving two-legged guests. Then, however, it was the principal inn in Norwich; and a great change had come over the state and condition of our inns since the time of Chaucer. In that day, inns had reached, in England, very nearly the climax of perfection. Hotels were an abomination unknown, although the name, descended from ancient times, still lingered in various parts of the country. Cleanliness, neatness, perfect ease, and independence characterized the inn of former years; the linen was white as snow; the food was generally of the best kind, however plain the cookery. There a man might take the world as it came; there he might pass his time as in a dream, obtruded upon by none of the hard realities of life, so long as he had in his purse wherewith to satisfy the demands of his host, which in those days were not very extravagant. There he might escape the impertinence, the annoyance, the importunity of the world. There he might riot or revel, muse or meditate, or read or write, or think or sleep, just as he pleased, without interruption. It afforded the most perfect species of liberty, the old English inn, without having any of the drawbacks of confusion and anarchy. No tax-gatherer ever came there, at least with the knowledge of the guests. The constable, even, was seen drinking his pot, or ladling out his punch, or smoking his pipe, with the other friendly persons round the bar, and, so long as order and decency were maintained, and perhaps a little longer, no one interfered with the quiet and ease that reigned within. The inn of the Half Moon, at the time I mention, was one of this sort; and toward it, in the first instance, as directed by others of experience, Ralph Woodhall took his way on his arrival in the city of Norwich, on a somewhat gloomy morning, about eleven o'clock. Before he took rest, however, or did more than brush his clothes from dust, and take off the heavy saddle-bags from their convenient position behind the saddle, to let his beast get a little refreshment and food, Ralph remounted, and rode away to another part of the town, higher up upon the Wansum. This was the old house, or palace of the old Dukes of Norfolk, in which, during their brief terms of residence in Norwich, they kept up in a limited sphere the state and dignity of a sovereign prince.

There had been some doubt in the mind of Ralph, when he arrived in the city, as to whether the nobleman on whom fancy, for the time, seemed to make his hopes depend, was in the town or not; but, as he passed along the streets, the number of servants which he saw in the Howard liveries, and the gayety and bustle which pervaded one quarter of the city, showed him that, so far as finding the duke, his first expectations were likely to be fulfilled. The antique gate-way, with a number of servants crowded under it--the wall surrounding the grounds extending to the river--the massive pile itself of the principal building, did not much impress him; for he thought it very much like one of the colleges at Cambridge, to which his eye was well accustomed. Appearing on horseback, and with a servant behind him, the gates were moved back by the retainers in the porch to give him admission into the court; and, descending there, he was led--while Stilling remained to look after the horses--to a little chamber on the ground floor called the Chamberlain's Office. There he explained his business by simply saying that he brought a letter for the duke from Lord Woodhall; and the grave-looking officer to whom he spoke, looking at the letter in his hand, led him into a waiting-room, where he found three other persons already in attendance on the duke's leisure. Each man was amusing the weary moments of expectation as best he might; one looking out of the window, which displayed an orchard in full beauty; one walking up and down the room, with eyes fixed upon the floor and hands behind the back; and one seated at a large table examining some books, which had been laid there, probably, to beguile the time. Patience and silence seemed to be the order of the day, and Ralph, after looking curiously at the splendid furniture which decorated even that plain room, betook himself to one of those volumes, which soon afforded him amusement to pass half an hour pleasantly. While he read, one after another of his companions in attendance was called out of the room, and at length, laying down the book, he fell into a revery, of that kind which often comes upon us at vacant moments--when brief summings up of the testimony borne by events to the progress of our fate, during a certain period just past, are made by memory, and left to the judgment of the mind, to see if any thing can be made of the case or not.

The great step was taken. Here he was, many miles from home, "seeking his fortune," as the term was then. He had entered the house of one who could at will advance his views or neglect his cause, with nothing to recommend him but one letter from a distant relation, and one from a person he did not know. Something, however, bearing on his destiny was to be decided soon, and he felt all that eager, fluttering anxiety of youth, which every man in early years must have experienced when the great object of the moment was in the balance. There was not much cause for hope, indeed;

and expectation, even under the exaggeration of youth, could hardly see space to stand upon; but love is a great fanner of the flame of hope; and love was always mingling a word with all Ralph's cogitations.

The lesser incidents, too, which had lately occurred, presented themselves to the young man's mind when the greater facts were discussed; the interview with the strange personage calling himself Moraber; the conduct of Lady Coldenham; the meeting with Gaunt Stilling, and the misadventure which had occurred to the latter on the road, passed in review. Of all these, the demeanor of his new servant, his circumstances, and his conduct, puzzled Ralph most. What was he? Why did he at once obey the order to follow him? Was there any secret brotherhood or association in the land, like that of the disciples of the old man of the mountains, which bound its members to follow implicitly the orders of an unknown superior? There had been at that time whispers of such a league; and, if Stilling was a member thereof, what dangers and obstructions might not his own course be brought among by retaining the services of a person over whose conduct another maintained so absolute and independent a control? Then, again, the man's demeanor had not been without remarkable points. Perfectly respectful he always was; but that he had his own particular notions, and liked them better than all others, he did not fail to show. He seemed to have no feeling of degradation from the office of servant which he assumed. He gave no vain reason for his obedience; but there was something in his manner which seemed to say, "I have taken upon me certain duties, and the only proper, the only honorable course, is to fulfill them to the very best of my ability. No honest task degrades a man; the vanity of shirking it, or the fault of neglecting its requirements when undertaken, may degrade. These are the only acts which can make the position of a servant degrading. He is as honorable as his master, if he does his duty as well." No task seemed too hard for him; the very words *menial services*, so often used obnoxiously by the mean and vulgar, he seemed to scorn. His pride was in doing well what he undertook. He appeared to feel that, in doing so, he made himself, in Nature's book, equal with all, superior to many placed continually above him by station and wealth. He would trust the care of the horses to none other; he was careful of his young master's wardrobe; he refused to sit down with him at table, even in small inns, where such a course was common, both in England and France.

All this showed a high mind and a clear intellect; but his character had other puzzling points. Sometimes--and, indeed, this seemed his general humor--he was as gay as the lark, full of glee and merriment; but ever and anon he would fall into deep reveries--fits of thought, deep, profound, even sad, from which it was difficult to rouse him.

Some days after the period of which I write, indeed, he received a letter by the carrier, which seemed to increase the frequency and intensity of these attacks of moodiness; but that had not occurred when Ralph sat in the room at the Duke of Norfolk's, as I have mentioned, and the temper or character of his servant had, to his eyes, all the first sharpness about it.

He was busily engaged in reflections upon all these things, when a stately servant, who had previously called the others out to the presence of the duke, came to summon him also, and led him, with slow and formal steps, to another room on the same floor. Little do the great of this world know how any stiff, haughty, or repulsive manner affects those who, reasonably or unreasonably, have been building up hopes upon their influence or kindness--what luster urbanity or gentleness gives to a favor intended to be conferred; how, by kind courtesy, a disappointment is softened and diminished. Very frequently, the man who will give thousands in charity will not spare a kind word, although it would relieve pangs a thousand-fold more bitter than any which gold can touch. Honor, high honor, to that man who does generous acts generously. There are some such in the world, and, thank God! I know them; but they are not many.

The manner of the Duke of Norfolk was freezing in the extreme. He received his young visitor standing; and, before hearing any thing he had to say, informed him, in a tone cold, though apologetic, that he was in some haste, as he had to go out. Ralph was the more surprised, as the duke had established, generally, a character for courtesy in his dealings with people of inferior rank; but he presented the letter of Lord Woodhall with the hope that that might produce some change in the great man's manner.

Such was not the case, however. The duke opened the letter, ran his eye hastily over it, as a somewhat tiresome ceremony, and then folding it up again, stood silent, as if expecting that Ralph would either say something or go. Seeing, however, that the young man remained silent likewise, he at length said, "Well, Mr. Woodhall, I must think over this, and will let you hear from me in a few days. Tell my chamberlain where you are to be found in Norwich."

"I do not think, my lord duke, that I shall be here very long," replied Ralph, making up his mind, with the rapid rashness of youth, to expect nothing more from the haughty nobleman before him; "I have another letter, however, which I may as well deliver to your grace now, lest I should not have an opportunity of seeing you again."

The duke seemed surprised, and not quite well pleased; but Ralph took out the letter which Stilling had brought him, put it in the nobleman's hand, and was about to retire. The moment the Duke of Norfolk saw the superscription, however, a great change came over his face. "Stay! stay!" he cried; "let me see what this letter contains before you go;" and he ran his eye quickly, but with evident attention, over the few lines within. Before he had quite done, he waved his hand toward a seat, saying, "Pray sit down, Mr. Woodhall," and then resumed the perusal. As soon as he had finished, he took a seat himself, and looking upon Ralph with a smiling countenance, inquired why he had not given him that letter first.

"Because, my lord duke," replied Ralph, "I thought the other from my cousin, Lord Woodhall, the most important. I do not actually know by whom the epistle you hold in your hand was written, it having been sent to me to deliver, without any other intimation; but I suspect that it came from a person so inferior in position to Lord Woodhall, that it might have less weight in your opinion than the other."

The duke smiled. "You were mistaken," he said; "we in the great world learn to estimate matters somewhat differently from others who have not mingled much with matters of general concern, and we give less weight than people generally imagine to rank and wealth. Lord Woodhall is a very excellent nobleman, and my particular good friend; but this gentleman," and he laid his hand significantly upon the paper, "is a very singular and extraordinary personage. Even in these days of infinite oddities he is very remarkable, and, besides his originality, he is a man of immense power of mind, strong will, vast patience, and unchangeable in his purposes; probably from a fixed opinion that certain things are to be, and that it is only required he should shape his course by them, and follow it perseveringly, in order to succeed in his endeavors. This turn has been given to his mind by a passion for judicial astrology, which he imbibed when he and I were fellow-students together at Oxford. He then belonged to Brazen Nose College, where that science, or pretended science, was a good deal cultivated, and although he never made a convert of me, yet I can not but admit that many of his predictions have had a very curious accomplishment. For instance, he named to me long ago, that a change, materially affecting the crown of England, would take place during the first week of February, one thousand six hundred and eighty-five. I read the prophecy to imply the death of the king, but throughout the whole of January his majesty remained perfectly well; and I saw him on the first of February without one token of decay, either in body or mind. I imagined my good friend's prediction would fail; when lo! came the startling news that he had been struck with apoplexy. You know the rest of the events of that week. His majesty died on the sixth, and a great change, indeed, took place."

The duke paused, and seemed to give his mind up to memory for some moments; and Ralph would not interrupt his reveries. At length he again broke silence, returning somewhat abruptly to the subject, and saying, "Moreover, my young friend, these two letters are written in a very different spirit. The first is a mere common letter of introduction, bespeaking my good offices for a young gentleman going to see the world. It is not even written in Lord Woodhall's own hand, though signed by him, and was never calculated to insure you more than merely the civility of an invitation to my house. The second, however, demands, in good broad terms, that I shall do whatever I can to promote your views, with sincerity and zeal; and, good faith, I am willing to do it, though the terms need not have been quite so imperative. First, however, I must know what those views are."

"I will explain them in a moment, my lord duke," replied Ralph; but the other cut him short, saying, "We shall not have time at present, for I am, in reality, going out upon business of some importance; I shall be back, however, in a few hours, and the best plan will be for you to come and take up your residence here for a fortnight or so. During that time we shall find plenty of opportunity for conversation, in the course of which I can learn all your intentions, and perhaps strike out some means of serving you. In the mean time, I will put you into the hands of my chamberlain, who will provide you with what rooms you need, and make you acquainted with the customs of the house."

Thus saying, the duke rang a small bell that stood upon the table, and summoned the chamberlain to his presence. Orders were cordially given for Ralph's hospitable entertainment, and leaving him in the hands of the officer, Norfolk went out to ride.

However far the duke might himself have unbent from his stateliness, the chamberlain remained as dignified as ever. Perfectly civil was he, indeed, for he had seen at a glance that the young stranger was high in the favor of his lord; but he was solemn and slow, with all the rigidity of a hackneyed official, putting a certain degree of state into the slightest movement, and uttering every word in a tone of ceremony. He inquired carefully what number of domestics Master Ralph Woodhall would bring with him, and finding that he was only to be accompanied by one, declared that that would render the arrangement of his apartments very easy, adding, with a pompous air, that gentlemen sometimes came accompanied by as many as twenty, which occasionally put the duke's officers to some inconvenience.

All, however, was at length arranged, a stable pointed out for the two horses, a small suite of rooms, at the western corner of the building, assigned to the master and his servant, and their names duly inscribed in the chamberlain's book.

This completed, Ralph took his departure, and returned to the inn, where Stilling was waiting his arrival, with some traces of anxiety upon his face.

"Well, sir, how has it gone?" he inquired, when Ralph appeared. "Is the duke courteous or not this morning? for the people here tell me his mood varies a good deal, according as he has many or few people to see; mighty civil to the first who come, somewhat short to the last."

"Matters have gone better than I could have expected," replied Ralph; "thanks, I believe, to the letter which you brought me, for till he saw that I can not say the duke showed any great urbanity."

"Ay, I knew that would do the business," replied Stilling.

"Why, I thought you did not know who it came from," observed Ralph

"True, I did not know," replied the man, laughing, "but I guessed. I have a rare bundle of guesses always about me, and they generally turn out tolerably right. But what is to come of it now, master! When shall we hear more? I do not like things to stick by the way."

"We shall hear more very soon, I trust," replied Ralph; "but, in the mean time, you must get ready, Stilling, to take up your abode with me at the duke's house."

"Hurrah!" cried Stilling, "that is progress, to have effected a lodgment on the walls already. But I won't lose a moment, sir, for that which is quick begun is quick ended, notwithstanding all that old women may say;" and away he went to lead forth the horses and replace the saddle-bags.

CHAPTER X

"If you please, sir," said Gaunt Stilling, on the second day after their arrival in Norwich, as he stood before his young master, who was seated reading, and had hardly raised his eyes at his entrance, "may I ask you a question?"

"Certainly," replied Ralph; "what is it, Stilling?"

"Why, only just this, sir," answered Stilling; "I should like to know if, before you set out, you mentioned my name to any one, or whether any one else knew that I was going in your service?"

"No one whatever, Stilling," replied Ralph, "except myself, our friend Moraber, and Mistress Margaret Woodhall, were at all acquainted with the fact; for I did not mention the subject to my father, as he might have imagined that I was about to launch into extravagance and encounter expenses incompatible with my small means, and, moreover, might have made himself uneasy during the whole period of my absence with this thought, which I should never have been able to remove from his mind, although I knew the impression to be wrong."

"Good, sir, good," replied Stilling; "and so now, by your leave and permission, I will be called Stilling no longer, but, as the old poet man says, 'your good servant ever;' I have my own reasons, sir."

"But I do not understand you," said Ralph; "do you wish to change your name, or rather take one that does not belong to you?"

"Yes, sir, any good traveling designation," replied the young man, gayly. "I am not of the rank or manners to dub myself captain; but any thing else will do as well."

"As far as I am concerned, it will," replied Ralph; "but do not the people of the house know your real name?"

"No, sir--no," replied Stilling; "I have waited till to-day to announce myself, and I know you have not betrayed me; for I was asked my name yesterday at supper at the third table, and begged time for consideration and preparation."

Ralph did not at the moment recollect that he had written the man's name with his own hand in the chamberlain's book, and he readily acceded to his wishes, not caring much by what name he went. Stilling fixed upon the designation of Tuckett--Jack Tuckett, and begged his master to call him so for the future, with which Ralph promised to comply unless memory played him an unpleasant trick, and brought back the old name when he was off his guard.

This was all settled, and for a time produced no consequences. Ralph did not choose to pry into the motives of this transformation; and, to say the truth, he was so occupied in thinking of the slow progress of his own affairs that he soon forgot the matter altogether, accustomed himself to call the servant Tuckett, and hardly remembered that he ever had another name. Slow progress! Oh, the eager hopes of youth, how they hurry us on to disappointing conclusions! He had been five days in the house of the Duke of Norfolk. He had seen more or less of that nobleman every day, and had been treated by him with kindness and distinction; but not a word had yet been said in regard to his views or prospects; and Ralph's spirit fretted within him to find the wheels move so much more slowly than he had expected.

At length one day the duke sent up a message to his room, importing that he was about, that morning, to set out upon a visit to a neighboring nobleman, at whose house the Earl of Sunderland was to meet him. He thought it might be advantageous to his young friend, he said, to be acquainted with that nobleman, and he would take him with him if he would consent to travel without a servant, as the house would be somewhat crowded.

Ralph smiled when he received the message, and immediately prepared to go. Stilling, or, as we must now call him, Jack Tuckett, seemed delighted with the arrangement, and asked permission, during his master's absence, to make an expedition of his own. His request was readily complied with; and the two parted not long after, Ralph to accompany the duke, and the other to go whithersoever his fancy led.

Nothing resulted from the interview with Lord Sunderland; and his character is too well known in history for me to dwell upon the impression he produced on Ralph's mind. The young man was naturally charmed with his winning address, and easy, unaffected manners. There was about him, too, a tone of superiority and confidence in his own opinions, which were somewhat impressive to inexperience. It is not to be wondered at, when men of great powers of mind, already forewarned of Sunderland's treacherous vacillation, yielded to the peculiar powers of fascination which he possessed, and believed him sincere and steady in his convictions, after he had been weighed a thousand times and found wanting, that a young man like Ralph Woodhall should be deceived by his pretensions to purity and truth.

The Duke of Norfolk, however, from to time read a comment upon the conduct of the statesman which was of service to his young friend; and several of the gentlemen who were present made observations upon Sunderland's professions, or told anecdotes of his former doings, which served in some degree to open Ralph's eyes. The time passed very pleasantly, however. Lord Sunderland seemed to have conceived a great friendship for the young country gentleman, would take a morning walk with him, and talk of classic lore and the stores of art in other lands with eloquence and information such as few possessed. But yet there was something unsatisfactory in the whole, which Ralph felt without being able to detect what it was--a want of something, probably of sincerity and frankness, which deprived his conversation of much of its charm.

At the end of six days the duke set out on his return, and the whole party reached Norwich somewhat late in the evening. Ralph found that his servant had not yet returned; but he was already a favorite in the household, and one of the duke's men came up to his room, and volunteered to perform the offices of "Mr. Tuckett."

"There are to be great doings to-night, sir," he said; "it is a ball night here. A great number of ladies and gentlemen have arrived from different parts to stay with his grace since you went; all the country round is invited, and the duke's carriages have gone out to bring in the company from the town. The state-rooms, too, are open, where every thing is of gold or silver, even to the tongs and pokers; so there will be a grand sight."

Ralph dressed himself as speedily as possible in the best array that his wardrobe would afford, and, receiving directions from the man who came to assist him as to the way toward the state apartments he had mentioned, descended without any of those emotions which vanity often produces in even the practiced in such scenes when they expect to play a conspicuous part. His mind was set upon higher objects; and he neither hoped nor wished to attract attention, or to win admiration in courtly halls. He had to descend--from the second floor of the house, where his rooms were situated--a large oaken stair-case, from which, at each landing-place, led away, in four directions, different corridors leading to numerous suites of apartments; and as, by the time he went down, guests were arriving thick, the galleries were thronged with gay groups, hurrying across or pausing for a moment to look over the balustrades at the parties entering the hall below.

Among the rest, Ralph stopped for an instant to gaze upon the brilliant moving scene, and, leaning over, bent his eyes upon the landing-place just beneath. Suddenly a figure passed across, the sight of which made him start and run down with a quick step. It was gone before he reached the landing; but if there was any sight in the eyes of love, that figure, he felt certain, was that of his Margaret.

He hurried on to the state apartments, where more than a hundred persons were already assembled, while the duke, all affability and kindness, was standing in the third saloon, receiving his guests, and saying some kind and courteous words to each. It was a bright and cheerful scene, and perhaps excelled in splendor the court of royalty itself; but Ralph had no eyes for any thing but the search which he made among the ever-increasing crowd for the figure he had seen. The magnificent pictures on the walls, the beautiful statuary ranged around--master-pieces of ancient and of modern art--the costly decorations on which the wealth and taste of several generations had been lavished, detained him not for a moment; but onward he passed, till he reached the room where the duke had placed himself. There he paused for an instant to salute the lord of the mansion, intending to hurry on immediately after; but the duke called him kindly to his side, giving him his Christian name as a mark of familiarity, and introduced him to the bishop and several of the most distinguished guests. Still Ralph was anxious to escape; but his noble patron had other business for him.

"Here, Ralph," he said, "this fair lady, to whom I present you, Hortensia, Lady Danvers, is anxious to see the bowling-green and wilderness illuminated on this fine night. I must, alas! remain here to receive all my coming guests, or I would be her guide myself. I can not, however, intrust her to any one who will supply my place with gallant courtesy better than yourself, my young friend. Madam, let me beg you to know and esteem my young friend, Ralph Woodhall, whose good qualities he will commend to you himself better than any words of mine could do."

The lady whom he addressed was young and beautiful, and looked younger even than she really was; for the features were all exceedingly small and delicately chiseled, the complexion brilliantly fair, while there was a world of youthful, speaking tenderness in her eyes, a sort of beseeching look, which seldom survives a long acquaintance with the great hardening world. She was magnificently dressed, but in a style peculiar to herself, approaching that of the earlier part of the last reign, rather than the stiffer mode which was already beginning to prevail; but her rich brown hair, looped up in great masses with diamonds, was arranged in a fashion which probably had never found favor in any country generally; for it required features such as her own, and a brow as beautiful as hers, to render it at all becoming. With her the effect was beautiful and picturesque, and she certainly was as lovely a creature, as she stood there by the duke's side, as the eye could well behold.

Nevertheless, Ralph would have given all that he possessed in the world to be free from the task of escorting her; but that could not be. He had no excuse ready, even if any excuse could have been available in such circumstances; and bowing low, he said, with the pardonable hypocrisy of society, that he should be delighted to be her guide. He knew not, in his ignorance of the ways of courtly life, whether he ought to offer her his arm or not, and he hesitated; but he saw many a gentleman and lady passing through the apartments arm in arm, and bending his head as she took a step forward toward the door, he asked, "Will you not lean on me?"

"With pleasure," she replied, taking his arm at once; and they walked on through that room and the next. It must have been difficult for the lady not to see that her companion's thoughts were not so exclusively given to herself as she had perhaps a right to expect, or to avoid noticing that his eyes often wandered from her beautiful face to different parts of the halls, as if looking for something. But woman is a strange creature, and very full of varieties. Some persons, of irritable and all-absorbing vanity, would have felt offended, and might have shown their anger. Not so Lady Danvers, however. What might have offended, or rather, I should say, disgusted her more, would have been the empty compliments and overcharged affectation of gallantry which were so common in that day. At all events, Ralph's demeanor had somewhat of the charm of novelty in it; and she seemed to apply herself diligently to show him that she was worthy of more attention than he paid her.

For some little time she was silent; but at length she said, in a low voice, "I think you must be looking for some one, Mr. Woodhall."

"Only my cousin, of whom I caught a glance upon the stairs," replied Ralph.

"And now you are wishing me far away," rejoined the lady, with a smile; "but come, let us look for him before we go to the wilderness; I am quite willing to join in the chase."

Ralph felt his rudeness; and, what perhaps was more to the purpose at that moment, he was convinced--for he had used his eyes well--that Margaret was not in the rooms. He had either been mistaken altogether in supposing he had seen her, or else she had gone to change her dress, which might, for aught he had remarked, been merely a traveling costume.

He hastened, then, to atone, saying, "Oh no! I will not lead you such a chase on any account; nor must you suppose any such rudeness in my thoughts. I wished but to say two words to my cousin. But it matters not; I shall find, I trust, another opportunity. Now let us go to the wilderness; this is our way."

"You are very strange," said the lady, thoughtfully; "I have given you a dozen opportunities of saying pretty things to me, and you have not taken advantage of one. I suppose there is not another man in the whole room who would have neglected any of them."

Ralph was about to put forth some apology, and to try to make some amends; but Lady Danvers would not suffer him to proceed, lifting her beautiful soft eyes to his face, and saying, "Stop! not a word of excuse; I like you all the better. For wits, courtiers, gallants, and fools I have a wonderful aversion."

"But at all events," replied Ralph, smiling, as they descended the stone steps to the bank of the Wansum, "you must at one time have liked courtiers better to choose one for your husband."

"My husband!" exclaimed the lady, with a clear, merry laugh; "I have no such incumbrance, Mr. Woodhall. I see you do not know much about me, although I know every thing about you. Now I will tell you all about myself, which may, perhaps, cheer your task for you. The duke called me Lady Danvers, for the best of all possible reasons, because I am Lady Danvers--but in my own right, and not as the appendage of any husband in Christendom. I and poor Henrietta Wentworth were in the same position, baronesses in our own right, and great friends, too, till she went away, though she is older than I am."

"Why do you call her poor Henrietta Wentworth?" asked Ralph; "I should think to be an independent peeress did not deserve much compassion."

"Oh, ignorant man!" cried his fair companion; "I did not think there was any one in the whole world who did not know that poor girl's history. I can not tell it to you fully, for there is much therein I would not wish to dwell on. Suffice it that she sacrificed all to love--rank, wealth, consideration, friends, home, country!"

"I envy her," said Ralph, in a serious tone; "methinks that there could be no greater happiness on earth than the opportunity of making such a sacrifice."

"For a worthy object," replied the lady, in as grave a tone as his own.

"And is he not worthy, for whom she has sacrificed all this?" demanded Ralph, eagerly.

"Not worthy of such a sacrifice in any way," said Lady Danvers, "except in love for her; there I believe he is perfect. Graceful, handsome, affable, kind, and brave in the field he is; but I fear much he is weak, vacillating, inconstant, and ungrateful to all but her: I speak of Monmouth."

"What, the duke?" asked Ralph.

"The same," replied the lady; and there the conversation stopped for a moment or two, while, passing over the bowling-green, which was surrounded by a ring of lights, as if to shine upon fairy revels on the greensward, they entered what was called the wilderness, where a number of mazy walks, illuminated by many tricornered lanterns, afforded ample opportunities for private meetings and whispered tales of love.

"This is exceedingly pretty," said the lady, looking around her over the scene, where the lanterns, shining through the green leaves, produced the effect of a garden lighted by glowworms.

"Yes," replied Ralph, in an absent tone; "but you said just now, Lady Danvers, that I knew little about you, while you knew every thing about me. The first was unhappily quite true; the second, I doubt not, was quite true also; but yet I can not well comprehend how any thing regarding so insignificant a person as myself can have reached your ladyship's ears."

"Now have I a great mind," replied Lady Danvers, "to punish you for all your misdeeds this night, by keeping you in darkness and mystery. I will even aggravate your suffering by telling you that I desired the duke to introduce you to me, and leave you to discover the interpretation for yourself."

"Nay, nay," said Ralph, "I am sure you will not be so cruel."

As he spoke, another party, conversing in gay, laughing tones, passed along a walk close to that which they were following, and only separated from it by a thin screen of hornbeam. The lady paused ere she replied; but when the others had passed, she said, "Well, well, I will be merciful, and spare you an unquiet night. You are the son of Mr. Robert Woodhall, of The Grange, the duke told me. I must explain: I asked him who you were as you crossed the room--for I thought you very handsome, of course; and I thought you better dressed than any other man there, because you had less gold lace and embroidery about you. However, the duke told me; and then I knew all about you directly. My dear mother, who left me here on earth some eighteen months ago, was the early friend of your mother, her constant companion in the days of girlhood, and she has often talked to me about her. She had her picture ever hanging in her room, and I have seen it a thousand times; but she always said it did her little justice--that she was the most beautiful creature in all the world. Then my mother would tell me how yours had chosen your father against the wishes of many of her friends, and neglected high station and courtly celebrity to become the wife of a poor gentleman on whom she had no fortune to bestow, and how, when she died and left him, he had abandoned all the paths of worldly ambition which he had opened for himself, and retired to his small estate with her only child. Once or twice in the year, a letter passed between your father and my mother, for they had both loved the same person, and both mourned her as long as they lived."

There was something so touching in her voice and manner as she told the little tale, that Ralph, hardly knowing what he did, took her fair hand and pressed it in his own. Lady Danvers seemed not at all offended, and entered fully into his feelings toward his mother.

"I am sure I should love your father very much," she added, "for I have read several of his letters--especially toward the last years of my own parent's life--and in them he spoke in as beautiful and touching affection of his wife and her loss as if she had not been dead a year. I am sure I should love him."

"I think you would," replied Ralph; "though that one deep grief, which he experienced so early, has made him very negligent of all those graces which I am told he at one time possessed. He is now immersed in studies, curious and abstruse, and heeds little else besides his books."

"Well, you see," replied Lady Danvers, "I have, at all events, an hereditary right to your friendship; and all I can say is, that if I can promote your views in any way, Mr. Woodhall, I shall be very happy."

"To have a right to call you friend, dear lady," replied Ralph, warmly, "is quite enough, without taxing your kindness further. The picture you have of my mother must be, I suppose, a copy of that which my father possesses; and yet I should like to see it."

"Oh, no, it is no copy," answered the lady; "she sat expressly at my mother's request, shortly after her marriage. It is very beautiful; the face so full of love, and tenderness and self-devotion. Hers was a noble sacrifice and I am sure, if she had possessed millions to give as well as her hand, she would not have hesitated. I can read it in her face."

"I am glad to hear you speak thus," replied Ralph; "the world judges hardly of such sacrifices. Her own relations blamed and cast her off."

"The world is very foolish in its estimates," replied Lady Danvers; "surely the best wealth, and jewels, and rank, and station are happiness and high qualities, peace of heart and contentment. Case me in gold, and I am no better, no happier; put me on a throne, I am no wiser, no better contented; but give me the society of those I love, health, and enough, and the riches of the world can add very little--their want take very little away. I would not be the slave to all this decoration--to the mere ornaments of the human frame or of human life, which I see the greater number of the women of this land become, for all that earth can give."

"Nor I either," replied Ralph; "but yet, dear lady, wealth and station are sometimes needful, not to happiness, but to the means of attaining that better wealth of the heart."

"Never, I should think," replied the lady. "Let us suppose a case," said Ralph. "Imagine that a man, in other respects not ill endowed, but wanting in riches and in high rank, dares to fix his eyes upon some 'bright particular star,' and hopes to win it; suppose even that he has gained love for love, what chance has he of being made happy--of obtaining her he loves, in short? Friends, relations, guardians interpose, obstacles of every kind arise, which can only be overcome by gaining that wealth and station, the want of which is the impediment."

"Not so, not so!" replied Lady Danvers, eagerly. "Let her he loves be nobly firm, and bold in affection. Let her do as your mother did; and, if there be competence, there will be happiness; but really, let us look about us. We are talking so eagerly," she said, while a warm blush fluttered over her cheek, "that people will say we are making love, and the duke will ask me about the gardens, and I shall be able to tell him nothing. Then will his grace have his good joke at poor me. However, Mr. Woodhall, whenever you like to see that picture, you can. It is at my seat in Somersetshire, and if I am absent when you pass that way, you have but to use my name, and the servants will show it to you. Bid them treat you hospitably, too, for their mistress's sake; now tell me, what is this we are coming to?"

"It is the fish-pond--illuminated, too, I see," replied Ralph; "let us go near the edge and look in. By day one can see down to the marble beneath. I know not whether this light is strong enough. Yes, it is; see how those gentlemen, in their gold and silver coats, swim quietly about, as if their watery world had no strife or contention in it. They always look to me like the prosperous and wealthy of this earth, who never seem to dream of all the strife, and care, and agony of body and of mind that is going on around them."

"Not so with all the prosperous!" replied the lady, in a tone almost reproachful; "those who are not quite so fortunate often do them an injustice. They can not see beneath the surface, or know not how often the heart, which has few or no sorrows of its own, bleeds for the sorrows of others. Yet so far you are right, I believe. Prosperity may have a tendency to harden the heart. Without feeling grief or care, imagination can not picture it distinctly, and we are in danger of forgetting, in our own tranquillity, the sorrows and the pangs which are not apparent to the eye."

They continued for a moment or two gazing into the clear water without noticing the groups that passed by. At length, however, a voice familiar to Ralph's ear said, loud enough for him to hear, "Yes, very lover-like, indeed! Do not disturb them."

He started; but the speaker was already going down one of the little alleys of the wilderness.

"Did you hear that?" said Lady Danvers, looking up with a blush and a smile; "it is time for us to go back, I think; not that I ever trouble myself much about people's wrong constructions; but it is as well not to give them cause for such observations."

Charming as she was, and kind, Ralph was very willing to return; but as they went, she gave him a frank invitation to visit her, either in London or the country, adding, with a laugh, "I have always some old aunt or ancient cousin of the house staying with me, so as to escape scandal, Mr. Woodhall; and remember, if I can at any time serve you, and perhaps I may be able, all the little influence I possess may be commanded by the son of my dear mother's friend."

Ralph thanked her warmly, eagerly; and they walked on through the mazy walks toward the house with somewhat slower steps, perhaps, than he would have taken had he been alone.

CHAPTER XI

There was an old white-haired man of distinguished mien standing by the Duke of Norfolk, and the latter said, with a good-humored smile, "You requested me, my lord, to take care of his fortunes. Now I have introduced him, this night, to the most beautiful, the most wealthy, and the most romantic young lady in the room, who knew something of his family, and seemed exceedingly interested in his fate. To make the matter more complete, I have sent them to take a walk together through the wilderness and by the bank of the river. Now, I look upon it as a hundred chances to one that they come back desperately in love with each other; for, as the dramatist has it, they have 'changed eyes' already. The lady has no one to control her, and, if I judge her rightly, she will some day or another bestow hand and fortune upon some poor gentleman of no rank, just to show the world how completely she despises the gifts the gods have given her."

"I am delighted, my lord duke," answered the other, "and trust with all my heart your anticipations may be fulfilled. Pray what is the lady's name?"

"Hortensia, Baroness Danvers," replied the duke. "She was once a great friend of poor Henrietta Wentworth, though somewhat more strict in her notions of propriety. I remember her weeping bitterly when told that Lady Wentworth had followed Monmouth. Before that, she would not believe any of the tales that were current. She is a good girl, but a fanciful little enthusiast."

There were only two other persons, besides Lord Woodhall, near enough to the Duke of Norfolk to hear his words. One was a very beautiful girl, who turned red and white alternately as the duke spoke, and the other was a young gentleman of no prepossessing mien, though the features of his face were generally good. He had a haggard and suspicious expression of countenance; and while the duke was concluding what he had to say of Lady Danvers, the young man addressed his fair companion, using a good number of the ribald expletives of the day, not very suitable to the ears of a lady.

"Demme, Margaret," he said, "that would never suit your brother, to have Master Ralph carry off the rich baroness. Gads zounds! I saw Henry fluttering round her in London like a blue and pink pigeon, and, depend upon it, he'll suffer no rivalry from a fellow like Ralph. He'll pink the bookworm in a minute, if there is any of that nonsense."

Margaret turned away with a look of disgust, but with a very pale cheek; and her father presented her to the duke, who received her with a graceful mingling of gallantry and respect. Lord Woodhall then introduced his kinsman, "Mr. Robert Woodhall, son of the late Lord Coldenham;" adding, with a well-satisfied look, "you see, my noble friend, that I have taken the liberty, in making this little detour on my road to London, to cast a number of my relations on your hospitality. My son Henry I think you have seen to-night."

"When monarchs make progresses," replied the duke, with a smile, "they must always be attended by their suite. Your son I saw half an hour ago; and if our friend Ralph would but return with his fair lady, we would have a family dance in the ball-room. Let me offer you my arm, Mistress Margaret; I think all the guests have arrived by this time."

When they reached the ball-room, they found Margaret's brother already engaged in the dance; and the duke and his party paused for some five or ten minutes, gazing upon the scene, while different groups of guests came forward, said a few words, and passed on. Margaret's eyes, however, were but little on the gay sight before her, and very frequently turned to the door by which they had entered with an anxious and eager glance. Ralph did not appear, however, and at length her cousin asked her to join in the dance with him. She could not refuse; and, taking their places, they were proceeding with one of the courtly dances of that day, Margaret with a pale cheek and inattentive mind, and Robert Woodhall with no great grace, but with some agility and skill, when two persons entered the room by the door exactly opposite to the dancers; and Lady Danvers, in all the splendor of her beauty, leaning listlessly on the arm of Ralph Woodhall, was before the eyes of Margaret.

At the same moment, Ralph saw her dancing with Robert Woodhall, and in spite of all he could do to command himself, his cheek grew fiery red. Margaret was fatigued with her long journey. She had been greatly agitated by the words which she had overheard from the lips of the Duke of Norfolk. She was one of those very few persons who undervalue themselves, and when she saw the resplendent beauty of Hortensia Danvers, arrayed and decorated by all that dress could do to heighten its effect, a chilly feeling of all the perils to which her love and happiness were to be exposed took possession of her. Her head became giddy; the objects swam before her eyes; her heart refused to beat and she sank fainting on the floor. The music was instantly stopped; a little crowd gathered round; and Ralph, letting Lady Danvers's arm drop from his own, sprang forward to render assistance. In so doing he came in contact with Robert Woodhall, who turned sharply upon him, exclaiming, "Demme, stand back, sir! You are impertinent! Who asked you to meddle?"

Ralph made no reply whatever, but took him by the collar with one hand, and forcibly drew him back into the center of the room. Then taking his place, he bent anxiously over Margaret, by whom her brother Henry was already standing.

The Duke of Norfolk had observed the whole scene, and had advanced toward the group gathered round Margaret, without, however, mingling with it. His voice was now heard exclaiming, "Carry the young lady out to her own room. She is only fainting with the heat, and will soon be better."

"Help me to carry her, Ralph," said Henry Woodhall, applying himself at once to the companion of his youth rather than to his cousin Robert.

They raised her in their arms and bore her out, Lord Woodhall following, and saying to those around, "She has only fainted--she has only fainted. The girl is not subject to such freaks; but that room was very hot. Pray do not follow--none of you--none of you. We shall bring her to herself very soon." Henry and Ralph carried their fair burden into an ante-room at some distance from the reception rooms, while an attendant ran away to call her own woman to her assistance, and as soon as they had placed her in a chair, Lord Woodhall said, "Now leave us, boys--leave us. I will soon bring her to herself. It is not the first time I have seen a woman faint in my life."

Henry obeyed his father's directions at once, but Ralph lingered for a moment, saying to the old nobleman, "Can I not render any assistance, my lord?"

"Only if you can contrive to unlace this stomacher, my dear boy," replied Lord Woodhall, who had been fumbling at the various lacings which went to complicate a lady's dress in those days, but apparently without much success "Margaret would not mind, I am sure. You have been always like a brother to her."

Ralph hastened to obey, and with hands which trembled with many emotions, and associations, dear but agitating, soon unfastened Margaret's dress and gave her fair bosom freer play. As he did so, the beautiful girl opened her eyes for a moment, fixing them with a look of thoughtful anxiety upon his face, and raised her hand faintly so that it lay upon his. Then, however, came the maid; and as he was once more desired by the old lord to leave himself and his daughter alone, the young man obeyed--reluctantly, it must be owned, and not without more than one glance turned back to her he was leaving. She was pale and insensible still, having fallen back into a fainting fit again almost as soon as she had opened her eyes; but the momentary look she had given him was not to be forgotten, and it was with regret that he quitted the room.

Instead of returning to the state apartments at once, the young gentleman wandered up and down the corridor for some minutes; but at length Lord Woodhall came forth with the welcome intelligence that Margaret had fully recovered; and with him Ralph returned to the ball-room.

In the mean time he had formed the subject of conversation in two of the different groups which that room contained. In one part Robert Woodhall was speaking eagerly with one or two gentlemen who surrounded him, saying, "He insulted me, sir--he insulted me; and he shall make me an apology, or I will know the reason why." The words were overheard by the Duke of Norfolk, who had just returned from bidding his guests go on with their dancing, assuring them that the little confusion which had occurred, had only been occasioned by a lady fainting from the heat, and ordering more windows to be opened to admit the fresh air. He immediately turned somewhat sharply toward Robert Woodhall, saying, "I beg your pardon, young gentleman, he did not insult you. You insulted him. He shall make you no apology, if he would remain my friend. Whether he will be content without an apology from you, must rest with himself. I shall not interfere."

At the other side of the room conversation of a different character was going on between the son of Lord Woodhall and the fair Lady Danvers. She had remained, after Ralph left her, on the same spot, watching, if the truth must be told, his proceedings with some interest, and suspecting, though not convinced of the truth. Henry Woodhall was an old acquaintance, but in her eyes nothing more; and when he approached her, as soon as he re-entered the ball-room, she inquired, "How is your sister?"

It was hypocrisy, I must needs admit; for had the question which first sprang to her lips been uttered, it would have been, "Where is your cousin?"

"Oh, she is getting better," replied Henry Woodhall, lightly; "ladies will faint, you know, most beautiful."

"Why, your cousin Ralph seems to take a deeper interest in the matter than you do," replied the lady, not seeking to make any mischief, but moved by a curiosity which perhaps had its source in some deeper motive still.

"Oh, they have been all their childhood together," replied Henry Woodhall; "Ralph is as much her brother, in all our eyes, as I am."

"I almost fancied it was something more than brotherly love," said Hortensia, in a low voice.

"Pooh! nothing of the kind," replied Henry Woodhall, in his gay, light tone. "Margaret is to be married to my cousin Robert, by the act in that case made and provided for

"'Uniting lands and money

In the holy estate of matrimony.'"

"But now tell me, beautiful lady," he continued, "will you dance with me?"

"Poor girl!" said Lady Danvers, with a sigh, not heeding his request at all.

"Why do you say poor girl?" asked Henry Woodhall.

"Because she ought to be a poor girl to marry your cousin Robert," replied Lady Danvers, bluntly, "and because she will be a poor girl if she does marry him."

"Marry him she will, assuredly," replied Henry. "These things always come to pass when the old people arrange them; and they do very well after all. You would be obliged to marry me, if your great-great-grandfather had arranged it with my great-great-grandmother."

"That I would not," replied Lady Danvers, "if all our ancestors had arranged it from Adam downward."

"Well, never mind that," replied Henry, laughing; "nobody asks you. The question at present is, Will you dance with me?"

"Then the answer is, No, I will not," replied Lady Danvers; "I shall not dance to-night."

"Then I shall look for some one else," answered Henry; and, turning gayly away, he left her.

Lady Danvers remained for a moment or two musing in the same place. She asked herself, Was there any love between Ralph and Margaret? The heightened color in his cheek when first his eyes fell on his fair cousin, she had not remarked, but she had seen the eager gaze which Margaret fixed first upon him and then upon herself, and the impetuous haste with which he had flown to her aid when she fainted. She argued, however, thus: "Perhaps the sight of a relation so kind and so noble in his feelings, at the moment when she was dancing with a man whom she could not love, forced upon her by her relations, may have moved feelings deep enough to overpower her. Perhaps Ralph's eagerness might be all very natural and right; nay, it *was* natural and right, in one brought up with the poor girl in fraternal affection such as Henry Woodhall had described. Perhaps--" But there was no end of perhapses. Lady Danvers was willing to believe that there was no love between the two, and did believe it; and yet she asked herself, when her musing came to an end, "What matters it to me whether there be love or not?"

Had she been seeing sights and dreaming dreams? It might be so; and certain it is, that among the sweetest of all those dreams which flit deceptive before man's eyes, from the cradle to the grave, are those which are so faint and intangible that we are not ourselves conscious of their passing till they have passed.

However that may be, and whatever silent streams of that peculiar current of the mind which runs between thought and feeling--partaking, like the mingled waters of the Rhine and Maine, of the distinct coloring of each--had been flowing through her brain, certain it is that she hung about in the ball-room, now in one place, now in another, avoiding all long conversation with any one till Ralph made his appearance again, and that soon after they were talking together as before. Her first questions were for Margaret; but Ralph had by this time recovered full command over himself, and knew how dangerous it might be for all his hopes to suffer the feelings of his heart to appear. He replied, therefore, in as cool a tone of indifference as he could assume, and exerted himself during the rest of the evening to appear at ease and unconcerned.

Margaret did not reappear. Robert Woodhall also quitted the ball-room, and was seen in it no more; but Henry continued dancing and talking, and more than once mingled gayly and good-humoredly in conversation with his cousin Ralph and the young baroness, seeming just as well pleased with the intimacy which had so suddenly sprung up between them as if he had taken part in introducing them to each other.

Lord Woodhall was well pleased also. He was not a man of very quick perceptions--no great schemer or arranger of plans; and, although he would have been very willing to see his son marry any woman on earth with the fortune of Lady Danvers, it had never struck him that the alliance was worth seeking for any member of his family till the notion was propounded to him, already arranged, by the Duke of Norfolk. Neither did he feel any inclination to meddle with it after finding it thus settled to his hand. All he thought was, that Ralph was a very lucky fellow in having such an opportunity afforded him.

Such were the feelings of several personages on the scene when supper was announced, and the guests sat down to one of the most splendid entertainments of the period. I need not pause to give any account of the supper, nor to tell how the guests were served on massive plate of silver gilt, nor how they drank out of goblets of pure gold. Is it not written in the book of chronicles of the house of Howard? and do we not know that even the pokers, the tongs, the shovels, and the fenders of the palace of Norwich were of solid silver?

Before the evening meal was completely ended, however, a servant bent over Henry Woodhall's chair and whispered something in his ear. That young gentleman remained at table for a few minutes longer, but as soon as he could find a good opportunity, he slipped away from the table and did not return.

Not long after, the duke and his friends rose from supper, and dancing recommenced, going on till night had far waned. In common courtesy, Ralph asked his fair companion of the evening to tread a measure with him, and her answer was very different from that which she had given to Henry Woodhall.

"I would with pleasure," she replied, "for I am fond of dancing; but I have refused several to-night, and among the rest your cousin Henry."

"Oh, Henry would not mind," replied Ralph; "he is hot in temper, but kind and good-humored; I will take the responsibility upon myself."

"No," replied Lady Danvers, "I said distinctly that I should not dance this evening, and therefore I will not. See what it is," she continued, in a gayer tone, "to neglect opportunity. If you had asked me while we were walking together in the wilderness, I would have danced with you at once, and then might have refused all other comers at my own will and pleasure; but now that I have declared my intention not to dance at all, I must not offend some very worthy people by dancing with any one."

"Well, if you do not dance, will you walk?" asked Ralph; "the air upon the terrace will be sweet and cool. There are many people walking there also."

"Be it so," replied Lady Danvers, with a smile; "the fresh air will do me good, for my head feels hot, and my brain somewhat giddy with the multitude of people crammed into the same room. There is nothing so strange as what people call pleasure; all who are here are seeking it in things where it does not dwell--nay, more, are trying to extract it from materials distasteful to most of them. What care they for dancing? What care they for the crowded ball-room? What care they for all the labor and trouble of dressing themselves forth for this grand occasion? It is always something else they are seeking than that which they pretend to be enjoying. Strange alchemy of the human mind, which changes lead into gold, and from things that are fatiguing, hurtful, or annoying, produces what is called pleasure, if not happiness. One dances to show a fine form or graceful teaching, not for any enjoyment of the dance. Another comes here to display a gown finer than her neighbor's; a third--who would rather have been in bed--to say that she was at the great ball, or perhaps," she added, laughing, "to prevent others from saying that she was not. I am beginning to think that every thing is hypocrisy in this world, Mr. Woodhall; is it not so?"

"God forbid!" replied Ralph; and quietly led her on to the terrace, where they wandered about for a few minutes. They soon, however, found their way down to the banks of the Wansum again, and walked musingly along, gazing upon the lights reflected in the water. Sometimes they talked together, sometimes they mused; but Lady Danvers leaned all the time upon his arm; and certainly, to the eyes of those who passed them, they seemed more like a pair of lovers happy in each other's affection than two persons who had met that night for the first time. At length the sounds of departure warned them to return; and as they parted, Hortensia said, "We shall meet again to-morrow."

CHAPTER XII

Is a room not very large, upon the upper floor but one of the Duke of Norfolk's palace in Norwich, sat Robert Woodhall by the side of a table on which were placed two large wax tapers. His hat had been thrown upon the ground at some distance; his sword and sword-belt lay upon the table; his head was bent forward as he reclined in the chair, and his left foot was thrown listlessly over the right.

I have described his features as good, though the expression of his face was unprepossessing, and there was now on it a thoughtful look, slightly varying from time to time, as if he were revolving some subject of much interest, or laying out some plan upon which much depended. Now a frown would gather on his brow; and now the frown would be chased by a smile; and now the smile would give place to a scornful curl of the lip, as if he were mentally sneering at some one present to his thoughts.

"Ay, Master Ralph!" he muttered, between his teeth, "we will fit you with something;" and then again he fell into silence. A moment or two after he muttered in the same tone, "Harry's a fool! He's as hot as pepper, though, when put up, and one can make something of that, perhaps."

Once more a moment or two passed without his saying any thing, and then came the words. "Yes, it must be that way if he has been tampering with Margaret's heart, and is now half won away from her by this bright Hortensia. Demme, it might be my game to let him win the young baroness, and make sure if Mistress Margaret myself. She is very handsome--would show well; and then her mother's fortune, that is all her own at once. No--zounds! I will not play that game; for, though I might win the stakes, yet he would carry off more still; and, by ----, he shall not triumph. My mother told me to avoid him through life; for that, if a struggle came between us, he might *throw me*: that was her word. Now we have run against each other, and the struggle must come. But we will see, mother mine which will throw the other. He may have the strength, but I have the trick. What the fiend can be keeping that lad? he has had time enough to learn the whole history of every body in the house."

Once more he relapsed into silence; but if he were waiting for any one, he had full a quarter of an hour to remain in expectation. At the end of that time a tall, powerful, but agile fellow, in the garb of a servant, entered the room, and with a sort of tip-toe, sliding, and noiseless step, approached the back of the young gentleman's chair. There standing he spoke over his shoulder, saying, "I have plenty of news for you, sir."

"You have had time enough to get it," replied Robert Woodhall, sharply; "speak out, and be quick."

"This cousin of yours is not here alone, as you thought, sir," said the man; "he has got a servant with him, and who do you think that servant is?"

"Nay, I know not, and what matters it?" rejoined his master; "though where the beggarly animal picked up a servant, or got money to keep him, I can not divine."

"He is none other, sir, but our old friend Gaunt Stilling," said the servant, by those few words causing his young master to start upon his feet with a look of vindictive fierceness which would have done honor to a tragedy-villain. The next instant, however, he sat down again with a laugh, saying, "That is impossible, you fool! That scoundrel Stilling went away with my pretty Kate, to take her out of my reach. I will find her, though. I heard the whole plan, and set three men to belabor him on the road, and bring her back. They failed in the latter, for she had gone on with her old fool of a father; but they succeeded in the former part of the business--at least they swore so, and if they cheated me, I will trounce them. It is impossible, I tell you. The men did overtake him, and one of them got a sharp poke in the shoulder from a companion of his. I saw the wound myself; and it was not such a scratch as a man might give himself, for the sake of a little bloody evidence to support a lie. What you tell me is impossible, I say."

"It is quite true, sir," said the man, in a soft, insinuating tone; "I will tell you all about it; but let me just say, in the mean time, sir, that if you had but condescended to trust me in the matter of the young lady, Mistress Kate, I would have had her back for you, and snug in the little cottage, within a single day."

"I never trust any body too much," replied Robert Woodhall, in a surly tone. "How the devil did you know any thing about the cottage?"

"Oh, I know every thing that goes on, sir," answered the servant, with a slight touch of self-sufficient confidence in his tone; "I believe you would find it better to trust one than many."

"Come, come, leave your preaching," cried Robert Woodhall, interrupting him sharply; "I do not desire to be schooled by such as you. You say this tale you tell me is true; I say it it impossible. Now make these two meet."

"Why, sir, you have been misinformed," replied the man. "Gaunt did not go with his sister, but the old man did. Gaunt stayed to go along, as servant, with your poor cousin Ralph; and it was Mr. Woodhall who slit Jack Naseby's arm. They had not much time to belabor Master Gaunt either, for they took to their heels and ran as soon as his master came to his rescue."

"Gaunt Stilling turned his servant?" said Robert Woodhall, in a tone of doubt and surprise; "I can not believe it, Roger. He is as proud as a prince, demme; he would be no man's servant."

"Oh, there are ways of taming pride, sir," answered the man. "It would not surprise me if you were to find means to tame the pride of both brother and sister."

"What is it you mean?" demanded his master, sternly. "Zounds! sir, do not trifle with me, or you shall suffer for it. Give me some connected account at once. Tell me what you have heard, and as you heard it."

"Well, sir, well," replied Roger, "I have both seen and heard. But, to give you a connected account, as you say: after I left you I went into the still-room, and pretended to have a defluxion which required some herb water. I soon got into conversation with the still-room maid, and then went with her to talk with the young ladies of the third table. I there heard that Mr. Ralph Woodhall had a servant with him who called himself Jack Tuckett, and that the said Jack had gone, or been sent by his master, on some expedition on horseback four or five days ago. Now I think I know every man's name within forty miles of Coldenham tolerably well, but I did not recollect such a person as Jack Tuckett among all my acquaintance. It sounds like a false name, too, sir; and so I determined I would go away to the duke's chamberlain and find out more. So, when I got to the chamberlain's office, I took off my hat, and bowed low, and the old gentleman said, with a grand air, 'What do you want, my man?' To which I replied, humbly, below my breath, 'My master ordered me to see that his name was rightly put down in the books, for there are more gentlemen than one who may be marked R. Woodhall.'"

"Come, be not so particular," cried his master, whose oaths and expletives shall be omitted for the future, or supplied by the reader's imagination rather than my pen. "Come to the point, sir."

"Well, sir, the point was that I saw the books," replied the worthy Roger, "and there I saw written Mr. Ralph Woodhall, and Gaunt Stilling, his man, with date and designation."

The Fate | 95

"It is impossible!" cried Robert Woodhall, in a tone of doubt rather than negation. "Why, but a few days ago he was bearding my mother like a lion--and it needs no less to beard her; and now, a servant to this poor, miserable cousin of mine, who has hardly money enough to keep himself in clean linen!"

"Well, sir, I was surprised too," replied the man, "though it must be a tough joke that surprises me; but just as I was crossing the stable yard, who should I see but Gaunt Stilling himself getting off that very good brown horse he rides, and leading him right into the stables. It was dark enough there, and I kept out of the way; but he caught sight of me, and all the menservants being busy in the house, he hallooed to me, 'Good friend, just hold my beast a minute, while I go in and get a lantern to look for the rack comb and brushes!' But I answered, in the voice of a Blunderbore, 'I'm no servant of the house; hold the beast yourself.' He gave me a benediction, tied his horse to the manger the best way he could, and away for a light. Then it, just came across me that I might find something out by a little feeling. So I went into the stable, missed a kick from a skittish mare, and, creeping up by the side of the new-come beast, who was as dull as a long journey could make him, I ran my hand over the saddle and its adjuncts. I found a pair of bags with padlocks on them, which there was no time to pick; and I found two horse-pistols at the saddle-bow, out of which it was not worth while to take the bullets; and I found a horseman's cloak, good broad-cloth enough it seemed to the feel, but it would not do to take it bodily, for people ask after their cloaks sometimes. I could not help feeling it, however, for it was so soft and good--ten times as soft as my lady gives her people--and as I felt it here and felt it there, I felt something crackle like paper. 'Here's a pocket,' said I; and I soon found it; and, gently insinuating my hand, I found these papers, which I brought incontinent to you."

Robert Woodhall took them, and looked at the first, which was a somewhat crumpled document, written on coarse paper, and seemingly a bill. He threw it down on the floor with a contemptuous look, which the servant immediately remarked and commented on.

"The next is more to the purpose, sir," he said.

"What! then you have examined them!" exclaimed his master, turning sharply upon him.

But Roger was not to be daunted easily; and he replied, with the utmost coolness, "Certainly, sir; I could not tell there might not be something immoral or irreligious in them, and I could not venture to bring you ribaldry."

His master laughed coarsely, and turned the paper, which was an open letter, till he could see the address. It was written in a very tolerable female hand, and was, in effect:

"To Master R. Woodhall.
"These from--"

Here the writer seemed to have been interrupted, for the writing broke short off.

Without ceremony, Robert Woodhall began to unfold the letter; but his servant observed, in a quiet tone, "I do not know, sir, whether it is for Mr. Ralph or you. That is a question. There is nothing in the letter to show--"

"What! then you have read it all, you infernal scoundrel!" exclaimed his master.

"Certainly, sir," replied the man, "every word."

"Then, by ----, I will--" cried Robert, with an angry look; but there he stopped, and, spreading out the sheet, read as follows:

"I am here in bondage, dearest love; if you do but love me half as much as you have sworn, come and deliver me. My father nor brother do not know all, or nearly all; but you know that the truth can not long be concealed. I am ready to fly with you, as you used to ask me, to the world's end: only come--and come as fast as possible. There is nothing to stop us here. Come, then, to your unhappy   Kate Stilling."

The place from which the letter was dated was A small town in Dorsetshire, and the date itself three days before.

Robert Woodhall smiled as he mused over those few lines, and then he turned to the address again, and seemed to consider it attentively, muttering, "Master R. Woodhall."

"You see, sir," said his servant, "one can not tell whether it is for you or your cousin, Master Ralph."

"What the devil do you mean?" cried his master, fixing his eyes eagerly upon him.

"Why simply, sir," replied the man, "that it would make a desperate good handle against him if it fell into the hands of the other."

"I think I understand you, Roger," said his master, in a much more placable tone; "but Ralph does not even know my fair Kate."

"We can not tell that, sir," answered the servant; "he was over at Coldenham lately."

"Only one day," replied Robert, "and soon got his answer from my mother."

"He was in the church with old Stilling, and in old Stilling's house," said the man; "that I know for sure."

"Was he?" exclaimed Robert, in a tone of much surprise; but, after a moment's thought, he added, "Ay, ay, to hire this young vagabond for a servant. But I understand what you mean, and perhaps may act upon it."

"Only be so good as to remember, sir," replied Roger, "that the letter was brought by his own servant over here, after being sent away, no one knows where, for several days; and the letter R may stand for Ralph as well as for Robert--or Roger either, for that matter."

His master laughed: "Would you make me jealous of Kate?" he said. "No, no, Roger, I understand all this clearly. Gaunt Stilling has gone over to see her while his master was absent with the duke. He has caught her writing this letter, and brought it away by force. Do you not see how the address breaks off? Perhaps he wishes to make use of it against me when he finds occasion; for my lady mother threatened me highly if I continued to persecute these people, as she called it. Luckily, the letter fell into good hands."

"Do you not think, sir, that those hands deserve some little lining?" asked the man, with a grin.

"They do--they do," replied Robert; "I am marvelous poor just now; but there is a guinea for you. You shall have more some day soon, if you continue to serve me as well. Now go and contrive to get my cousin Hal to come and speak with me as soon as possible. This letter, perhaps, may serve me much in one way; but I have another matter in hand which will need quick attention."

The man bowed low and retired, but he expressed no thanks for the present he had received; and when he had reached the other side of the door, he tossed up the piece of coin with a contemptuous air, saying, "A guinea!"

CHAPTER XIII

"Well, Robert, what is your important business?" demanded Henry Woodhall, entering his cousin's room with a look of haste and impatience. "Be quick, for I want to return to the ball."

"The ball will be over before we have done Henry," replied his cousin, in a grave and emphatic tone; "I have several things to say to you of importance."

"In the way of homily?" asked Henry Woodhall, laughing; "come, then, put off your solemnity, Bob, and let us hear what it is."

Thus saying, he threw himself into a chair, and his cousin replied, "Some things I have to say affect myself alone; some affect you and me; some affect you only."

"First, second, and to conclude," said the gay young man. "Why, what is all this? How comes it that my rattle-pated, dissolute, latitudinarian cousin Robert has, all of a sudden, become metamorphosed into a parson? Where are your demmes and your zoundses? Where are your remarkable oaths, and your satin embroidery blasphemy? Why, Robert, you must be in love, or have taken physic, had the cholic, or the heartache. They tell me that powdered unicorn's horn is a sovereign thing for clearing the brain of melancholic humors, and that a few grains of mummy, taken in goat's whey, will purge the liver of black bile. Let me commend them to your consideration."

"All very well laughing, Hal," replied Robert; "but this is no laughing matter, by ----."

"Come, come, there's an oath!" cried his cousin; "the patient is getting better. Well, if we are not to laugh, what are we to cry about?"

"About being made fools of by a raw Cambridge student," replied his cousin, bitterly; "about being cheated, deceived, betrayed--about having all your father's plans and my mother's overthrown--about your losing the hand of a rich and beautiful heiress, and my losing my future wife's heart."

"Well-a-day, well-a-day!" cried Henry Woodhall, "this is a serious matter. But let us hear the particulars. Imprimis, about your future wife's heart; by which, I suppose, you mean the heart, or muscular pin-cushion, of my sister Margaret. But first let me observe, Bob, before you proceed, that Maggy is not quite certainly your future wife. There is many a slip between the cup and the lip, Robert; and that matter is not quite settled yet."

"Quite settled between your father and my mother," replied Robert Woodhall, "and quite settled as far as I am concerned. With regard to Margaret, the matter may be different; for I am certain that this mean, pitiful fellow, Ralph, has been trifling with her affections, and has won them too."

"Awkward for you!" replied his cousin, "and one reason the more for my saying this matter is not settled between you and Maggy. I tell you fairly, Robert, I will have a say in any thing wherein she is concerned, and you shall not have her hand unless between this and then you show yourself more worthy of her."

"How will you prevent it?" asked Robert Woodhall, in a sharp, almost fierce tone.

"By running you through the liver, if need be," replied Henry Woodhall; "I tell you, Robert, that as you two stand just now, you with your vices and Ralph with his poverty, I would rather see him Margaret's husband than you."

Robert Woodhall fixed his eyes full upon his cousin's face, and contemplated him for a moment or two in silence, while a dark, malignant smile gradually came upon his lip. "You love hypocrites, I think, Henry?" he said, at length.

"No. I hate them," replied the other, sharply.

"You can not say that I have any hypocrisy," rejoined his cousin; "all that I do, be it bad or good, is open, in the face of day. I am frank and bold at least. But are you sure that this young lad, on whom you pin your faith, has not learned hypocrisy at Cambridge as well as Greek and Latin? Are you sure that his heart is not as mercenary as a money-lender's? that his conduct is not as foul and corrupt as a street prostitute's? that his hypocrisy is not as great as a non-juring preacher's?"

"Pooh, pooh!" said Henry Woodhall, "I have known him from infancy: we have been boys--have grown up men together. We have been like brothers, and his thoughts are as common to me as to himself."

Still that same dark smile hung upon the lips of Robert Woodhall as he listened.

There was something triumphant in it, a sort of cool self-confidence, which conveyed, before he even spoke, the idea that he possessed the means of overthrowing all the arguments opposed to him in a moment.

"Well," he said, "let us look a little at Mr. Ralph's real conduct, and see whether it be such as you quite approve. Men have singular opinions on these subjects. Your own are somewhat curious; and perhaps you may admire all this. First, taking advantage of your father's hospitality and kindness, he makes love to Margaret, and wins her heart; then--"

"Stay, stay!" cried his cousin; "of that we have no proof but your own jealousy; and, if there be any thing between them, it is more than probable that they have mutually grown up to love each other, and then some casual word or accidental circumstance has betrayed the secret of each breast to the other. I can not blame him, Robert. Margaret is a little angel, and any man might well love her. But still, I say, we have no proof of this but your jealousy."

"My jealousy! Henry," replied Robert, with a sneer which he could not repress, though it injured his own cause; "I have no jealousy, good cousin. I am not in the predicament. However, even were it so, that is a matter very easily settled. Ask Margaret herself. Press her closely, and either by her looks or words you will come at the truth. But, for the moment, let us suppose that it is so; I would not blame him either, were there any real love in the case; for, though I do not know much of the heroic passion, yet I have heard that it sometimes drives men mad. But if there has been no real love on his part; if he has been moved only by mercenary motives; if he has been ready at any moment to sacrifice her when he saw the prospect of greater fortune than her own; if, the moment he has seen this young Baroness Danvers, he has cast off all thought of Margaret, and paraded their intimacy openly, in order that the poor girl might be satisfied at once of his treachery; if he has pursued Lady Danvers the more eagerly because the world gave out that you were to have her hand, would you think this honest, honorable, kind in your generous, excellent cousin Ralph?"

"No, no," replied Henry Woodhall, fiercely, "I should think it base, pitiful, mean, deserving instant chastisement. As to the matter with Hortensia Danvers, I care not one straw. Let him win her and wear her if he will. I never thought of her--never thought of marriage at all--never shall, probably, till I find my mustachio turning gray, or have got the gout in my right foot. Then is the time for matrimony and a warm dressing-gown; but with Margaret he shall not trifle; and, if he do, he shall answer for it. On this subject I will make full inquiry from the dear girl herself. I shall know in a moment, for I have been well accustomed to read her looks. It can not be done to-night, however, for she has gone to rest. Have you aught else to say?"

"Nothing that I hold of very much importance," replied Robert; "two things, however, may as well be mentioned. First, he insulted me grossly when I was endeavoring to aid your sister after she fainted."

"That is your own affair," cried Henry Woodhall; "you can send him your cartel, and that is soon settled."

"You are mistaken," replied Robert, somewhat gloomily; "the Duke of Norfolk has laid me under an obligation to forbear, and given me to understand that he will have his eye continually upon me."

"Humph!" said Henry Woodhall, with a slight accent of contempt, for, to say truth, he did not hold his cousin's courage very highly, "What is number two?"

"It is a mere nothing in my eyes," answered Robert, smarting a little from his cousin's tone, "and doubtless you will think nothing of it either; for your sanctified men are abundant in charity to peccadilloes of the kind--especially when they are committed by themselves or their near relations. It is only this, that while making love to Margaret, and doubtless vowing his whole heart to her, he was amusing himself in another manner with a country girl in the neighborhood--nay, do not look contemptuous and unbelieving; of this I have the proof in my own hands. Nay, more, since he has been here--as, it would seem, the young lady is in a difficult position--he has sent his own servant over to see her, and bring him news of her estate."

"Why, he has no servant," replied Henry Woodhall. "He went away without one. That I heard at The Grange, for I thought to offer him my own lad Brown, that he might appear the better here."

"True--quite true," replied his cousin, with a laugh; "he kept the matter very quiet; for he would not have his father know of the politic arrangement. Oh, he is the most frank and candid of men! The way he managed was this: he made compensation for the sister's ruin by taking the brother into his high and mighty service. Other potentates and lordly men have done the same. Then, to conceal the transaction, he made the lad join him on the road, and uses him now as the go-between of himself and the sister."

"And can you prove all this?" asked Henry Woodhall, in a grave tone.

"Every word of it, step by step," replied Robert; "but I attach no importance to it."

"I do," answered Henry, sternly; "I must hear the proofs."

"Good," said Robert; and, rising, he opened the door, exclaiming, "Roger, see if you can find some servant of the Duke of Norfolk's, and ask him to come hither for a moment. Any one will do."

He then closed the door, seated himself, and remained silent, internally enjoying the varied but painful emotions which sent their traces like cloud-shadows over the face of his nobler cousin. There was something in the mental torture which he had inflicted that pleased him well, for Henry had galled him often, and he now had his revenge.

At length the door of the room opened, and one of the duke's servants was introduced, with a look of some surprise and curiosity. "You sent for me, gentlemen," he said; "how can I serve you?"

"I only wish to ask you a question or two." said Robert Woodhall. "Pray tell me, has my good cousin, Master Ralph Woodhall, a servant here with him?"

"I think he is absent, sir," replied the man, "on some business of his master's."

Robert Woodhall smiled, and then asked, "Had he one with him when he arrived?"

"Oh yes, sir," replied the servant, "a man who calls himself Jack Tuckett; but he has been away for about a week, I think. I have not seen him at the third table."

"Thank you, that will do," replied Robert Woodhall. The man departed, and the young gentleman then called in his own servant Roger. "Now, Roger," he said, "examine this letter accurately. You admitted that you read it. Now see if it be the same, in every respect, that you gave to me about an hour ago."

The man took the letter, opened it deliberately, read it all through, and then handed it back to his master, saying, "It is the same."

Robert threw it over to his cousin, who read it hastily, and then, turning sharply to the man, demanded, "How came you by this letter? Who gave it to you?"

"Tell the truth, I command you, Roger," cried his master; "the plain, straightforward, unadorned truth."

"Certainly, sir," replied the man; then turning toward Henry, he added, "Nobody gave it to me; I picked it up."

"That is a lie, Roger," said his master. "I insist on your telling the truth as you told it to me--about this letter at least. I do not wish you to compromise others; and whatever you say that may compromise yourself shall be forgotten, and you forgiven."

"Very well, sir, I close the bargain," replied Roger, with the coolest impudence. "If the truth must be told, then, I was in the stable-yard to-night, when I saw Mr. Ralph's servant come in. I was rather anxious to know where he had been gone so long, and seeing him go away for a lantern, I thought I might as well investigate whether he had got any thing particular about his saddle. I could make nothing of that, but I found that he had thrown his horseman's cloak over the beast's shoulder, and in the pocket I discovered the old bill I showed you and that letter, which I perused carefully, and then brought to you. But I do hope, sir, you will send it to Master Ralph, for I am afraid there will be a fuss about it."

"We will take care of that, Roger," replied his master. "Have you any questions to ask him, Henry?"

"No," replied the other; "he is a d----d scoundrel. But how do you make out the brothership? This billet is signed Kate Stilling; the other man said Ralph's servant was called Jack Tuckett."

"A traveling name, sir, a traveling name," replied Roger, mingling in the conversation; "I know the man quite well, and have seen his pretty sister Kate more than once. He may call himself Jack Tuckett at the third table, if he likes, but his real name is Gaunt Stilling, and so you will find him written down in the chamberlain's book, for I saw it myself. He was for a couple of years a soldier in the Tangier regiment, and very likely called himself Jack Tuckett there, for that honorable corps did not like to always go by their own names."

"Go away," said Henry, sharply; and Roger quitted the room.

"There are now two things I have to ascertain," said Henry Woodhall, composing himself with a strong effort, which gave a stern rigidity to his manner; "first, whether Master Ralph Woodhall has been trifling with the affections of my sister. Secondly, whether the name of Gaunt Stilling is to be found, as his servant, in the chamberlain's books here."

Robert nodded his head, but was silent, and the other went on. "All this must be done to-morrow, for it is too late to-night; and as soon as I am satisfied, we will converse further, Robert; for Ralph must be taught, if he have done these things, that they do not go without their reward. If I have done you injustice, my good cousin, I am very sorry for it; perhaps it may be so; for when we find that we have been bitterly mistaken in one man, we may suspect that we have been as bitterly mistaken in another. Good-by for the present."

"Good night," replied Robert, who would not add another word, for fear of lessening the impression he had produced; and they parted.

CHAPTER XIV

Early in the morning of the day after that of which we have just been speaking, a young gentleman walked up and down the terrace, on the garden side of the Duke of Norfolk's palace in Norwich. His eyes were generally bent upon the ground, but ever, when he turned, he raised them for a moment to one particular window on the second floor of the building. His walk continued for fully half an hour uninterrupted. The guests and the servants had been up late, and nobody felt himself inclined to rise betimes except that young gentleman, who, to say truth, had not closed his eyes all night. All the windows of the house were still defended from the attack of the morning sun by the large gray wooden shutters which folded over them from the outside. At length a solitary housemaid appeared at one of the doors which opened on the terrace, sweeping out a quantity of dust, mingled with flowers, and bugles, and other gew-gaws, without noticing at all whether with them might not be mingled diamonds, or rubies, or other precious things.

Shortly after, the window toward which the young gentleman's eyes had been so frequently turned was opened, and the shutters thrown back, in the act of doing which a maid's head and shoulders appeared. Instantly the young gentleman stopped, saying, "Tell Margaret, Vernon, that I wish to speak with her as soon as she can admit me."

"Very well, sir," replied the maid, and withdrew her head.

Henry Woodhall took two or three more turns up and down the terrace, and then brushing hastily past the girl who was sweeping out the hall, he mounted the stair-case and knocked at his sister's door. The maid admitted him, and was about to recommence her labors upon the toilet of Margaret, who was seated before a table near the window, with her beautiful hair hanging in large masses over her shoulders. But Henry turned toward her, saying, in an impetuous tone, "Leave us, Vernon! I wish to speak with my sister alone. You shall come back in a few minutes."

Margaret had started up at the sharp sound of her brother's voice, feeling some degree of alarm, which was only increased by the strange change which she perceived upon his usually placable and good-humored countenance. The moment, however, that the waiting-woman had retired and closed the door, Henry's whole aspect softened. Margaret was still frightened, however; and, throwing her beautiful arms round his neck, she said, "What is the matter, Henry? You frighten me."

Henry put one arm round her waist, led her gently back to her chair, and seated himself by her side. Then again drawing her nearer to his heart, he said, in the kindest and tenderest tone, "Dearest Margaret, I have come to comfort and console you. You and I are the only children of the house, Margaret. I have always loved you better than any thing on earth, and have seemed to feel no wish or hope separate from your happiness. Let us, dear Margaret, have confidence in one another; and you will always find that you may rely upon me as a stay and counselor in any moment of difficulty, and that I will think of your happiness without any consideration of avarice, ambition, or prejudice, which may have weight with others."

Margaret hid her face upon his shoulder; but he could see the cheek, and temple, and the fair, delicately-chiseled ear glowing like an evening sunset.

"You need not tell me, Margaret," continued Henry; "I know and see how it is with you and Ralph. But only speak, dear girl--only let me know how this came about. Has he sought you eagerly? Has he taught you to conceal this from my father and me till this moment? Has he instilled into your mind lessons of concealment from those who love you best? Has he taken advantage of my father's kindness secretly to win your heart, without a brother's knowledge, and against a parent's will?"

"Oh heavens, no! No, no," cried Margaret, raising her head and gazing on her brother's face; and then, with warm, impetuous words, which I can not repeat, for they were all confused, almost incoherent, but all very natural, she poured forth the whole tale of her love, showing how, from early years, almost from infancy, she and Ralph had become attached to each other; how little kindnesses, and some important services, and frequent communication, and the interchange of mutual thought, had ripened early regard into fraternal affection, and warmed fraternal affection into mature love. Then she told him how by the merest accident, their mutual feelings had become known to each other, and how they had trembled, and dreaded, and agreed that it was in vain to hope, and had determined to part; how, in consequence of this resolution, Ralph had remained one whole vacation at his college; and how they fancied, in the end, they could meet calmly, and forget their love; and how, when they did meet, they found that passion was stronger than reason, and that it was in vain to hope that the memory of first true love could ever be obliterated. Then she added that Ralph had determined to go forth and seek his fortune, lighted on his way by the hope of winning her, and how he had not even bound her by any engagement, except that deep, strong bond of the heart, which she fondly fancied could never be severed; and then she once more hid her face on her brother's bosom, and tears told the rest.

Henry was a great deal moved. "His crime is not so great," he said, thoughtfully.

"Crime! crime!" repeated Margaret; "what do you mean, Henry?"

"Yes, crime," answered her brother; "for it is a crime, Margaret, to trifle with affections such as yours."

As he held her to his heart, he felt her shudder at the confirmation of the fears she herself had entertained. But Henry went on, determined to say all at once, in order to spare the pain of after explanations.

"There is more besides this, Margaret," he said; "more besides his conduct to you and Lady Danvers. There are other affections he can trifle with--other hearts he can break, Margaret. I am moved by no pride, no family prejudice, no desire of wealth. You could be happy with small means with a man who deserved you; but I tell you, my dear sister, you must think of this man no more, for he deserves you not."

"Other hearts he can break!" said Margaret, in a low, sad tone; "I do not comprehend you, Henry."

"There, read that letter, Margaret," said her brother, putting the billet he had received from their cousin into his sister's hands.

Margaret gazed at it, read it by fits and snatches, and then said, "I know not what this means--Kate Stilling! Who is Kate Stilling?"

"An unhappy peasant girl," replied her brother; "look at the back, Margaret. It was brought by his own servant after a long absence, and fell into my hands by chance."

Margaret turned the paper, and, as her eyes rested upon the words of the address, she sank slowly down into the chair from which she had just before risen, and the letter dropped upon the floor.

Henry thought she had fainted again, and took a step to call for assistance, but Margaret's voice stopped him.

"Stay, Henry, stay, I beseech you," she cried; "say not a word of this to any one, if you do love me indeed. Let us never talk of it but when we are alone together. You shall henceforth know every thought of my breast--Only--only beseech ray father to quit this place at once. Tell him I shall be ill here; tell him I shall die;" and, starting up with a burst of uncontrollable emotion, she sprang to the side of her bed, cast herself upon her knees, and, burying her face in the coverings, sobbed loud and vehemently.

Henry gazed upon his sister for a moment with feelings of deep sympathy and compassion, and then hurrying out of the room, found her waiting-woman near the door.

"Go in to your lady, Vernon," he said; "comfort her and soothe her, but say no word of her state to any one; for I have had to grieve her much, and it would only double her grief if others were to know it."

Thus saying, he strode on and sought the higher chamber which had been assigned to his cousin Robert. The latter was still in bed and asleep, but Henry soon roused him.

"I have inquired, Robert," he said, as soon as the eyes of his cousin were fully open; "I have inquired, and the whole of the tale you told me is but too true. Ralph is a scoundrel and a hypocrite, and must be punished. Get up; you must bear him a billet from me."

"No need of such great hurry, Hal," replied Robert, in his usual affected tone. "Demme, Ralph is not a wild goose that will take wing every time you fire near him. He will stay here as long as the bright baroness does, believe me."

"But I must go," replied Henry; "ay, and this very day. Margaret must be here no longer. Last night my father hesitated whether to go on this morning or to stay another day. A word from me will turn the balance, and that word I will speak."

"Your plan is a bad one, Hal," said his cousin; "if you attempt to bring your enemy to the ground this morning, you will be frustrated, depend upon it. All the world is up and busy; the Duke of Norfolk has eyes upon us all; there will be no slipping away unobserved for such a time as would be needful to get out of Norwich. No, no, you must go more cautiously to work."

"But Margaret has besought me earnestly to have her taken hence at once," replied Henry; "she says she will die if she stays, and, on my life, I think she says the truth."

"Well, have her taken hence," replied Robert; "let her and your father go, and let us stay behind; or, better still, let us all go; it will lull suspicion."

"Four-and-twenty hours shall not pass ere I have satisfaction upon Ralph Woodhall," replied Henry, vehemently.

"No need that they should," answered his cousin; "only hear me out. Send your cartel this morning before you set out; take it for granted at once that this ambitious youth will not refuse his good cousin a meeting at the sword's point, and name the wilderness as the place, at any hour of the night when you can be sure, by the almanac, that the moon is up. Give him a hint that, though you seem to be going Londonward, you will be back for the pleasure of pinking his doublet; and bid him come to the ground alone, as you will do."

Henry Woodhall mused for some time over this plan, but eventually agreed to follow his cousin's suggestions; and Robert, springing from his bed, soon produced writing materials for drawing up the challenge. Henry sat down to the table, and wrote for a few moments in a fine, bold hand, and when he had concluded, read the letter aloud to his cousin as follows:

"Sir,--Your conduct, which I have had the sorrow and misfortune of discovering lately, and of which you yourself must be conscious; the evil uses which you have made of my father's unsuspecting hospitality and kindness, and the pain and discomfort which you have occasioned in my family, compel me not only to inform you that I can no longer look upon you as a relation, but to require that you give me immediate satisfaction for the injuries you have inflicted. The circumstances in which I am placed drive me to abridge the usual courtesies upon this occasion, for which I pray your excuse. To avoid all publicity and the chance of interference, I shall apparently take my departure from Norwich this day; but you will not fail to find me in the wilderness of the duke's house, near the fish-pond, this evening at ten, when there will be sufficient moonlight for our purpose. I send you inclosed the length of my sword; and if you be a man of courage, for which I give you credit, you will be at the spot appointed, and alone, as I shall be.

"I have the honor to subscribe myself your most obedient and very humble servant,

""Henry Woodhall."

"Let me see, let me see," said Robert; and, taking the note from his cousin's hand, he read it over very considerately, pausing and pondering upon every word. There were some things that he could have well wished omitted; but, upon the whole, it was better than he expected--that is to say, more suitable to his purpose--and, after some consideration, he determined to let it go without alteration. "Master Ralph," he thought, "will fancy that the whole weight of the offense is having made love to my pretty Lady Margaret contrary to the will and wishes of papa and brother: that can hardly be explained away, I think. Nevertheless, doubtless he will endeavor to explain it as best he can. He will not like fighting the brother, for whatever comes of it must be ill for him. I must contrive to stop all explanations, and bring them to the point of the sword. There, whatever they may do will be done for me."

This last thought carried on his mind for some little time in a different direction. An important subject of consideration started itself; but he reserved it for future thought, and brought back his mind to the affair of the present. He saw that he must prevent any communication between the cousins, as explanation, if it did not absolutely lead to the discovery of his villainy, would, at all events, frustrate his object, and throw suspicion on his character. To do so, however, was very easy. Henry's absence till the hour of meeting was all that was needful on one part, and that was already arranged. The only chance of another turn being given to the whole affair was, that Ralph, with his frank and open nature, might set out, as soon as he received the challenge, to follow Lord Woodhall and his family, meet all charges boldly, and explain his whole conduct. Some means, he thought, must be devised to prevent such an occurrence; but he determined to leave that also for after consideration, to obtain from Henry the task of delivering his letter, and to delay its execution till after Lord Woodhall's departure.

"Who shall I send it by?" said his cousin, interrupting his reverie's, somewhat impatiently.

"Oh, I will take it, of course," replied Robert; "I think the best plan will be, Henry, for me to remain here another day; I can then get Master Ralph's answer."

"Remain or not, as you like," replied Henry Woodhall; "but his answer I will have before I quit this place--if any answer indeed is to be given. I appoint a meeting. Any man of courage or honor will feel himself obliged to be there, without further question. Ralph is undoubtedly a man of courage; I have seen him tried; but he may not like to fight me in this cause; and I will have yea or nay."

Robert felt that he had made a false step, but he hastened to retrieve it by another stroke of his art.

"Well, then," he said, "let us send it by my servant Roger; he is skillful in all small diplomacies. He shall be here in a moment. Fold it up, and seal it with your largest seal, remember, while I throw on a dressing-gown and seek for my good man."

Henry Woodhall sat down to the table, and his cousin left the room. Close to his own door he met his man Roger, coquetting with a pretty-looking waiting-woman somewhat over-dressed. He had no hesitation, however, in breaking through their sweet conversation by calling Master Roger to the window at the further end of the corridor.

"Who is that?" he asked, fixing his eyes upon the girl, as she retreated toward the head of the stairs.

"Only Lady Danvers's waiting-woman," answered Roger, with a simper; "she is a sweet creature, and uncommonly kind."

"Ah!" said his master; "now listen to me;" and he proceeded in a low voice to give the man the instructions which he thought needful. He repeated them over twice with great precision, and each time Roger bowed his head and said, "It shall be done, sir." How he fulfilled his mission I shall now proceed to show.

Robert Woodhall returned at once to his own room, saying as he entered, "I can not find the scoundrel; but he will be here soon, for he knows my hour, and that I won't endure negligence."

Henry Woodhall rose with a look of impatience, and walked up and down the room. A few minutes after, there was a knock at the door, and the servant entered.

"You are late," said his master, in an affectedly sharp tone.

"No, sir, to a minute," replied Roger; "the castle clock is now striking."

"Well, that matters not," cried Henry; "take this letter to the room of Master Ralph Woodhall, and bring me back an answer, if he thinks fit to send one."

"Instantly, sir," said the man, taking the note with a very humble bow; and, with a look of perfect unconsciousness, he quitted the room. He then directed his course at once toward the apartment of Ralph, but he communed with himself as he went. "A guinea!" he said; "a guinea! and something more in prospect! Upon my soul, my honorable master is generous and free of his money. Hang me if I do not spoil this little scheme for him, just to show him that he can not work without me. But I must be cautious, so that he does not find out who did it."

He put the letter in his pocket, and walked straight on to Ralph's door, where he knocked.

Now most of the rooms in the duke's palace at Norwich had ante-rooms to them, which was the case here. Thus the door was opened, not by Ralph Woodhall himself, but by no less a person than Gaunt Stilling; and the servants of the two cousins stood face to face, eyeing each other for a moment with a somewhat sinister expression, like two quarrelsome dogs meeting suddenly at the corner of a street and deliberating, ere they set to, as to which shall give the first bite.

"Good morning to you, Mr. Stilling," said Roger, who was the first to drop his tail, if I may follow out my simile; for a soldier of the Tangier regiment might well be considered a very formidable opponent. "Let us forget all grudges. I have had no share, for my part, in doing you any wrong; and I now bear a message from my master to yours--not very willingly, for, to say the truth, I don't do much of my master's work willingly at all; but a man must gain his bread, you know."

"What is your message?" asked Gaunt Stilling, sharply, adding something, muttered between his teeth, which the other did not hear.

"My master told me to say," replied Roger, "that he will be obliged if your master will be in this room of his at noon to-day, as he has something to say to him at that hour."

"Very well, so be it," replied Gaunt Stilling, and was then about to close the door, which he held in his hand, in the other man's face. A sudden change of thought seemed to come across him, however, and he opened it wider than before, saying, "Harkee, Roger, I do not believe you are so bad as the rest of them. I never saw you at our house with your scoundrel master; and, if you take my advice, you will quit his service as soon as possible, otherwise bad luck may befall you."

"Find me another place first, Mr. Stilling," replied Roger; "but, however, I will talk more with you of it by-and-by. I dare say we shall soon meet; and I do not like my place much, I can tell you, in any way."

Gaunt Stilling nodded his head and shut the door.

Robert Woodhall's servant then directed his steps quite in a different direction from his master's chamber, found out Lady Danvers's waiting-woman on the floor below, and whispered a word in her ear.

"A challenge!" cried the maid.

"Yes," replied Roger, in a solemn tone, "about some words which passed between them last night in the ball-room."

"And when are they going to fight?" cried the young lady.

"Some time in the afternoon." replied Roger; "but the hour I did not hear, for I was talking with a pretty little gill-flirt, of whom you know something, in the passage. She was as cruel as Queen Mary, and made me lose the best part of the story. Can I find you again in an hour?"

"Not you," cried the girl, with a coquettish air.

"I am obliged to go now," said Roger, "but I will hunt the house for you very soon. Mind you don't tell any one what I have told you."

"Oh dear, no," replied the girl, "I would not tell any one for the world;" and away she went, and told her mistress every word.

In the mean time Roger made his way back to his master's room, having calculated--for he was a great calculator--that the little interlude which had just passed would precisely fill up the lapse of time that might have been consumed in reading the letter of which he was the bearer, if he had delivered it. He entered without ceremony; and, as he expected, the first question was, "Have you taken the letter?"

"Yes, sir," replied Roger, mentally adding, "and brought it back again."

"What was the answer?" demanded Robert Woodhall.

"Very short, sir," replied Roger; "all that was said was 'Very well, so be it.'"

"So I say too," cried Henry Woodhall; "so be it, Master Ralph. I knew he would not flinch, Robert; but now I will go and get my father and Margaret off as soon as possible, and return and join you here from our first halting-place."

"Good," replied Robert, regarding his cousin with a somewhat supercilious smile, which the other could not help remarking. His thoughts, however, were busy with other things, and he made no inquiry regarding the cause, but at once quitted the room.

Robert remained seated, with his eyes fixed upon the table, and for some moments he was motionless as well as silent. There are people, however, who, when thought is very strong within them, love to have some active demonstration of the conclusions at which they have arrived. Robert Woodhall raised both his hands, and with the index finger of the right touched first one and then another of the left-hand, pausing between the second and third, and then going on to the third and fourth.

"So," he said; "ay, so."

At that moment his eye rested upon his servant Roger, and he exclaimed, angrily, "What are you lingering for? quit the room."

"I thought you might want me, sir," replied the man; "and you told me to bring the letter back again, and deliver it to you."

Thus saying, he placed the challenge before his master, and retreated to the ante-room, where he paused for an instant to consider what he termed "the finger work."

"That is to say, as plain as it can speak," said Roger to himself, imitating his master's gesticulations, "finger one, Henry kills Ralph; finger two, a troublesome rival out of my way, and I revenged by another man's sword--very good. Finger three, Ralph kills Henry; finger four, a better man than myself taken out of the world, an everlasting barrier put between Master Ralph and Mistress Margaret, Lord Woodhall without an heir, and I Baron Woodhall on his death--very good, indeed! Clever, Master Robert, clever! I did not think you had so much wit; but there are other witty people in the world as well as yourself."

CHAPTER XV

Within two hours after the events of which I have just spoken, the family of Lord Woodhall, that is to say, himself, his son, and daughter, took leave of the Duke of Norfolk, and, followed by a great mob of servants, mounted on horseback as was the custom in those days, set out in the family coach on the road to London. Robert Woodhall remained behind upon some one of the many excuses for any thing that he liked to do, which he was never without. He waited for a full hour, however, before he proceeded to take advantage of the absence of his family, remaining quietly in his own room all the morning, and cogitating with considerable satisfaction upon the probable result of the arrangements he had made.

About noon, however, he called his servant Roger, gave him the challenge, and told him to carry it to Mr. Ralph Woodhall. He did not choose to take it himself; for Ralph, he knew was somewhat impetuous, and the pass of a sword between them might soon have given an entirely new face to the whole state of affairs. He was cautious, too--very cautious; and in giving the letter into the hands of his servant, he said, "You need not tell him that I am still here. Let him think that I have gone with the rest, as he was not about when they departed. If he asks, you may say I will certainly be back to-night."

"I understand, sir, I understand," replied Roger, and away he went with the letter.

On knocking at Ralph Woodhall's door--carrying this time the letter openly in his hand--Roger was once more encountered by Gaunt Stilling, who received him very graciously, and asked him to come into the ante-room.

"What have you got there?" asked Stilling, pointing to the letter.

"An epistle for your master," replied Roger, with a certain significant smile, "which is to be delivered immediately, Master Stilling."

"Mr. Ralph Woodhall is not here now," replied the other; "he was sent by the duke to escort Lady Danvers on her way home."

"I know that as well as you do," answered Roger; "I saw him go some time before our people; but I only obey orders, Master Stilling. Did you give him the message I left?"

"Certainly," replied Stilling; "and he answered as became him, 'that if your master had any thing to say to him, he must wait his time and convenience.'"

"Proud!" said Roger, with a laugh; "proud, but quite right! I must give you the letter, however, though I suspect it will not reach him in time for its purpose."

"He will be back before nightfall," replied Gaunt Stilling, emphatically; "of that you may assure your master. Pray, what is the purport of the letter, as you seem to know all about it?"

"A challenge--nothing but a challenge," replied Roger, with a jaunty air.

"Time and place appointed?" asked Stilling, quite quietly; "I suppose you know that too?"

"Oh yes," replied Roger; "I do not think my master ought to have any secrets from so faithful a person as myself, and therefore, to the best of my abilities, I remedy his negligence when he forgets to tell me any thing. You see the letter is very convenient--folded up in haste, and the ends quite open. Just take a peep. There you will see--Place, the fish-pond at the end of the wilderness--Time, ten o'clock to-night, when the moon is well up--Length of sword, twenty-eight inches."

"Ralph Woodhall will not stand upon an inch or two," replied Gaunt Stilling, with a grim smile. "You may tell your master, on my assurance, that Mr. Ralph will be back before sundown, and will not fail to be on the spot named at the hour appointed. Is your master here?"

Roger had the greatest possible inclination, for once in his life, to tell the truth; but the reader will remark, that the telling of the truth in this instance would have been nearly equal in value to telling a lie, as it was a betrayal of his master's confidence, which might have been as satisfactory to him. However, the fear of something occurring to expose his disobedience overweighed other considerations, and he replied, "No, he has gone away, but he will come back with Mr. Henry to-night."

"Good," said Gaunt Stilling, "good--a pleasant afternoon to you, Master Roger."

"What?" asked the servant, in some apparent surprise at the valediction.

"I only said good afternoon to you," answered Gaunt Stilling, coolly. "I wish to be left alone."

This significant hint was sufficient, and Roger took his departure to inform his master that Mr. Ralph Woodhall would undoubtedly return before night, and would be at the place appointed. Robert was well satisfied, but Gaunt Stilling was not completely so. He walked up and down the room several times, thinking deeply, and often muttering to himself, "One push of a sword," he said, "and the account is settled--God speed the good lad's arm. Oh, if he had but used the sword as much as I have! Yet he seems to fence well."

He then looked very hard at the letter several times, as if he had a strong inclination to pry into the contents; but at length he muttered, "No, no, I remember what he said upon the road. I will not do a dirty action." Then, after having thought for a minute or two more, and felt, perhaps, very eager to see the whole, he exclaimed, "Nay, I will put it on his table. There he will find it when he comes back."

Let us pass over a few hours; for long details will not suit the conclusion of a chapter, and we must hurry to the end of the first act of this strange, eventful history.

It was night, and nearly ten o'clock. There were two persons in Robert Woodhall's room, and his servant Roger standing on the outside of the door.

"No, no," said Henry Woodhall, whose face was somewhat pale and haggard, "I go alone. I insist that you do not come with me, Robert, nor follow me. Push over the light; I wish to seal this letter."

"For whom is it intended?" asked his cousin, somewhat eagerly.

"For the Duke of Norfolk," replied Henry; and he then added, in a calm and easy tone, "The issue of such encounters is always uncertain. The night is darker than I expected; and I may chance to fall. If so, I wish the duke to know all about this affair. If I live, I can explain all myself."

"I will take care that it shall be delivered to him in case of such unlooked-for misfortune," replied Robert, in a tone of very well simulated apprehension.

"Your pardon, my good cousin," said Henry; "my own servant is below, and shall have orders to give it to the duke if I do not return. There, there," he continued, seeing that his cousin was about to remonstrate, "I will have my way, and have not time to dispute."

He took out his watch and said, "Eight minutes." Then sealing the letter, he lifted his hat from the table, made sure that his sword moved easily in its sheath, and, shaking his cousin's hand, without another word quitted the room.

Robert opened the door and listened, and it were vain to say that his heart did not beat. As soon as he heard his cousin's step upon the stairs, he drew his servant into the room, and whispered, with a ghastly look and eager eye, "Follow him, Roger, follow him at a distance, to the fish-pond at the end of the wilderness. See what happens, and bring me information instantly of the result."

The man departed without reply, but there was a curious sort of smile upon his lip as he walked along the corridor. A quarter of an hour passed, during which Robert continued to stride slowly up and down his room, with his hands clasped tight together, his eyes straining upon the floor as if they would have burst from his head, and his cheek of an ashy paleness. The spirit of Cain was in his heart. He felt--he knew, that at that moment he was committing murder. But the fiery torture of that deed--commencing generally in rage and ending in remorse, with but one momentary point for act between them--was to him protracted through all those long, long minutes. At length he heard a step coming with lightning speed up the stairs, and the next instant his servant burst into the room. There was no smile upon his face now. It was ghastly and full of horror: he panted for breath.

"Speak! speak!" cried his master; "what has happened?"

"He is killed, sir," replied the man.

"Who? who?" demanded Robert, aloud, forgetting all caution.

"Mr. Henry, I believe--nay, I am sure," answered Roger; "the night is dark: there is a thin mist all over the ground by the side of the river: I could see nothing till I got very near; but I heard the swords grating. After I came in sight, there were but three passes, and then Mr. Henry fell and lay quite still. Mr. Ralph is the taller, is he not?"

"Yes--yes," replied his master; "Henry was my height, Ralph much taller."

"Then Mr. Henry is gone," replied the man, "for it was the short one who fell. The business must have got abroad, for a number of the duke's people were hurrying out--Hark! they are bringing him up hither."

"Take the body to the room where he slept last night," said the voice of the chamberlain upon the stairs; "I will go and inform my lord duke."

CHAPTER XVI

In the vast, immeasurable depth of thought, there are so many resources, that one would suppose it were quite unnecessary for any one to repeat himself or to copy others, let him write as much as he will; and yet we see continually men of considerable powers of mind borrowing largely--I might even say systematically--from the works of ancient or cotemporary writers: not always the identical words, though sometimes those; not always the identical thought, though sometimes that; but, more generally, the ideas suggested by the thoughts of others, and so intimately blended with them as to be inseparable--judging themselves safe from the accusation of plagiarism upon the same plea which was put forth by a thief indicted for stealing a scarf, who proved he had only taken the gold fringe. I know many men who never compose--and they are men who write much, and well--without having open around them many works of precisely the same character as that which they are writing. It is a dangerous habit, and much to be avoided. Indeed, we pray against it every day when we nay, "Lead us not into temptation."

As to repeating one's self, it is no very great crime, perhaps, for I never heard that robbing Peter to pay Paul was punishable under any law or statute, and the multitude of offenders in this sense, in all ages, and in all circumstances, if not an excuse, is a palliation, showing the frailty of human nature, and that we are as frail as others--but no more. The cause of this self-repetition, probably, is not a paucity of ideas, not an infertility of fancy, not a want of imagination or invention, but that, like children sent daily to draw water from a stream, we get into the habit of dropping our buckets into that same immeasurable depth of thought exactly at the same place; and though it be not exactly the same water as that which we drew up the day before it is very similar in quality and flavor, a little clearer or a little more turbid, as the case may be.

Now this dissertation--which may be considered as an introduction or preface to the second division of my history--has been brought about, has had its rise, origin, source, in an anxious and careful endeavor to avoid, if possible, introducing into this work the two solitary horsemen--one upon a white horse--which, by one mode or another, have found their way into probably one out of three of all the books I have written; and I need hardly tell the reader that the name of these books is legion. They are, perhaps, too many; but, though I must die, some of them will live--I know it, I feel it; and I must continue to write while this spirit is in this body.

To say truth, I do not know why I should wish to get rid of my two horsemen, especially the one on the white horse. Wouvermans always had a white horse in all his pictures; and I do not see why I should not put my signature, my emblem, my monogram, in my paper and ink pictures as well as any painter of them all. I am not sure that other authors do not do the same thing--that Lytton has not always, or very nearly, a philosophizing libertine--Dickens, a very charming young girl, with dear little pockets; and Lever, a bold dragoon. Nevertheless, upon my life, if I can help it, we will not have in this work the two horsemen and the white horse, albeit, in after times--when my name is placed with Homer and Shakspeare, or in any other more likely position--there may arise serious and acrimonious disputes as to the real authorship of the book, from its wanting my own peculiar and distinctive mark and characteristic.

But here, while writing about plagiarism, I have been myself a plagiary; and it shall not remain without acknowledgment, having suffered somewhat in that sort myself. Hear, my excellent friend, Leigh Hunt, soul of mild goodness, honest truth, and gentle brightness! I acknowledge that I stole from you the defensive image of Wouvermans's white horse, which you incautiously put within my reach, on one bright night of long, dreamy conversation, when our ideas of many things, wide as the poles asunder, met suddenly without clashing, or produced but a cool, quiet spark--as the white stones which children rub together in dark corners emit a soft, phosphorescent gleam, that serves but to light their little noses.

CHAPTER XVII

The call was very sudden. Ralph Woodhall was taken quite by surprise. He had calculated upon finding some opportunity, during the day, of quiet conversation with his Margaret; and now to be desired by his friend and patron, the Duke of Norfolk, to escort Lady Danvers upon her road westward, caused him some trouble and anxiety. He knew not how to refuse, however; for the duke informed him that intimation had been received of tumults on the road, and the fair Hortensia herself was present, looking as beautiful as ever, but pale and considerably agitated, and apparently alarmed. In such circumstances there was no showing even any hesitation, and, turning to the lady, he said, "If you will but wait for me five minutes, Lady Danvers, I will be ready. I wish to say a few words to my cousin, who must be up by this time, and--"

"Oh, there will be plenty of time for that after you return, Master Woodhall," said the duke. "Lord Woodhall announced last night his intention of remaining till to-morrow or the next day. So sure was I of your prompt readiness, that I took the liberty of ordering your horse to be saddled, and he now stands at the door, with five of my own servants ready to accompany our fair friend's carriage."

This was said with some stateliness, and Ralph evidently saw that there was something unexplained.

"I will get my hat and gloves, then," he said, "and be ready to escort Lady Danvers at once."

"I will send for them," replied the duke; and, raising his voice, he called a servant, saying, "Minton, get Mr. Woodhall's hat and gloves."

Ralph smiled, but made no reply; and as soon as the servant returned with what he had been sent for, he followed the duke, who, with ancient courtesy, conducted the lady to her carriage, and kissed her fair hand as he placed her in it, whispering, at the same time, "You see I have obeyed your injunctions to the letter; but take care of your reputation, dear lady."

Hortensia blushed to the eyes, but answered gayly, "Never fear that, my lord duke; I do right, and defy scandal."

The carriage moved on, and Ralph Woodhall followed it, with the Duke of Norfolk's servants and those of the fair baroness following him. Throughout the first five miles of the journey poor Margaret might have seen him with relief and satisfaction to her own heart. Thoughtful and abstracted, he kept near the carriage, it is true, but he never once approached its side. He rode on at the slow, uneasy pace which was necessary to keep up with, but not pass by the heavy vehicle; with eyes turned toward the ground and a somewhat contracted brow. He was not sullen, for his was a frank and cheerful heart; and, though he was grieved to be deprived of Margaret's society even for a few hours when he could have enjoyed it without peril to himself or her, that would never have clouded his bright look, when he sacrificed his wishes to be of service to another. But there appeared something strange to him in all that had lately passed--something that roused suspicions of a vague, unpleasant kind--that showed him he was made an instrument of for some purpose which was carefully concealed from himself.

"Could it be at the desire of Lord Woodhall that he was sent away?" he asked himself. "Could *his* love for Margaret, or Margaret's love for him, have been discovered?" Perhaps it might be so; and the intention of the parties might be to remove him away from the house upon some fair excuse till she was gone.

The thought was very bitter to him; but yet his mind clung to it; and the more he reflected, the more probable the supposition seemed. There were objections, it is true. That the Duke of Norfolk should have condescended to have mingled himself with such a deceit, was not at all likely; and he could not imagine for one moment that Lady Danvers would have knowingly lent herself to it. All the opinions she had expressed the night before--her whole conduct--her whole manner--her very look, were opposed to it; and yet the anxiety to hurry him away, to prevent him from speaking with any of his relations, or even seeing them before he went, the few whispered words that passed between the duke and Hortensia, which he had remarked, although he did not hear them distinctly, all seemed to tend to such a conclusion, and puzzled him sorely. He revolved the whole in his mind, first turning the argument one way, and then another--at one time convinced, and at another doubting. Thus he rode on pondering, as I have said, for some miles, when suddenly the sound of a horse's feet coming rapidly behind attracted his ear, and he turned and looked round. The servants of the Duke of Norfolk were in the way, so that he could not see who approached; but the moment after, doubt was ended by his own man Gaunt Stilling riding up.

"What is the matter?" asked Ralph, as the servant drew close to his side. "Has any thing gone amiss?"

"I heard you had gone away for the morning, sir," replied the man, respectfully, "and as you had left your riding-sword and taken your small sword, and had forgotten your cloak, I made bold to ride after you with them."

Ralph unfastened the dangling, inconvenient weapon he carried, gave it back to the man, and put on the other sword--more serviceable on horseback--which he had brought. Then, pausing for a moment, he suffered him to strap the folded riding-cloak to the back of the saddle without dismounting, and seeing him linger, asked, "Is there any thing more?"

Gaunt Stilling approached as close as he could, and spoke several sentences to his master in a whisper. Ralph turned, and put a question or two in the same tone, with an expression of some, but not great, surprise on his face. The man replied, and it was only the dumb-show which the Duke of Norfolk's servants witnessed. At length the young gentleman said aloud, "I will certainly be back before nightfall, unless some very unexpected circumstances occur to render it impossible, but, at all events, before bedtime."

Gaunt Stilling took off his hat gracefully enough, and rode away, directing his horse toward Norwich; and, after giving nearly half an hour more to deep meditation, apparently not of the most pleasant character, Ralph rode up to the side of the carriage, and commenced what he would fain have made an easy conversation with its fair inmate.

While this little event occurred, and these thoughts and considerations had been passing in his mind, he had himself been the object of some interest and anxiety to Lady Danvers. She attributed, indeed, his thoughtful, gloomy mood, and want of ordinary gallantly, to very different feelings from those which were really in his breast.

"He has received the challenge," she thought, "and is fearful he won't get back in time;" and then, addressing the maid, who sat opposite, she said, "Look out, and tell me what he is doing now."

"Just the same as before, my lady," replied the girl, "looking down at his horse's neck, as if he were counting the hairs in the mane, and gloomy enough he looks too."

"We must prevent him from escaping, Alice," said her mistress; "but I know not well how to manage to detain him, till it is too late for him to go back."

"Trust to chance, my lady," replied the waiting-woman; "it is a rare book, that chapter of accidents, if one knows how to read it rightly. But I dare say the duke has told his own people how to manage it. I saw him speaking with Master Wilton, the head groom, who goes with us. I should not wonder if the young gentleman's horse cast a shoe, or went dead lame, or something of that kind."

Lady Danvers smiled, but replied, "I will not trust to that, Alice. The duke seemed more indifferent about the matter than I expected. He said that boys would fight, but that to please me he would prevent this affair. I trust to his word as far as his ability goes, for he is a man of honor; but I do not think he will be very active in the business."

"Oh dear," replied the maid, "I should think, for my part, he would be glad enough to stop two handsome young gentlemen from cutting each other's throats on his own ground. I do hate the sight of those swords; and if I were king, I would have them all taken from them, and locked up against a time of war. But the duke certainly can not like such things."

Hortensia Danvers shook her head. "Neither you nor I, Alice," she said, "can understand men's feelings about these things; we have a great objection to be cut, or wounded, or hurt in any way, and bloodshed is naturally horrible to us. But no man cares much about such things in his own case, and, of course, can not be expected to care more in the case of others."

It was at this moment that Ralph rode up to the side of the carriage, saying, with an effort, "The roads are bad, notwithstanding the fine weather; but I fear we shall have rain, for there is much mist lying on the low ground."

"I do not think that is a sign of rain," replied Lady Danvers; "but I am no good judge of signs and seasons."

"Would that I were," replied Ralph; "for there are many that I do not understand."

"I must not pretend to be interpreter," replied Lady Danvers, in a gay tone; "however, if you wish me to act the Sibyl, propound your questions, and I will try. You must take the oracle for what it is worth, and remember that all such answers always read two ways. But would it not be better for you to give your horse to one of the men, and take a seat here beside me till we arrive at some point of danger, when, of course, my knight will mount on horseback and deliver me?"

"With all my heart," replied Ralph; "then I can question the prophetess at ease."

Thus saying, he ordered the coachman to stop, dismounted, and entered the carriage.

"You mentioned danger just now," he said, as soon as they were going forward again. "Now tell me, dear Lady Danvers, do you really think there is any danger?"

"Undoubtedly," replied Lady Danvers; "both I and the duke thought so, or you would not have been with me now."

"But have you had any intelligence which should make you fear?" asked Ralph.

"Distinct and certain," answered the fair lady. "It is true I am somewhat of a timid nature, and am apt, perhaps, to be frightened occasionally without cause; but such is not the case with his grace of Norfolk, and he judged that my apprehensions were very reasonable."

"May I ask where the danger lies, and in what it consists?" inquired Ralph.

"Nay, I do not know that I can give you a consistent account of the whole matter," replied Hortensia, with a quiet smile; "but we heard of much discord and quarreling, and that there was likely to be a fight."

"Indeed!" replied Ralph, with an air so perfectly unconscious that Lady Danvers began to ask herself if she had been misled by her maid's information, or if he was acting the hypocrite to perfection.

"Have you had no cause to suppose such things are likely to take place?" she asked.

"None whatever," he replied; "so little so, indeed, that I almost fancied, from the extremely pressing hurry in which I was dispatched upon this pleasant task, that the duke did not only desire to confer upon me the honor and happiness of escorting you, but also to get me out of the way for a time."

Hortensia raised her beautiful eyes to his face, and fixed them there while she inquired, "Do you know of any motive he could have for such a proceeding?"

"I can fix upon none in particular, and have been puzzling myself to divine one," replied Ralph; but, at the same time, he colored highly, and Hortensia was satisfied.

A silence of some minutes ensued; and then the lady, with all her quiet gayety, resumed the conversation: "I do think--to use a housemaid's mode of asseveration," she said, "that you are the most ungallant young man that I ever met with--I don't say discourteous, for your manner is fair enough, Master Ralph Woodhall; but I do not believe that there is one man to be found in court, camp, or city, who would have gone about to discover any cause for his being sent on a journey with me, or who would not, if forced to take it, have sworn most devoutly on the Holy Evangelists that it was the most blessed chance that ever befell him--whether he thought it so or not, Ralph Woodhall--you understand, whether he thought it so or not."

Ralph felt that he had in some degree failed in politeness, and he replied, "No one, dear lady, would have told you so more readily, and no one would have felt it more sincerely than myself, upon any other day than this; but I had to-day something important to do, which rendered what would otherwise have been a true pleasure, the cause of some slight embarrassment; but you see I am too straightforward to be courtly, even when I do my best."

"I like you all the better," replied Lady Danvers, frankly; "but now let us talk of something else. I dare say and hope that you will get back in plenty of time to do all that you want to do, if it be right and proper: if it be not, I hope you won't; for I am certainly not going to give you up, and send you back again sooner than I please, because you are cross at being taken away from Norwich. Be therefore exceedingly civil and amusing during the whole of the rest of the journey, in the hope that your chains may thereby be broken all the speedier."

Ralph thought that her philosophy was a good one, and exerted himself to cast off the feeling of disappointment, and to make himself as agreeable as possible for the rest of the way. He succeeded very well, although, to speak the truth, he did so greatly by the assistance of Hortensia who put forth all her powers to amuse the hour. Thus passed the time upon the long and weary way which lies between Norwich and the western part of the county. It is not very picturesque even now, displaying but little beauty and little variety, except the beauty of exceedingly well cultivated fields, and the variety of oxen and sheep, sportsmen and dogs. But culture could then hardly be said to have begun; and it was not a sporting season of the year. There was no inducement, therefore, for the lady and her companion to turn their eyes from the interior of the carriage; and, to say sooth, if Ralph desired a lovely prospect, he could not have had one more beautiful than the face and form of her who sat beside him. He could not but feel, too, the fascination of her look and manner; and her conversation, gay, light, and playful as it was, had frequently running through it, like dark veins in the clear white marble, a strain of melancholy which rendered it still more charming. It was like a light, blithesome bird, that dips its wings for an instant in a cool stream, only to rise again refreshed and brightened.

Slowly as the coach proceeded--and it was one of those large, lumbering, gilded vehicles which we can not imagine to have traveled at the rate of more than four miles an hour--five hours had been consumed ere the party reached the little town of ----.

Ralph was glad to see it, for he thought he should be there dismissed; and yet there were feelings of regret at parting with that fair and charming girl--feelings which, could Margaret have seen them really as they were, would have given her neither pain nor offense. It was now between two and three o'clock, and there was a good deal of gayety and bustle in the town, the streets crowded, wagons and market-carts obstructing the way, and countrymen riding rough-looking horses, with their tails tied up to keep them out of the mud. With some difficulty the carriage moved along the road; and Ralph remounted his horse in order to give directions for clearing the way. They reached at length the inn door, where the horses were to be fed and to rest for an hour or two. Ralph handed Lady Danvers from the carriage, and was leading her through a little crowd which had gathered before the inn, when he remarked that, although the appearance of such a vehicle in a remote place might well attract attention, the eyes of the mob were principally turned in another direction, as if watching for some object coming down the street.

"Dear me! my lady, there is something going on," said Mistress Alice, the waiting-maid; "what can it be about?"

Hortensia made no reply, but, quitting Ralph's arm upon the step, walked hastily into the house, and then whispered to the maid, "Send the duke's head groom to me at once."

The landlord was, in the mean time, bowing low; and his good dame, with abundant keys, and more than one pin-cushion by her side, was courtesying to the ground, ready to show the beautiful lady to her chamber.

"What is the matter without?" asked Lady Danvers; "the people seem a good deal excited."

"Oh, it is nothing at all," replied the landlady, "only a Nonconformist gentleman who has been examined by the magistrates. They are taking him away to the jail, and the people do not like it. I should not wonder if there were to be a riot to-night; for the Whigs have the upper hand in this town, and they don't bear patiently all that is going on."

Hortensia turned and looked through the doorway into the street. She saw Ralph standing on the steps, and a crowd passing hurriedly on before him. The next instant, however, she beheld him spring forward, and heard him exclaim. "Why do you strike the man, sir? You are exceeding your duty. He can not go faster than he does."

What was answered she did not hear; and the steps of the inn were almost instantly covered with a multitude of people, who shut out from her sight what was passing beyond.

"Come up, my lady--come up stairs," cried the landlord; "they will make bad work of it."

Hortensia followed up the stairs as fast as the landlord could go; and, shown into a large and handsome room which faced the street, she ran forward, threw open the window, and looked out. The sign-board of the inn was in the way, so that she could not see the exact spot where Ralph stood; but she heard angry words and fierce tones going on below, and a moment after, stones began to fly and cudgels to wave. But the next instant the sound of Ralph's voice rose up over the din, exclaiming, clear and loud, "Keep the peace--keep the peace! Suffer the constables to do their duty according to law; and you, sirs, take care that you do not exceed the law, as you have done already by striking this gentleman when he was making no resistance."

Though he spoke loud, his tone was so quiet, and his words so reasonable, that Lady Danvers entertained no apprehension regarding his conduct or his safety, and, taking one glance over the crowd to a spot where she saw her maid standing on the opposite side of the road, afraid to make her way back to the inn, the lady withdrew into the room to avoid the stones which were flying thicker than was pleasant.

The loud and angry speaking continued for several minutes, and once a stone came into the room where Hortensia was sitting; but no one came near her, for the excitement of the scene without had affected even the people of the inn, and it is probable that neither her own servants nor those of the Duke of Norfolk could force their way up to the door. At length, however, a nimble step was heard upon the stairs, and the head groom, whom she had sent for, appeared with an eager and excited countenance. He doffed his hat as he entered the room, saying at once, "They have taken him away before the magistrates, my lady; but Mistress Alice said you wanted me."

"Who? who?" demanded Lady Danvers; "of whom do you speak?"

"Mr. Ralph, my lady," replied the man. "We would have rescued him with the strong hand, and beaten the constables all to mortar; but he would not let us, and ordered us all to keep the peace. But I had better run up at once with the rest, to see that he is fairly dealt by."

"Ay, do so, do so," cried Hortensia, at first, eagerly; but then immediately she fell into a fit of thought, and as the man was quitting the room, called him back, saying, "Stay, Wilton--Wilton! we may turn this to advantage, perhaps."

The man seemed surprised and confounded, but the lady beckoned him to come nearer, saying, "I have no time for explanations, Master Wilton, but you must do what you can, without endangering Mr. Woodhall's safety or character, to turn this matter so as to keep him here till to-morrow morning. In a word, the Duke of Norfolk sent him here with me to keep him out of the way. There was some quarrel going on between him and another gentleman in the house, and his grace wished for time to arrange it before he returned."

"I understand, my lady, I understand," replied the man, with a shrewd nod of the head. "His grace gave me a little hint, but I did not think of turning this to profit. I'll manage it--I'll manage it;" and away he went at full speed, saying to himself, "My lady does not mind having a handsome young man to sit with her all the evening, I'll warrant, though they do say she has refused scores of great people already. Well, there is no knowing womankind."

He overtook Ralph walking quietly up the street between two constables, who, from an intimation of his strength which they had received, kept at a respectful distance from him. A number of men and boys were following close, with an unnecessary trot; and all the servants of the Duke of Norfolk who had come into the town with the carriage, as well as one or two of Lady Danvers's people, and several women and children, were following at a little distance behind. Wilton made his way through all these, and kept close to Ralph's elbow till the party reached the justice room (which was, in fact, the parlor of an alehouse), and the prisoner was ushered into the presence of the justices, who, booted and spurred, and with their horse-whips in their hands, were just ready to leave the place and ride away. There were three of them present, and two of them looked exceedingly rueful at the prospect of more business. The third, however, rapping out a great oath, cast himself back into his seat again, and laid his horse-whip on the table. "Why, what the devil--" he said; "you look like a gentleman, sir. Curse my buttons, what have they brought you here for?"

"They can best tell you themselves, sir," answered Ralph.

"Don't you go to church? Don't you take the sacrament? Are you a Nonconformist?"

"I go to church and take the sacrament as regularly as most men," replied Ralph; "and Nonconformist I am none, having been brought up in the Church of England from my infancy."

"Pox take you, then," exclaimed the choleric fat justice, addressing the constables, "what did you bring this gentleman here for?"

The charge was then formally made by the two constables, imputing to Ralph the serious offenses of riot and an attempt to rescue their prisoner.

Ralph, in reply, simply told his own story. The constables, he said, had treated an old and respectable-looking man with unjustifiable harshness, irritated apparently by the great crowd which had collected. One of them had even struck him with his staff, upon the pretense of making him go on, although he was offering no resistance.

"That was Doggett, I'll be sworn," said the magistrate, looking round at his two brethren; "I told you all Doggett would get us into a scrape some day."

Doggett, however, was not present, having gone to lodge his prisoner in jail for re-examination; and the magistrate continued, turning to Ralph Woodhall, and saying, "Well, sir, but who are you? What's your station, rank, profession? What do you know of this prisoner who you say was maltreated?"

"I know nothing of him whatever," replied Ralph, "except that he was maltreated, and that I told the man who struck him he exceeded his duty. As to my name, rank, station, et cetera, my name is Ralph Woodhall, a distant relation of a nobleman of that name, without any rank but that of a Master of Arts, without any condition which can particularly designate me but that of being at present a guest of the Duke of Norfolk, and having undertaken, at his request, to escort Lady Danvers on a part of her way to the West."

The magistrates all looked very blank, for the Duke of Norfolk was the great man in those parts; and great men, whether good men or not, obtained much more deference in those days than at present. The business would have probably ended in a dismissal of the charge and a rebuke to the constables; but Master Wilton, who was a shrewd Yorkshireman, from which county the principal grooms in great families were then generally selected, chose his moment well, and, stepping forward, said, "What Master

Woodhall says your worships, is quite true, and I can prove it, if I had time to bring forward my witnesses. I am head groom to his grace of Norfolk, who is the dearest friend of this young gentleman. If your worships like to put off the case until I can get the people together who saw it all, I will be 'sponsible that Mr. Ralph will be here at any time you like to-morrow."

The magistrates looked wise; but Ralph exclaimed, with a somewhat sharp gesticulation of impatience, "I would a great deal rather have the case decided at once. I have business which calls me back to Norwich."

"This is a very serious charge, sir," said one of the magistrates who had not yet spoken--an ill-tempered man, rendered cross by having been detained; "recollect, sir, that if we decide against you on a charge of riot and attempt to rescue, we shall have to commit you to prison for trial."

"I have plenty of witnesses, too, if they talk of witnesses," said one of the constables. "I can prove that there was a riot, and that he had a hand in it. I suppose his being a friend of the Duke of Norfolk is no great matter here."

This part of the discussion was the most unpleasant part to Ralph Woodhall. The prospect of being committed to prison if he urged the case forward at that moment was, of course, more unpleasant to him than that of being detained for the whole day; but, nevertheless, he urged, in a few words, that the witnesses might be speedily collected, as they could not be far off, and that the duke expected his return that night.

"That is of no consequence to us, sir," said the chairman of the magistrates, with solemn dignity; "and we can not wait here all the evening collecting witnesses. We must adjourn the hearing till to-morrow morning, and, in the mean time, should be sorry to do any thing harsh, if we could be quite certain that you will be here present at the hour appointed."

"I'll pawn my body and soul, your worship," said Wilton, "that he does not stir out of the town to-night, and if he do, you can come and take me out of the duke's stables, and lose me my wages and my place."

"Will you give your word of honor, sir," asked the magistrate, addressing Ralph, "that you will appear at the hour appointed?"

There seemed no help for it, and Ralph replied, "I will, if the hour be an early one."

"Nine o'clock," replied the magistrate, with a laugh; "we are all early men. I hold you to your word, then; and you too, Master What's-your-name. Clerk, make out the bail-bond for him; we won't be too particular as to the property."

Once more, there was no help for it; and it is good policy in life, as Ralph well knew, to submit patiently to that for which there is no help. The clerk, however, was tediously slow--people always are slow when we want them to be quick, and by the time the whole business was concluded, and the young gentleman had once more issued forth into the air, the clock in the old steeple was striking five.

A little crowd had gathered about the doors of the justice room, and they greeted Ralph when he appeared at liberty with a warm-hearted cheer. He got clear of the people as soon as he could, however, and, followed by the servants of the Duke of Norfolk and Lady Danvers, made his way back to the inn. A day from which he had expected some of those golden moments which are the treasures of the heart, had nearly passed by without affording him one look of her he loved.

CHAPTER XVIII

How often, as society is constituted, does the passing of one single hour affect the whole of the hours that gather into life. A moment is sometimes enough; but it is more frequently an hour--two hours--an evening.

I wonder if it was so with the patriarchs. I rather think not: for if so, they would not have lived so long. If Methuselah had gone on at the rail-road pace at which we live in modern days--if he had crowded into each day of life the same amount of thought, sensation, act, event, which now fills up the space of every four-and-twenty hours, between seventeen and seventy, the whole history of the world, in its hundred thousand folio tomes, would have been a joke to the annals of his existence. But we make a great mistake if we think those old gentlemen, in any thing, lived as fast as we do; and this, I feel sure, was the secret of their longevity.

Oh no, they moved from place to place, with their flocks and herds, traveling *not* much more than five or six miles a day. They struck their tents in the morning; they pitched them in the evening; they milked their cows, tended their "much cattle," and the day was done. Sometimes they did not even strike their tents at all, but remained upon one spot, till, like the locusts, they had eaten up every green thing. An occasional combat with a lion or a bear--a fight with a neighboring herdsman, or the procuration of venison "to make savory meat," was an event agreeably diversifying the monotony of existence; and I have a strong notion that thought and feeling marched at as slow a rate as all the rest.

Thus was it, probably, that their thoughts were so grand, their feelings so powerful. In mighty masses, they moved slow; but whatever they touched they overwhelmed.

We, on the contrary, can never go too fast; forgetting that there is but a certain portion of life allotted to every man, and that life is not mere time, measured by suns or moons, but a certain amount of action, event, idea, sensation. We crowd more into seven days than a patriarch put into seven years; and then we wonder that life is so brief, that so little time has been allowed us.

There was an evening--a long evening--before Ralph Woodhall and Hortensia Danvers. What might they not have done in that space of time? How completely, under many circumstances, might it have altered the whole course of the fate of both; and it did affect their fate considerably: perhaps not in event, perhaps not in that course and conduct of external life which is open to the eye of the world, which consists of act, and influences others, but much in that internal life, where thought and feeling are the actors, where spirit speaks to spirit, and their proceedings are only open to the eye of consciousness.

But let me tell, and as briefly as possible, for I must hurry on to other things, what did actually take place.

When Ralph returned to the inn, he was led at once by the landlord, with every demonstration of the most profound respect, to the apartments which had been assigned to Lady Danvers. He found one of the servants of the Duke of Norfolk with her, one of her own men, and her own waiting-woman; and he saw, at a glance, by the sparkling look with which she gave him her hand, that she had heard all, and had approved what he had done. He was somewhat surprised to see, indeed, the state and condition of the room into which he was shown. It had been understood that Lady Danvers was to go on that night, as soon as her horses had been refreshed; but now, every thing seemed prepared for her longer stay.

Hortensia had an art of giving any place of her temporary abode an air of graceful refinement which was very charming, and it was done with a rapidity and precision which could only be accomplished by the aid of the fairy or order. The room was a large, old-fashioned, dingy room, well-furnished enough, and reserved for persons of high degree who might chance occasionally to visit the house; but since Hortensia Danvers entered it, the furniture had been rearranged, a number of little articles of taste and ornament had been taken by the maid from her baggage, and laid about upon the tables with apparently a careless care. Here was seen the book of Common Prayer, in its cover of crimson velvet, with silver clasps; there a beautifully finished miniature in a golden frame. In other places were seen materials for writing, arranged in quaintly-formed stands of the workmanship of the fifteenth century, while all the flowers that could be procured in the neighborhood decorated different parts of the room. The maid was still busy with these arrangements, under her lady's direction, when Ralph entered, and gazed round with a look of wonder.

His fair young companion seemed to enjoy his surprise, and asked, in a cheerful tone, if she had not decorated the room gayly.

"You have, indeed, sweet lady," he answered; "but is not all this labor thrown away? I thought you were going forward this evening."

"So thought I," replied Lady Danvers, "till you chose to get yourself apprehended by constables, Master Woodhall. Then, as you had courteously come so far to take care of me, I found myself bound in courtesy to stay to take care of you. You would not have had me go on and leave you in the hands of the Philistines, surely? I have just heard how it has all ended for the time; but, over and above a wish to know how the matter goes with you to-morrow, it is too late now, at half past five, to think of moving my quarters for the night. I therefore invite you to sup with me here, and to spend such portion of your time with me, in this dull solitude, as you can withdraw from more weighty occupations."

She spoke in a gay and jesting tone; and seeing a certain look of uneasiness upon Ralph's countenance, which she justly attributed to the thought of being detained--though she misunderstood entirely the circumstances which rendered the detention painful--she added, "Moreover, I lay my commands upon you to clear your countenance instantly, to submit with a good grace to the will of Fate, to cast off all thought of repining at being cooped up for a whole evening with Hortensia Danvers, and, if possible, to make yourself exceedingly agreeable, and more civil than ordinary. Alice, you stay here," she continued, addressing the waiting-maid, who seemed about to quit the room; and then, with a laughing look to Ralph, she added, "It is as well that she should have the benefit of our learned conversation, both for her own instruction and the instruction of others."

Ralph could not help smiling; and, seating himself beside her in one of the window seats, he made up his mind to do as she bade him, to think no more of what could not be avoided, and to let the present pass as agreeably as might be.

There was no very romantic scene before them: a wide old street, with the quaint gables of the houses turned to the highway; edifices of wood, with galleries and sometimes stair-cases running over the outside; edifices of stone and brick--for the country afforded both--with flights of steps descending from the path to the reception rooms. There was the market cross in the middle of the highway, where the latter grew wide, about twenty yards above the inn door, enlarging into a sort of market square, and the church tower a hundred yards beyond, with a group of boys playing at marbles before the gate by which the dead were borne into the cemetery, and wrangling over their game as fiercely as if they had tasted human blood. Some knots of people still lingered in the streets, gossiping sagely over the events which had just passed, and presaging more sagely still the events which were to come; and numerous carts and wagons, with their loads still packed, or ready for removal, occupied a considerable portion of the street. It was like a dream of the age fading away and ready to give place to a period fresher, stiffer, more practical.

Yet over the whole there hung a light, misty haze of sunshine and vapor commingled, not uncommon on an English afternoon, and not unlike the dim, magnifying fog which shrouds from the eager eye the transition from the present to the future.

"How richly the sunshine streams down the street upon that old carved cross and the straw-strewn market-place!" said Ralph.

"All the more bright because we see not whence it comes," replied Hortensia; "and the warmer--to the eye, at least--for passing through an atmosphere grosser than that from which it issues. What is it most like, Ralph--like woman's love, or Heaven's bounty, or the rays of Hope, that stream between the close dwellings of man's earthly aspirations, gilding the straws upon his onward way, and making the stones on his path shine like jewels?"

"Like woman's love, methinks," said Ralph, "because, as you say, it pours from sources we do not see, brightens the dimmer air that it pervades, and often lends a luster to worthless objects, which shine in its light alone."

"True," said the lady, with a sigh; "but see, it catches on the cross upon the steeple-top, and makes it shine as if with fire."

"It will rest there longest," replied her companion; "shining after all is dark below."

"Even so," said the lady, retiring from the window; "I love the shaded light of a quiet room better than the wide, garish sunshine abroad. Come, let us talk of other days, when you and I were boy and girl, and knew not of each other's being, and chased butterflies, and sought to catch the rainbow, and did all that the common bond of nature uses to link withal the human hearts through the wide world in one community of universal sympathy in early years. Tell me, Ralph Woodhall, why is it that all mankind, thus one in happy youth, should part so widely in maturer years--part in feeling and in thought, in conduct and in course, in object and in means?"

"Because," replied Ralph, "at least so I suppose, infancy is one general starting-point from which all the roads diverge, leading further and further asunder."

"Till all guide us to the great precipice which surrounds our arena on every side," said the lady, "and we take the leap from points wide apart. But we are getting dull, Mr. Woodhall. Do you remember your mother?"

"But faintly," replied Ralph, "yet brightly too, though it may seem a contradiction. The long look back through life is to me like the prospect down that street, where there are many long, shadowy spaces in which I can see nothing clearly, while every here and there comes a bright gleam of light, displaying every thing as vividly as in mid-day."

"Memory! memory!" said the lady; "it is ever like the setting sun."

"Sometimes," continued Ralph, "the objects furthest off seem to catch the light of that sun of memory most brightly; and where a dark lapse of shadow intervenes, the objects beyond are the most brilliant. One of my earliest recollections is of having been taken into a large room, dimly lighted by a shaded lamp, and seeing a pale, beautiful face pillowed on my father's arm. I remember being lifted up by a nurse upon the side of the bed, and my father's raising gently that fair, faded form, while my mother cast her arms around me, and I heard her say, 'God bless and keep thee, my child;' and then some tears fell upon my face, and I was carried away. All around that scene is dark and obscure; but it is as clear to memory as the events of yesterday."

"It may be that such is the happiest parting," said Lady Danvers, shading her eyes with her hand. "It is very sad to watch the decreasing strength, to gaze anxiously upon the waning color, to listen terrified to the panting breath, to see the eyes we love lose their light, and to mark the dull, awful change steal over the face once warm and eager with affection. Yet who can tell? Each one has his sorrow; Nature's lamp is only lighted to go out, and leave the heart it cheered in darkness. What matters it if it be suddenly extinguished by some harsh wind, or slowly flicker out for failing oil? Come, let us be more cheerful; let us talk of the gay, great world, or of country scenes and happy life at home. Surely we may find some more cheering themes than death or sunset."

"Both have a morrow," replied Ralph; and then he tried, with some success, to vary the conversation with lighter topics; but still the somber tone which it had at first assumed spread through it all a quiet, gentle melancholy, which was not without its danger to one heart there. Ralph had but little knowledge of the world--none of courts or courtly scenes. By nature he was a gentleman--by habit, by thought, by feeling. His collegiate life had not been long enough to stiffen or to harden, and his studies had been directed to all those things which embellish as well as enrich the mind. Thus his conversation was new--almost strange to Hortensia's ears--unlike aught she had heard before, yet full of sympathies with much in her own heart and mind; and for several hours the time passed sweetly, till toward half past eight Ralph rose to retire.

"Surely," she thought, "all danger of an angry meeting must have gone by for to-day;" and, perhaps, with too strong a consciousness that she would willingly have detained him longer, she let him go.

Shortly after, an undefinable feeling of dread took possession of her. "There is no knowing," she thought, "what men in their intemperate courage may do to satisfy themselves upon their point of honor. Alice!" she cried aloud, "go and see for Mr. Ralph Woodhall; tell him I want him--that I had forgotten something which I wished to say."

"Lord! my lady, I dare say he is gone to bed," replied the girl.

"Ascertain, at all events," said Lady Danvers; "ask one of the duke's servants."

The waiting-woman left the room, and remained away for some five minutes. When she returned, she said, with a laugh, unconscious of her mistress's anxiety, "The young gentleman has gone forth, my lady--to amuse himself in the town, I'll warrant. But Master Wilton says he will give him your ladyship's message as soon as he returns."

Lady Danvers sat up for more than one hour, but Ralph did not make his appearance; and with a heavy heart she at length retired to rest.

CHAPTER XIX

"It is hopeless," said the Duke of Norfolk, sadly, as he stood by the side of the bed on which they had laid the body of Henry Woodhall, and let the cold hand, which he had taken in his own, sink slowly down by the dead man's side.

"Quite hopeless, I fear, your grace," replied a surgeon, who stood on the other side. "The sword, I suspect, has passed right through his heart."

"Did not some one say that Mr. Robert Woodhall is still in the house?" inquired the duke; "why is he not here? Has any one told him?"

"He knows it, your grace," answered one of his servants, who had aided to bear in the body; "his own servant went up to inform him; I saw him pass that way in haste."

"Has any one seen Mr. Ralph Woodhall?" inquired the duke; but no one replied; and he sent up to Ralph's room to ascertain if he had returned.

In a moment or two the messenger appeared again, saying, "He is not there, your grace. His servant says that he went away this morning with Lady Danvers, and he has not yet returned."

The duke mused thoughtfully, and then made inquiries as to whether the wilderness and the grounds adjacent had been searched, observing, at the same time, "This poor youth has evidently fallen in a duel, for when he went away this morning he concealed his intention of coming back. Nevertheless, it is right we should know his opponent, that we may ascertain if the circumstances of the combat were all fair."

"The poor young gentleman's servant is below, your grace," said the chamberlain, "but I would not let him come up till I had your commands."

"Bring him here--bring him hither at once," said the duke; "perhaps he can throw some light on this sad affair."

The man was immediately brought into the room, a tall, stout, fresh-colored, good-looking fellow; but he turned ashy pale when his eye fell upon the breathless form of his master; and, without noticing any one in the room, he advanced to the bedside, while the tears rose thick in his eyes, exclaiming, "Alas! alas! poor Master Henry! a better gentleman did not live. Little did I think, when you told me to give the letter early to-morrow, what you were going to do to-night, or I would have stopped it one way or another. But your father will have vengeance upon him who killed you, if it cost him his heart's blood, or I don't know him."

"Of what letter do you speak, my good friend?" asked the duke; "is it one from this poor young gentleman to his father?"

"No, your grace," replied the man, drawing forth a letter from his pocket, but apparently hesitating as to whether he should deliver it, "I am to give it to your grace to-morrow."

"Give it to me," said the duke, in a tone of authority; "no time like the present;" and, taking the letter, he opened it at once. The contents were as follows:

"My Lord Duke,

"A quarrel having taken place between myself and my cousin, Mr. Ralph Woodhall, which we are to void to-night, in the manner which befits gentlemen of our station, and as the issue of such encounters is always uncertain, I write you these few lines, to be delivered in case matters should go unfavorably with myself. Although I think he has behaved ill in some affairs of domestic concern, and has certainly caused great pain and uneasiness in my family, for which I have demanded satisfaction this night, I hold Ralph to be a man of honor; and I beg to inform you that the challenge was given by myself, in such terms that he could not refuse to accept it; that I appointed the meeting to take place by moonlight, in order to avoid the eyes which I had reason to believe were upon us; and that it was at my express desire that no witnesses or seconds were present. I say this, lest, from the above circumstances, some undeserved imputation should fall upon the character of my cousin. From my knowledge of him, during many years, you may rest assured, whatever is the result, that all has passed honorably and fairly between us; and, so long as I have life, I beg you, my lord duke, to believe me, your grace's most faithful and obedient servant, Henry Woodhall."

The duke mused much over this letter, and hesitated, in some degree, how he should act. He doubted not, from the warm and impetuous temper of Lord Woodhall, that the servant's words would prove prophetic, and that the old nobleman would suffer nothing to stand in the way of his vengeance.

"I must have time for thought," he said to himself. "This youth, Ralph, has given his fair guardian the slip, it seems. Well, I can not blame him; I should most likely have done the same myself in his circumstances. He should have stayed, however, to confront what he has done--and yet, perhaps not. It is better as it is. His presence would have been very embarrassing."

As he thus thought, with his eyes fixed upon the door, Robert Woodhall suddenly entered the room, and the duke, though not a very acute man, could not help remarking that a sudden change came upon the young man's countenance even as he passed the threshold. The expression of his face, at the moment he pushed the door open, was any thing but one of dissatisfaction; there was even a faint smile upon his lip, although his face was pale enough. But a look of deep sadness was assumed in a moment; and, advancing to his noble host, he first apologized, in good set form, for not having come sooner, alleging that he had been partly undressed when the news arrived, which, the reader knows, was false.

The duke replied by pointing to the corpse, and saying, somewhat stiffly, "This is a sad sight, sir; I hope you have had no share in urging this quarrel forward, and think it might have been better if you had taken means to prevent its fatal termination. By good advice, such matters are sometimes obviated."

"Ah! poor Henry!" cried Robert, with a look at the dead body, and a shudder, which was natural enough; "I do assure your grace that I had nothing to do with this squabble at all. Henry wrote the challenge with his own hand; I did not even bear it to my cousin Ralph; and surely a man of honor like yourself would not have me betray a secret intrusted in full confidence to my keeping."

"And yet," said the duke, sternly, "at the very moment when your two near relations were about to shed each other's blood, you were undressing to go to bed!"

Robert colored whether he would or not; but he excused himself by another lie.

"I did not know the precise hour, my lord duke," he answered; "Henry only gave me half his confidence. He would not even leave a letter, which he wrote to your grace, to my care. He acted in every thing for himself."

"Perhaps he did right," replied the duke, somewhat bitterly, for there was that in the young man's conduct and demeanor which did not please him--nay, which excited suspicions, just in themselves, though not very definite.

"I think it will be better, Mr. Woodhall." he continued, "for you to mount on horseback, as early as may be to-morrow morning, and break the tidings of this unfortunate affair to poor Lord Woodhall."

"I will go at once, my lord duke," replied Robert.

"That is needless," replied the duke, in a grave, melancholy tone; "you would but break in upon his rest. Do not rob an aged man of one night of calm repose that he can enjoy; do not add more hours of bitterness to the many bitter hours he must endure. I will write to him myself, by your hands, and you shall have the letter by the gray of the dawn to-morrow. That will be time enough."

"But will your grace take no means to cause the apprehension of the murderer?" demanded Robert Woodhall, with a look of well-assumed surprise.

"Murderer!" said the duke; "do you mean your cousin, sir?"

"He was my cousin, sir," replied Robert, a good deal nettled by the duke's tone, "but I shall regard him as my cousin no longer; and a man who drives another by his bad conduct to call him to the field, and then slays him, I can only look upon as a murderer, be he my cousin or not."

"That dead hand there," said the duke, pointing to the corpse, "wrote, while yet in life, a full exculpation of his adversary's conduct in the affair of the duel, at least. Ralph Woodhall was only acting, it would seem, as any man of honor would have acted, and those who best deserve the name of murderers are they who urge on petty quarrels to a fatal result."

"Your grace's opinion seems harsh of me," said Robert Woodhall, with feelings of rage he could hardly repress.

"I have not forgotten," replied the Duke of Norfolk, "that the first quarrel last night was between yourself and your cousin Ralph. What may have been your conduct since I do not pretend to say; but certain I am, that until Henry Woodhall quitted the supper-table, he and his cousin were upon the most friendly terms, and I am not aware that they met afterward until this last fatal occasion."

Thus saying, he turned and left the room, giving some necessary directions to his servants as he descended the stairs.

Robert Woodhall remained standing at the foot of the bed, with his eyes gloomily fixed upon the floor. Several of the attendants still continued in the room; but they all drew back from the young gentleman with a feeling of dislike and suspicion, for which they might have found it difficult to assign a cause, though undoubtedly the duke's words gave direction to their thoughts. There are instincts, however, in the human breast; and those instincts, probably, had some share in the feelings of the men who surrounded Robert Woodhall.

He remained there, I have said, with his eyes fixed gloomily upon the floor--not upon the corpse; but he was roused from his revery by the voice of the surgeon, who still stood by the bedside, and who said, "Mr. Woodhall, will you come here for a moment?"

Robert approached him slowly, and then the old man said, in a peculiar tone, "Will you put your hand upon the breast of your poor cousin?"

"No," cried Robert Woodhall, almost fiercely; and, turning sharply on his heel, he quitted the room.

About two hours after the events I have just related, the Duke of Norfolk was seated in his own fine library, with lights and papers before him, but quite alone. The door opened, and his chamberlain appeared, saying, "Here is the young man, your grace; he had not gone to bed."

The chamberlain had been followed into the room by Gaunt Stilling, whose large, massive brow was very heavy, as if with deep grief. The duke waved his hand to the chamberlain, and that officer withdrew to the other side of the door, keeping watch there, but not approaching too close.

"Your master has not returned yet, I hear," said the duke, fixing his eyes upon Stilling's face.

"He has not, my lord duke," replied the other, gravely.

"This is a serious affair," said the duke; "and I fear that the consequences may be very serious to your master. Lord Woodhall is a man of much influence at court, and of a warm and vehement temper. This young gentleman who has been killed was the general favorite."

"And well he deserved to be so!" cried Gaunt Stilling, warmly; "he was not perfect--no man is; but, as people of his rank go, there were few like him. Had it been his cousin Robert, who would have cared? but Fate seems to make mistakes sometimes, as well as others. The good are taken and the bad are left."

The duke listened quietly to this outburst of feeling, and then inquired if the man thought he could tell where his master was to be found.

"I think I can find him, your grace," replied Gaunt Stilling; "but I will not say where, if any evil is to come of it."

"I do not wish to know where," answered the Duke of Norfolk. "If you can find him, well. Bear him this letter from me; and it will be as well to take with you as much of his baggage as you can, for I think it will be inexpedient for him to return hither for some time, till this storm has blown by. I will find means to befriend him during his absence."

"What am I to do with the rest of the baggage, my lord duke?" asked Gaunt Stilling; "there is a good deal more than a horse-load."

"There is a carrier crossing the country, I think, to-morrow," the duke replied; "the chamberlain will give you surer information. You can send the superfluous baggage by him to any place you like, northward or westward--perhaps it would be better to send it to his father's house; but my people will see it expedited, if you will give it into their charge."

Gaunt Stilling bowed, took the packet which the duke held in his hand, and which deserved that epithet rather than the name of letter, and withdrew in silence. But he did not set out immediately. An hour was spent in packing up the baggage of his master, and another hour in writing a long letter, which, when finished and sealed, he placed in another half sheet of paper, on the inner side of which he wrote a few lines to his father, and put old Stilling's address, at Coldenham, upon the whole. This, together with the larger trunk-mails, he delivered to the duke's night porter, to be forwarded by the chamberlain on the following day; and then, after making some inquiries as to the shortest roads, he placed the two pair of saddle-bags upon his horse, and set out in the same direction which had been taken by his master and Lady Danvers on the preceding morning.

It was by this time nearly four o'clock, and until daylight Stilling rode as fast as he could go, except where, every now and then, he met with a corner, or a turning of which he did not feel very sure. When daylight did break, and the laborers began to trudge forth into the fields, he found that he had gone somewhat out of his way, which obliged him to retrace his steps for nearly a couple of miles. He then proceeded more cautiously, but contrived to reach the little town where Lady Danvers was a few minutes before nine. At the inn he asked eagerly for his master, having some fear, indeed, that Ralph might have passed him while he had been wandering wide of the proper track.

The reply, however, satisfied him; for the landlord stated that the young gentleman, Mr. Woodhall, had that moment gone down to the justice room, with all the Duke of Norfolk's servants. Thither Stilling followed him, as soon as he had given his horse into the hands of the hostler, and placed his bags in security. Round the door there was a small crowd, as usual; but the stout young fellow elbowed his way in, and arrived just at the moment when the fat magistrate in the chair was announcing the decision of the bench.

"There is no pretense whatever," said the justice, "at least such is the opinion of myself and my brethren, for detaining Mr. Ralph Woodhall even for an hour. It is clearly shown, by a multitude of witnesses, that he endeavored to calm the riot rather than to excite it, and that the brutal conduct of the constable Doggett was the sole cause of any commotion; for which brutal conduct we have determined to reprimand the said Doggett, and he is reprimanded accordingly. Mr. Woodhall, you are at liberty, and we hope that your detention may not prove inconvenient."

Ralph was about to make some reply, but Stilling, stepping forward, placed the packet in his hand, saying, "From his grace of Norfolk, sir--in haste."

Ralph took it, and was breaking the seal, when Gaunt Stilling whispered, "You had better read it in private, sir, for there is matter of much moment in it."

Hurrying out of the justice roam, Ralph returned to the inn, sought his own chamber, and opened the packet.

It contained several sealed letters, addressed to different gentlemen in Dorsetshire and Somersetshire, and for himself a brief note to the following effect:

"My Young Friend,

"After finishing the inclosed, I have but a moment to write to you, but it is absolutely necessary for your safety, for your present comfort, and your future happiness, that you should leave this part of the country as speedily as possible. The anger of Lord Woodhall, when all is made known to him, will be excited, as you may well suppose, to the very highest pitch of fury. He has immense influence at court, and can destroy you. I am not sure that it would not be better and safer for you to betake yourself to Holland for a time; in which idea I have inclosed for you a letter for a gentleman at the Hague, who will show you kindness.

"You may trust upon my doing all I can for you during your absence, both out of consideration for yourself and our friend Moraber.

"You can consult Lady Danvers in the West as to the best means of keeping yourself concealed till this storm has blown by; but, whatever you may think of the circumstances in which you are placed, believe that my judgment is best, and take the advice of your sincere friend,

"Norfolk."

Ralph gazed at the letter for several minutes with a pale cheek and anxious eye but then some one knocked at his door, and the voice of one of Lady Danvers's servants said, "My lady, sir, wishes to speak with you immediately."

"I will come in a moment," replied Ralph; and, folding up the Duke of Norfolk's letter once more, he proceeded with it in his hand to Hortensia's apartments.

CHAPTER XX

In one of the largest houses of that day in London, and in that fashionable suburb which lay in the immediate vicinity of the palace, sat a young lady in deep mourning, weeping bitterly. She was quite alone in her own room; and the face, once almost ruddy with the hue of country health, looked now pale and delicate. The wits about the court, who by any chance had seen her, either at her father's residence or during a former visit to the court, had not failed to have their remark, their jest, or their gallant speech upon the occasion of her altered appearance.

One man, of exceedingly refined taste, declared that she looked far more lovely since she had cast away what he called that "very vivid rose," which made her look like a lovely dairy-maid.

Another replied that his lordship was fonder, he believed, of lilies than of roses.

Another rejoined that these were not lilies, but faded roses; and another declared that his two noble friends made it out clearly that the lady had the gift of weeping rose-water for her brother's death, as it was evidently by the process of distillation she had become so pale.

Little did any of the gay mockers know all the sources of poor Margaret's tears. True, she wept much for her brother's death. She had loved him well, as he had loved her. There had been something in his frank and generous nature peculiarly attractive to a heart like hers. Even his rashness, his vehemence, which were occasionally excessive, were all tempered toward her, and had only the effect of making her shrinkingly withhold from him the one great secret of her life. The thought that that secret love might have been the near, or even the remote cause of her brother's violent death, added double bitterness to her tears. But this was not all. Margaret wept for her lover as well as for her brother--wept for the slayer as well as the slain. She knew, with a certainty that might have made her swear to the fact, that the provocation must have been great indeed that could induce Ralph to draw the sword upon her brother Henry; she felt for the severe struggle which must have taken place in his mind before he sought the fatal spot. She felt for all that he must have experienced when their swords crossed and Henry fell. She felt for all he must have endured in the anguish of his flight, and for all he was still enduring, wherever he might have sought refuge.

"Remorse and despair, both in one," she said; "these must be his portion now, poor Ralph: remorse for having taken my brother's life, and despair for having by his own act placed an impassable bar between us forever. Oh, yes! whatever they may tell me, I know, I feel he loves me still. If he have, indeed, trifled for an hour with this bright and beautiful Hortensia Danvers, when he saw my poor Henry lying on the grass, all his love for Margaret has returned, I am certain. No man can forget the love of early years so easily-- at least not Ralph. I know what he will feel, I know what he will think; and sure I am that no one here, not even myself or my father, will weep for poor Henry as bitterly as he does."

Oh! abiding confidence of woman's love, what is like thee? No other passion--no other feeling--no other thought pervades the whole of being, takes possession of every faculty, clings to the heart, rules and subjugates the mind, sets reason, and argument, and conviction at defiance like thee. It must be true love, though not the paltry passion, the half-indifferent liking, the admiration warmed a little by propinquity and habit, the convenient, half mercenary, half ambitious tenderness. None of those lukewarm mixtures of heart and brain, which stand white-gloved and orange-flowered before the altar of a fashionable church, and are recorded under the desecrated name of love, to have that very record blotted out, ere a few short years are over, by the bitter drops of regret or the burning spots of shame. No, no; it must be true, full, wholehearted love--the love that gets a grasp upon the very soul--the love that is immortal as the soul itself.

And such was Margaret's love for her pool cousin. For him she wept as much as for her brother Henry; for she felt and knew that his life was dead if his body lived, and that the fallen man was happier than he whose existence was prolonged.

At that moment Margaret thought little of herself or of her own future fate. She was of an unselfish nature; and her first thoughts were never--as so many's are--of the cares, anxieties, and griefs which the events of the day might bring upon herself. Imagination would indeed, from time to time, force upon her some recollection of her own fate and situation--dim, hovering phantoms, wandering the extreme verge of thought, but never coming near enough to be tangible. But, for the time, her feelings rather than her thoughts were alive principally to the fate of her brother and of her lover. Of her father, it is true, she thought often and painfully; but his deep grief might have affected her more, had it been of a character more like her own. But there was an eager, fiery fierceness in it, with which she could have no sympathy. He called down curses upon the head of him who had deprived him of his son; he vowed vengeance--ay, and sought it; and declared that life only should bound his purposes of revenge. Margaret, indeed, did not give much credence to such vows. Without having studied it, without having even thought of it, she knew her father's character well. It had sunk into her mind, as it were, making its impress, from infancy upward, more and more deeply every year. She knew him to be warm-hearted, kind, generous, passionate, somewhat careless, not without ability, but without consistency, if not continuity of purpose. She had never seen any passion maintain a long and powerful influence over him, however vehement might be the outburst at first. Grief, from which man usually flies the most eagerly, as his natural enemy--as the enemy of all his desires at every period of life--had had a greater hold upon him than any other affection of his mind to which she had ever seen him subject. She remembered well the period of her mother's death, which had occurred some five or six years before, and how long afterward a deep, brooding melancholy had hung over Lord Woodhall, how slow was his return to cheerfulness, how frequently the fits of gloom would come back. But even that had passed away, and she doubted not that this present frantic rage against poor unhappy Ralph would pass away likewise. She somewhat feared, indeed, what might be the result when the violence of passion should subside; when that which for the time seemed to bear away grief upon its fiery wings should sink down either gratified or wearied out, and leave him alone in sorrow and desolation. Then, she knew, would be the struggle; then, when he daily saw the empty place at the table, when he missed the beloved face, when he heard no more the cheerful voice, when the presence which was sunshine to him, and the gallant bearing in which he took such a pride, were all found wanting; when the house looked vacant and lonely, and the meals cheerless and solitary, and the evenings went by unenlivened, and the day ended with the knowledge that he was gone--then, she thought, when her mind turned in that direction, then will sorrow be fully felt in all its heavy weight; then will the anguish which is now divided by rage bow him to the earth; and then must be the time for me to struggle with my own griefs, in order to lighten his. Now it would be vain to say a word. To oppose his wrath against poor Ralph would be madness; to offer him consolation, as vain.

From time to time these thoughts came upon her, and, even sad and bitter as they were, they offered her some relief; for the others--those I have described before--were so much more intense and painful, that any thing which led her mind away to other things was a blessing for the time. She might have looked round all the world for some surpassing woe, without finding any which could compare in her heart with that which the death of her brother, by the hand of her lover, had inflicted. They were both so dear--so unutterably dear--they were both so linked with every affection, and every memory, and every hope, that the one, who was dead to all, and the other, who must be dead to her, left the once flowery landscape of life, which had lain so lately smiling before her, nothing but a dark, desolate wilderness. It was like a fair scene just torn by an earthquake, and bearing not one trace of its former aspect.

It was over such thoughts that she was now weeping, somewhat more than a fortnight after her brother's death. Her father had gone forth, still moved by the same fierce desire of vengeance, to move every power of the court to gratify that burning thirst; for those were days in which influence and even wealth--money, base, corrupted money--made the very scales of justice quiver. He had been more harsh and ferocious that day than usual; he had dwelt upon the particulars of her poor brother's death with a painful, lingering minuteness, which tore poor Margaret's heart. He seemed anxious to lash his resentment to such a pitch that it would bear all before it, and he left the house declaring that he would bring Ralph to the gallows, or perish. This scene, as he had walked up and down the room, looking angrily at the floor, and every now and then stopping to add some bitter or painful word more, was full in Margaret's mind when she retired to her own chamber, and there sat down to weep as I have described. It was one of the darkest hours which had fallen upon her since her brother's death; for the probability of her lover's being found and taken--being brought to trial--being condemned-- was brought more painfully home to her heart than it had ever been before. All seemed darkness and despair around her. What should she do in such a case? she asked herself. How should she act? Throw herself at her father's feet, and beseech him to forbear, and be merciful? She knew it was vain--all vain. She might as well beseech the hurricane. Should she leave him whom she so dearly loved to perish unseen, unsupported, unconsoled? She knew her own heart would perish also. Should she fly to him, cast off all restraint, make her fate with his, interpose between her father and his vengeance, and say, "Strike him through me?" But her brother's spirit seemed to stand in the way of the very thought, crying, "Margaret, Margaret he slew me."

Poor Margaret could but weep; and bitterly, painfully did she weep; but while the tears were still streaming as rapidly as ever down her cheeks, there was a light tap at the door, and, without waiting to be told, her maid entered the room. She was an old and faithful servant, who had waited many years upon her mother; somewhat stiff, indeed, but full of love for all the children of the house; one of those old attached servants of an English household, which are hardly to be found in any other land. She had wept over the death of poor Master Henry, as she called him, as bitterly as any one; but she had shared Margaret's feelings rather than those of the old lord. She had loved Henry well; but she loved Ralph nearly as well, for she had known him from the cradle; had known his mother, and every one who had known her had loved her. Ralph had always, too, shown a great attachment to her. As a child, he would sit with his arms round her neck, and call her, in his infant prattle, "his Dody"--her name was Dora Vernon; and the very first comfort which Margaret had received came from her lips, very shortly after the fatal news arrived.

"Do not take on so, Mistress Margaret," she said, adhering still to the term mistress, which was but beginning to decline; "the dead can never be brought back by weeping; and if your tears are for the living, as I can't help thinking they be in part, I dare say, if you knew all, Master Ralph is not so much to blame as you think. I don't see, for my own part, why the good old lord goes on so madly against poor Master Ralph. He fought two men in his day himself, and killed one of them, and he would not have a gentleman refuse to fight, I am sure, when he was asked. Master Henry, God rest him! was hot and passionate enough, as you know; and, I dare say, he provoked poor Ralph more than he could bear. Perhaps he was deceived about something, and wouldn't listen to reason about it, for he took up things very hastily, and all things are not as they seem at first; and I am sure Master Ralph would not give real cause of offense to man or woman either, for he is as good, and kind, and noble-hearted a lad as any in all the world. But if people will not listen to reason, and hear things explained, what can one do? and that was always Master Henry's way: a word and a blow, and the blow came first."

I have said that this speech, somewhat incoherent as it was, had comforted Margaret greatly and it gave her comfort in more ways than one. She remembered the letter which Henry had shown her, and the impression which it had produced upon her mind; and a doubt, a thought, a hope that they might both have been deceived--that the letter was either a fabrication, or might be explained, arose, and grew stronger and stronger every moment. What right had she to judge him unheard? she asked herself--what right had Henry? and, knowing the weakness of her brother's temper, his rashness, and punctiliousness upon the point of honor, she easily conceived that he actually compelled Ralph to draw his sword, without listening to any thing he might say in his own defense.

The sight, therefore, of her good Dora was now pleasant to her; and she did not even try to wipe away the tears that she was shedding when she entered, but, holding out her arms to her, leaned her head upon her shoulder, and wept there.

"There, there, my dear child," said the good woman, "you have been sorry enough; and don't you be afraid of all that the old lord says. He'll not do half that he thinks. It's poor, powerless work when old men begin to swagger. I heard him going on when you were in the withdrawing-room with him; but he'll do nothing; and I dare to say that Master Ralph will easily show that he was driven to do what he did. And now, my bird, wipe your eyes, there's a dear child. Here's a little saucy boy down stairs wants to see you; he has been out there over the way for an hour, till the old lord went out, and then he came over and asked for you. Harrison sent for me, but the lad won't talk to any one but you, for he has got a letter to deliver into your own hand, he says--a love-letter, I don't doubt;" and the old woman laughed a little. "I don't doubt that it's a love-letter, for it isn't in Master Ralph's hand--that was my hope at first--but it's a great, sprawling, twisting hand, and the boy's all decked out as fine as a groat--a sort of page-looking lad, with a band of feathers round his hat, quite fantastical."

"Send him away," said Margaret, sadly; "I will not see him; I have naught to do with love-letters, Dora."

"But you can not tell it is a love-letter," replied the waiting-woman; "that was only my fancy; and, indeed, my dear child, you should see him, for he won't give it to any body but you; and you can not tell what it may be about, and it's always right to look at a letter; and it is but civil."

"Well, bring him up," replied Margaret; "but stay you here, Dora, till he is gone."

The boy was brought up so rapidly, that, had Margaret been in a very observing mood, she might have suspected he had not been very far from the door while the conversation just detailed was passing between her and her woman; but she only noticed that he came; that he was a gay-looking boy of some thirteen or fourteen years of age, very much like what Dora had described; that he asked her carefully, ere he gave the letter, whether she was Mistress Margaret Woodhall. Her mind was too much occupied with other thoughts to notice or attend to any thing more.

She answered his question in the affirmative, took the letter, and then, gently bowing her head, dismissed the boy, saying, "I will send my reply, if this should require one."

"Well, I do think," said Dora, "seeing he is so smart a youth, I would have tried to find out where he came from. Letters do not always tell who sent them, and--"

"Nonsense--nonsense, Dora!" said Margaret. "I care not whom it comes from, nor whence it comes;" and, much to the good woman's inconvenience, she continued to hold the letter unopened in her hand, gazing upon the ground, and falling gradually into thought.

"Well, really!" exclaimed Dora Vernon, after she had waited some five minutes; and Margaret, rather startled by the sharpness of the sounds than clearly understanding their meaning, languidly opened the letter, and fixed her eye upon the page.

The moment she did so the whole expression of her face altered; her eyes recovered their brightness, and fixed eagerly on the lines beneath them; the color mounted up into her cheek; her lip lost its dejected stillness, and bent into a sweet, hopeful smile; and then, as if there were magic in the ending lines, she started up, let the paper drop, and pressed her hand tight upon her heart.

Dora pounced upon the letter in an instant, took it up unchidden or forbid, and gazed at the words it contained. They were large enough, Heaven knows; but still her spectacles were habitually needful; and, retreating a step, for fear her young lady should attempt to stop her, she mounted them on her nose, and read:

"Fear not, my child," so the letter ran, "fear not! Fate has done its work with your poor brother. It could not be otherwise. It was doomed to be so. I warned you, you would have many trials; but fear not--shrink not. More must yet come; but they will pass away, and though a multitude of obstacles may seem to stand between you and happiness, yet shrink not--doubt not! Your fate depends upon yourself. The stars do not rule, but counsel you. Be firm--be true--be happy!

"Above all, doubt not him who loves you. Trust to tried affection and long-known truth; and be assured that he who may now seem guilty is innocent as yourself. He who seems most innocent is guilty. You sent not to me in the hour of need as I bade you; but I watch over you, and come to your comfort, even when you seek me not. Be firm and true.   Moraber."

"Goodness gracious! if that is not the wise man in the old tower!" exclaimed Dora, when she had arrived at the name, and made it out with some difficulty; "Lord bless me! Mistress Margaret, how can he know any thing about you?"

Margaret had sunk into her chair again, without an effort to prevent the good woman from reading the letter; and, in deep thought, made no reply to the question till Dora had repeated it twice.

"You talked to me much about him, Dora," she replied, at length; "I went to see him--that is all."

"And never told me a word!" muttered Dora. "Ah, my pretty child, I can guess, dear one--I can guess, my bird. Well, love sees with his own eyes; and I say not they are bad ones, though folks call him blind. He's no bad judge, I wot, though he judges not as old lords and great people judge. Marry! they would have people men and women of the world's making, not of God's; but you can't fashion flesh and blood like a coach or a coat. Nature says shall, and who shall gainsay her? Love's not a loose cloak to fit every one; and it's a garment which can but be bought once and won't turn. Don't tear it, my dear, for patch it you can't; and old Moraber is right, depend upon it--he always is."

"Pray God he is so now," replied Margaret, fervently; and then, throwing her arms round Dora, in a wild burst of strong emotion, she wept again as profusely as ever, but far more happily.

How the heart catches at the least assurance of that which it longs to believe! Oh, dry and dusty earth of which we are made, how soon is it fired by the least spark of hope! I remember hearing of that famous lost Greek fire, how, one time, spilled by accident in the baths of a great city, no effort could put it out; it burned through theaters and dwelling-places, through the great church, through its stone pavement, down to the very graves beneath. And this is Hope, unextinguishable even into the tomb. Does it end even there? I know not. But beyond is the first world of reality, where Hope, the wanderer, meets her sister Joy.

Yes, from so slight and frail an assurance as that of the strange, wild letter she had just received, Margaret's thought-world was relighted; the darkness passed in part away; she dared to look forward; she dared to withdraw her eyes from her brother's tomb; she boldly said to herself, "Come what may, I will be firm and true."

But, as a consequence of that letter, another comfort, not more substantial, not more sustaining, but still infinitely great, was afforded her. Her old servant's words showed her that the secret of her heart had been penetrated--that no glowing explanation--no timid hesitation--no word--no sign was needed further--that she had some one to confide in, some one to counsel and to aid. The counsel might not be the wisest, the aid not the most powerful, but she stood no longer alone in the sorrow of her own heart.

CHAPTER XXI

We left Ralph Woodhall proceeding toward the apartments of Hortensia Danvers with the Duke of Norfolk's letter in his hand. He seemed puzzled and confused, but his determination was soon taken. "I might have foreseen this," he said to himself; "it could not be long concealed; and I must bear my destiny. But I will not encounter the good old lord with any attempt at justification. The Duke of Norfolk is perhaps right: it would be better for me to be absent for a time, seeking fortune in the West, or perhaps in Holland, till the first burst of wrath has passed. I can trust to Margaret's love."

With these thoughts he entered the sitting-room of Lady Danvers, where he found her standing by a table, dressed for her journey, and looking toward the door, as if anxious for his coming.

"Well, they have set you free," she said; "but I have been in some fear about you, not that you would not appear at the time, if you could, but that you might not be able. I sent to ask you to speak with me last night, but, to my surprise, found you were absent."

She spoke with a peculiar emphasis, and Ralph replied, in a faint, melancholy tone, "I was absent for some hours, Lady Danvers--how employed, I may find another opportunity of telling you. At present, let me show you this letter from the Duke of Norfolk. I have, unfortunately, incurred the anger of my noble relation, Lord Woodhall; he is a good man, but violent to an exceeding degree when excited; and the duke advises me strongly to hurry away into the West till I can take ship for Holland. There is his letter; you can read what he says."

"No need--no need," replied Lady Danvers, putting the letter aside; "I know it all--all that has happened. Poor young man! Well may you speak in so sad a tone, Mr. Woodhall. But the duke is right. There is no resource for you but to keep in retirement for a time, till this has passed over. Depend upon it, Lord Woodhall will move heaven and earth to ruin you. To the West? I am going to the West; but my course will be too slow; you must set off instantly."

"So I propose," replied Ralph, "though to what exact spot I shall turn my steps I do not exactly know; that is a part of the country I am unacquainted with."

"I will decide it for you," replied Hortensia; "let it be Danvers's New Church. Stay! let me give you a letter to my steward, who is the man of all others to aid you, and to take means for insuring your safety."

"Nay, dear Lady Danvers," replied Ralph, "I am under no such great apprehension as you seem to think; I have done nothing that any man of heart would not have done, or that any man of honor might not have done. I would fain, it is true, avoid all personal collision with Lord Woodhall in his present state of rage; but for my personal safety I have no fear; he is a man of too much honor to resent what has occurred by any unworthy means."

"There is no knowing--there is no knowing," said Lady Danvers; "your life is too precious to others--to your father, to be lightly risked. Is your horse in a fit state to carry you? If not, take one from my servants; they are well mounted, and their beasts must be quite fresh by this time."

"Oh, mine is quite fit and strong," replied Ralph; "the little journey he has had can have had but little effect upon so strong and tried an animal."

"Well, I will write the letter," replied Lady Danvers, with the same eager and quick manner in which she had hitherto been speaking. "You go and order your servant, who is arrived. I am told, to get all things ready. Alice! Alice! bring me back the ink and paper."

Ralph hastened to follow her suggestion, and found Gaunt Stilling in somewhat sharp conversation with a man considerably taller than himself, but who seemed to stand in considerable awe of him.

"Get you back to Norwich, Master Roger," said Stilling, in a more angry tone than Ralph had ever heard him use before. "If I find you watching our movements, I will break every bone in your skin, and take that as an installment of what your master owes me."

"I must wait till I have baited my horse, Master Stilling," replied the servant.

"I should like to know what the devil brought you here," cried the other; but he was interrupted by the call of his master, and only paused to add, "Mind what I have said; I am not one to be trifled with, as you ought to know by this time."

Ralph gave his orders rapidly, then returned to his own room for a few moments, and then once more sought Hortensia for the letter she had promised. It was written, sealed, and addressed to "Master William Drayton, Danvers's New Church, by Harstock, Dorset."

She placed it in Ralph's hands, gazing at him with a look of deep and melancholy interest. There was also an air of hesitation about her as she asked, "Is all ready?"

"I dare say it is by this time," replied Ralph. "Accept my best thanks, dear Lady Danvers, for all the kind interest you have taken in me, especially in these painful circumstances in which I am placed."

She waved her hand almost impatiently, saying, "Not a word--not a word, my good friend; but there is one thing more I wish to say--" Again she hesitated, but then added quickly, and in a tone of kindly feeling, "Ralph, I look upon you as a relation--I can not regard your mother's son in any other light; you came away with me hastily yesterday; you had no time to provide funds for a long journey--No false delicacy between you and me."

Ralph took her hand and raised it to his lips, and as he did so he thought that it trembled very much. "Thanks--a thousand thanks," he said; "and I would accept your kind offer as frankly as it is made, but I have quite enough here, Lady Danvers; my servant has brought a large part of my baggage with him, and I have there all the little store which was to last me for six months."

"Well, well--go, then," she said; "do not delay a moment, for I am apprehensive till you are out of the old lord's reach. We shall meet again, my friend, and talk over all these details more at leisure. At present, nothing is to be done but to part as soon as possible."

Again Ralph kissed her hand, which was beautiful enough; though, to say truth, her lip was the more tempting of the two. He was soon in the stable-yard, and found his horse saddled and the baggage all arranged. In another moment he was riding out under the archway of the inn, and remarked a face gazing from a little window at the side, which commanded a view both of the stable-yard and of the street. Gaunt Stilling shook his fist at it as they passed, and, while his master paused to say a few words to the Duke of Norfolk's servants who were gathered round the gate, laid his finger significantly on the hilt of a good strong sword, which by this time he had added to his traveling equipage. Ralph was then turning his horse to the right hand, in the direction of the western road; but Gaunt Stilling rode up to his side, saying, in a low voice, "This way, sir; we are watched, and must give them the slip. I can find the way, I think, by the back lanes, as they have directed me. After we get past Ely, I know every rood of the road for a hundred miles."

Ralph readily followed his suggestion, but inquired, after riding a few yards, "Who is watching us? One of Lord Woodhall's people?"

"No!" replied Stilling, in his quaint, bluff way; "knave Robert's knave Roger."

"I wish to heaven it was his master instead," said Ralph, with a quick glow of the cheek and flash of the eye.

"Ay, so do I," answered Gaunt Stilling, gloomily; "but he always contrives to put some one else in his place when that place is a dangerous one. Every man has his time, however, and his is waiting for him."

He then relapsed into silence, and they pursued their way without interruption. Nothing remarkable occurred upon the road throughout the whole journey, though, as the reader knows, it led them across nearly the widest part of Great Britain. Ralph himself was silent and melancholy, and many painful considerations pressed upon his mind, withdrawing it from that enjoyment of changing scene and rapid motion which a young and ardent heart like his might well have experienced in traversing the beautiful counties which lie between Norfolk and Dorsetshire. His thoughts were almost entirely of Margaret. He saw little--he observed little--and conversation he had none; for Gaunt Stilling, though evidently a man superior, by education, to his class, and who had received the education of the world as well as of books, was taciturn and gloomy. He had never spoken much, and what he had said was generally brief and blunt; but now he hardly uttered a word, and remained usually totally apart from all other servants or society of any kind in the inns where they chanced to stop on the road. Ralph remarked, too, that when his bill was brought to him at any of these places, no charge was ever made for his servant or his servant's horse; and the strange circumstances in which the man had been placed with him came back, from time to time, upon his mind with a feeling not altogether agreeable. That he had been useful, serviceable, ay, and zealous in his service, Ralph fully felt; but it was unpleasant to him to have such gratuitous attendance, especially where it involved no light expense to the person rendering it. He determined he would have some explanations upon this subject with Gaunt Stilling; but the man's taciturnity, his own busy thoughts, and the rapidity with which they passed from place to place, made him delay the execution of his intention till they reached the place of their temporary sojourn.

Upon the frontiers of Somersetshire and Dorsetshire, Gaunt Stilling seemed to enter upon a well-known land. He had before displayed a very good knowledge of the country lying between the Isle of Ely and the Mendip Hills--an extent sufficient to try his geographical information--but now not a single lane or by-road was unknown to him. He was aware where comfortable inns could be found in the most remote parts of the country-- not at that time well cultivated or largely populated; and Ralph could not help thinking that, if it were really necessary for him to play at hide and seek at all--which he began to doubt--he could not have a better instructor in the game than his good companion.

Still, however, Gaunt Stilling maintained the same dull silence; answered in monosyllables, though civilly, and never exceeded above two or three words except once, when, crossing the beautiful Mendip Hills, he said, "I have brought you forty miles out of the way, sir, not for the sake of giving you that fine view, but for the purpose of avoiding the lands of old Lady Coldenham. I should be soon known there; and you would be found out through me. Then the news would fly across the country as rapidly as possible."

"I really do not see the need of such extreme precaution," replied Ralph, musing.

"Don't you, sir?" said Gaunt Stilling, and there the conversation dropped; for Ralph did not think it needful to enter into the particulars of his situation with his taciturn servant, and knew not how far the facts might have been bruited abroad in the household of the Duke of Norfolk.

At length, one afternoon, about a couple of hours before sunset, they passed through a long, deep lane, sunk beneath the level of the neighboring fields, and overhung by tall and shady trees in the full richness of their summer foliage. Even at those spots where the head of a horseman rose above the bank, no view of the country was to be obtained; for rich orchards, already beginning to glow with their blossoms, spread all along on either side for more than a mile. At the end of a quarter of a mile's riding, the sunshine was seen streaming up the end of the lane; and in a few minutes more Ralph stood upon the verge of a gentle descent, where the eye ranged free along one of the most beautiful valleys he ever beheld. A considerable portion of the ground in front was laid out as a park, with sloping lawns, and large ancient trees on both sides of a stream of some extent, which ran rapidly, dashing and sparkling, down the dell. An old gray bridge, too, was seen here and there along the course of the stream--even in the wilder land, which spread forth beyond the limits of the park; and on an elevated spot some two hundred yards from the river appeared a large stone edifice, perhaps of the reign of Henry the Seventh or Eighth, for it bore some of the characteristics of the best period of Tudor architecture.

At the distance of about a bow-shot from the house, but within the limits of the park, rose a beautiful church, from the bosom of a small grove of trees. Not less than three centuries and a half before, it might have deserved the name of New Church; for even if any architect could have been found to imitate so perfectly the inimitable early English architecture, the lichens and mosses, the hue of the stone, and the crumbling of the antique moldings, would have clearly denoted how long it had been constructed.

"There is Danvers's New Church, sir," said Gaunt Stilling; "but we must take a little round to get to the gates."

"It seems a peaceful spot enough," said Ralph, in reply.

"Peaceful?" murmured Gaunt Stilling. "Is there such a thing as peace?"

In a few minutes more they had entered the park and were riding up to the house, under the old stone gate-way of which were sitting a hale, good-looking, well-dressed man, past the middle age, and an elderly woman, with a young child reading a horn-book at their feet.

"That is Master Drayton, I take it," said Gaunt Stilling; and, riding up, Ralph dismounted and presented Lady Danvers's letter.

"This is for me," said the man upon the steps, opening the letter; "I suppose my lady will soon be coming."

At the same moment he unfolded the sheet, and fixed his eyes upon the contents. They seemed to startle him; for although he said, as a sort of comment while he read, "Of course--certainly--to be sure," his broad brow was contracted, and his whole face assumed a hesitating look.

"You are quite welcome, sir," he said, when he had done, "and I will do the best I can for you. My lady's orders shall be obeyed to the utmost of my power; but I can't resist the law, you know."

"Resist the law!" exclaimed Ralph; "surely Lady Danvers does not ask you to do that! and there could be no necessity on my account."

"Well, sir, you know best," replied Mr. Drayton, "but I think it will be best if you would just step into this room, and talk with me for a moment;" and, opening the door of the house, he led the way to a small ante-room off the great hall. When there, he said, after having closed the door, "What I meant just now, sir, was merely that I would do every thing, as in duty bound, to hide you; but that, if officers should come to take you, I could not think myself justified in resisting with a strong hand."

"Officers come to take me?" said Ralph, completely bewildered; "there must be some mistake, my good sir. May I be permitted to look at Lady Danvers's letter!"

"Oh, certainly, sir," replied the steward; "there is nothing that you need not see;" and he placed the letter in Ralph's hand, who read as follows:

"Master Drayton,

"This will be given into your hands by Mr. Ralph Woodhall, the son of my poor mother's dearest friend, and consequently mine. You will show him every attention in your power, and let him make use of Danvers's New Church as if it were his own, providing suitably all things for himself and his servant. It will be necessary to keep good watch around the place, and not suffer him to be at all molested by any one, as he has had the misfortune of killing in a duel his cousin, the son of Lord Woodhall, who is highly incensed against him."

Ralph let the paper fall from his hand, and gazed upon Mr. Drayton with a look of unmingled astonishment. "In the name of Heaven!" he exclaimed, "what is the meaning of this? Henry Woodhall killed in a duel! and by me! I can not believe my senses when I see such an assertion under the hand of Lady Danvers. She must have been grossly and terribly misled--but there must be some foundation for this;" and, opening the door vehemently, he made his way to the outer porch, and called aloud, "Stilling! Stilling!"

The man, who was leading the horses up and down, returned to the door, and Ralph at once demanded, "What is this? Lady Danvers, in her letter to Mr. Drayton here, declares that my cousin Henry has been killed in a duel."

"Well, sir, did you not know it?" asked Stilling, in a cold tone.

"Know it!" exclaimed Ralph; "how in Heaven's name should I know it? You never mentioned the subject to me during the whole course of the journey."

"I thought it would be too painful a subject, sir," replied the man, with a very peculiar look; "you had the Duke of Norfolk's letter."

"The duke never mentioned a word of it," said Ralph. "Good God! this will drive me mad;" and, turning on his heel, he walked back into the house, followed by Mr. Drayton, and, casting himself into a chair, covered his eyes with his hands in an agony of grief and consternation.

Gaunt Stilling tied the horses to an iron railing and followed him quietly; and good Mr. Drayton, as much moved to attention and respect toward the young gentleman by the agony he saw him suffer as by his lady's letter, did all that he could think of to comfort and console him. It was not much he could think of, it is true, for he was a man of material thoughts and habits. He could tell the number of acres, roods, and poles in every farm upon the estate, and how they should be cultivated. He knew the condition and the wants of every laborer, every tenant; and he tried his best to ameliorate the one, and to diminish the other. But to deal with deep sorrow--to soothe an intelligent mind and feeling heart, were tasks above or beyond his scope. At best--and it was his only resource--he might try to divert the thoughts of one afflicted from the causes of grief. He had done so with many a mendicant at the hall door--for he was no harsh and cruel deputy despot--and he tried at least to add comfort to gifts. He did the same even now. He even teased Ralph about bed-rooms, and first and second tables, and what he would require during his stay; till at length he pressed him so hard upon these subjects, that Ralph rose and followed him to the rooms he proposed to show him with a gloomy air and heavy step, from which all the elasticity of youth seemed gone.

Gaunt Stilling looked after him with a hesitating, uncertain expression of countenance, as if he did not know whether to follow him or not. But, after a moment's consideration, he turned round, led the horses to the stables, and after having given them, with some directions, into the hands of a country lad whom he found there, returned to the house and sought out his master, whom he found sitting sorrowfully alone, Mr. Drayton having quitted him in order to make the necessary preparations.

The moment Gaunt Stilling entered the room, Ralph motioned him to shut the door, and said, "Now tell me more of this sad affair, Stilling. I am calmer now; and though I do wish you had spoken to me on the subject as we came hither, by which you would have stopped my journey entirely, yet I dare say you were under the same mistake which it seems has been made by others."

"Why, sir," replied the servant, in a tone of some feeling, "I saw you very melancholy and sad, and, as the duke himself had written to you, I naturally concluded that you were right well aware of all. You may easily judge that, the death of Mr. Henry Woodhall was the subject of talk with the whole of the duke's house; and when he had written to you, I could not presume to speak to you on the subject without your speaking to me."

"The duke's letter I must have misunderstood entirely," replied Ralph; "fearful of wounding my feelings, it would seem, he wrote in vague general terms of unfortunate events and unhappy circumstances. My imagination, utterly ignorant of what had taken place, fixed upon other events and circumstances--but all that matters not. Now I would know the whole. It would seem that they attributed poor Henry's death to me?"

"Yes, sir, every body thought so," replied Gaunt Stilling. "They said that Mr. Woodhall had discovered that you and his sister were in love with each other, contrary to the wishes of the family; that he had challenged you, and that you had killed him."

"But you must have known better," said Ralph, somewhat sternly; and the man's countenance fell, and his brow became clouded, as if the tone of the master, whom he served gratuitously, had wounded his pride.

Ralph went on, however, saying, "You should have contradicted it at once, Stilling. The duke might be deceived; for he could not tell that I had not returned secretly; but you must have known I never re-entered my room from the time I quitted it in the morning."

"Yes, sir," replied Stilling, in a quiet tone; "but there was no need of re-entering your room. You had a sword with you, and had but to ride back, fight your adversary, and disappear."

"True--true," replied his master; "But did you really think I had done so?"

Gaunt Stilling hesitated, but replied at length, "I certainly did not, sir; but I was in no circumstances to speak my mind. Every thing, indeed, seemed against your having done so, in my mind, till the morning after."

"And what happened then to make you change your opinion?" asked Ralph.

"Why, I heard at the inn where Lady Danvers stopped," replied Stilling, "that you had gone out about half past eight o'clock, and had not been seen by any body for some hours. Now the duel took place between ten and eleven; and, with a quick-going horse, you might easily have got to Norwich within the time."

Ralph pressed his hand upon his brow, saying, as if in reply to some question which had arisen in his own mind, "That explains it--that explains it all. How Lady Danvers could have imagined that I had been guilty of this act, I was at a loss to comprehend; but now I see it all."

"Guilty! sir," said Gaunt Stilling, whose old soldier's habits made him view such events in a very different light from that in which his master regarded them; "no great guilt, I think, in killing a man in fair and open combat, without advantage--especially when he was the person to seek it."

"We may think differently," replied Ralph, "but this, at least, I will tell you, Stilling, that if my hand had shed poor Henry's blood in such a quarrel as this, I never should forgive myself to my dying day. Leave me now, Stilling. You will be well taken care of here; and I will send for you soon, to seek for any further information I may want. At present, my mind is all in wild confusion; and I must try to calm my thoughts, and decide upon what is to be done next. My first impulse is to set off at once for London, to clear myself of this deed."

"Better give the horses some rest, sir," said Gaunt Stilling; "we have come at a rattling pace; and they won't do much more just at present. Besides, it would be well to think whether you could clear yourself so easily as to prevent disagreeable consequences. Four or five months' imprisonment, waiting for trial, is no very agreeable thing, and the very fact of your running away here in such haste would require a good deal of explanation, for other people might not understand it quite as well as you do yourself."

Ralph looked at him earnestly, and asked, in a low, deep voice, "You surely do not believe me guilty still?"

"Not in the least, sir," replied the man, frankly. "I am quite sure you are not; and I can even give a guess, and a pretty shrewd one, as to what was the mistake which made you follow the duke's advice so readily; but all I think, is, that other people may not understand the matter so easily, and that, in order to clear yourself, in a hurry, of this accusation, you might be forced to explain other matters, which might be unpleasant for you to touch upon."

"I will think over it--I will think over it," replied Ralph; and Gaunt Stilling, seeing him fall into a deep revery, quietly left the room.

CHAPTER XXII

Candles were lighted in a small, beautiful room at Danvers's New Church, and Ralph Woodhall sat at a table covered with delicacies which he could little have expected to find, at that season of the year, in that remote place. He gave small heed to them, however. He ate what was merely needful for sustenance, and drank several glasses of fine old wine, which were pressed upon him by the care of two old servants of the Danvers family--blue bottles, as they were called in those days--who, with less to do at any time than they altogether liked, were left behind by their lady in the country, when she journeyed far, in consideration of their age, which they themselves were not apt to believe in very much. They thought themselves strong and hearty as ever, and able to do any sort of work which might be assigned to them. But Hortensia was not one to overtask any one's willingness; and she had more consideration for their years than they had themselves. Right glad were they, then, to pay every attention to a favored guest during her absence; and old men, being very often apt at calculation, and especially at putting two stray ends of circumstances together and linking them, as it were, with cobbler's wax, reasoned internally upon the probability of the handsome young stranger--in regard to whose fortune and fate they knew nothing--becoming, ere long, their legitimate lord and master.

Toward the end of the meal, when some early fruits, at that time brought to perfection with great difficulty and at vast expense, had been put upon the table, Mr. Drayton himself appeared, and stood for a moment by the side of Ralph's chair, excusing the scantiness of the dinner on the ground of the short time allowed for preparation.

"We shall treat you better to-morrow, sir," he said; "but, in the mean time, is there any wine in the cellar you would like better? The keys are always left with me, and there is some very rich Burgundy, as well as Bordeaux wine of the finest quality--even imperial Tokay; for my late lord was a great judge, and the wines have only improved since his death, which, come Martinmas, will be thirteen years."

"Nothing more, Mr. Drayton--nothing more, thank you," replied Ralph; "I have had quite enough, and all has been very good."

"Perhaps, sir, you would like to look through the house," said Mr. Drayton, determined not to leave the young stranger to his own bitter thoughts if he could help it; "it is a curious old place, and, to my mind, looks better by candlelight than at any other time. I think old places always do; for there is something about them which makes one feel that their real light is gone, and that they can only be viewed pleasantly by something manufactured and modern. I think you would like to see it."

"Very well," replied Ralph, in an indifferent tone; "I will accompany you, Mr. Drayton, when you like."

"This minute, if you please, sir, if you have done your wine," replied Mr. Drayton. "Stay! I will call people to take the lights on before, and we will go through the whole suites of apartments, beginning with the yellow guest chamber, and going on to the green guest chamber, and the blue guest chamber."

"Yellow, and green, and blue guests!" said Ralph; "methinks that there must have been some heavier hearts than even my own here."

"Oh, sir, it is but a name," replied the good man; "and I dare say what we call the rooms has little to do with those who sleep in them. But now, sir, I will be ready in a moment;" and, ordering one of the menservants to take up two of the lights and precede them, he led the way with a step as slow and solemn as if the place had been a nunnery, and he had feared to interrupt the devout orisons of its inmates.

I will not detain the reader with much particular account of the various rooms and passages through which Ralph was led, but simply dwell upon the general aspect of the place, which was solemn, stately, and meditative. The effect, too, was heightened by every ornament and decoration to be seen, for the late Lord Danvers had a consummate knowledge and a real taste for art. Thus along the old corridor, which had been converted to the purposes of a picture gallery, the young gentleman was led, pausing every now and then to examine more closely one or other of the portraits which hung upon the wall. The whole history of each was well known to Mr. Drayton, who gave it in full to his young companion--not, perhaps, without a little embellishment, in order to keep his attention engaged. At first Ralph walked listlessly enough; but gradually his mind assumed an interest in the subjects which were laid before him, and he stopped several times to gaze at the different portraits as he passed by, asking the names and history of the personages. Some were by Sir Peter Lely--some were by Vandyck; and the collection went as far back even as Holbein. The Danvers family, of course, figured conspicuously. There were Danverses of all ages, from the infant swathed up like an Egyptian mummy, to the white-bearded senior in his high-backed chair; men in suits of armor, with pages holding the casque, and a horse looking over the left shoulder; gentlemen in long gowns and venerable ruffs, and ladies in stiff bodices, or with collars buttoned up to the chin. But there were also a number of portraits representing persons either allied to the family by blood or affection, or figuring remarkably in history. Howards there were many--Percys not a few; and, in fact, the records of each age since the family rose to distinction had their representative on the walls. Among the rest were two full-length, portraits of ladies in the early spring of life. One was represented standing with a large Spanish fan in her hand, while a grayhound, raised upon his hind feet, and with his curling tail dropping gracefully nearly to the ground, had his fore feet upon a table supporting a globe of gold and silver fishes, which he seemed to be eyeing with intense curiosity and some appetite. The face of the lady was exquisitely beautiful; and Ralph had no occasion to inquire the name of the original, for the likeness to Hortensia was so strong, though the hair was a shade less dark, that no one who had seen her could fail to recognize her mother. The other portrait was of a somewhat taller lady, leaning upon a marble urn, which had something sepulchral in its character. Her eyes were raised, so as to seem gazing directly at the spectator; and her right hand was stretched out, as if she were offering it to the figure in the other picture. In those eyes there was that deep, intense expression which is never seen--no, never-- except in persons whose feelings are strong and permanent; and the painter had caught that look, and expressed it with wonderful power, making even the beauty of the features and of the coloring subservient to that. It was a face that Ralph knew well; and to see the portrait of his own mother side by side with that of the late Lady Danvers, made him feel indeed as if there were nearer bonds between him and Hortensia than any thing like a sudden friendship or the acquaintance of a few short days could twine.

"I must always feel toward her as a brother," he thought; "and she has nobly proved toward me that she regards me as such. One of my first acts must be to disabuse her mind of the idea that I would so lightly draw my sword against my cousin Henry's life."

Then turning to Mr. Drayton, he asked, "Is there any picture of Lady Danvers here?"

"Only one, sir, in her own morning room," replied the steward; "it was taken when she was quite a child, and she would never sit for one afterward. This is the room;" and, taking a step or two forward, he opened a door on the left.

The lights the servant carried slowly penetrated the gloom, and Ralph gazed round with deep interest at the arrangement of the place where so fair and interesting a creature as Hortensia made her ordinary abode. Nowhere could his eye rest without finding some proof of her fine taste, and of a certain spirit of order, neatness, and decoration rarely met with in one so young. Antique cabinets of ebony, with silver hinges and locks, were in several parts of the room, containing, doubtless, many little treasures of virtù. A large table in the middle, supported by richly-carved and twisted columns of dark-black oak, was covered with miniatures, carvings in ivory, pieces of rare china, curious ancient ornaments, one or two small books in very antique bindings, and two or three small statues in bronze or ivory, which might, perhaps, have employed the hand of Cellini or Bologna. There, too, were a number of specimens of the cinqui-cento art, placed beneath glass covers to keep them from the dust; a crucifixion in ivory, where the intense passion of the expression seemed to make the dead material live; a drinking-cup of silver, from the sides of which stood out in bold relief some scores of figures holding up wreaths of flowers to the brim, as if to catch the drops of wine that might rim over, and every figure differing from the other, but anatomically perfect and full of grace; a salt-cellar of gold, used probably at high festivals in days of yore, where, on a large cockle-shell, intended to contain the salt, stood the figure of Neptune waving his trident over the heads of two sea-horses, while round about were exquisitely grouped, with arms sometimes linked together, sometimes cast round each other's necks or shoulders in every different attitude that can be conceived, the numberless deities of the wave.

On the walls around, between the various cabinets and the windows, were a number of small and beautiful pictures from the hands of the greatest masters. They were principally landscapes though here and there a figure-piece of the Dutch or Flemish school found admittance, where the subject fitted it for a lady's eyes. There was only one large picture in the room, and that was the portrait of a young girl, some what fancifully dressed, putting aside with her hand the green leaves and branches of a tree, and seeming to look out from the shadowy bower beneath upon those who gazed upon her in return. The face was full of life, and light, and intelligence, and joy. Youth was evidently holding revel in her heart, and the spirit of the free green-wood seemed over all. Although Lady Danvers's eyes had deeper things in them now--although the expression was now generally more thoughtful, more timid, and the form, there in the bud, had blossomed into womanly loveliness, yet Ralph had no difficulty in recognizing Hortensia in the delicate features and wild graces of the child. He paused longer there, and with deeper interest than he had done any where else; and as the servant continued to hold up the lights before him, and Mr. Drayton stood a step behind, a slight smile came upon the face of the latter, arising apparently from some conclusions that he was drawing in his own mind.

"This is my lady's dressing-room," he said, after a while, opening a door beyond, "and this is her bed-room."

Ralph followed, and gazed round. Here, it was evident, the same spirit resided; but the bed-room itself was very simply arranged. There was a fire-place for a wood-fire, with a mantel, piece of rich white marble, supported by two beautiful columns; and the andirons, according to the ancient mode, were decorated with two large dogs' heads beautifully sculptured in brass. Above the mantel-piece was another picture of the late Lady Danvers. The chairs were of green velvet, and the hangings of the bed the same. The pillow and the sheet were edged with lace; and as Ralph gazed at the spot where Hortensia laid her head to rest, he said to himself, with a strange feeling that he did not stop to analyze, "May peace and happiness ever rest there with her!"

Turning away with the good steward, he proceeded through a number of other rooms; but, though the house had some historical associations, and a number of those old dreamy stair-cases, passages, and halls, which filled the unoccupied mind with strange imaginings, no part had such an interest for him as that which he had visited first; and he returned to the room in which he had been sitting with the more painful feelings busy in his heart, but mingled with some pleasanter thoughts, by all that he had seen in the apartments of Hortensia.

"I will now, Mr. Drayton," he said, "write some letters, and then retire to rest."

"Ay, sir, it is always better," said Mr. Drayton, in that commonplace tone which somewhat jars with strong emotions, "to write a letter at night, take counsel with one's pillow, and read it over before one sends it in the morning. It seems my lady has made some mistake about this duel, and it has taken you by surprise. You had better think well, sir, before you act in any way, for one does not always do the wisest when one acts in a hurry."

"True--true, Mr. Drayton," said Ralph, in an absent tone, "I will think before I act; but still I must not suffer an imputation to rest upon me which I do not deserve;" and, after having procured writing materials, he proceeded to indite several letters, of which I shall only give one as a specimen. It was addressed to Lord Woodhall, and was to the following effect:

"My honored and very dear Lord,

"I have this evening, and only this evening, learned the sad and terrible event which has occurred in your family, and which has deprived me not only of a very dear relation, but of one who has been my friend from boyhood. Though your lordship's grief must naturally be greater than that of any other person, believe me that mine, upon receiving this intelligence, would have been hard enough to bear without any aggravation. But coupled with the sad information comes the strange tidings that by some mistake, to me unaccountable, my name has been mingled with the transaction which deprived you of your dear son, and me of my friend and cousin. I can not leave you to suppose for one moment that I would have drawn my sword upon your son; but I have further to declare that there was no quarrel or dispute between us whatsoever; that we parted on the night of Wednesday last in perfect friendship and good feeling; and that I have never either seen or heard from him since, as I set out early on the morning of Thursday to escort Lady Danvers westward, and have never been in Norwich from that hour to this. Nay, more, it is utterly impossible that I could have been there, as I am willing to prove at any time, by accounting for every moment of my time, and producing persons who were with me. If, notwithstanding my most solemn assurance, your lordship still entertains doubts of the fact I mention, which can not be removed by private investigation, I am not at all unwilling to abide fair and open trial; and if I do not show that there was no possibility whatsoever of my having been on the spot, and at the hour where and when the unfortunate transaction took place, let me be condemned as a murderer.

"One thing, however, I would fain avoid, which is lengthened imprisonment; but if it is publicly given forth on what day the charge against me can be tried, I pledge you my word of honor, as a man and a gentleman, I will come forward at the place named, and surrender myself to abide the result.

"With the hope that God may comfort you in the sad affliction with which He has been pleased to visit you, and that He may shower every blessing upon yourself and your daughter, I have the honor to subscribe myself, my lord, your lordship's most faithful and humble servant,

"Ralph Woodhall."

Another letter of similar import was addressed to the Duke of Norfolk, another to his own father, and another to Lady Danvers.

He would fain have written to Margaret also, but paused, hesitated, and finally abandoned his intention.

When these were all concluded, he sent for Gaunt Stilling, to consult with him as to the best means of dispatching the letters from that part of the country, communications by post being in those days not very rapid and not very secure.

"I will have them conveyed, sir," said Stilling, taking the letters, "though Norwich and London are far apart, and Lincolnshire a good way off too; but if the object of these letters is what I guess, I think you might save yourself the trouble and expense, which will not be small."

"What do you guess the object is?" asked Ralph.

The man paused for an instant, and then answered, "To tell all these people that you are not the man who killed Mr Henry Woodhall."

"Do you not think it worth my while to clear myself of shedding my cousin's blood?" asked Ralph, with some feeling of anger at the man's cool tone.

"Certainly, sir," replied Stilling; "but I think it is done already, in all probability. Either you do not know well the person who first placed me with you, or he has not told you how his eyes are always on those in whom he takes an interest. His eyes need no perspective glasses, sir, and he is just as well aware of the whole facts as you or I--better, indeed, most likely, than either of us. Nor will he let the knowledge sleep, depend upon it. He will make your cause good with those who are most concerned, whether you ask him or not."

Ralph smiled faintly. "You seem to have great faith," he said; "but I must not trust to any thing like a chance in such matters. I should like the letters to go."

"Well, sir, they shall go," replied Gaunt Stilling; "but one must trust to chance in all matters. For instance, I must give this letter for London to the king's post: there's a chance of his being stopped on the way. This must be sent to Lady Danvers by a special messenger, who is just as likely to miss her as not. The Duke of Norfolk will be gone from Norwich by this time, and--"

Ralph waved his hand somewhat impatiently. "I wish them to go," he said; "there is no chance, at least, of the messenger not reaching London."

"The greatest in the world," answered Gaunt Stilling; "but I see, sir, that you are not aware of all that is going on. Do you know that the country between this and London is all in a flame? If civil war has not broken out already, it won't be long first, and depend upon it that no letter will reach London, without being stopped and examined, for this month to come. I haven't got all the particulars right, but you shall hear more to-morrow morning, for I have got friends in Lyme, where this matter first broke out, and I have sent over a boy to inquire."

"Give me the letters," said Ralph Woodhall, "and I will decide to-morrow, when we have heard more."

Thus saying, he took them back, determined, on account of the difficulties Stilling threw in his way, to see them dispatched himself. The news of insurrection made but small impression upon his mind at the moment, occupied so fully as it was by personal feelings; but he asked a few questions in an indifferent tone; and, receiving nothing but a report of vague rumors, to which he attached but little importance, he retired to bed, determined to rise early on the following morning, and transact his business for himself.

CHAPTER XXIII

The most capricious gift of heaven is sleep--That is a very bad expression--unphilosophical--not logical; but yet it expresses what I mean, perhaps, better than any other form I could have used. A gift can not be capricious, though the giver may; and yet, in this instance, the giver is never capricious, and the gift, as if instinct with life, and will, and perversity itself, seems to have no rule, no regularity, no consequence of effect.

One is always inclined to repeat or copy the opening of Young's Night Thoughts when one speaks of sleep; and yet the owl-poet, soft and solemn as he was, did not always direct his thoughts aright. Sleep does not always "his ready visit pay where Fortune smiles;" nor does he always forsake the wretched to light on lids unsullied by a tear. Far, far from it. Shakspeare knew the world, waking and sleeping, better than Young; for sleep does often "knit up the raveled sleave of care," and bestows his balmy blessing, as the gift of Heaven, upon wearied eyelids, and aching hearts, and care-worn brains, which naught of earth earthly could ever soothe. Ay, and he does so, too, in circumstances where the blessed boon could never be expected; unless man could calculate finely, and to the utmost nicety, all the varied shades of the heart's feelings, all the different hues of the mind's thoughts, all the delicate outlines of the body's sensations, and balance the harmonies existing through the whole as in a goldsmith's scale.

Ralph Woodhall lay down to rest--to rest, mark me, I say--not to sleep. Sleep he never calculated upon. His mind was as busy and as active when his head touched the pillow as his body had been during the four or five days preceding. But his body was weary; there was a dull numbness in his limbs, an oppressive weight upon his corporeal energies that pressed them down, and he thought he could find repose, though not slumber. In a moment, however, there came a vacancy of thought--a dead leaden lapse in mind's existence--a space in which intellect and feeling were still and silent. Suddenly the mind or the heart, I know not which, woke up, and the body itself was roused by the start of its companions. He raised himself upon his arm, gazed wildly round upon the darkness, half remembered, half forgot where he was, sunk slowly back upon his pillow, and slept profoundly.

His sleep was long as well as deep. The morning sun rose and shone into the room; the summer birds began their song, and caroled at his window all unheard; his servant came in, gazed at, but would not wake him, and retired, saying to himself, "Would that I could sleep so;" the breakfast table was laid in the small room below; the church clock even struck nine, and Ralph was sleeping still.

It was not exhaustion of body, for he was accustomed to hard and robust exercise, often repeated, long continued; but it was exhaustion of body and mind together.

The immortal spirit, bound up in the fleshy clay, partakes of the infirmity of its fellowship; and that which, liberate from earth, must necessarily be unconscious of weariness or needful of repose, when linked in the bond of life with dust, feels a part of the weight which hangs upon its mortal brother. Both were weary with Ralph Woodhall--both slept. There was an utter vacancy of all things in that dull, leaden repose. There was no movement--no tossing to and fro--no murmuring of the lips--no dream--no thought--no feeling, waking. All was still. The beating of the heart went on--the mere mechanism of life was there: the wheel was not still, the silver chain was not broken; there was existence without life--without the living life, deprived of which existence is but a gap in time.

It was nearly ten when he awoke; but then, the shortened shadow on the floor, the brightness of the sunshine as it streamed through the window with its warm, yellowish, unempurpled light, showed him how long he had slept; and he proceeded to dress himself eagerly and in haste.

As he stood by the window at the toilet table, bestowing no great pains upon his attire--for mind had by this time recovered the full mastery of her mortal ally--he saw a horseman crossing with speed the open space of the park which lay between the house and the little bridge that spanned the river some half a mile further up The man was dressed in the livery of Lady Danvers, which, as most liveries were in those days, was somewhat gay, if not gaudy; and the horse seemed tired enough to require frequently the whip and spur.

Ralph took no great heed, for his mind was busy within its own peculiar sphere of thought, and sent forth few scouts to notice what was passing without. He saw the man gallop up to the terrace and pass round to the back of the house, without any comment, even merely mental. He did not ask himself who he could be, why he rode so fast, or what intelligence he brought. It was but to him that a something had arrived at the mansion-- that a horse and man had passed rapidly before his eyes, and that they were gone. He was still absorbed in the thoughts of the preceding day, when a gentle knock at the door roused him, and, turning round, he saw Mr. Drayton entering with some letters in his hand.

"I beg pardon for intruding, sir," said the steward, with a bow of profound respect; "but a servant has brought some letters from my lady, among which is this one for yourself, marked, 'with the utmost speed.' I therefore made bold to break in upon your rest, for your servant told me you were still sleeping."

"I thank you, Mr. Drayton," replied Ralph; "I have a good deal overslept myself. What says your lady?"

"But little to me, sir," replied the steward, "except to give you this letter immediately, and to send the other to Lady Di Fullerton, who often stays here; but I thought this needed immediate notice, and therefore, as I have said, I brought it up."

Ralph took the letter with more indifference than Mr. Drayton thought altogether proper toward the hand and seal of his fair influential mistress, and then, having opened it, he read as follows:

"I write to you in haste, dear friend, for since you left me I have heard much which requires to be spoken of between you and me immediately. Some mistakes have evidently been committed--where or how I can not stop to inquire; and it is needful, before you take any step whatever, that you should consult with some one, even though it be so humble a counselor as myself. There are more dangers surrounding you than you at all imagine, very different from those which alarmed me on the day that you left me, and which have now passed away from my mind. These can not be explained by letter; but you must now--I enjoin and require you, by courtesy and gallantry, which I know you possess, if you would but show them--to remain a close prisoner in my house till you see me without doing act or deed which can bring any one to know where you are concealed. I may add that there are warrants out against you for crimes less merciable than the simply fighting of a duel, and that you must not be found at present, till the doubts and fears which shake men's minds have passed away. Do not suppose that I will keep you long waiting, although I do not choose to commit the facts of which I am cognizant to the peril of a letter; but I am following you as rapidly as may be, bold in my independence, and, I trust, in my right purposes. Nevertheless, to escape the world's forked tongue, I have written to an amiable but antique cousin--married and widowed--to come over to Danvers's New Church. Should she arrive before myself, show her all courtesy and kindness, and believe me, if you will let me be so, your kind sister,

"Hortensia Danvers."

Ralph studied the letter with much attention; read and re-read every sentence several times, and ultimately resolved to abide by the counsel it contained, and to await the coming of his fair hostess ere he took any step whatever. It was evident--so he argued--that Lady Danvers was disabused of the idea that he had killed his cousin Henry in a duel; but what were the circumstances of peril to which she alluded, he could not divine.

Could it be, he asked himself, that the influence of Lord Woodhall, attributing to him his son's death, had been exerted with such effect as to have a factitious accusation of some other offense against the laws brought against him to secure vengeance? Such an idea would never occur to any Englishman in the present day, and the very mention of it would be laughed to scorn. But we must recollect that this was no vain and improbable fancy in the times of which we are speaking. Trumped-up charges, for the purpose of destroying a political adversary or a private enemy, had been for more than twenty years, and still were, as common as daisies; nor had such villainy yet reached its height; for the three succeeding years displayed an amount of villainous practices of this kind which probably never before, and certainly never after, stained the history of any Christian country. Courts of law, too, were notoriously corrupt; judges were bought, sold, and influenced. Scroggs and Jeffries had befouled the judgment-seat; attorneys general were at the beck and call of every political enmity or court intrigue; and corrupt sheriffs selected, packed, and instructed the juries of the day on the basest motives for the most infamous purposes. It was no chimera of the imagination, then, that Ralph Woodhall dreaded, but a real and substantial danger, which might affect any man who had incurred the enmity of power and influence.

There could be no great harm done, he thought, by delay; and he determined not to send the letters which he had written on the preceding evening till Lady Danvers had arrived.

On questioning the man who had brought her letters, he found that she might be expected in two days more; and, to follow her directions exactly, he took a strong resolution to confine himself to the house till after he was made more fully aware of the peril that menaced him.

But alas for human resolutions, and for the young man's above all! Ralph was uneasy and restless. The anxiety of his mind left him no repose. He tried to read, and the fine library of Danvers's New Church afforded ample opportunity; but he soon found that the delight in books was for the time gone. He thought of Margaret, and of his poor cousin Henry, and, with a feeling of sympathy and pity, of old Lord Woodhall himself. He knew well that the first effect of his son's violent death would be to produce rage and a thirst for vengeance, which might be turned against him by the slightest accident; but he knew also that this would subside, and that profound grief would take the place of anger, and very probably affect the old man's health, if not his intellect.

He paced up and down the room. He gazed forth from the window, full of thought. He tasted very little of the dinner set before him. He looked at his watch often to see how the dull day went. In fact, to use a vulgar but significant expression, "he could settle to nothing."

At length, as the sun began to go down, he felt that longing for the free, open air which is so hard to be resisted. He persuaded himself that there could be no harm in wandering out into the park. He would go no further, he thought; and, as he had seen no one throughout the whole livelong day but the servants coming to and fro, or a game-keeper, with a gun on his shoulder, crossing the wide expanse within the walls, his walk, he fancied, was likely to be solitary and uninterrupted. Resolution soon gave way under such reasoning, and out he went, wandering quietly along, and soon losing himself amid the scattered trees and undulations of the ground. It is very pleasant to lose one's self sometimes, to shake us free from every thing habitual, to lose sight of houses and men, and the busy scene of mortal coil, to comrade with nature, and see naught but nature's handiwork around; and Ralph certainly had ample opportunity of doing so; for, quitting the path, and taking his way across the green turf, he was soon out of sight of the house, and wandering on among the old fantastic hawthorns, with the fern waving its plumes up to his knees, and here and there a chestnut or an oak spreading its green branches over his head. Every now and then a rabbit or a hare would dart away from his foot, and cunningly gallop through the tall, concealing fern, marking its course by a long wavy line. A herd of deer, here and there, would stand and gaze at him as he passed, keeping him at a fearful distance, or trot away with increasing speed if he came suddenly near. A solitary doe, too, started up as he approached her lair among the longest leaves, and scampered off in a different direction from the herd; and Ralph would moralize upon her somewhat in the vein of Jacques, asking himself what she had done to be thus shut out from fellowship with her kind--what offense she had committed against the laws and proprieties of the deer.

There were all these things around him, but there was no trace of man. If the scene had ever been embellished by man's hand, the vestiges of his handiwork had passed away, and it all seemed Nature's doing. Clouds, too, were flitting over the sky--large, grand, fleecy summer clouds, low down in the air, and looking like the island of the Laputan sages. Ralph's fancy played with them too. He made flying thrones of them, and winged chariots, and longed to have some enchanter's spell to call one down to receive him and float away upon that soft, calm coach till he could step gently down at Margaret's side.

This pleasant amusement of the mind--this refreshing solitude had no long time to last. After walking about half a mile through the fern, the wall of the park appeared in sight, and Ralph, turning a little to the left, resolved to follow its course and return to the house by the other side. He soon heard voices speaking beyond the wall, however, and judged rightly that beyond it lay some public road. An instant after, as he looked on, he saw a figure leap the wall at the distance of about a hundred yards further up the hill, and immediately crouch down among the fern and long grass which was there particularly tall. Ralph paused for a moment to watch what would follow, and, standing under an old chestnut-tree, could see without being seen. Running feet were heard immediately after, and then the head and shoulders of a man appeared above the wall. After gazing quickly round, the last comer exclaimed, "He has run on! he has run on! he must have either taken down over the bridge, or among the cottages by old Mother Diamond's."

Thus saying, he let go his hold of the wall and disappeared; and Ralph could hear the sound of many persons running fast and calling to each other as they went. His curiosity was excited by the scene he had witnessed, and he connected it in his own mind with some vague information which Gaunt Stilling had brought him in the morning of a rising on the sea-board of Dorsetshire, which Ralph had judged from the man's account to be of no greater importance than a riot in a country town. He walked straightforward, then, toward the spot where the man who had leaped the wall lay concealed, when the stranger started upon his feet with a large horse-pistol in his hand, warning him to stand back: "I will not be taken by a single man," he said; "I will die first, with arms in my hand."

"I do not seek to take you, my good friend," replied Ralph, in a calm tone; "I have no commission for such a thing. But you had belter put up your pistol; for, if you should be foolish enough to fire it, it would bring back to the spot those who apparently are seeking you, and servants and game-keepers enough to render your other arms useless."

"Then will you swear not to touch me if I do put it up--not to attempt to take me, I mean," said the stranger, after having eyed him attentively for a moment.

"I will give you my honor," replied Ralph, "and that must satisfy you; but I should much like to know, if you please, what you are doing here within the walls of this park, where I imagine you have no business, and where you are exceedingly likely to be apprehended as a deer-stealer?"

"I am the most unfortunate of men," cried the other, "and only escaped one peril to fall into another. Sir, I assure you I came not to steal your deer, but merely to escape from those bloodhounds of a tyrant who are following me to death."

Lamentable as his reply was, there was something almost ludicrous in the tone in which it was delivered, and Ralph smiled slightly as he replied, "The deer are not mine, my good friend, nor am I the proprietor of this park, but merely a guest at the house."

He was going on, when the other interrupted him with a theatrical gesture, saying, "Then I beseech you, sir, if you have any generosity or chivalry in your disposition, aid an unfortunate stranger, who is only persecuted on account of his political and religious opinions. I have committed no crime. They can charge me with no other fault but that of hating tyranny and popery."

"If that be all your offense," replied Ralph, "there is many a man in the land who would be chargeable with the same, and myself among the rest. But I really know not how to serve you, unless it be by leading you to a way out of the park, in a different direction from that which your pursuers have taken. I saw a gate a few minutes ago, up the stream. They have gone down below toward the bridge, and will very likely search the park when they find themselves disappointed there. You had better follow me, therefore, as fast as possible, in order to have a fair start."

"Without delay--without delay," replied the stranger, waving his hand in what he conceived a very graceful manner; and, pursuing his course onward by the wall, Ralph conducted him toward a gate of the park, which was visible from the house. As they went, the stranger, who seemed somewhat given to babble, entered into more conversation than the young gentleman perhaps desired. Nor was the style exactly well suited to compensate for the defects of the manner. His language was a mixture of bad French and somewhat vulgar English, with the assistance, every now and then, of a word or two of Low Dutch; and in this jargon he went on to inform Ralph of a variety of particulars which, had our young friend's loyalty been very rampant, might have induced him to cause his arrest upon the spot. He boasted that a fortnight would not pass before the crown of England was upon the head of a good, true Protestant king; that the whole land was rising in favor of the legitimate heir to the throne, and that the army itself was full of disaffection to the reigning monarch.

Ralph interrupted him as soon as he could, half inclined to believe that he was insane, and only anxious to get rid of him as soon as possible; but, before they reached the gate toward which their steps were directed, they were encountered by a game-keeper, who stopped full in their way, looking at them both sternly as they approached.

Suddenly, however, the man's face changed, and he exclaimed with a laugh, "Ah, Tom Dare! when did you come back from beyond sea? I thought you dared not venture. Why, do you know, man, you are proclaimed, and all the lads of Taunton are looking for you?"

Tom Dare, as the keeper called him, had at first shrunk into himself in evident consternation; but the last words seemed to rouse him, and, resuming his high-flown tone, he answered, "They shall soon find me, for I am going there tout droit."

"But who is this gentleman?" asked the keeper, looking at Ralph with some degree of suspicion, and addressing his question to the man he called Tom Dare.

Ralph, however, took upon himself to answer, saying, "I am a guest of Lady Danvers, my good friend, and finding this person in the park, I undertook to show him the way to the gate."

"Oh, sir, you are the gentleman staying at the house," said the keeper, doffing his hat; "as to Tommy Dare here, the sooner he is out of the park the better--indeed, I don't know what he does here at all."

To this uncivil speech Mr. Dare only replied by a rueful shake of the head, and by some muttered words in regard to a certain lady of Babylon who had a very unpleasant reputation. In the mean time he sped on, however, the game-keeper turning in the direction of the gate also, as if to see him out of the park. There was an air of doubt and hesitation about the keeper's face, and once or twice he muttered to himself, "I don't know--I'm not sure but I ought--but, hang it, one's own townsman! No, no, I can't do it."

As soon as they came in sight of the gate at the upper part of the park, both Ralph and the keeper stopped, and the latter said, "There's the gate, Master Dare; and I'll give you a word of advice: take care of your neck if you get to Taunton. I don't believe you'll find the folks bide any nonsense there, especially when there are riots going on in the country."

Mr. Dare, who was a step or two in advance, waved his hand solemnly, and Ralph thought he could hear the word "Fool" uttered in a low tone. The fugitive hurried on, however, and passed the gates, and Ralph turned back with the game-keeper on his way to the house.

"Who is that man?" he asked, as they proceeded.

"He is a bad fellow, sir," replied the game-keeper, somewhat abruptly; "his name is Thomas Dare, who had at one time a little money in Taunton, my native town, but he could not keep himself quiet, for he was a great talker and orator, as they call them, and got a number of folks into a scrape in the last king's reign, then left them to shift for themselves, and ran away to Holland. I am not at all sure that I ought not, by rights, to have apprehended him, for he is a proclaimed outlaw, and is here for no good, depend upon it."

Ralph made no comment, but strolled back again toward the house, feeling a little dissatisfied with himself for not having adhered to his resolution of the morning. The sun was setting when he reached the door, purpling the slopes of the park, and making the river glow like a ruby. Another day had passed; and as he stood there and looked for a moment round, he could not help thinking of how different was the scene, and the spot, and the circumstances in which that day had gone by, from any thing he could have anticipated but a few weeks before.

CHAPTER XXIV

The mansion of Danvers's New Church, when Ralph entered it, seemed silent and solitary enough. It was too large for a small household, such as now tenanted it. The steward's apartments were far away, the rooms of the inferior servants still further distant, and, entering the small saloon in which he had passed the morning, Ralph felt as if he were the only inhabitant of the house. The evening light, now tinged with the gray of night, shone in at the window; the paintings on the walls had become dim and indistinct; shade after shade came melancholy over the sky; and the ticking of a clock upon the stairs would have been the only sound that broke the stillness, had it not been for the note of a distant blackbird singing from beneath a bush. Ralph felt his spirits depressed, and was not sorry when one of the old servants entered the room, bearing two letters in his hand.

"This is for you, sir, I suppose," he said; "Harry has just brought it back from Lady Di Fullerton, with this other for my lady against her return."

Ralph took the letter which the man handed to him--a small, delicate note, perfumed and sealed; but it was too dark by this time even to read the address, and he had to wait till lights were brought. When they had been set upon the table, he bade the good man send his servant to him.

"He borrowed a horse from Mr. Drayton, sir," replied the man, "and rode away about twelve o'clock. He has not come back yet, I believe."

"I remember--I remember," replied Ralph: "he asked leave to go to see some of his friends;" and then, turning to the note, he examined the back, which bore,

"To the Honorable Gentleman at present residing at Danvers's New Church."

Within were written a few complimentary lines in the French language, expressing the regret of Lady Diana Fullerton that she could not have the extreme pleasure of doing the honors of her relative's house to Lady Danvers's guest, as she had been for some time too seriously unwell to venture out of her own dressing-room. Plenty of polite and courtly expressions were employed; but the main fact was, that there was no chance of Lady Fullerton being able to give her society and countenance to Hortensia during Ralph's stay at Danvers's New Church.

To say the truth, Ralph did not very much embarrass himself with reflections upon this derangement of Lady Danvers's plans. He was young, inexperienced in the world, and a college life of those days was not at all likely to open the eyes of a young man to the proprieties of society. He saw no more reason why he should not stay in the same house with Hortensia than stay in the same street; and it must be remembered, also, that that horrible cloak of decorum, which but too frequently covers, like charity, a multitude of sins, was a thing hardly known in those days, when the phrensied license of the Restoration was but just giving place to the colder and more covert debaucheries which succeeded. He quietly tore to pieces Lady Diana Fullerton's note with very little reverence, and, casting the subject from his mind, let his thoughts rest again, with some of that impatience for action which is peculiar to youth, upon the death of his poor cousin Henry, and the anguish which he knew Margaret must be feeling both for her brother and for himself, if she believed him guilty. He longed to fly to her, to console her, to comfort her, to assure her of his innocence, and of his ever-enduring affection; but how rarely is it that Fate allows us to do any thing that we long to do. Had not even the warning of Lady Danvers kept him in inactivity, he would not have dared either to visit or to write to her whom he so much loved. He did not know if their attachment to each other had been really made known or not; for, although he had at first imagined that the anxiety of the Duke of Norfolk and Hortensia to remove him from the vicinity of Lord Woodhall was occasioned by a discovery which he knew would excite the old lord's highest indignation, even without any of those insinuations which Robert Woodhall was too likely to add, yet that anxiety was now explained in another manner, and his and Margaret's mutual love might be still unknown, and their happiness periled by any indiscreet act.

Thought, so rapid in itself that it can girdle the great earth ere the leviathan can swim a mile, makes time often pass rapidly along with it. The evening wore away insensibly, broken by only one solitary ramble through the galleries and rooms which he had visited the night before. That ramble, indeed, occupied some time, because there were many of the pictures which interested him; and more than once he stood with the light in his hand gazing at the face of departed greatness or beauty, and comparing what he knew of the life passed away with the permanent expression of the countenance.

It has always given me a strange sensation to go through an ancient portrait-gallery, and see the faces of the dead looking down at me from the wall--living, as it were, again in the spiritual world of art. Their acts may be recorded on the page of history--their thoughts, their words transmitted to us even in their own hands; but these are voices without substance, vague shadows of a name. It is only the hand of the painter or the sculptor, that can give us the definite and the clear. On the broad brow, in the liquid eye, in the curl of the lip, in the dimpled cheek, in the poise of the figure, in the very fall of the hand, we read more of men's character, or more of its truths, than in all that they have written--even, than in all that they have done. Men write for the world, and often act for the world. Circumstances control them--events rule them. Few, if any, are not at some time, if not at all times, acting a part; and even where passion has spurned all governance, and the fiery deed of love or hate has seemed in its bright glare to reveal the very inner secrets of the heart, still no one can tell how that heart may have been affected by events of which we know nothing--how many motives, sensations, feelings, passions, accidents, may have prompted and mingled with the deeds which we only see in their harsh whole. But, upon the face and form, we are fond to think that Nature has herself written the description of her handiwork. There, with some experience, and but very little skill, by indications as small as the letters of a book, we can read much of the mind, the heart, the character, which no other page can ever display; and, at the same time, the likeness of the fleshly tabernacle of the spirit stands before us, so that all which can be known of the mixed being is at once in presence.

Oh, great Lavater! every one is more or less a physiognomist.

Ralph gazed, then, upon those faces with association very busy in his mind. Or, again, he would pause before a sunny landscape, and let the eye rest upon the golden skies, or wander through the far-prolonged vales, or pause among the deep groves of trees, watching the nymph bathing in the limpid stream, or the ancient armament sailing up, amid columns, and trophies, and palaces, to an imagined city; and the poetry of painting would wake in his heart as many bright images as ever were called up by verse or the lyre.

Again, he would go on, and, feeling free in the solitude, he ventured once more into Hortensia's own apartments. But this time he got no further than her picture. It had certainly something fascinating in it, for he stood and gazed on that bright face, bursting through the branches, in its wild, gay youth, and comparing it, line by line, with the features which memory preserved; and as he did so, imagination was busy too. He asked himself, what were the events, what the course of life, which had subdued and chastened the light hilarity there displayed--what was it that, like Undine's love, had given a soul to the wild spirit sparkling there? He did not puzzle, though he did not satisfy himself; he enjoyed the wanderings of his own imagination round the pleasant theme, and when at length he turned away to retire to rest, he said to himself, "She must always have been very lovely."

Let us not ask if Hortensia shared his dreams with Margaret. We have no right to lift up sleep's shadowy curtain, and see the fairy sports of fancies freed from the control of will and reason. He slept, and doubtless he dreamed too; but he woke early, ere the sun had so far climbed the eastern hill as to overtop the wood, and while the slant rays were still pouring in golden splendor through the branches of the trees.

As he paused to look through the open window after having dressed himself, his eye passed over the park to the valley beyond, and, where the open ground stretched out from the banks of the stream up the sides of the hills, he was surprised to see a number of horsemen, in groups of two or three together, cantering lightly hither and thither, as if in sport. It was no season for hunting; but he thought that perhaps they might be flying a hawk, and he watched them with some interest till he convinced himself that that supposition was incorrect.

A moment after he saw a single figure on horseback riding up the broad road from the great gates to the house, and as it came nearer he recognized his servant, Gaunt Stilling, who had been absent since noon of the day before.

"Perhaps he brings me some intelligence," thought Ralph; and, descending to the small saloon, he ordered his breakfast to be brought. Still Gaunt Stilling did not come; and at length, after having waited ample time for him to tend his horse, his young master sent for him. When he appeared, Ralph was a good deal struck with something strange in the man's looks. He seemed worn, fatigued, and thin, and his apparel was dusty with the road; but that was not all. He was gloomy, abstracted, more taciturn than usual. Even in the midst of a sentence he would fix his eyes upon the ground, and seemingly fall into a deep revery.

"Do you know who those horsemen are, whom I saw just now riding down in the valley?" asked Ralph, after a few other questions of no moment.

"No, sir," replied Stilling; "I saw them, but did not heed them."

"They seemed at one time to be hawking," said Ralph. "Have you heard any further intelligence from Lyme, Stilling!"

"None, sir," answered the servant; "I have been forty miles the other way. I met that scoundrel, Thomas Dare, this morning, who might have told me, perhaps, but--" and he left the sentence unconcluded, remaining, as it were, lost in thought.

"But what?" asked his master.

The man started and looked up. "Oh, merely that I was busy with other thoughts, sir--that the man is a rascal, and that we passed each other with only 'Give you good-day, Master Stilling'--'Go to the devil, Thomas Dare.'"

Something had evidently gone wrong with Stilling; but, as he did not seem inclined to speak of it, Ralph, though he felt interested, merely said, "I hope you had good news of your family, Stilling?"

"The worst in the world," replied the man, abruptly. "I thought the worst had come some time ago, yet this is worse; but, so help me Heaven--" and again he broke off his speech and relapsed into silence. This time, however, his silence was not without significance, for he clinched both his hands tight, as if struggling with some strong passion.

"I am very sorry to hear this," replied Ralph, in a feeling tone. "Can I do any thing to assist you, Stilling? I need not tell you that I am most willing, if it be possible."

The man looked up more brightly, and replied, "Not at present, sir, but the time may come--Hark! there is Lady Danvers, I suppose; I heard of her upon the road."

The sounds which had attracted his attention were produced by horses' feet upon the gravel, and the moment after the great bell rang out loud. Without taking note of the fact that there had been no sound of carriage wheels, Ralph rose hastily and ran through the hall to the door, in order to assist his beautiful hostess as she alighted. He was surprised to see, however, when he opened the door, a party of some ten or twelve horsemen, three of whom had dismounted, while another, far taller and much handsomer than any of the rest, was in the act of alighting also. One groom held his horse; another supported his stirrup; and there was something dignified and graceful in his whole air which instantly attracted Ralph's chief attention toward him. He wore a star and broad ribbon, and over his heavy riding-boots a pair of golden spurs, and his whole dress was splendid, though subdued in coloring by good taste.

Before any questions could be asked, the steward and two or three of the old servants were by Ralph's side, and finding that he had been mistaken in his expectations, the young gentleman retired into the house, leaving Mr. Drayton to reply to any inquiries. Ralph heard a fine melodious voice, however, ask if Lady Danvers were then in Dorsetshire, and Mr. Drayton replied in the negative.

"I have a letter for her from an old friend," replied the stranger, "and would wish to add a few lines myself, if you will furnish me with materials for writing. Nay, more, I am inclined to tax your hospitality so far, sir, as to ask for some refreshment for my men and horses, and some breakfast for myself--you know me, I presume?"

"I do, your grace," replied Mr. Drayton, "and, of course, whatever the house affords is at your service."

"Well, then, I will walk in here and write," replied the other, advancing toward the room in which Ralph then was.

Mr. Drayton seemed puzzled how to act; but, before he could decide, the stranger had entered the room, and stood face to face with Ralph Woodhall. He bowed courteously, but with a look of some surprise; and the good steward thought fit to take upon himself the task of introducing Ralph as "Mr. Woodhall, a friend of my lady's family, sir, who is staying for a time at the house."

He did not mention the name of the new visitor; but while he hurried away to procure pen, ink, and paper, the gentleman who had come in seated himself calmly at the table, and entered easily into conversation. His very appearance was a recommendation; and his demeanor was so graceful, that, even had his conversation been less happy than it was, there would still have been an irresistible charm about it; but his words were well chosen; his expressions what I may call picturesque, if not poetical; and there was a touch of that vivacity which often passed for wit at the court of the second Charles. He asked a number of questions, but none of them impertinent or intrusive. He spoke of the house, and the grounds, and the beauty of the park; said he had been there when he was a boy, but had nearly forgotten it, and expressed a wish, before he went, to walk over the house.

"I shall have much pleasure in conducting you, sir," replied Ralph, "for during the short time of my stay here, I have more than once wandered over the building, and felt much interest in all that it contains."

"Then you are not well acquainted with the place?" said the other; but, without waiting for a reply to what was in reality a question, he added, "Let us go. Doubtless they will be a long while in finding pen, ink, and paper. I have always found it so, here in Dorsetshire, since my return."

They walked out into the hall together, where two or three gentlemen stood booted and spurred. They uncovered their heads as soon as the other appeared; and one of them, advancing a step, addressed him, saying, "It is all clear, your grace, on the way to Taunton, and the intelligence in that quarter is satisfactory."

"Good," replied the other. "This want of cavalry is inconvenient. What says Mr. Dare as to the levies about Taunton?"

"He had not yet reached the town, my lord duke, when his messenger came away," was the reply; "but he promises much--more, I fear, than he will perform; for his reception in some of the small villages by the way has been so good, that he looks upon it as a conquered country already. He is a braggadocio, if ever there was one."

"He is a good creature, notwithstanding," replied the duke; "light and gay in danger, and cheerful in all circumstances--a little given to boast and assume, perhaps; but still his gayety and confidence throw a light upon our expedition, which I wish we had a little more."

"Shall I give any orders regarding the march to-morrow?" inquired the other gentleman.

"I think not," said Ralph's companion; "we must wait for these Taunton levies, or some surer information. It will not do to leave all resources behind us till we have the certainty of support in advance. But make yourself easy, gallant friend; time, I trust, will be our ally, and not our enemy."

There was something uncommonly easy and placable, though confident in the speaker's tone and manner; and Ralph, though he had divined from the first that he was speaking with the Duke of Monmouth, began to doubt whether his supposition was correct, for he had not calculated accurately how far adversity can tame both the highest and the lightest spirit.

After this brief conversation, they passed on through the house, speaking calmly and cheerfully of the various objects which it presented to their eyes, as if there were no such thing as strife, and warfare, and bloodshed in the world. The duke walked the suites of splendid rooms and the long-drawn-out lines of corridors as if he were treading the drawing-rooms of some peaceful palace, with a calm sort of meditative gentleness, not unmixed with dignity, which beseemed him well. In his whole demeanor, carriage, and appearance, he was every inch a prince; and his very abstinence from all reference to political topics seemed to Ralph a recommendation of his cause. He appeared as tranquilly confident of his rights as if nothing more was required than to show himself to win all hearts in his support. Had he always maintained this happy trust, he would have been a greater, a happier, perhaps a more successful man.

The duke asked several questions, however, tending to elicit his young companion's opinions; and, finding him a stanch Protestant, though of the Episcopal Church, and a strong enemy of all tyranny, civil or religious, he ventured gradually to allude distantly to his own enterprise, and to hint--without asking it--that the assistance of every gallant gentleman was an object he desired.

Ralph was silent, from very many varied motives. He gave neither encouragement nor the reverse, judging more sanely than the duke of the circumstances which surrounded them, and entertaining many doubts whether, if Monmouth, by one of those strange accidents which sometimes influence the course of great events, should succeed in dethroning James, his own elevation to sovereignty would be acceptable to the great body of the people of the realm. To himself, notwithstanding the fascination of Monmouth's manner, he felt that such would not be the case; and he knew that in the hearts of Englishmen there is a fund of steady, determined loyalty, a hereditary love for an ancient line of kings, which it requires the insanity of great oppression to shake or overthrew.

The Duke of Monmouth (for he it was) did not press the subject by any means far, seeming to feel it beneath him to canvass for the aid of any individual. He might know, too, that much eagerness displays small confidence; and at this moment of his career it was a part of Monmouth's policy to appear full of good assurance.

He returned to the small room below, then, after commenting in the tone of a connoisseur upon some of the pictures, and in that of a gay courtier upon others, and finding writing materials ready, sat down and wrote a few lines upon a sheet of paper, in which he inclosed another letter he had brought with him. He sealed and then addressed the whole to "Hortensia, Baroness Danvers;" and then placing it in Ralph's hand, he said, with a gay smile, "I will trust this to your good care for speedy delivery, sir. If you be a lover, it comes from no rival; if you be a friend, it comes from a friend no less sincere; if you be a relation, there are lines within it from one who has loved the person addressed as sincerely as any relative could love. Nay, my good sir," he continued, turning to Mr. Drayton, who entered, followed by several servants bearing food in a rich service of plate, "you treat my humble state too royally; but the time may come when I can acknowledge your courtesy better. Mr. Woodhall, will you partake?"

The duke's breakfast was not half concluded, when one of his followers, from without, came in suddenly and without ceremony, and spoke a word to Monmouth in a low tone over the back of his chair.

The duke started up, and gazed at him for an instant with a look of horror and consternation.

"What!" he exclaimed; "what did you say? shot Thomas Dare--in the streets of Lyme--on a dispute about a horse?"

"Too true, indeed, your grace," replied the other; "shot him dead; the ball passed through his brain."

"By the Lord that lives!" cried Monmouth, "these turbulent men shall find that he who claims to rule a realm like this, can at least rule a handful who pretend to obey. Have out the horses there! I must not lose a moment."

Ever energetic, and often right, in purpose, Monmouth hurried to depart, only to show how weak he could be in act, how amenable to the weak counsels of others. Brave as a lion in the field--often timid in the council--not without skill as the general--ever misled as the politician and the man.

As, about to mount his horse, he turned away from the door, he looked round to Ralph with a pleasant smile, saying, "Remember my commission--I trust to you."

"I will not fail, your grace," replied Ralph.

They were few and simple words, but their effects were more important.

CHAPTER XXV

"Ah, poor gentleman!" said Mr. Drayton, as the cavalcade passed quickly down the tortuous road through the park toward the gates, "I remember the time well when he went through the western counties in a sort of triumph like; when men and maidens turned out of every village and every town to meet him; when his horse's feet trod upon nothing but flowers, and the ringing of the bells kept all the country in a noise. Feasted at Longleet, met by all the gentry of the land, harangued by every corporation, the people made an idol of him, and the great men could not show him too much honor; I fear he will find it different now."

"Do you think the people have lost their love for him, then?" demanded Ralph, anxious to hear more of events which were passing so near, without any certainty having reached his ears.

"Not a whit, sir," answered the steward, "not a whit, if you mean the common people. They are more constant than gentlemen think. Why, they are flocking into Lyme in thousands, I am told. But with the gentry it is different. They courted him for interest--at least one half of them--and now for interest they will keep aloof. The Tories will stick by the crown right or wrong; and Whig gentlemen have a great notion of looking well before they leap. I would take any fair bet that the good duke will not find five men above the rank of a yeoman to join him before he fights a battle and wins it--if ever that should happen."

Ralph made no reply, although he doubted not that Mr. Drayton's anticipations were too true. He inquired, indeed, what was taking place in the country round; but the rumors--which were all that the steward could relate--were, as is always the case on such occasions, confused and various; and, after a time, Ralph begged the worthy man to send him his servant Stilling, in order to renew the conversation which had been broken off by Monmouth's arrival.

Mr. Drayton seemed to hesitate for an instant, and then said, frankly, "I think you had better let him alone, sir, just at present. Something has gone very wrong with him, that is clear. I saw him a minute or two ago walking up and down the stable-yard, and pinching his hands one in the other as if he would have screwed the blood out of his fingers' points. Poor fellow! I remember him a gay, blithesome lad in an attorney's office at Dorchester--a good education he had, Gaunt Stilling--but then the old lady got him a commission in the Tangier regiment, and he went away. He's mightily changed now; and yet he can't be much over thirty."

"So much?" said Ralph, in a tone of surprise; "but tell me, Master Drayton, do you know any thing of the cause of his present distress of mind? You seem to be well acquainted with his family."

"I have known them many years, sir," replied the steward, with a grave face. "As to what is the matter now, I don't exactly know any thing. The carrier brought over word some three weeks ago that his sister had been sent away from Lincolnshire by the old man, to get her from a young gentleman who wished to wrong her. The father brought her half the way, and her uncle went the other half to meet her. Now I fancy Gaunt has been over to see her. It's a bad business, I'm afraid; and the gentleman's name they talked of was the same as yours, sir."

As he spoke he fixed his eyes with an inquiring look upon Ralph's face, and the young gentleman felt himself redden as he recollected all he had seen and heard at Coldenham. He fancied, too, that there was some suspicion in the steward's eyes; and he hastened to reply, "Not mine exactly, sir, for there is no other of the name of Ralph Woodhall that I know; and I never saw poor Stilling's sister but once, and then only for a moment."

He spoke somewhat sharply, and Drayton replied in an apologetic tone, saying, "I beg pardon, sir; I did not at all mean that you were the gentleman--indeed I knew you were not; but I thought it might be some relation."

"Possibly," replied Ralph, not quite satisfied yet; "I know nothing of this matter, however; for, with the exception of the poor cousin whom I have lately lost, and his father, I have been on no terms of intimacy with any of my male relations."

"They are of high rank, sir, I believe," replied the steward, in a tone of inquiry.

But Ralph merely bowed his head, thinking it not necessary to enter into any part of his family history with a mere stranger. After a moment's pause, he said, "I will take your advice, Mr. Drayton, and leave poor Stilling alone for a time; but I think it would be as well to divert his thoughts after a short period from painful subjects of contemplation. I wish, therefore, that you would, without my sending for him, let him know that I wish him to go out in the afternoon and ascertain what is doing in the country. Tell him that I desire very precise and accurate information as to the movements of the

Duke of Monmouth's forces and those of the king, for it can not be supposed that a large body in actual rebellion will be suffered much longer to move about the country unopposed."

"I don't know, sir," answered Mr. Drayton, shaking his head; "but sometimes governments are taken napping, and I think the only chance for the good duke would be to push on upon London at once. Bold counsels would bring many a man to his standard, for there is something catching in boldness as well as in fear. I doubt, however, that Stilling will learn much; for I have men all about who would bring me any tidings that are to be got, and they bring me nothing certain."

"I should wish him to go, nevertheless," replied Ralph, "It would serve to occupy his mind, and may, perhaps, furnish us with information even more valuable to your lady than myself."

The steward bowed and withdrew, and for an hour or two Ralph amused himself as best he might. To have seen him one would have supposed him of as idle a nature as ever existed. He opened no books; he had no inclination or application to read. He looked at no pictures, unless it were those of imagination. His mind had harder realities to deal with than those which any canvas can display. The greater part of his time was passed in gazing forth from the windows upon the wide, wavy scene without, which afforded, as it were, a stage sufficiently extensive and ample for all persons in the drama of fancy to play their several parts before his eyes. Oh, how memory and imagination conjured up, from the depths of the past, from the depths of the future, scenes and characters which might all bear their share in the tragedy about to be performed in the land! A gloomy anticipation, a dark but too true shadowing forth of the stern, terrible acts that were about to take place, visited the young man's mind; and he felt that sensation of awe, that sublime, dreadful expectation, which is experienced by a spectator viewing from a height the thunder-cloud marching onward over a sunny land, soon to be left desolate, or the tempest riding over a calm sea, and piling up the glassy waters into surges full of shipwreck and of death.

The minutes glided by almost unnoted; and then, seating himself again at a table, a strange fancy seized him of writing down the thoughts of the moment--the reflections--the anticipations, which rose one by one as he considered the circumstances that surrounded him.

It was a dangerous amusement. Written thoughts, as undigested--as carelessly recorded--as immaturely gathered--as inconsequent and undirected, had aided not a little, in the last reign, to bring the head of the gallant Sydney to the scaffold; but yet the impulse was upon him; and he did not even strive to resist it, but eat and thought, and wrote, and thought, and wrote again.

The day had declined, and evening was not far off, when Gaunt Stilling entered the room abruptly, saying, "There has been a bit of a battle, sir, at Bridport, and the duke's troops have been repulsed. It was plowman against plowman, and the duke's plowmen would have won the day if Lord Grey and his horse had not ran at the first fire."

"Who is Lord Grey?" asked Ralph, in a quiet tone.

"Oh, the duke's general of horse," answered Stilling, with a laugh. "A gentleman very bold in words, and brave enough, they say, in presence of a hangman or a judge; but he does not like the nasty smell of gunpowder, and eschews push of pike."

"Have you any other tidings?" inquired his master.

"Oh yes, plenty," answered Stilling; "the Duke of Albemarle--who is more, by-the-way, of a monk than his father--is marching to attack the duke with the militia. He will be beaten, of course; for, where Monmouth is in person, the people will fight like wolves, and he is no bad general either. That will be a feather in his cap, and may bring some people in. But then Feversham is marching down with three or four regular regiments--my old comrades among the rest. Now Monmouth is worth twenty Frenchmen, and Feversham is only fit for a court supper; but then there is Churchill with the Blues already in the field, and he will give the good duke some trouble, or I mistake my man. But I forgot to tell you, sir, that my Lady Danvers was coming down the hill as I passed; and she will be here in a minute or two, for they were going at a great rate, not liking, I suspect, the sounds of war that were whizzing all round them."

"Indeed!" exclaimed Ralph, starting up eagerly; "I will go to meet her. She comes by the western gates, I suppose?"

"Oh yes, sir, by the west," replied Gaunt Stilling, gazing after his master as he hurried toward the door; and then, as the young gentleman disappeared, the man muttered between his teeth, "Fickle--fickle, like all the rest. What matters it what falls upon him--they are all alike. This girl has captivated his eye, and little cares he how many hearts he breaks. Ah! what a cursed thing it is to be a gentleman, and what fools those are who strive to rise above humble station, to be a prey to the next bigger beast than themselves!"

In the mean while, without hearing or heeding his servant's comments, Ralph had snatched up his hat which lay in the passage, and hurried out down the walks toward the great gates. The little cavalcade was already in sight--the great lumbering vehicle, and the horsemen who accompanied and followed it. It were vain to say that Ralph did not behold it joyfully, or that the coming of Hortensia was not pleasant to him. At the very lowest estimate, it was an agreeable relief to the dull monotony of the life he had been leading. But then there was much more: her grace, her beauty, the charm of her manner and her conversation, shed a light around, like that of the sunshine, which brings out the beauty of even the dullest scenes, when it can reach and enrich them with its varying splendor. With her, too, he could consult, confer, and determine; and action, which seemed to him like life, promised to commence with her coming.

With well-pleased looks, then, he hurried on, and met the carriage half way through the park. He did not approach unmarked; for, whether she expected him or not, Hortensia saw him afar, and bade the coachman stop. When he came near, she alighted, looking, as he thought, more beautiful than ever; and placing her hand within his arm, directed the rest to go on, saying she would walk up to the house. There was a sweet, tender placidity in her look--a gently-moved calmness, which was very lovely in itself; and as she leaned upon Ralph's arm, while the servants hurried on, obeying with due discretion the orders they had received, she looked up in her young companion's face, as if to see how much he had suffered--what ravages thought and remorse had effected in his appearance since they parted.

Her first question, however, referred to things very different from the subject which was uppermost in her thoughts. "I hope," she said, "that my cousin, Lady Di Fullerton, has taken good care of you. Ralph, I have been a sad, weary time upon the journey; but coaches move slowly."

"I doubt not, dear Lady Danvers," replied Ralph, with a faint smile, "that Lady Diana would have taken good care of me had she been here; but--"

"Is she not here?" exclaimed Hortensia, in an eager tone, with the blood suddenly rushing up into her cheek, more from surprise and the sudden pressure of many strange considerations in her mind than from any great disappointment or annoyance. "Why did she not come? She must have received my letter?"

"She was too, ill to come," replied Ralph; "but I fear my stay may be inconvenient to you--perhaps not quite right. There can be no harm or danger in my going forward at once on my way."

"Ralph," exclaimed Hortensia, in a somewhat reproachful tone, "you do not think me so weak--so foolish! Surely, if my good name be so frail a thing as not to bear the giving shelter in an hour of danger to the son of my mother's dearest friend, it were little worth the keeping. You stay, Ralph--

you stay, if you have any regard for me! No, no, it matters not. I asked my good cousin out of deference to the cold world's opinion. Having done that, I have done enough."

Well may prophets, and, by their tongues, the great Creator of the human heart, declare that it is the most deceitful of all things; for any one who has ever rendered the secrets of the dark, mysterious cavern of his own bosom objective to the analysis of reason, must have recoiled from the scrutiny, deterred by the fearful complications which the eye, at one glance, can perceive. How far--and how far willingly--Lady Danvers was deceiving herself, it is hardly necessary to inquire. It is quite unnecessary, and would be useless, to attempt to trace all the tortuous and darkling passages by which the deception crept along. Certain it is, however, she had persuaded herself that the son of her mother's dearest friend--of her adopted sister-- stood toward her almost in the relation of a brother; that she could not do too much for him; that she could do nothing within the bounds of modesty and honor that was not justifiable and justified in the bright, clear, piercing eye of heaven.

Strong in the rectitude and purity of her own purpose, she cared little for the dull, dark, earthy eye of the world. But she little recollected that there is a misty, shadowy land, between the pellucid light above and the coarse darkness below, where the phantoms of associations hover between the two--ever beheld from the one realm, and sometimes too clearly displayed to the other. She did not ask herself--she did not venture to ask herself--what personal feelings, what mortal affections were stealing in and mingling unperceived with the calm, unselfish, soulful memories which had first drawn her thoughts to Ralph Woodhall. She knew not--she would not know--that there was any difference whatsoever in her feelings toward him, as they walked there in her own park side by side, from those with which she had first beheld him at the Duke of Norfolk's house, a stranger in all but memories. She loved to call him to herself--to think of him in her own mind as her brother Ralph. Oh, cunning heart, how skillful art thou even in snatching the artifice of indistinct words to veil thy workings from the deceived eye of thy master. She would not have called him Mr. Woodhall now for the world. It would have broken the spell--destroyed the illusion. He would have been no longer her brother, but her lover--or him whom she loved. The very thought that her heart could have been so far given, as it really was, to one who had never sought or asked it, would have been death to her; for, with all the warm tenderness of her feelings, the deep, strong, enthusiastic tone of her affections, she had every quality of a true woman: that nearest approach to the angel which the latter world has ever seen.

Let the cold argue against such things. Let the worldly. Argue, ye bound up, molded, fettered in the strong conventionalities of a false and factitious state; ye who are tutored from the nursery to the altar, to bend your wills and crush your hearts before the great world's god, Convenience. In that age--base, corrupt, debased as it was--one of the worst that earth has ever seen--in the reaction--in the rebellion of man's heart and soul against the iron tyranny of a cold and false fanaticism, there were glorious instances of pure and true devotion, of strong and deep affection, of passion above license, of morality beyond decorum, which are rarely seen now when the fire of fanaticism is extinguished, and the rigid rules of a cynical religion have been superseded by the gilded but unsubstantial fetters of an eye serving propriety. Nay, more, the most licentious chronicle of the scandals of that age, the witty scoffer at every virtue, the pleasant companion of every vice, has been the one to record some of the brightest exceptions to the system in which he moved and had his being.

The freedom of the times; the liberty of thought and action in which she had been brought up; the independence of all conventional forms, except those of courtly ceremony, which prevailed during the whole time of her youth; the very dangers, difficulties, intrigues, cabals, slaughter, agitation, and extraordinary circumstances which marked the latter years of Charles the Second, had rendered Hortensia independent, from a very early period, of the world's opinion; and in the case of Ralph Woodhall, she had already paid it more deference than she was ever inclined to pay.

True, had she asked her own heart why she had yielded thus far to a power she contemned and despised, she might have found there was a weakness in her own bosom which counseled caution. But she would ask her own heart nothing, as I have before said. Like an unskillful general, in the certainty of some strong points--honor, uprightness, purity, and truth-- she thought her position impregnable, and made no allowance for the easy slope of passion, or the covert ways of love.

Thus onward she walked with Ralph, repelling the very thought of his quitting her house on account of what the world might say with utter scorn. I know not whether the thought ever presented itself to her mind that there was an easy way of silencing the tongue of scandal by uniting their fate forever; I rather think not; but I am quite sure that such a thought never crossed the mind of Ralph. However, if she was satisfied, he had no cause to be otherwise; for he was not such a Quixote in delicacy as to fear that which, with her better knowledge, she did not fear.

He laughed gayly, then--more gayly than he had done for many a day--saying, "Well, dear Lady Danvers, I only sought to show my devotion to your will by my readiness to go, rather than put you in unpleasant circumstances; but, at the same time, I must tell you that no such dangers exist in my case as you have been led to suppose. My poor cousin Henry, by whosesoever hand he fell, owes not his death to me. I would have sacrificed any thing but honor rather than have crossed swords with him. My long absence from the inn, which perhaps you may have heard of, and which might have given time, though barely, for me to return to Norwich, can be every moment accounted for."

"Ay, that is what has puzzled me," said Hortensia, before he had quite concluded what he had to say; "two different accusations have been brought against you--at first sight incompatible with each other: the one, that you went back to Norwich, fought, and slew your cousin Henry; the other, that you passed several hours in comforting and consoling the unhappy family of the poor Nonconformist minister. But I made anxious inquiry of the people at the inn, and none could tell me at what hour you returned. They said you must have stabled and groomed your horse yourself; and I concluded that some mistake had been made about the hour of the duel; for every thing I had heard before we set out, and every thing contained in the Duke of Norfolk's private letter to myself, seemed to prove that such a duel had taken place."

"I never quitted the town," replied Ralph; "I never took my horse from the stable; and in regard to the duel, I had not the most remote idea that such a lamentable event had taken place till I arrived in these domains."

"Nay, I doubt you not in the least," replied Hortensia; "but, though guiltless of your cousin's death, and though you could prove your innocence completely, which might be more difficult than you imagine, your situation would still be one of imminent peril, and you must not think of stirring from this house so long as you can be here in safety--how long that may be, in these distracted times, who can say?"

"But what is the peril, dear lady?" asked Ralph; "my innocence of my cousin's death can surely be easily proved, for I can account for every moment of my time."

"Did any one see you return to the inn?" asked Lady Danvers; "I made inquiries, and all the servants of the house assured me that such was not the case."

Ralph mused for a moment or two, and then replied, "It is very strange; I do not recollect having seen any one. I entered by the door from the stable-yard, saw a light burning in the entrance, took it up, and went straight to my own room."

"At what hour was this?" asked Hortensia.

"I can not well say," replied Ralph; "it must have been after ten, but I think before eleven."

"The duke's letter to myself," replied Lady Danvers, "said the hour of the duel was some time between ten and twelve. Now, Ralph, consider upon what nice calculations your fate might depend. Those who know you well will have no doubt; but those who do not know you--a prejudiced judge--perhaps a packed jury, will at all events suspect, and if they do suspect, your death would be the consequence."

"Nay, I can not think that," answered Ralph Woodhall; "duels occur every day; and where there is no dishonorable act accompanying them, we never hear of any such severity."

"But you deny the duel," said Lady Danvers; "you can not admit that it took place, if it did not. Yet certain is it that your cousin sent you a challenge for that very hour--that he met some one--that the meeting took place at night--that there were no witnesses--and that he was killed. Your very denial of the meeting would be construed into a consciousness of guilt in the transaction."

The color had been mounting higher and higher in Ralph's cheek every moment, as he saw the extraordinary complication of circumstances which rendered it difficult for him to prove his innocence, and was almost led to fancy that Hortensia believed him guilty still. "Upon my honor as a man, and my faith as a Christian, dear Lady Danvers," he said, "I had no share in this transaction whatsoever."

Hortensia laid her beautiful hand gently on his arm, and replied, looking full in his face, "And upon my honor and faith, Ralph Woodhall, I believe you; but I mentioned other perils besides these. The magistrates, it is true, dismissed the charge against you of attempting to rescue old Mr. Calloway, the Nonconformist preacher; but hardly had you left the town, when it was discovered that you had passed a considerable portion of the night with the family of that poor, persecuted man. You know how severe the laws are upon that subject, and how tyrannically they are exercised. It was proved that several other persons had visited the house that night as well as yourself; they were all arrested and committed to prison. A new charge of attending a night conventicle, contrary to law, was preferred against you, and a warrant was immediately issued for your apprehension. The case would be a perilous one at any time; but since this rash insurrection by the Duke of Monmouth, the great leader of the Calvinistic party, the dangers would be incalculable, even were not the matter complicated by other serious accusations. Nay, nay, you must stay here, Ralph, till we may find means of getting you out of the country. Monmouth must be mad, I think, or fearfully misinformed."

We often find that when the mind is bewildered by considerations too intricately tangled and commixed to be easily separated and reduced to order, it receives the first pretext that presents itself to fly to some other theme, however irrelevant or unimportant, as if to refresh itself before it returns to its more laborious task. Such was probably the case with Ralph Woodhall; for, without pursuing the subject of his own fate further, he said, "I forgot to mention that the Duke of Monmouth was here this morning, and stayed for more than an hour."

"Indeed!" exclaimed Lady Danvers, in a tone of no very great satisfaction; "I wish he had stayed away. I can never forgive him."

"He also left a packet for you," said Ralph, "committing it to my charge, and saying that it contained a letter for you from an old and dear friend, who still loved you well."

"Alas! alas!" replied Lady Danvers, "poor Henrietta! where once she loves, she loves forever. Love has been her ruin and her blight; for she was never taught that there are higher and holier things than even love. Let us go in, Ralph; I must read her letter, for she is still very dear to me."

CHAPTER XXVI

"At the house of Lady Danvers, say you? on the far edge of Dorsetshire?" said the voice of an old man, tremulous, and eager with strong passion.

"Yes, my dear lord," replied Robert Woodhall, "at Danvers's New Church, a place where a strong-armed man could pitch a crown piece into three counties. He has doubtless chosen that retreat, partly because he fancies a warrant may be easily evaded, partly--"

"But are you sure, Robert--quite sure?" asked Lord Woodhall; "do not let us make another mistake."

"I am quite sure," answered his young cousin; "I have the news from three of our own people who have seen him there. You know my mother's place lies at no great distance, and the whole country round rings with the rumor that he is to be married to Lady Danvers--the cause, probably, of his taking the life of a better man than himself."

"Married to the gallows first!" cried Lord Woodhall, vehemently. "Call a servant, boy; bid him bring my hat and cloak. I will away to the king. Monmouth lies about there, they say; he was last heard of marching toward Exeter. Feversham and Churchill are after him, and the troops may serve our purpose as well as the king's."

"Shall I attend you, sir?" said Robert.

"No, no," answered the old lord; "stay here till I come back. Go and comfort poor Margaret. She bears up a little now, but still weeps often. It will gladden her heart to hear that there is a chance of catching her brother's murderer at last."

A slight, hardly perceptible smile curled upon Robert Woodhall's lip; but, turning away to conceal the emotions of which he was conscious, he called Lord Woodhall's servants to their master, and then saw him deferentially to the door.

There are as great varieties in love as in any other passion; seldom found altogether pure, it is mixed with a thousand various alloys, some more, some less congenial to itself. Now it must not be supposed that Robert Woodhall was altogether without love of a certain kind for his fair cousin Margaret. True, it was of a coarse nature, even in its very origin. Her beauty--her fresh, warm, healthful loveliness, had its attractions for a man who, even before he could count manhood, had sated himself with licentious pleasures. But even this baser sort of love was mingled with many other feelings. Ambition had its share, and avarice; and, strange to say, spite and revenge too. He saw that Margaret did not love him; he felt intuitively that she would never love him; but that conviction diminished not in the least the ardor of his pursuit. It prompted a desire to pain, to grieve her, whenever he could do so without appearing as the active agent, but took not the least from the desire to possess her as his wife, nor shook his resolution to attain that object by any means, however base.

Quietly walking up the stairs, he entered the room where she usually sat during the morning, but found it vacant. He sat for a few minutes, gazing forth from the window into the street, till the door opened, and Margaret herself appeared. With a cold inclination of the head, she was about to withdraw immediately. But her cousin called to her, saying, "Margaret, Margaret, I have something to tell you from your father. He wishes you to stay with me till his return, when he will give you further tidings."

Margaret obeyed at once, entered, sat down, and drew an embroidery frame toward her.

"Very satisfactory intelligence has been received this morning," said Robert Woodhall, "which my lord, your father, has gone to make the most of. We have discovered the place where poor Henry's murderer lies concealed."

The tears rose in Margaret's beautiful eyes, but still she would not hear Ralph called by such a name. "You have no right, sir," she said, "so boldly to announce my cousin Ralph a murderer till he has been proved so."

Robert Woodhall saw her emotion with infinite pleasure, but he answered in a quiet tone, though with a slightly-curled lip, "I did not know that there was any doubt of it."

"Great doubt," replied Margaret; "I, for one, do not believe that Ralph would ever draw his sword against poor Henry; and there are others, wiser, and better able to judge than myself, who do not believe it either."

"Indeed!" exclaimed Robert Woodhall, with unfeigned surprise; "pray who?"

"For one, the Duke of Norfolk," answered Margaret.

"You astonish me," said Robert, musing; "then pray whom do you and the good duke suspect?"

There was something contemptuous and bitter in his tone, which kindled a momentary anger in Margaret's breast, and she answered, "No one in particular, Robert Woodhall; but we should suspect you just as soon as poor Ralph. Pray where is he, if you have discovered?"

One of his slight, shrewd, sarcastic smiles came upon Robert Woodhall's face; and he answered, "He is at Danvers's New Church, the seat of the fair Hortensia, to whom he is about to be married, if the hangman does not previously perform for him a ceremony of a different kind."

"Unfeeling, heartless man!" exclaimed Margaret, rising, with her face flushed, to quit the room; but Robert placed himself in her way, saying, "Your father wishes you to stay here until he returns.--Why do you call me unfeeling, Margaret? I did not intend to either offend or grieve you."

Margaret returned and seated herself, but when he again asked the question, she replied, "If my father wishes me to remain, I will remain; but I remain not to converse with you, Robert Woodhall. I tell you, I doubt you--nay, more, I do not believe you. More than once I have detected you in saying things that were untrue; and I will now know, as soon as my father returns, whether it was his wish or will that I should remain with one whose society is unpleasant to me."

The pale, somewhat yellowish tinge of Robert Woodhall's face gave way to burning red. He felt that he was understood--unmasked by a woman--by a mere girl; and there is no offense so bitter to a villain as to have his character unveiled.

"I will repay you," he thought, "I will repay you!" but, at the same time, he would have given a good deal to have escaped from the room, in order to meet Lord Woodhall ere he saw his daughter, and to guard against the questions she might ask. He suffered some minutes to pass however, for the purpose of covering his maneuver, but then rising, he said, "Your father is longer than I expected. I fear I must go; I have an engagement."

Grief is a great teacher of the human heart; and Margaret had learned much since first she was presented to the reader. "Your pardon Robert Woodhall," she said; "you stay here till my father returns. What you have told me is either true or false. If it be true, you are bound to remain with me, as I was commanded to remain with you--Nay, not a word! Sit down, or I will call those who will make you."

She was nearer to the door than himself, and she moved toward it, and laid her hand upon the latch.

Before Robert Woodhall could recover from his surprise, the voice of the old lord sounded below, and the next moment his step was heard upon the stairs. Margaret stood quietly by the door. Her cousin did not venture to move; but few human hearts have felt the rage which filled his at that moment. A minute after, Lord Woodhall entered the room, and ere he could speak of any thing else, Margaret exclaimed, with a boldness unusual with her, especially in speaking to her parent, "My dear lord and father, this gentleman tells me that it was your command I should remain here with him till you returned. I beseech you tell me whether this is true or false; I do not believe it."

"False!" cried the old lord, sharply; "I never said such a word. What is the meaning of this, sir?"

"Only a little lover's artifice, my dear lord," replied Robert Woodhall, with a pleasant smile; "I did but stretch your words a little. You said I was to go and stay with her till you came back, and I chose to read your meaning that she was to stay with me."

"Lover!" said Margaret, with a bitter emphasis, and was turning to quit the room, when the old lord detained her by the hand, saying, "Oh, is that all? Stay, stay, Margaret, this is no very unforgiveable offense--stay! I have news for you."

"I hope good news, my lord," said Robert Woodhall. "The king, I trust, has entered into your views?"

"As warmly as heart could wish," replied the old nobleman. "Feversham has received his commands to order Colonel Kirke to occupy Danvers's New Church with his regiment, and to arrest the fugitive. The object is to be concealed, and the occupation of the house and village to pass for a mere military operation till they have got the murderer in their hands; otherwise he might escape us again, boy, in the troubled state of the country."

"Your lordship calls him murderer," said Robert Woodhall, quietly, eager to make mischief between the parent and the child, "but Mistress Margaret objects to my use of that term, and says she does not believe Ralph Woodhall committed the act."

"How is that--how is that?--not believe?" cried Lord Woodhall, turning toward his daughter, and dropping her hand.

"The Duke of Norfolk does not believe it, my lord," replied Margaret; "I received a letter from him this morning with the trinkets I left behind me in my room at Norwich. He says that he has reason to believe some great mistake has been committed, and that my cousin Ralph is quite free from all participation in the deed."

"Who does he suspect, then?" demanded Lord Woodhall.

"I will bring you his letter, my father," replied Margaret, fixing her eyes firmly upon the face of Robert Woodhall; "you will there see that he suspects a very different person, and will comprehend why to remain in that gentleman's society was most unpleasant to your daughter."

"What does he say--what does he say? No need of the letter just now," cried the impetuous old lord; "I can read that afterward: tell me the substance of what he says."

"I have told you part, my father," replied Margaret; "but he adds that it is clearly proved there was no quarrel between Ralph and poor Henry, though there was between Ralph and Master Robert Woodhall. He says they parted perfectly friends at supper; that they never met afterward during the whole night; that no challenge was ever actually delivered to Ralph; and that he has good reason to believe, from circumstances which have lately come to his knowledge, that my cousin never returned to Norwich after he himself had sent him away to escort Lady Danvers on her journey. He says, indeed, that to have done so, in the circumstances of which he is personally cognizant, implies almost an impossibility. The duke adds," continued Margaret, with a voice which trembled a little at the gravity of the words she was about to utter, "that undoubtedly Robert Woodhall attempted to produce a quarrel between Ralph and my poor brother; and he remarks that Henry's death could be of no possible advantage to Ralph, but that it might be to other persons."

Lord Woodhall glared round with a look of bewildered rage; but Robert caught the ball at the rebound with great skill. "His grace of Norfolk must think that you take a great interest, Mistress Margaret, in your *poor* cousin Ralph," he said; "but that is of no matter. Strange as it may seem, my dear lord, I am very glad that this foolish suspicion has been so plainly stated. An innocent man laughs at such things; he does not run away from investigation. Indeed, did not the duke's dislike of myself blind him, he could not fail to see how ridiculous all this is. Henry's own letter to the duke himself, which you have seen, shows that the challenge was given and accepted; and I can prove easily, not only that I never quitted my room that night, but that I did all in my power to dissuade Henry from the course that he was following. He was headstrong, and would have his own way. My servant can prove many of these facts. He is in the house; call him up and examine him. I wish no previous interview with him; I have no lesson to teach him."

The man was called; but he had already taught himself his own lesson; and he mentioned those facts only, of all that occurred at Norwich, which could show his master's character in the fairest light.

Lord Woodhall was quite satisfied, but Margaret was not. She had a sort of instinct in this case, and it led her right.

CHAPTER XXVII

Some days had passed at Danvers's New Church; and I must not dwell upon their passing. "Time warns me to be brief," as worthy clergymen say in long-composed sermons, where no reference to time existed in the act of composition. But time, and the end of the volume apparent to the view (which are to an author what time and the end of life ought to be to every man), warn me that I *must* be brief. Several days had passed at Danvers's New Church since Hortensia Danvers and Ralph Woodhall had entered that house arm in arm. Fill up the time as you will, reader. I can not dwell upon it. Very little passed of any consequence. We well know how bulky trifles will become when we are trying to pack closely the portmanteau of the present. A child's toy will take up more room than a volume of philosophy, and a blown India rubber ball occupy ten times more space than all the essays of John Locke. Those days had been filled with trifles. They formed a period of little or no progress. Country gentlemen had come in--esquires, and justices, and barons, and lords of high degree--to offer their services and compliments to the young, graceful, beautiful Lady Danvers, upon her return to her ancestral home. Country gossips had flocked thither to see, and hear, and know all that was going on; for certain reports had been carried about by the tongue of Rumor as to the sojourn of a young and handsome cavalier within the walls of Danvers's New Church.

At first Hortensia was somewhat puzzled what to do; for, with all her readiness--which proceeded more from simple purity and rectitude of purpose, enlightened by a bright, clear mind, than any worldly wisdom--she could not help feeling that she was commencing a struggle against a very muddy but turbulent torrent called the world, which would require a stout heart to stem it.

If she refused to receive such visitors, she was certain to subject herself to misconstruction. If she appeared with Ralph, there was still a danger of misconstruction, and peril to him likewise. She resolved to receive them all; and she did so, with quiet ease, and calm, though somewhat cold demeanor, which rebuked curiosity, and put calumny at fault. She would not suffer Ralph, however, to appear, impressing upon him strongly the necessity of concealment for his own safety, and taking such means as her knowledge of the country, and her more general experience of the world and the world's ways, enabled her to adopt of finding some means of conveying him secretly to the coast of Holland. Every morning servants on horseback went out to different ports on the western shores of England. Every evening servants returned, bringing no satisfactory tidings. Nearly one half of life is consumed in emptinesses, and three quarters, at least, in emptinesses and disappointments taken together. So it was at Danvers's New Church.

But still a little progress was made--a very little. Nevertheless, it is worth while recording. It may be asked if Hortensia, when the consciousness came upon her that she had to swim, as it were, against the stream of the world's opinion, did not sometimes say to herself, "Ralph's arm may at any time save me, and bear me safe to shore."

I do not think she did so, for it was a subject upon which she did not like her thoughts to rest. She was fain to believe, and did believe, that she was actuated by no feeling but one, a sincere, unmingled desire of freeing a man whom she esteemed, the son of her mother's best friend, from perils and difficulties undeserved. And yet there were various little incidents-- very indefinite--very intangible--a word dropped row and then--a deep fit of thought after the name of Margaret Woodhall had been mentioned- -a grave and solemn earnestness of manner in protesting that nothing on earth could have induced him to draw his sword against Henry Woodhall, which, like the light gusts of the evening wind, bringing up misty clouds upon the western sky, cast over Hortensia's contemplated future a vague, uncertain gloom, from which she was pleased to turn her eyes, and rejoice in the sunshine of the present, when she and Ralph spent the evening alone together in her wide, tastefully-furnished withdrawing-room, sometimes reading authors whom we venerate as the fathers of the poetry and prose of England, but who were then hardly consecrated by the hand of Time; or singing, and playing upon instruments then in vogue, music which might strike us, perhaps, in the present day, as poor in the harmony, but which had a freshness, a vigor in the melody that is rarely to be found in this all-steaming age.

True, in the darkness of the night, Hortensia would often lay awake for hours, not indulging in apprehensive or regretful thoughts--not even, like the patriarch, struggling with the angel of Hope to win a boon at last from the Giver of all happiness, but watching, like a warder upon a tower, to prevent the entrance of any of the enemies that flocked continually forward to obtain admittance into the fortress of the mind.

Sometimes, wearied with this dark, silent strife, she would wake her maid, who now slept in the same room, and bid her strike a light and give her a book to while away the tedious hours till daylight came. This done, the maid would creep again to bed, and fall in a moment into dreamless, heavy slumber, the envy of the highborn lady lying near.

It was thus one night--I call the period of darkness night--when Hortensia, after reading for some time, placed the book beneath her pillow, raised her fair, beautiful arm, as children will do, under her head, and with the rich curls of her unfilleted hair falling over it, and partly shrouding her face, was trying to obtain a brief, refreshing draught of that sweet, calm, morning sleep, which often visits us just in the sober-colored dawn of day, when she heard the trotting of a horse; and the moment after, the great bell rang sharply.

No one answered, and several minutes passed; but then the bell rang again; and shortly after, slow and tardy steps were heard pacing the marble hall toward the great door.

A gray light was by this time stealing into the room; and Hortensia, partly roused again, exclaimed, between sleep and waking, "Alice! Alice! some one is ringing the great bell. Throw on some clothes, and go and ask what is the matter."

The girl was already awake, for she had slept long and well; and the ringing of the bell had roused her. She was soon partly dressed and gone, and Hortensia heard her talking with the old porter over the balustrade of the stair-case. The interrogatory seemed to deviate into a gossip; and when the maid returned, saying, "Nothing but some letters, my lady, brought by a messenger for Mr. Ralph Woodhall," Hortensia was fast asleep, and unconscious of the words spoken.

When she again awoke, some two hours afterward, she made further inquiries, and on being informed of what had occurred, hastened to dress herself as rapidly as possible.

On descending to the breakfast-room (or little hall, as it was called at that time, in her dwelling), she found three letters addressed to Ralph Woodhall lying undelivered on the table. The porter had not thought it worth while to wake the young gentleman, he said; and Hortensia at once dispatched a messenger to her guest, who appeared soon after with the letters open in his hand.

"Any news? any tidings?" asked Hortensia, eagerly. "The sight of those letters frightens me; for it is clear some one has discovered the place of your retreat, and our secret is no longer safe."

"It has been discovered, indeed," replied Ralph, "but how I know not. However, two of these letters are to warn me that this place is no longer safe for me. There is one of them."

As he spoke, he gave into the hands of Lady Danvers a sheet of somewhat coarse paper, on which were written a few lines in a bold hand. She read them attentively, and then, raising her eyes to his face, inquired, "Who is this person who signs himself Moraber?"

"I can hardly tell you," replied Ralph; "he is a strange, solitary being, of whose history I know nothing, except that he was a college companion of the Duke of Norfolk--gave himself up, from a very early period, to the study of judicial astrology, and seems, by that or some other means, to have obtained a very strange degree of knowledge regarding the fortunes and feelings of a great multitude of persons. You will see in another letter, which I will show you in a moment, that he takes no slight interest in my own affairs, and has done me justice in matters where even those who loved me well were inclined to doubt me."

"But from whom is that very long letter? if my curiosity be pardonable," asked Hortensia, pointing to a sheet of foolscap closely covered.

"This is from my good father," replied Ralph, with a smile; "and if you will take the trouble of deciphering the first few sentences, you will see, dear lady, that one brought up in such principles was not likely to take his cousin's life in a duel."

Lady Danvers took the letter and read what follows:

"Dear Son,--I have been in a state of anguish of mind not to be described from Wednesday last, the twenty-second of the month, till this present Tuesday, the twenty-eighth. I had heard, and that from authority which appeared not to be doubted, that you had been mad enough to engage in a duel, notwithstanding all the principles which I have endeavored to instill into your mind; that you had killed your adversary, and that the slain man was your cousin Henry. Now I have ever held, and have endeavored to teach you to hold, that dueling is not only murder, but murder of the most aggravated kind. The slaughter of the man may take place by accident--by a hasty blow in a moment of passion--in self-defense, when suddenly assailed--or in a general tumult or commotion; and in these cases the law of man--and, let us not doubt, the law of God also--deals leniently. But in the case of a duel, there is no sound and legitimate excuse whatsoever for the man who slays another. He has time for reflection, therefore the act is deliberate and premeditated. He goes out to kill, and he kills. Nor is it any mitigation whatsoever of his offense that his adversary came there with the same purpose toward himself; for the crime of the one can never excuse the crime of the other. Still less is it an excuse that dueling is a custom of society; for every Christian and every philosopher must perceive that this custom of society is in itself a criminal one, a proof of its barbarism rather than its civilization; and he who sanctions it by his example, commits, in addition to the particular crime of murder, a general offense against society and mankind by encouraging and perpetuating a criminal habit which all good men should unite to put down. Thus, to the eyes of God, and to the eyes of all reasoning men likewise, the act of killing another in a duel is the most aggravated kind of murder; for the evil is not confined to the offense, but spreads round as a diffusible poison, affecting detrimentally the whole mass of society. There are but three occasions in which any man is justified in taking the life of another: in actual defense of his own life--in defense of his country--and in obedience to the laws of his country. All other cases are murder. Now you may easily conceive, my dear son, how much pain it gave me to think for one whole week that my son was a murderer. I have this day, however, received from a person calling himself Moraber, whom you must have heard of in our neighborhood, the most strong and solemn assurance that you are innocent of this terrible offense--that you did not fight your cousin, and that he was slain by some other hand. I believe the information to be correct, for my informant is above suspicion; but yet I beseech you, if it be possible, write me the same assurance, that my mind may be freed completely from anguish such as I have never known--nay, not even when it pleased Heaven to take from me your beloved mother."

The writing went on for several pages further; but Lady Danvers stopped there, and returned the letter to Ralph, saying, "I agree with him entirely, Ralph. But to return to this Moraber. What can he know of any thing that is taking place here? He tells you that immediate flight is necessary to your safety; that you have but two days to execute it after the receipt of his letter; yet the letter is itself nearly a fortnight old."

"I have still surer information than that," replied Ralph. "Here is another letter, which I will show to no eyes but your own, dear Lady Danvers. After all your kindness and generosity toward me, however, I can keep back no secret of my heart from you."

Again Lady Danvers took the letter he offered, and read. It was brief, hastily written in a woman's hand, and to the following effect:

"An opportunity has suddenly presented itself, dear Ralph, of sending to you a few lines, and I seize it, first, to assure you that, notwithstanding all that men accuse you of, I do not believe one word of the tale. Your love for Margaret would never suffer you to slay her brother. Secondly, I write to tell you that dangers of various kinds menace you where you are. Your place of concealment has been discovered. Orders will be dispatched this very night to the troops marching against the Duke of Monmouth, to occupy Danvers's New Church as a military post, and apprehend you if you are found there. Fly immediately! and, if possible, till the storm is passed, take refuge across the sea. The dear and beautiful lady with whom you are will doubtless be able to provide you with the means of escape, and if so, will merit more than, even at present, the eternal gratitude of your own

"Margaret."

Strange and beautiful were the changes of expression which came over the face of Hortensia Danvers as she read those words. The very first sentence called the warm blood rushing into her cheek, like the light of the morning sun kindling the white clouds on the horizon. Then the glow faded away again. Back, back to the heart every warm, thrilling drop was withdrawn, and her beautiful face remained pale as that of a marble statue, while her eyes fixed upon the lines as if every word had been a fate to her who read. Even after she had done, she held up the letter still in her hand, gazing at it in deep silence.

"I must tell you, dear Lady Danvers," said Ralph, in his inexperience not reading her looks aright, "I must tell you that my cousin Margaret and myself have loved each other warmly from childhood, and that it was the hope--a hope almost insane--of winning her father's consent to our union that led me forth to seek my fortune in the wide world--"

"Here--take it! take it!" said Hortensia, putting the letter in his hand; "I will be back directly; all this news confounds me; I must think--alone and in quiet. I will be back soon, and we will decide upon something."

Again the warm blood rushed into her cheek, as if some sudden thought, for which she took shame to herself, crossed her mind secretly, and she added, in a faltering voice, "To have my house occupied by troops! I will be back presently."

For nearly half an hour Ralph walked up and down the hall alone; but then, with a slow and somewhat languid step, Hortensia rejoined him, and seated herself near the table. Not a trace of tears was upon her cheek; she had evidently not been weeping, but she was still as pale as alabaster, though her eyes beamed with even more light than usual. Was it that there had been a deadly struggle of passions in her heart? that she had been the victor? that the light of triumph was in her eyes, but that the exhaustion of combat well-nigh overpowered even the conqueror? Perhaps so; but certainly she betrayed no evidence of the struggle in her manner toward Ralph. She was as kind, as warm, as eager as ever.

He had still the roll of letters in his hand, and, pointing to them, she said, with her sweet smile and musical voice, "I must do something, Ralph, to win this dear girl's gratitude, as she trusts to me. Let me see the letter again."

He gave it to her. She read it through, and then murmuring, "May she be happy!" pressed her lips upon Margaret's name. When she gave it back to Ralph, there was a single tear upon it, and that was all she shed.

"Now," said Hortensia, gayly, "we must to counsel, to see if we can not out-maneuver our enemies. There is further down the coast a little port called Seaton, where there used to be large and very safe boats which they called luggers. I was a great favorite there with the good fishermen when I was a child, and methinks, if we can reach that port, it would be very easy to hire one of these boats, if not to convey you to the coast of France or Holland, at least to land you at some other English port where you may find a vessel ready to sail."

"Perhaps I had better set out at once," said Ralph; "my horse is quite fresh now, and, with some one to guide me, I could reach the port rapidly."

"No, no, that will never do," replied Lady Danvers; "the country is all covered with troops, and you will be stopped to a certainty. I will tell you how we must manage. During the day we will send forth people in all directions to ascertain what roads are clear. Then, toward evening, we will set out in my carriage, as it were, for an hour's drive round the place. No one dare stop me; and after that we shall have darkness to befriend us. We can take the roads we know to be open, and as your friend Moraber gives you two whole days, we shall be within the limit."

"Nay, nay," said Ralph, "I will not have you peril yourself for me. That must not be, dear Lady Danvers."

"Well, I will convoy you part of the way," said Hortensia. "Let your servant ride on to Seaton, obtain information there, and meet us on the road. One of my people can mount your horse; and when you need the beast, the man can get upon the carriage to return. This will be the surest way; and if we obtain good intelligence, I shall run no risk, nor you either, I trust, Ralph."

So was it settled; and the same evening Ralph and Hortensia began a pilgrimage which will require a chapter to itself.

CHAPTER XXVIII

There had been very few visitors to Danvers's New Church during the morning. Something had kept every one away but the parson of the parish, and an old lady of the village, who held a sort of middle station between the gentry and the yeomanry of the country, and prided herself upon knowing all the affairs of both. Trustworthy servants, however, had been coming and going all the day; and they brought intelligence which showed that a considerable circuit must be taken round the town of Axminster, in order to avoid the two contending parties in the western counties, then actually coming to hard blows with each other.

About four o'clock Gaunt Stilling set off on horseback for Seaton, the way to which he knew well, and his business at which place was explained to him easily. He was to meet Lady Danvers and Ralph a little to the eastward of Axminster, and let them know the result of his inquiries at Seaton; but his instructions were totally independent of the various scouts which had been sent forth, and the rumors which Hortensia received from the latter were somewhat contradictory, especially toward the close of the day.

Nevertheless, about an hour before sunset, the great lumbering carriage was brought round to the door; the lady and Ralph entered it; and, followed by several armed servants on horseback, they took their way toward the upper gates, by a road not quite so much frequented as either the lower road or the foot-path which crossed the park below the house. It was a soft and not unpleasant evening, such as one often finds in that climate, with a misty, hazy sort of air, through which the sun struggled from time to time, shedding a rosy light over the whole scene around.

Hortensia was somewhat silent, and evidently anxious--I do not mean to say frightened, for she was unconscious of any personal danger--but the perils of her companion seemed to weigh upon her; and when she did converse, her whole conversation consisted of inquiries, consultations, and advice as to the best means of passing on undetected till an assured place of safety should be reached. Every consideration seemed merged in that one. There was no longer the light, lark-like flight of fancy which had often, in the leisure hours preceding, carried away the mind of Ralph Woodhall into far etherial fields of space; there was no longer the calm, thoughtful, yet not unimaginative wandering of the spirit through more familiar scenes filled with association, where, side by side, they had gone on over the leas, and through the meadows of ordinary life, drawing as much essence of dream from a cowslip, or a primrose, or a violet, as bolder efforts of the fancy would extract from the high mountain or the floating cloud. All was now hard, dry matter of necessity and business. That was the only difference between the communion of the preceding days and that of the present; but it was great.

The edge of the sky grew rosy; the sun set; the night came. The misty clouds, from which had dropped, occasionally, large tears upon the earth, passed away like gloomy thoughts from a bright mind; and star by star came out in the refreshed sky, and looked down upon the earth in melancholy calmness.

Alone, and side by side, Hortensia Danvers and Ralph Woodhall wended slowly on. I must not pretend to look into her bosom; the eye of man never did. There may be some women who can divine what mysterious things were passing therein, but even of women, not all.

It were vain to say that at that moment--which to him seemed the real parting moment--Ralph Woodhall did not feel many deep, many strong emotions at the thought of being severed, perhaps forever, from one so beautiful, so gentle, so generous, so kind. It is too rare to find pure, disinterested friendship on the earth for one of a high heart to meet with it untouched. He forgot himself--his fate--his peril--the pressing urgency of petty circumstances--the momentary dangers that beset his way--the trifling incidents that at every step might change his destiny for good or ill. He thought only of Hortensia; and yet with such thoughts that Margaret might have seen them all, joined them, and shared them.

There was a deep silence for a considerable length of time. Had there been any other soul within the carriage, not sharing in their thoughts, to him it would have seemed very long. To them it was all too brief for the crowded feelings they forced into it.

At length Ralph could refrain no more. He took Hortensia's hand in his: he pressed it to his lips, and said, "Oh, dear Lady Danvers, how can I ever thank you sufficiently--how can I ever explain to you all I feel. Your kindness--your many acts of kindness, have come upon me like a torrent, so rapidly that I have had no time to breathe or think till this moment; and now, when I still feel the full force of all, we are going to part for God knows how long!"

"Hush!" said Hortensia, in a low, agitated voice; "hush!" and for a single instant she leaned her fair brow upon his shoulder; then raising it calmly, she added, "Ralph, my dear brother, we must not think of any thing which can withdraw our attention from the present perilous hour. If you escape happily and well--as God in his great mercy grant--tell your Margaret, with Hortensia's love, that she did all in her power to save and aid you--nay, tell her," she added, in a more cheerful tone--though there was a touch of fluttering effort about it too--"nay, tell her that in after years, perhaps, when storms have vanished and the skies are clear, Hortensia will come to visit you both in your happiness and claim the gratitude she promised, and, then rejoicing, will talk of days of sorrow and of peril passed away."

Silence fell upon them again. Was that a sob? It was very like one.

Whatever it was, it was drowned the moment after in the rattle of musketry; there was a flash, too--distant, but near enough to show suddenly the tower of a large Cathedral-looking church, long lines of houses, and stacks of chimneys, and undulating hedgerows, and wavy-outlined trees. The next moment--not in one volley, but in an irregular running fire--shot after shot was heard, sometimes single, sometimes two or three together, sometimes as if from whole platoons, while quick reiterated flashes ran along all the hedgerows within sight, and then the roar of a cannon or two was heard, with a shrill sound of fifes and drums.

In an instant Ralph's hand was upon the door of the carriage, and before Hortensia could beseech him to forbear, he had sprang out.

"Here, Jones, give me my horse!" he cried. "Turn round the carriage, and away back with all speed! What! is the lane too narrow? On before there seems a wider space. Stay! I will ride on and see. Coachman, you must get your mistress out of this peril as speedily as possible. Come after me slowly; some one put the cushions against the front windows; you, men on horseback, gather round the carriage--take no part with any one, but defend your lady."

Then dashing forward, he was for a moment lost in the darkness, till his voice was heard shouting, "Here! here is room to turn;" and the coachman hurried on his horses at the utmost speed to a place where a wide, open space, with a gate leading into a field, seemed to give a chance of wheeling round the lumbering vehicle.

At that moment, however, just as the four horses, somewhat restive with the noise and confusion, were plunging and rearing, and a man on foot was striving to turn the heads of the leaders round, the whole evolution was interrupted by a number of men in military garb, but not array, running as if for life up the lane, and dashing against the horses and the carriage.

One of the fugitives exclaimed, evidently mistaking Ralph, who had his sword drawn, for some one else, "All's lost, my lord, all's lost--Monmouth has won the day, and the men are running like devils."

Thus saying, he flung his musket into the ditch and ran on, only to be succeeded by another still more terrified, who had already denuded himself of cap and weapons, and was struggling to get out of a military jacket which seemed to cling to him like the coat of Nessus. He cried, "Monmouth! Monmouth! The Protestant religion forever, and d--n papacy, and prelacy, and the pope of Rome!"

"Here! draw up across the lane!" cried Ralph, addressing the horsemen who accompanied the carriage; "keep a sufficient space clear for the coach to turn; let another footman go to the head of the horses--get them quickly round--soothe them, soothe them!"

At that moment a sharp volley came up the lane, and one of the balls rattled against the carriage. Ralph spurred instantly toward the side, but, ere he reached it, his horse staggered and sunk upon its haunches.

"You are not hurt, Hortensia?" he said, springing from the saddle. "Oh God! you are not hurt?"

"No, no," she cried, "but you're wounded, Ralph."

"Not in the least," he answered; "it is but the horse;" and, running forward, he aided with better skill in turning the carriage round.

While thus employed, a party of horsemen of distinguished mien galloped up the lane, and one of them, with a hat loaded with plumes, paused for an instant to ask, "Whose carriage is this? In Heaven's name, how came you here?"

"We were going to Axminster," replied Ralph, "but suppose it is in the hands of the Duke of Monmouth. We can hardly get the carriage round."

"As difficult as I have found it to take Axminster with two regiments of boobies and a handful of plowmen," replied the other. "I fear we can not stay to help you. If you fall into the hands of Monmouth, give him the Duke of Albemarle's compliments, and say I hope we shall meet again some day soon."

"Come, come, my lord, this is no time for jesting," said another of the horsemen; and the party rode on, leaving the ground clearer than it had been before.

A few moments only were now required to turn the carriage completely; but the lane was deep and muddy, and little progress was likely to be made, while it seemed certain that pursued and pursuers would still be urging their course along the very path which it was necessary to follow in order to reach Danvers's New Church.

Ralph gave a look at his horse, but the poor beast was now stretched out with his head flat in the clay, and it was necessary to drag him out of the road before the carriage could pass. This consumed some time, and several fugitives hurried by, exclaiming as they went, "They are coming! They are coming! You had better make haste."

At length the carcass of the horse was removed, and, taking the pistols from the holsters, Ralph approached the side of the carriage, saying, "I know not whether I can best give you protection by mounting another horse and riding by your side, or--"

"No, no, come in, come in," said Hortensia. "I need some one with me--I am foolishly frightened."

Ralph instantly opened the door, but, turning to the men ere he entered, he said, "Draw round as close as possible; each keep a cocked pistol in his hand. Bid every one stand off, saying we are peaceful travelers avoiding the affray. Be firm, but forbear any violence. Now, coachman, drive on as fast as you can go."

Thus saying, he entered the carriage and seated himself by Hortensia's side, while the coachman plied the whip with terrified vehemence, and the horses dashed on quicker than probably they had ever been known to go before. In the rumbling and rattling of the wheels, and their grating through the stones and mud, the sounds from without--although there was still firing, and shouting, and running going on all around--were not very distinctly heard; but there were some clear, sweet, musical tones fell distinctly enough upon Ralph's ear: "Oh, Ralph, tell me--assure me that you are not hurt," said Hortensia. "I am sure I saw you reel upon the horse as if a ball had struck you."

"It was the horse who staggered and fell," replied Ralph; "I can assure you I am not hurt at all."

"Thank God!" said Hortensia, with a deep sigh; and Ralph went on to add, "I feared you might be hurt, for I heard a bullet strike the carriage."

"Did it?" said Hortensia; "I was not aware of it. It did not come near me; and I was looking out, and thinking how wildly you men expose yourselves unnecessarily, more than of any thing else."

"Not unnecessarily," replied Ralph, "depend upon it; it needs some one to command under such circumstances."

"And that you did right well, most certainly," replied Lady Danvers, assuming a tone of gayety not very congenial to her feelings; "I could have fancied you a general, and think, indeed, you should have been a soldier. But what are we to do now? What is to become of us?"

"We must go back to Danvers's New Church at once," replied Ralph. "We have no other choice; and I must try my fortune alone early to-morrow morning. It is strange we have heard nothing of Gaunt Stilling."

Hortensia did not reply, and after a moment Ralph added, "The firing seems further off now, to the east of the town. I strongly suspect Monmouth will not pursue his advantage--his troops are too raw. Is any thing the matter? You do not speak."

"No, Ralph, no," she answered; "my heart is very full with many mingled feelings; some joy--as, for instance, at our escape from danger--some apprehension, some sorrow; but I trust that to-morrow will bring better fortune, and that, ere night, I shall hear that you are safe, Ralph."

She called him Ralph twice in the same short answer, and it was pleasant to his ear; but she had remarked that from the moment when he sprang from the carriage he had given her no name whatever, except once that of Hortensia. He would not--he dared not, call her so again, after the first excitement was over, and yet, with the warm sound upon his lips, he could not bring them to utter a colder name. Their thoughts were both upon the same subject at the same moment.

The sound of the firing had nearly ceased. The fugitives who were still passing were few and scattered, and the moon was rising slowly in the east, and silvering over the heaven behind a wooded hill, and a tall, ancient-looking farmhouse upon a high, stony bank, when suddenly a loud voice cried, "Halt! who goes there?"

The coachman instantly pulled in his reins, and Ralph, putting his head out of the carriage, replied, "Friends! whose post is this? Standoff, for the men are armed, and we want no more confusion."

"What friends?" demanded the sentry.

"Lady Danvers and her servants," replied Ralph, knowing the announcement could do no one any harm but himself. "She is seeking to return to her own house, as she finds she can not get to Axminster. Who commands at this post, fellow, I ask again?"

"George Monk, duke of Albemarle," replied the militiaman, stoutly; "and, I can tell you, you must stop till he says that you can go on, for if you come a step further, I will shoot one of your great coach horses."

CHAPTER XXIX

The sentinel who spoke the words with which the last chapter concluded was placed in a little hollow way, or cut in the steep bank through which the lane had to wind on in order to pass over the hill. He was evidently a country boor of the Duke of Albemarle's militia, unacquainted with military service, and as likely as not to put his threat of shooting one of the coach-horses in execution. But before Ralph could think of what was next to be done, or Lady Danvers could say a word, a figure was seen to drop down from the bank behind the poor soldier, seize him by the throat, and with very little ceremony wrench his musket out of his hands, taking special care to allow him no opportunity of discharging it in the struggle.

"A pretty fellow you are, to stop a lady's carriage on the king's highway," cried a voice which Ralph recognized right well. "There! go and tell the duke what you've been doing, and get well punished for your pains. He never told you to stop Lady Danvers's carriage, I'm sure."

Thus saying, Gaunt Stilling shook the powder out of the pan of the man's musket, and, giving him a kick behind, sent him running up toward the farmhouse I have mentioned.

"Quick, my lady," said the servant; "you had better drive back to Danvers's New Church as fast as possible. You can not pass any other way; I will overtake you soon; jog along, Master Coachman."

He sprang up the bank again as he spoke, and the carriage moved forward.

It is probable that the Duke of Albemarle, who was of a more jovial temper than his renowned father, only laughed at the sentry's mishap. Certain it is, he gave no orders for pursuing the carriage of Lady Danvers; and Ralph and his fair companion continued their journey uninterrupted. That journey was slow in its progress, however, and it was nearly two o'clock in the morning before the carriage entered the park. The moon, which had risen clear, had become dim and cloudy--not altogether obscured, indeed, but partially vailed in thin clouds, amid which her rays formed a broad yellow halo, auguring ill of the coming weather. The beautiful park itself, the dark trees, the solemn old house standing on its eminence, all had a sad and gloomy aspect in that sort of dreary twilight, and with a wearied frame, and a heart not happy, the buoyant spirit of Hortensia fell. She sat silent and thoughtful by Ralph's side, and more than once felt that she could weep and find relief in tears if she were alone.

She restrained them, however, and strove to look cheerful when Ralph at length aided her to alight at her own door.

"Ah, my lady," said Mr. Drayton, "I'm glad to see you back, for rumors have come in of a battle near Axminster."

"In the midst of which we have been, Drayton," replied his lady.

"Oh, a mere skirmish, madam," said Gaunt Stilling, advancing from the hall door; "but I have some news to give you and my master, for which I will crave your attention as soon as may be."

"Come in here, come in here," said Hortensia, turning toward the little room in which Ralph had made his principal abode during her absence.

"If you are going to use the coach to-morrow, my lady," said the coachman, coming up the steps, "I had better get the carpenter and the blacksmith up at once, for two bullets have gone right into the hind axle-tree."

"We can use some other lighter carriage," said Lady Danvers, thoughtfully; "the vis-à-vis--"

"Lord bless you, my lady, it would be knocked all to pieces." said the coachman; "and, besides, that can't be, for it is in Lunnun, and all the other carriages, for that matter."

"Well, then, Harrison, get this mended as well as you can, without sending up to the village. Now, Master Stilling;" and, accompanied by Ralph, she bade the man who followed shut the door.

"I'm very sorry, sir," said Gaunt Stilling, addressing his master, "that I could not get back in time to stop your going on; but I was met and turned at every point, like a hare by the grayhounds, so that I was three times as long as I need otherwise have been. However, it's quite useless going to Seaton; for an embargo has been laid on all the boats, and the Tory magistrates are strong in the village. I have found out, however, from some of the old boatmen, that there is a much better chance in the Bristol Channel. You mustn't go to Bristol itself, for Lord Pembroke is there, and he has probably got his orders with regard to you; but if you can cut across to any of the little ports, or to Bridgewater, you are sure to find a ship, and seamen ready enough. It will cost a good sum, though, they say."

"That matters not." said Lady Danvers. "But are you sure that he can pass?"

"There is nothing sure in this world, dear lady," said Ralph, "unless it be woman's kindness; but in such matters we must take our chance, do the best we can, and leave the rest to the will of Heaven."

"If I could have a fresh horse to-morrow, my lady," said Gaunt Stilling, "I will undertake to make sure of a path. My own beast will rest in the mean time, and my master and I can set out at night--only it would be a great deal better for you to stay here, if I may be so bold, for we shall get on twice as last on horseback, and not draw so many eyes."

"But it may be dangerous for him to remain here," said Hortensia; and, looking round to Ralph, she asked, in a low voice, "May I tell him what we have heard?"

"Oh yes, we can confide in him entirely," replied Ralph; adding, "The truth is, Stilling, we have information that this house is to be occupied by the king's troops, with a special injunction to apprehend me if I am found within its walls. Orders have been already sent to Lord Feversham to that effect."

"Lord Feversham is a gentleman, if not a soldier," answered Gaunt Stilling, with a laugh, "and he will do every thing ceremoniously. It would be no hard matter to bamboozle him. I would undertake to pass my master upon him for a cardinal in disguise--but I thought, sir, you had two whole days to come and go upon?"

"What! then you have heard from our friend in Lincolnshire too?" said Ralph.

"Yes, sir," replied the man, "and you may depend upon what he says. Lord Feversham is near three days' march upon the right--at least he was this morning; and if you can but keep yourself still and quiet in the house, there is no fear till I come back. He has no horse to spare; and he could not move infantry down in time, let them go as fast as they will. My plan was to let them get in advance of us, and then pass in their rear; but if they are to occupy this house, that will not do, and we must get in the rear of Monmouth instead. He is certain to move forward from Axminster, I suppose, after his successful skirmish, which he fought cleverly enough, if he had but known how to draw good use out of it afterward. I shall hear what he is doing, however, to-morrow, and if he marches toward Bath, as I think likely, we can easily cut across behind him, and get to the coast before a battle is fought."

"Do you think, then, he will fight a general battle?" asked Ralph.

"Oh, beyond doubt," answered Gaunt Stilling; "his men are bad enough, it is true, and badly armed too; but then it does not require old Greeks to beat a coxcomb like Feversham. They tell me, however, that Churchill is there, and Oglethorpe, and the Tangier regiment, and Dumbarton's; and it would require men who had smelt powder to fight those fellows."

There was a knock at the door at this moment, which interrupted the conversation for a time; the worthy steward, partly moved, perhaps, by curiosity, partly by anxiety for his lady's health, having come to inquire whether she would not take some refreshment after her fatiguing journey.

Brief consultation between Ralph and Hortensia during supper confirmed the resolution, already half taken, to follow the counsels of Gaunt Stilling, and Lady Danvers even submitted to the necessity of letting her young guest seek safety alone, without offering a word of objection to that which she believed would prove most favorable to his purpose.

A horse was accordingly ordered for Stilling, to be ready early on the following morning, and Ralph and Hortensia parted to seek repose.

The following day broke dull and heavily. Drops of rain fell from time to time; the sky was covered with a mantle of gray cloud. The whole aspect of Nature was well in harmony with the feelings of two dear friends about to part in peril and anxiety--to part, with a dark, uncertain future before them--without any knowledge to guide hope as to the when, and the where, and the how they were ever to meet again.

How often is it, even when hands are clasped, and eyes are bright with expectation, and lips murmur hopefully, "We shall soon meet again," that grim Fate stands sternly by, and puts in the dark word of contradiction, "Never!" But there are sadder partings--partings where the word of Fate is heard like thunder--and partings where, though the word be not actually spoken, yet the frown upon the forehead of Destiny fills the heart with dread, and wild, unhopeful doubt.

Such was the parting for which Hortensia prepared herself; but, happily for her, there was much to be done to fill up the intervening hours. The best horse of her stable had to be selected for Ralph's use to supply the place of that which he had lost; and then she had to persuade, to insist, to argue with him on the matter of receiving from her the means of hiring a vessel, at whatever cost, to carry him to the Dutch coast.

It is very strange; three days before, he would have had no hesitation whatsoever in profiting by her kindness at once; but now, he strove to avoid--to evade it. He assured her he had enough--that he had all he wanted, even while he was calculating in his own mind what amount he could obtain for the various trinkets he possessed. I will not try to look into his motives, for he would not look into them himself, although he carried his refusal almost to a point of coldness. It was only in the end, when Hortensia, with a faltering voice, said, "For Margaret's sake, Ralph," that he yielded even in part, and accepted assistance which she thought infinitely small.

She made up her mind, however, as to the means of foiling his false delicacy, as she called it; and she proceeded to execute her plan as soon as she was left alone. It is true that she would fain have had him stay with her the whole day. Each minute seemed valuable; they were the last drops in the flask. But he had to write a letter to his father; and though it was not long, the time that it occupied was the dullest of the day to Hortensia. To occupy a part of it, however, she sent for her steward as soon as she was alone.

"I know not, Master Drayton," she said, "what rents you have got in, but there are circumstances existing which will speedily require more money than I have brought with me. I dare say you recollect quite well my mother's friend, Mistress Woodhall, for you must have been with my father before her death."

"Oh, quite well, my lady," replied Mr. Drayton, "and a beautiful creature she was."

"Now this young gentleman that is here is her son," continued Hortensia, "and I feel toward him and would act toward him as a sister, if he would but let me. From circumstances not necessary to mention more than I have done before, it is needful that he should go to Holland as fast as possible. Now you can easily judge that to hire a vessel for that voyage will in these present times cost very dear. He thinks he has got quite enough. I know that he has not; but he will accept no more; therefore I must contrive to place the necessary funds in the hands of his servant Stilling, if you think the man is to be trusted."

"Oh, perfectly, my lady, perfectly," replied Mr. Drayton. "How much does your ladyship think will be required?"

"Not less than five hundred pounds," replied Lady Danvers.

"I have not so much in the house," said Mr. Drayton, somewhat surprised, "but I will easily procure it in the course of the day, and will get all that I can in gold, as most convenient to carry; but the tenants often pay their rents in great heaps of silver, which takes hours to count. When will it be needed, my lady?"

"Before nightfall, at all events," replied Lady Danvers. "When you have got it, Mr. Drayton, give it into the hands of the good man Stilling, for his master's use. You had better, perhaps, take a receipt for it, and tell him to employ it at once in case of any difficulty being made about the hire of a vessel. You are sure you can trust him?"

"Oh, quite sure," replied Mr. Drayton; "ha is very moody and somewhat passionate, but as honest a man as ever lived."

When this conversation was over, Hortensia passed the next half hour as best she might, sadly and thoughtfully enough, walking up and down the terrace before the house in despite of the drops of rain which fell from time to time. At length she was joined by Ralph, and strove steadily to appear cheerful, if not happy. They conversed of many things--some bright--some dark--some pertinent to the occasion and the circumstances--some wandering far away into realms where thought but too often did not keep pace with words.

Thus passed away hour after hour; and though, to vary the time, Hortensia and Ralph sat down to the usual meals, but little food was taken, and thought and conversation went on as before.

At length, about an hour before sunset, as they were sitting in a large, beautifully-furnished corner room, which commanded two views of the park, they heard the sound of a horse's feet coming at speed, and Ralph went to the window, saying, "Here is Stilling, returned, I suppose--No! it is a stranger, in a military dress."

The man pushed his horse up the terrace, and rang the great bell without dismounting; and Hortensia, opening the door of the room, which was near the head of the stairs, listened eagerly.

Slowly the old porter swung back the heavy house door, and a voice from without said, "Here is a letter addressed to the Right Honorable Lady Hortensia, Baroness Danvers--come, take it, for I must be on to Dorchester."

"Who is it from?" asked the old porter, not hurrying his steps in the least.

"From the Earl of Feversham," replied the soldier; "I have had hard work to find this out-of-the-way place."

"Won't you dismount and take a glass of ale?" inquired the porter; but the man replied, "No, no, I must not stay;" and, turning his horse, he trotted quickly away.

"These are tidings, Ralph," said Hortensia; "let us go and see what they are;" and, descending to the floor below, she met the old man with the letter in his hand. She refrained from opening it till she and Ralph were again alone, but then perused the few lines it contained eagerly. They were written in French, the earl's native language, and contained the usual amount of unmeaning compliment and prettiness. Stripped of all verbiage, however, the purport of the letter was to inform Lady Danvers, as in gallantry and duty bound, that the position of Lord Feversham's forces and his line of march compelled him, most unwillingly, to occupy her house and park as a military post of much importance. "I have given the strictest orders," continued the earl, "that your beautiful ladyship be not put to the slightest uneasiness or inconvenience; but as the receiving of a large body of infantry without notice might embarrass you, I have thought fit, in due devotion to your beautiful eyes, to overlook a little the strict line of military duty, in order to give you intimation a whole day beforehand, that the gallant Colonel Kirke, with the Tangier regiment, will crave your hospitality to-morrow at some period between the hours of four and seven, post meridian. We trust very soon to come at the end of these rebellions, and, in the mean time, I commend myself, my lady, to your good graces and favorable consideration. Feversham."

The eyes of Ralph and Hortensia instantly turned to the date of the letter, and, with a feeling of relief, they perceived that it had been written on the morning of the same day, so that four-and-twenty hours were clear before them.

"Do you know any thing of this Colonel Kirke?" asked Ralph.

"Nothing whatever," replied Hortensia; "but I know the Tangier regiment does not bear the best name in the world."

"Of its qualities," said Ralph, with a smile, "we can get full, though perhaps not unprejudiced information from Stilling when he returns, for he once served in this very corps. He can not be long now, I suppose."

Nor was he; for he must have passed Lord Feversham's messenger very nearly at the gates of the park, and the letter had not been read ten minutes when he entered the room.

"Well, Stilling, what news?" said his master; "I was beginning to be somewhat anxious for your return."

"Plenty of time, sir--plenty of time," said Gaunt Stilling, "and my news is good. A schooner or a brig can certainly be hired in the Channel, and at no very hard rate. The way, too, is open, for Monmouth is moving to the eastward, as I expected. The people behind him are all in his favor, and the magistrates are powerless. No warrants run there. Still, as parties of troops are scouring about here and there--no one knows where--it will be better to take the low horse road, which leaves Taunton and all those towns on one side. I was only afraid that some of the king's officers might have occupied the little hamlet at St. Mary's, in order to command that road, and that Monmouth might have left it behind unnoticed, thinking he could force it at any time. I find, however, that a part of Oglethorpe's corps, which was quartered there, retreated this morning for fear they should be cut off, so that the way is clear and easy to Bridgewater, where we shall be sure to hear of ships."

"We shall have ample time, too," replied Ralph, "for Colonel Kirke will certainly not be here before four o'clock to-morrow afternoon."

"Colonel Kirke! Colonel Kirke!" exclaimed Gaunt Stilling, with an air of consternation; "is he coming here?"

"So we are informed by Lord Feversham," said Hortensia. "Do you know any thing of that gentleman?"

"God's life! my lady, quite enough," replied Gaunt Stilling; "pray forgive me, but who is coming with him?"

"The Tangier regiment, which he commands, I believe," answered Lady Danvers. "You know something of them, Mr. Woodhall tells me."

"I know this, my lady," replied Gaunt Stilling, "that if they come here, and Kirke at their head, this house is no place for you, or any lady or poor girl either. It is impossible, sir," he continued, turning to Ralph, "that Lady Danvers can remain here, if Kirke and these Tangier men are coming. I served with them for three years in Africa; and if I had been inclined to disbelieve in the existence of a devil, I should have had no doubt afterward, for I had more than four hundred real ones all round me, and the arch fiend at their head. I beg your pardon, my lady, for speaking so plainly, especially as not long ago I was all for having you stay here, and letting Mr. Woodhall and myself find our way alone. But now I see it can not be done. You must not remain an hour, nay, not ten minutes in the same house with Kirke and the Tangier men. There is no knowing what they have done, and what they will dare to do--Oh, if I could but tell you all I know! You must either come with us, or let us see you to some place of safety."

Lady Danvers smiled somewhat sadly. "I fear I must not come with you," she said, "if you mean to Holland; but I have friends both in the neighborhood of Wells and Bristol who will gladly give me refuge."

"Then, madam, if you will take my advice," replied Gaunt Stilling, "you will take care of your plate, and all the pretty little knickknacks that I see lying about all over the house, or you will find clear boards when you come back again."

"I will order all the rooms to be locked up," said Hortensia, "except those where the men must sleep."

"The Tangier regiment don't mind locks, my lady," said Gaunt Stilling, gravely. "There is always an excuse for breaking a lock, especially when there are Nonjurors and Dissenters about. Doors would open very fast, and with two or three hundred witnesses you would have two or three hundred accomplices. Ask Tom if his brother's a thief! No, no, my lady, take my advice; put every thing of value into small drawers which would not hold an infant, or they'll break in to see if there's a Dissenting minister. Consign all your plate to the plate-chests; and, when you come back, you may think yourself very lucky if you do not find the eyes of your grandfather bored with a pike, or the portrait of your mother shot through with a musket, just to see if there be not a concealed door behind the canvas. Feed them well, or they will feed themselves better; and disperse all the women of the household over the parish--that is to say, under eighty. The men must take care of themselves, and a hard time enough they will have of it--some heads broken, if not driven in, before you come back, I will warrant."

"You lay me out work for a long time, Master Stilling," answered Hortensia; "what is to be done, Ralph?"

"Take his advice, dear lady," replied Ralph Woodhall. "Let me aid you in your arrangements, at once and immediately. Then lie down and take a short repose, and let us set off before daylight to-morrow. We will see you safe to Wells, and I shall depart with a lighter heart."

Gaunt Stilling did not appear to be quite satisfied, but he made no observation; and various servants being called, Lady Danvers explained to Mr. Drayton that she was under the necessity of quitting her own dwelling, as she had received information from Lord Feversham that Danvers's New Church was about to be occupied as a military post by Colonel Kirke and the Tangier regiment.

"Odd bless my life! my dear lady, that's bad news indeed," cried the old man, rubbing his hands in an agony of perplexity; "why, it is the worst regiment in the whole service--nothing like it in all the civilized world--a mere band of licensed robbers and plunderers, especially their colonel--gracious! what shall we do with all the things that are about?"

"We must lock them up safely," said Lady Danvers; "and that was one reason of my sending for you, Mr. Drayton. We must all set to work as hard as possible; the carriage and horses must be round at the door before three. But I will not take more men with me than is needful. My maid Alice must go. The rest of the women you had better disperse among the farmhouses and in the neighboring villages till the storm has blown by; and you must take the best care of these men who are coming that you can."

CHAPTER XXX

It was wonderful to see how soon, with a little order and a right good-will, all the rooms were cleared of the rich and delicate ornaments which filled them. The girl Alice, well trained by her mistress, did good service in this way, and at length all was completed. Four servants, besides Gaunt Stilling, were selected to accompany the carriage, and, after a few minutes' quiet conversation with Ralph, Hortensia retired to seek some repose. Her last words were, as they parted, "This is a strange life, Ralph."

How often it is that such little truisms give the clew to long, deep, intricate, undisplayed trains of thought, which have been going on in silence and secrecy for a long time before the common place result, in which most meditations end, is expressed.

Lady Danvers's words led the mind of Ralph on a journey fully as long and various as her own had previously been traveling, and, after giving a few directions to his servant, he cast himself into a chair, and passed the night in sleepless silence, till the faint gray of the early morning began to tinge the eastern sky. From time to time he had heard steps in the house throughout the night, and before the hour appointed Hortensia was down and ready to proceed.

There are various characteristics which give the men who possess them great power and influence over their fellows. Promptitude and decision, even though they approach rashness; firmness and determination, even when they touch upon obstinacy; great knowledge of the world and wide experience, are pre-eminent among these; and, by a combination of all three, Gaunt Stilling had obtained an ascendency among the servants of Lady Danvers which rendered him at once the leader and commander, as it were, of the little party which surrounded the carriage as it wended on. Two men he threw forward in advance, at the distance of some five hundred yards from each other, to gain intelligence and report to him in case of need. He himself rode a little before the carriage, and the other two men placed themselves one at each door, or portière, as it was the custom then to call it, one leading Ralph's horse by the bridle. The morning was peculiarly fine--bright, glowing, and beautiful--the colors of the sunrise unusually vivid; but the feathery clouds over head soon began to mass together. The sun lost his splendor, became dull and heavy-eyed, and then disappeared behind a shroud of vapor. First came on a thick, drizzling rain; then a heavy, continuous pour, pitting the dry ground, and then forming miniature torrents by the road side.

The carriage was much more heavily laden than on the preceding journey, and slowly and laboriously it went on, wallowing through the thick mud, and often seeming to pause, as if to rest itself, in the gutters which channeled the way. Progress was very tardy; hour after hour went by, and still every scene was familiar to the eyes of Hortensia. She knew this house, and that farm, and the church upon the hill, and the little village inn with its jolly host, and she could almost tell the exact distance from spot to spot. The slowness of their progress alarmed her; and after going on for four hours, and indulging in a fit of deep thought, she turned suddenly to Ralph, saying, "Indeed, I think you had better mount your horse, and ride away with your man. I shall reach Wells in safety, without doubt; but I fear every moment we may meet with Colonel Kirke, or some other of the king's officers, and the consequences might be dangerous to you. Have you not remarked that one of the men has ridden back several times to speak with your servant? We are now approaching the turning toward St. Mary's, and really we had better part here."

It cost her a great effort to utter those words, but it cost Ralph none to reply.

"I will leave you on no account," he said, "till I see you safely in your cousin's house at Wells; I should ill repay your kindness were I to act so selfish a part. A lady traveling in such scenes of confusion needs all the protection she can have; the danger to myself I do not think great. If we are rightly informed, Kirke's men will be marching on a different road; and as to the men moving rapidly backward and forward, it is but to keep up the communication from front to rear. We move slowly, indeed," he added; "but I never expected to accomplish the journey in less than three days, and with these roads it will probably take four."

"Four!" exclaimed Hortensia; "why, I have ridden the distance in one. Heaven knows what may happen in four days."

The words were still upon her lips when Gaunt Stilling rode up to the carriage and looked in, saying, as if in an inquiring tone, "I think we had better turn a little way up the lane to St. Mary's, sir, for I find from the reports that there is a good large party of the king's troops at a village about a mile before us. They halted there last night, but where they are going this morning the people do not seem to know. The carriage can get up the lane for about half a mile, and the two first sharp turnings will hide it from this road. There is a field near there where we can wheel about when we have obtained intelligence that the troops have marched on."

Ralph and Hortensia agreed to the proposal, and directions were given to the coachman accordingly. But Gaunt Stilling had reckoned without his host. Not fifty yards after the carriage had turned into the lane, a deep, unmended hollow, almost deserving the name of a pit, presented itself in the road. The horses dashed over--one stumbling and nearly falling--the heavy and overladen vehicle plunged in, with a shock first to the fore, then to the hind wheels; the injured axle-tree, not well mended, gave way, and the carriage stuck fast and immovable.

It was evident, in an instant, that the accident was beyond repair, at least for a long time; and while Ralph and Hortensia stood by the side of the vehicle, in no slight embarrassment and dismay, a distant beat of drums was heard, and one of the horsemen, who had been sent on the high road to bring his fellow from the front, came up at a quick pace, saying, "They tell me these are Kirke's lambs, my lady."

"You had better avoid that flock, madam," said Gaunt Stilling; "we can all be seen from the road; and I would not have them find you here for a good deal."

"But what is to be done?" exclaimed Ralph, impatiently; "they are already marching, it would seem; the carriage can not be repaired for hours, and Lady Danvers can not go on on foot."

"No, but she can on horseback," answered Gaunt Stilling.

"But there is no lady's saddle," replied Ralph; "her dress is not fitted for riding."

"Oh, that has all been taken care of," answered Gaunt Stilling, with a grin, "if Mistress Alice followed my counsel, and the coachman Harrison did what I told him. I knew quite well we should have some accident before we had done, and that my lady would likely have to mount on horseback and ride for it. As to the drum, that's only the muster-drum, and they won't march for this half hour; and, if people have not forgotten, there's a pad for my lady's riding on the carriage, and an amazon skirt, as they call it, under the cushion."

"The velvet pad is up behind," growled the coachman, who had been gazing disconsolately at his broken vehicle.

"I put the skirt in," cried the maid; "I always do what I'm told."

"But what am I to do with you, my poor Alice, if I ride away?" said Lady Danvers.

"Oh, never mind me, my lady," replied the maid, "I'm not a bit afraid of them. If they say a word to me, I'll scratch their eyes out. Or I can walk along down the lane till I get to some cottage, and hide myself there till they have plundered the coach and gone by."

"Why, I should think you had known them of old, Mistress Alice, you hit them off so pat," said Gaunt Stilling; "but you won't find a cottage for a long way, I can tell you. However, if you and the men get into that little wood, and hide yourselves there, it is a thousand to one that they don't seek for you. The picking of the carriage will take them some time, and Kirke won't let them stop long."

"I sha'n't get into the woods," said the sturdy coachman; "I'll stand by the carriage."

"And I'll stick by the horses," said one of the men; "the girl can hide herself in the wood, if she likes--I won't."

"Then, my brave lads, I'll stay with you," answered Gaunt Stilling. "I know these men, and perhaps can do more with them than any of you. I know Master Kirke, too, and he knows me. However, do not let us waste time in talking;" and, turning to Ralph, he added, "You and the lady, and one of the men, had better ride on, sir, as fast as may be; I will follow you as soon as I can, and reach you where you stop for the night. Perhaps we can get the carriage repaired so as to go on to-morrow. Harrison, get the pad on the lightest going of the horses. Alice, set your little fingers going about your lady's dress."

"Marry, you're familiar!" said the maid, searching under the cushions of the carriage; and, at the same time, Ralph replied, "But I do not know the way, Stilling."

"I do--I do!" exclaimed Hortensia; "only tell me, is it the second or third turning you take to the right?"

"The fourth, my lady," replied Gaunt Stilling; "don't take the third, or it may lead you into the lion's jaws; the fourth turning, and then ride straight on. You go in one line for sixteen miles till you come to a cross-road with a good inn. There, my lady, I think you'll need rest; and there, God willing, I'll bring you news. Now, pretty Mistress Alice, have you got the skirt?"

"Yes, here it is; but what my lady is to do without her hat and feather, I can't tell."

Hortensia smiled, but made no answer; and her extemporaneous toilet was soon completed.

The pad by this time had been placed upon one of the servant's horses, and Ralph lifted his beautiful companion into the saddle, not without some haste and anxiety, for the sound of fifes and drams playing a march was distinctly heard, and it was clear that Colonel Kirke and the Tangier regiment were moving down the road. As soon as she was safely seated, he sprang upon his own horse's back, and Hortensia, shaking her rein lightly, with a look in which sadness checkered strangely one of her gay smiles of olden days, put the beast into a canter, saying, "Now, Ralph, for a gallop, such as I used to enjoy so much when I was a girl."

CHAPTER XXXI

The roads were bad, and heavy with rain which had fallen during the night, but still Ralph and Hortensia kept up the quick pace at which they had set out for some six or seven miles. They spoke little, but the rapid motion seemed to animate and cheer them both; and at length Hortensia drew in her rein, her color revived by the air and exercise, and a brighter look of hope in her beautiful eye.

"I think we must have distanced them, Ralph," said Hortensia, "and we can ride on more quietly now."

"I trust there is no danger at present," answered Ralph; "and though, dear lady, you seem as if you were boon companion of the huntress goddess, it may be better to spare the horses."

"One of Diana's maidens I suppose I was destined to be," replied Hortensia; and then, as if to take away the point from her words, she added, "I was ever very fond of hunting, I remember, when a child--except, indeed, the catching of the beast, which I could never bear. The shrill scream of a poor hare when caught by the dogs, banished me at length from the hunting-field forever."

She fell into thought again for a moment, and then lifting up her eyes to her companion's face, she said, "We are very foolish, Ralph, I think--you--I--every body."

"Indeed!" said Ralph, smiling; "why think you so?"

"Because," replied Hortensia, "not content with all the great and ugly evils with which Fate has crammed this mortal abode of ours, we set up looking-glasses all round them in our minds to multiply them by reflection. Is not this foolish, Ralph?"

"Methinks it is," answered her companion; "but I believe the reason of it is that we wish to see them on every side, to see if we can not diminish them or cast them out."

"Vain effort!" replied Hortensia. "Our path is straight on; we can not turn aside from it. The ills that lie upon it must be encountered in front, and there is no use in watching for them till they are within reach. Let us be wise,

Ralph, if it be but for this day. Let us enjoy the present as far as we can. You think no more of a dark past or a gloomy future, and I will cast from my mind many a heavy thought and anxious care which the world's eye shall never behold. See! the sun is breaking out from behind the clouds, mottling the livery of the sky with gold. Let us fancy that in a calm, peaceful land, in a softened summer day, with nothing but prosperity round us, a happy home before us in which to rest, a short but bright vista of pleasant, youthful hours behind us, and light and loveliness on every side--let us fancy, I say, that we are taking a morning's ride for mere enjoyment. Can you do your part?"

"I will try," replied Ralph, "and, indeed, dear lady, as you say, it is the wisest plan. I have turned all the events of these last few days in my mind during this whole morning, and during the greater part of last night too; but thought has come to no result; and, as you see, the best-devised plans are frustrated in the moment of execution. I really feel inclined to be a fatalist, and to think that Destiny is leading me on blindfold, struggle how I may."

"Perhaps so," replied Hortensia; "but you are already breaking our compact, and moralizing upon things that be. Let us get into dreamland, Ralph; it is the mind's best refuge. You never were in France, or Italy, or Greece, I think; never saw the seven sober, united provinces, nor dwelt among the stiff and boorish aristocracy of Germany?"

"Never," replied Ralph, "never;" but yet the very name of these places turned his thoughts, as Hortensia intended, into another channel; and the two continued, not without an effort, indeed, to discuss subjects the least possibly connected with their own fate or the circumstances of the moment. Often--very often would thought recur to painful themes; the distant barking of a dog--the wild, joyous galloping of a horse in a neighboring field, would startle and alarm with the thought of fresh danger; but then, each time this occurred, the effort to banish the night-mare of the moment would be less difficult, till at length they nearly succeeded in forgetting all that they wished to forget.

Thus the time passed more pleasantly, and the road seemed shorter and less wearisome than it might have done had they yielded greater attention to pains and anxieties. That which Hortensia counseled and was practicing, has been, through the history of the world, one of the great secrets of philosophy and fortitude. The stoic bore his shame, the martyr his anguish, by thinking of something else; and great would be the blessing to man if he could attain to such mastery over his own mind as to give no more thought to any painful circumstance than is absolutely necessary to safety.

Ralph's heart was well guarded, indeed, or it could not have gone through that journey with Hortensia in safety; not so much from the beauty of her person, or the charm of her conversation, or the sweetness of her voice, or the high-hearted mind which seemed to pour a sort of halo of light around her, as from the deep thoughts of her--her character--her fate--which that long, dreamy ride suggested. He was thinking of her continually, even while conversing with her on indifferent things--thinking of her, not in a manner that could have pained Margaret if she had seen all his thoughts, but thinking of her far more than Margaret would perhaps have liked. The words which gave his mind that direction were those which Hortensia herself had used in speaking of herself, when she promised, for the enjoyment of the moment, to cast away from her mind "many a heavy thought and deep anxiety which the world could never see;" and on this text he went on, discoursing with himself, as I have said, even while he was striving to keep up a gay, wandering conversation with her.

The way seemed short, and neither Ralph nor Hortensia could believe that they had gone sixteen miles from the turning of the road when they saw, at length, a large, good-looking inn standing at a corner where two ways crossed. That which they were traveling themselves was a mere lane. The other, which traversed it, was evidently a high road, and Ralph said, "I hope we are right. We surely can not have come so many miles already?"

Hortensia looked up at him with a gay smile, and pointing to his horse, replied, "The poor uncommunicative beasts know better, Ralph; see you, your horse hangs his head, and both think they will be much the better of corn and water. Hark you, Peter," she continued, turning to the servant who had followed them, "ride up to yon inn door, and ask how far this is from St. Mary's. That will give us some indication of the distance we have come. But mind, mention not my name or Mr. Woodhall's on any account. It might be very dangerous to me, Peter, and I think you love your mistress well enough not to risk her safety by any indiscretion."

"I won't say a word, my lady," replied the good man, pulling off his hat as he rode forward.

In two or three minutes more, Ralph and Hortensia were seated quietly in a comfortable small room of an old-fashioned inn, with an old-fashioned landlord waiting upon them. He was full of attention, and often took his snowy night-cap in his hand, uncovering his bald head to guests whom he saw were worthy of reverence.

"Dinner shall be placed before you, my lord and my lady, in a moment," he said. "You have just come at the nick of time, for we had a great banquet ordered for Master Jenkins and his friends. He was to be married the day after to-morrow to pretty Mistress Betty Parker of the Grange; but those soldiers who came down to join Oglethorpe's regiment last night carried him off with them for disaffection--foul fall them! His only fault, if it was a fault, was too much affection--for Mistress Betty Parker. He would have given her up his whole soul and substance; and as to his being a Nonconformist, he was as good a Churchman as any in these parts, was baptized by old Doctor Hicks, and confirmed by the Bishop of Wells. But I'll show you your bed-room, my lord and my lady. It is all quite snug and comfortable, in here, out of this parlor," and he threw open a door leading into a very nice room beyond.

"You make a mistake, my good friend," said Ralph, while Hortensia's face glowed with painful crimson. "I am not this lady's husband, but merely protecting her on her journey in these dangerous times."

"Well, sir, I hope you soon may be," said the pertinacious host. "You couldn't have a better, nor she either, for that matter, I'm sure--Good gracious! the lady's crying--Dear me, madam, I'm very sorry--I beg pardon a thousand times--I'm a foolish old man and must chatter."

"Never mind, never mind, my good man," replied Hortensia, drying her eyes. "It is I who am foolish; but I have been subject to much fatigue and anxiety to-day. We had very nearly fallen in with a band of these lawless soldiers who are about, and I was obliged to leave my carriage on the road, broken down, and ride on under this kind friend's protection."

"Oh, well, if that is all, he can have the bed-room just opposite, where he can come to you in a moment if you want him," said the host, and again Hortensia's face glowed like a rose.

"If I stay the night, I may need that for my maid," she replied; "the girl will come on as soon as possible. I dare say you can find him a room somewhere else."

"I have none so good," said the landlord. "Twenty-five is rather damp, and number seven--"

"Never mind, never mind," said Ralph, "any one will do for me. These must be for the Lady Hortensia and her maid--Now go and hurry dinner as fast as possible."

The old man turned toward the door, but stopped suddenly, and looked round with a bright expression, as if a good thought struck him,

"Won't it be better," he said, "to have a bed put into my lady's room for the maid?"

"Exactly--exactly," said Ralph; "that will do very well."

"Capital--capital," cried the old landlord, snapping his fingers with an air of triumph; "that hits it exactly; then you can have the opposite room, and comfort them both if they should need it."

Ralph could bear no more, and burst into a fit of laughter, in which, to say sooth, Hortensia joined, although she was not very sure whether she should laugh or weep again.

The old man looked in some surprise, and left the room with a somewhat sheepish air.

As soon as he was gone, Hortensia raised her eyes to Ralph's face with an expression of much anxiety, rendered almost whimsical by the faint glow of merriment that still lingered like sunset round their lips. "This will not do, Ralph," she said, in a timid tone; "I hope my people will come and join us soon; but I must not--I fear I must not travel with you alone, though God knows, and you know, that our feelings toward each other would not shrink from the scrutiny of all the world."

Ralph took her hand and pressed his lips upon it. "You have been pained too much on, my account already," he said; "but I must and will see you safe to your journey's end, Hortensia. If your maid does not join you at once, I doubt not we can engage some honest girl here to fill her place for the time, and accompany you on the way to-morrow. No one who knows you could doubt you for an instant."

"But what may not Margaret think?" asked Lady Danvers, turning very pale.

"Margaret's thoughts are all generous," replied Ralph; "and if she knew you as I do, she would almost worship you for your kindness to me."

"Without a doubt or a suspicion?" asked Hortensia, sadly.

"Without a shadow or a cloud to dim her confidence," replied Ralph, boldly. "Others might insinuate what Margaret would not believe; but I feel it now, dear Lady Danvers, to be a duty to you, to her, and to myself, as soon as I can find an opportunity, to write to my dear cousin, and tell her all the generous, noble, disinterested kindness you have shown to me. It is risking a good deal, perhaps, but I think I can find the means of conveying the letter to her secretly."

"Perhaps I may find courage to write to her also," replied Hortensia, thoughtfully. "A woman, in a woman's letter, soon reads a woman's heart; and mine I don't wish to conceal--from her eyes, at least. She will understand me."

Ralph pressed her hand kindly in his own. His brow was clear and calm; his eye expressed, perhaps, esteem, regard, affection, but not passion, and he answered, "She *will* understand you as I understand you; she will be grateful to you as I am grateful to you; and she will neither doubt, nor fear, nor hesitate, but comprehend you, most excellent and amiable of human beings, as you will ever be comprehended and loved by one who esteems you more than any other being upon earth but her with whom his whole fate and existence has been linked from early childhood."

Heaven knows what it was in his words, but Hortensia bowed her head till it touched her hands upon the table, and burst into so vehement a fit of sobbing, that Ralph, after in vain endeavoring to soothe her or even to attract her attention to himself, called loudly from the door for help, and soon brought the landlord's wife and daughter to the assistance of his fair companion.

The peculiar situation in which they were placed prevented him from carrying her himself to her bed-room; but he had soon after the happiness of hearing that she was calmer and better; and for an hour or two he waited tranquilly, in the pleasant and quiet abode which they had found, for some news of all they had left behind them on the road.

Hortensia had just rejoined him--had just made one of those excuses which women often make for any agitation they betray when emotion overpowers habitual self-command, saying that she had overcalculated her strength, and that the fatigue which she had lately undergone had affected her more than she had expected.

"The truth is, I suppose, Ralph," she said, "I have been acting the fine court lady too much of late, and in cities and crowds have lost somewhat of the dairy-maid health I used to boast of in days of yore. I must abandon such enfeebling scenes, and once more ride my fifteen or twenty miles in the day, as I used to do; for I am resolved not to be a languishing dame till my hair begins to turn gray, and not even then if I can help it."

They were gazing forth from the window, which, looking over a low copse on the opposite side of the road, gave a beautiful view of that rich and beautiful country, which extends for many miles along the borders of Somerset and Devonshire--a land which probably my eyes will never see again, but which will be present to my mind to the last hour of life. The garden of England well may they call it; and when they say that, surely they mean the garden of the world. The sun was shining fitfully; the clouds, broken, were drifting away on a swift wind; the trees and fields were sparkling with the past rain, and the soft exhalation of the warm earth marked out the aerial perspective of every far-receding slope more tenderly than usual. From the refreshed earth the air rose up loaded with perfume, and the note of the blackbird poured rich and musical from the covert, as if to keep scent, and sight, and sound in harmony. They had not gazed for above two minutes, however, and Hortensia had hardly had time to ask her own heart how and why it was that Nature's own world was so bright, and beautiful, and peaceful, while man's was so full of ruggedness and thorns, when the sight of Gaunt Stilling trotting up quickly to the door, and quite alone, called the attention both of herself and her companion.

The man asked some questions quickly of an hostler who was standing by the horse-trough, gave him some large saddle-bags to carry into the house, and then dismounting, entered the inn. A moment after, he was in the presence of his master and Lady Danvers, and Ralph argued at once, from the expression of his face, that matters had gone wrong with him. Nevertheless, his words did not convey any evil tidings.

"Lucky you didn't stop, my lady," he said, addressing Hortensia, "for we were very likely to have a fight for it, and two shots were fired, which did no damage to any thing but the carriage. However, we have saved it from actual plunder, though I believe Kirke's lambs have filched two or three things of no very great importance."

"But where is the carriage?" asked Ralph; "and where is Lady Danvers's maid?"

"It will be impossible to get the carriage repaired at all till to-morrow," replied Gaunt Stilling, "and it may be night then before it is ready but we contrived at last to get it drawn up into the yard of a good farmer, who will take care of it, and the men and all, and Mistress Alice to boot, till they can set off to Wells. As to the young woman, my lady," he said, with a laugh, "you should have her taught to ride; for we could find no possible way of getting her on here, or I would have brought her with me. We contrived a capital sort of pad saddle for her, and mounted her tolerably well; but no sooner was she on upon one side than she was off upon the other. So the matter was in vain; for I knew my horse would have enough to do to bring one here alone, otherwise I would have brought her on a pillion behind me. I have brought a heap of things for your ladyship, however, which the girl crammed into a big pair of bags I bought from the farmer."

"Have you heard any news of the other forces that are marching?" asked Ralph; "it is absolutely necessary that we should get some accurate intelligence."

"Hard to be found, sir," replied Gaunt Stilling; "I don't think much that there are more than three men among the king's troops who know which way they are marching, or what they are doing, and Feversham is not one of them. If Monmouth had but one good regiment of foot and a handful of horse, he would beat them all in detail; he must win a battle or he's lost, however, for they're pressing him back upon the sea just by their dead weight."

"But can he win a battle with such ill-disciplined and ill-armed forces as he has?" inquired Ralph.

"I don't rightly know, sir," replied Stilling. "His men are bad enough, in all conscience; but the king's are not much better--Feversham, an idle, effeminate fop--vain, too, as a peacock; the men a set of drunken marauders, only fit to scour a conquered country, and the officers, for the most part a set of dissolute, enfeebled libertines, who know as much of tactics or campaigning as that table. Your cousin, Lord Coldenham, is one of them, sir. I think it would not take a very strong man to knock down a whole regiment of such, like a child's house of cards. But there is Churchill," he added, "and Oglethorpe, and Dumbarton's regiment, and the Blues. Monmouth will fall down there if they come across him. His only chance would be to beat Feversham first, and then push on to London. A battle won and a forward march would make many cold friends warm ones."

"But have you been able to obtain no intelligence, then, which may guide us?" asked his master; "I care not for myself, Stilling, if I could see Lady Danvers safely at Wells."

"Ay, that is the thing, sir," answered Stilling; "for the whole country is in a state of commotion, and it is almost equally dangerous to move or to sit still. The whole roads to the south and east are in a state you can form no idea of. Every sort of outrage is being committed. Nothing is safe, nobody is respected. The landlords are ruined by having men quartered upon them. The villages are plundered. The farmer's horses are all taken to draw the baggage-wagons and artillery, and you would suppose not only that martial law was proclaimed, but that the whole land was given up to pillage. It is as bad as Tangier; and it was only because Kirke knew me, and I knew Kirke, that her ladyship's carriage was spared. When I told him that if he did not keep up some discipline about the carriage at least, some secrets might come out he might not like to have public, I could see him fingering his pistol, as if he did not well know whether to shoot me or bid his men march on; but I had a pistol too, and my hand upon it, and I think that settled the question with him. However, all I can say is, we must go on very carefully to-morrow, for nobody seems to know which way Monmouth has turned. I dare say we shall hear, however, as we proceed, and as to the rest, we must trust to the chapter of accidents. Now, with your good leave, sir, I will go and get something to eat, for I have neither had bit nor sup since last night, and my horse is nearly as badly off as his master."

Gaunt Stilling withdrew, and Ralph and Hortensia were left alone to consult over the somewhat cheerless prospects before them. To stay where they were for that night seemed inevitable; and, following Ralph's suggestion, Lady Danvers sent for the good woman of the house, to inquire if some young woman could not be procured in the neighborhood to act in the capacity of her maid for a few days. The landlady willingly agreed that her own daughter should sleep in Hortensia's room, and attend upon her that night, but no consideration would induce her to allow the girl to quit her home on the following day.

Inquiries were then made in the village, which lay about a quarter of a mile down the road; but all proved vain. The terror which the various bodies of troops had occasioned rendered every parent anxious to keep his child at home; and Hortensia was obliged to make up her mind to undergo any evil construction that the world might put upon her conduct, as she was placed in a position from which, however unpleasant, there was no escape.

It would be tedious to trace the adventures of the next two or three days, for they only consisted of embarrassments and disappointments very similar to those which have been already noticed. Whichever way Ralph and Hortensia directed their steps, intelligence reached them that some body of troops lay between them and the place they sought to reach; and, turned at every point, several days were lost in fruitless wanderings, which only brought them nearer to the Bristol Channel, and further both from Wells and Hortensia's own dwelling.

Sometimes a feeling of despair would come over Ralph, and he more than once thought of seeking out the quarters of his cousin Lord Coldenham, of whose presence with the royal forces he was now assured, and trusting to his honor to find means of conveying Lady Danvers safely on her way. But when he proposed such a plan to her, she rejected it at once in a manner which admitted of no further argument.

CHAPTER XXXII

In a room which we have before described in Coldenham Castle sat the same stately, proud-looking, majestic dame to whom Ralph Woodhall had paid a brief visit of ceremony before his final departure from his father's house. The unconcealed gray hair upon the broad, powerful, masculine brow, added not less, perhaps, to the grave dignity of her aspect, than the keen, finely-cut features, and the stern black eye. There was a look of some discontent upon her countenance as she opened, one after another, a number of letters which had been placed upon the table before her, but no doubt, no hesitation, no remorse; and yet she might very well have felt all, or either.

"Not caught him yet?" she said, bitterly; "God's my life, thief-takers must have lost their skill! But they must have him soon. I have tracked him to his lair, and it seems they have unearthed him. Surely they can run him down now. It must be this foolish confusion in the country about Monmouth which has favored his evasion. Methinks I will go over myself. Men are but women nowadays, and it is time that women should act the part of men. I will soon find means to catch him. I fear me Coldenham is too weak and soft, and the old lord too rash and hasty; Robert, though the best head among them, too politic and wily. It needs to see clearly, and judge wisely, and strike boldly. A keen sword is of no great use without a strong hand. I will soon do it if I go; and let me but catch him, I will so pile up crimes upon his head that he will need a wiser jury than England can afford to set him free."

This was partly murmured in distinct words, partly thought; and while her meditation on that subject continued, she retained in her hand unopened the next letter of the pile, hardly regarding it. When she had done, she looked for a moment at the back, and said, "The old man's hand! Why does he write to me, I wonder?" and, tearing open the seal, she read the contents. They seemed to affect her more than she expected, for one of those strange changes came over her countenance which I have before described.

"Ha!" she exclaimed, "ha! how sits the wind now?" and, turning to the beginning, she re-read the letter to an end. It was to the following effect, and much more brief than good Mr. Woodhall's epistles usually were:

"My dear Lady and Cousin,

"I write to you because I am informed, on authority which to me would be beyond doubt as proof of any other assertion, that, although no one should be better aware than yourself of the innocence of my son Ralph in the matter of his cousin Henry Woodhall's death, you are urging on our kinsman Lord Woodhall to persecute him with great severity, and also are engaged in seeking causes of offense which may render him obnoxious to the court, and perhaps even prejudice him before a jury. This information having been communicated to me without any injunction to secrecy, I think it but just to yourself and to my son--although I believe that some error must exist--to make known to you the fact, in order that you may at once give immediate contradiction to the report, should it be false. Should it be out of your power to contradict it, however--which I do not believe--I have to warn you that the consequences to yourself may be more dangerous than you imagine; that all your proceedings in this case will be at once brought to light; and that many things, now apparently buried forever in the darkness of the past, may have to be brought forward in the eye of day. Trusting that, with the firmness and decision which belong to your character, you will at once deny the truth of the information which has reached me, I beg to subscribe myself, et cetera."

Lady Coldenham gazed upon the paper with a look in which many an evil expression mingled with surprise. "Insolent old fool!" was her first exclamation; "does he dare? Who could have told him of this? his fellow-simpleton, Lord Woodhall himself, I suppose. Nay, nay, there can be no communication between them. It must have come from some other source; whence, I can not divine. The old man Stilling surely could not--nay, how could he? he knows not of it. It is very strange. And this threat, too. The son threatened, and he shall rue it. The father threatens, and he may rue it too. Deny the truth? Nay, I will confirm it with 'the firmness and determination which belong to me.' It is time that I should know to what these menaces tend. If I am to have a foe, let me meet him in front;" and, taking up a pen, she wrote hastily upon a sheet of paper a few bold lines to the following effect:

"Sir,--What I dare to do, I dare to avow. Your son Ralph murdered his cousin Henry Woodhall. I have urged, and shall urge Lord Woodhall, the bereaved father, to suffer no weak remains of affection for an unworthy object to prevent him from punishing the offender to the utmost. I, for one, should prefer to have a man hanged out of my family, rather than to have a murderer left living in it. Your cousin,

"Esther Coldenham."

This done and the letter sealed, she rang the silver bell upon her table, and, as soon as a servant appeared, handed him the tender epistle, saying, "Dispatch that by a messenger immediately."

"May it please your ladyship," replied the man, "Mr. Woodhall's messenger is waiting."

"Then let him have it and be gone," replied Lady Coldenham; "his master can't have my answer too soon."

When she was again alone, Lady Coldenham once more read her cousin's letter, and it seemed less satisfactory to her than even at first; for, with all the evil passions which it evidently stirred up, and which painted themselves upon her countenance, there was an expression of doubt, of hesitation, of dread, which that face had seldom, if ever, before borne.

She had great power over herself, however. She was resolute, persevering, undaunted in purpose. Little had she ever scrupled to do in life; and no fear had ever got sufficient hold upon her to deter her from any act on which she had determined.

Whatever it was she dreaded on the present occasion, she suffered not the impression to remain upon her mind for more than a few moments. Then, casting it from her as something that was used and done with, she turned to the letters again, perused all those which she had not read before, made notes upon such as referred to business, and then calmly and deliberately ordered every thing to be prepared for a journey into Dorsetshire within three hours. Her own arrangements were very rapidly made, and the early time of dinner was approaching, when the peculiar servant who attended upon that room entered with another letter in his hand. Lady Coldenham took it and looked at the address. The moment she did so, a paleness came over her face; and the man could see that her hand shook as she broke the seal. He did not venture to remain, however, and retired with his usual noiseless step. But the door was not yet quite closed when he heard a cry, as if of pain, and then the sound of a heavy fall, and, running hastily back, he found his mistress stretched senseless on the floor. The letter lay wide open at a little distance from her, and he thought fit to look at it before he called for aid. Only one word, written in a fine, bold hand, in the middle of the page, was to be seen. It was, "Beware!" and, as he could make nothing of it, he called the waiting-woman and the housekeeper, and a number of other servants, who soon, by their united efforts, brought Lady Coldenham to herself. For a moment or two after her eyes opened, she lay quite still where they had placed her; but then, as if moved by some sudden passion, she started up, snatched the letter from the floor, and uttered some wild and whirling words which no one could rightly comprehend.

"It is false!" she cried; "it is a forgery! They are in a league to frighten me; but they shall find themselves mistaken. Ay, they shall find themselves mistaken!" and, after tearing the letter into a thousand pieces, she sunk slowly into a chair, and leaned her head upon her hand.

"Is the coach come?" she asked, as if not fully aware of how short a space of time had elapsed since she gave her orders.

"No, my lady," replied the waiting-woman "it is not time yet. But, as your ladyship has not been well, would it not be better to delay your journey till to-morrow?"

"Not an hour--not a minute!" replied Lady Coldenham, sternly; and, rising up from her chair as stately as ever, she said, "You may withdraw. Let me know when dinner is ready."

CHAPTER XXXIII

The sun set slowly, and somewhat dimly too over a wide, extensive, melancholy-looking plain in the west of England. Two persons gazed over the wide expanse from the windows of a tolerably comfortable farmhouse situated on the first slope of a rising ground to the eastward. Nothing could appear more dreary and hopeless than the aspect of the scene before their eyes. The general face of the country for some miles to the westward was completely flat, rather hollowed out than otherwise, looking much like a Dutch landscape, where a wide tract of country, rescued from the sea, continually forces upon the mind of the spectator the impression that at any time the sea may break in again and recover its own. I know few things more desolate in appearance than one of these Dutch landscapes late in the autumn or early in the spring. There is a sort of marshy, fenny feel in the very look, which makes the mind shiver and creep, as if it got the ague before the body was sensible of it. But even a Dutch landscape had the advantage over that which lay beneath the eye of the traveler. The manifold wind-mills, with their arms waving in the breeze, which give a sort of merry activity to most of the Dutch pictures, were here wanting. The curious old manorial houses, very often furnished with draw-bridge and portcullis, and with clumps of old trees around them, were not to be seen. Here and there, indeed, marked out by the falling of the light and shade, a little elevated piece of ground, apparently but a few yards wide, though in reality much more extensive, rose up as a sort of island a few feet above the dull level of the plain; and there almost invariably appeared the spire of a little village church, with a low cottage or two scattered among the orchards, and the squire's or parson's house domineering over the rest. All these houses, however, in which men and women dwelt--in which every human passion had its sway--in which loves, and hates, and hopes, and ambitions, and envy, and pride, and jealousy, and enmity, and strife, and mortal struggle existed as well as in the midst of courts, seemed, to the eyes that looked upon them from the height, no larger than the smallest of a child's playthings, so completely did they sink into insignificance--lost, as it were, in the vast expanse around.

Dim, dim was the aspect of the whole scene. The setting sun, half vailed in cloud, yet partially seen through the gray covering of the sky, looked pale and wan, and of evil augury. No rosy glow accompanied his descent, till his lower limb touched the very verge of the horizon, and then two or three blood-red streaks marked the death of day, without affording one hope of brighter looks to-morrow. There were none of those strong contrasts, those deep blue shadows, and warm yellow lights, brought forth by the changeful aspect of the April or October day; but the utmost variation in the depth of hue served but to throw out, in very slight relief, the little hamlet-covered elevations I have mentioned. Perhaps, indeed, this effect was produced more by the long lines of light mist that rose up from the lower parts of the ground than by any contrast of light and shade; and the dull, leaden, cheerless, rayless look of the whole was only rendered more oppressive by two or three tall wreaths of bluish smoke which rose up here and there, several miles apart, marked out the distances, and showed how wide was the space beneath the eye.

"Somewhere here," said Ralph, "must have lain, I think, the famous isle of the Æthelings, so celebrated in our Saxon history; for this was the great marsh--at that time nearly covered with water in the winter--into which the Danes could never penetrate."

"It looks, indeed, a sad and gloomy place--the refuge of despair," replied Hortensia; and then allowing her eyes to run forward over some twelve or fourteen miles of ground, they rested upon a spot where, against the western sky, rose up a number of irregular white masses, crowned by a very tall steeple, which looked as solitary and melancholy as a column in a wilderness.

"That must be Bridgewater, I suppose," said Hortensia.

"I fancy so," answered Ralph, "but I can not tell. We will ask the good farmer;" and he was turning toward the other side of the room, where stood the door, when Hortensia stayed him, saying, "Nay, do not leave me, Ralph; I am very sad to-night. I know not why it is; but I suppose these long journeyings and wearing anxiety have fatigued me much--fatigued mind, and heart, and soul, and spirit, more than the body, for these frail limbs do not feel so weary as after the first day's journey; but there is nothing like the weariness of the spirit. It matters little whether it be Bridgewater or not--let it be what it may. We shall learn more to-morrow--"

The moment after, with a little spice of that caprice which the weariness of the spirit that she talked of often gives, Hortensia added, "If that be Bridgewater, and the villages we see there be occupied by the king's troops, as the people say, they must have somehow passed us; and I should think that we could get across the country to Bristol or Bath early to-morrow. Of course, if Monmouth is before them, they will call in all stragglers and detachments, and the road in their rear must be clear."

"I have good hope it will prove so," replied Ralph; "but if the intelligence we have heard to-night be correct, your own house at Danvers's New Church must be free of these marauders. Nothing is more probable than that Lord Feversham should order Kirke, as the people told us, to join him again by forced marches."

"I wish Stilling would return," said Lady Danvers, with a sigh. "We have fed so long upon the bitter bread of uncertainty, that I am marvelous tired of the diet, Ralph."

"He has not yet been gone half an hour," replied Ralph Woodhall. "Take my counsel, dear lady: go and lie down to rest for a few hours, and as soon as Stilling returns I will send and let you know what news he brings. If I judge right, there will be some one up in the house all night, for the good people are evidently anxious and alarmed in consequence of the near presence of the soldiery."

"If I sleep at all," replied Hortensia, "it shall be in this large chair. Though the back be as tall and stiff as a monument, yet there, ready for any event, I shall rest more quietly than in a bed. I like this sober evening twilight--this sort of middle state of sight, where there is nothing very bright, and nothing very dark, like the calm, even hue of happy mediocrity. Forbid me candles at an hour such as this. I could go on, methinks, musing and pondering in this light for ever, if it would but last--or till the night of age and death fell upon me."

Her quiet melancholy dream ended with the opening of the door; and the good farmer's wife entered, saying, in a broad, Somersetshire dialect, "Come, young folks, don't you sit moping here in the dark. I've got something ready all hot for your supper down below. A plenty of roasted eggs and some bacon, and some good dough cakes as ever were baked. It's poor feeding for such as you, I dare say; but it's the best we can give, and it's given right hearty."

"And so will we partake of it," said Hortensia, rising and laying her hand upon the good woman's arm. "Come, Ralph, let us go to supper; we can employ our time worse, even in sitting thinking sadly here."

"Well, thou art a dear, beautiful lady! and there's the very best cider in the country to boot," said the farmer's wife, walking down the stairs by the side of her fair guest.

Hortensia did not see the connection between herself and the cider; but she asked no questions, and was soon seated at the farmer's supper-table, where, in addition to himself, his wife, and her two guests, were half a score of plowmen and maid-servants, all very decorous in their behavior, though simple and rough enough in their manner.

The conversation turned naturally enough to the situation of Monmouth and the king's troops, and some speculations were indulged in as to the result of the struggle going on. It was evident that the good farmer was a Tory at heart, although he took especial care to guard the expression of his opinions.

"Lord bless you! my lady," he said, in answer to some observation of Hortensia, "there will be no battle. The duke can't afford to fight such men as he's got before him--that's to say, the duke or King Monmouth, as they call him; and I can't tell, of course, which is right. But he's strengthening himself in Bridgewater, they say; and I know he sent for a great number of our lads round about, to help to cut rines and throw up dikes. He'll soon be obliged to give them all up, I've a notion; but nobody can tell, after all. War and love are the two most uncertain things that are, and I do not know which is the worst, for my part."

"Love," said Hortensia, smiling; "for, besides being bad in itself, as you say, it often leads to war, which is another evil."

"Lord bless you! my lady, love's a very good thing in its way, when it's young and fresh," said the farmer's wife, with a merry laugh. "It's not like beer, the better for being kept, that is true; but all those sweet liquors grow sour when they get stale; and so love's no worse than the rest of them. Isn't it so, father?"

The jolly farmer shook his sides with a hearty laugh, but replied, with a better compliment than courts could afford, "Such as thou never gets stale, my dear old girl; for there's a sweet spirit in the heart of thee that won't let a drop in thy veins grow sour, and the longer thou art kept the better."

The conversation served somewhat to cheer; but still both Ralph and Hortensia were anxious for the return of Gaunt Stilling; and Lady Danvers would not consent to retire to rest before information was received of what was the course to be pursued in the morning. After the supper was over, they went up again together to the room above, and seated themselves by the window, while the good farmer's wife followed them with a single lamp, and sat making stockings, and every now and then saying a word or two, calculated, as she thought, to keep their spirits up.

Ralph and Hortensia said little, but gazed on the scene before them, with the stars twinkling faintly above, and the wide expanse of Sedgemoor nearly vailed in mist, looking like a dim, uncertain sea.

"Ay, we none of us can rest to-night," said the old woman; and then, after a pause and two or three more stitches, she continued. "That's because we all feel as if something were going to happen; and something must happen, too, very soon--I'm sure of that. They've got too near to part without tearing each other."

"It is sad to think of," said Hortensia; "perhaps to-morrow may bring fate to many hundreds of honest men who ought to be friends and brethren."

"Likely, my lady," replied the farmer's wife; and there the conversation dropped.

"Farmer Bacon thinks they are going to have a siege," said the good dame, after about half an hour's silence; "but I don't think they'll wait for that slow work."

"I should think Lord Feversham would hardly give the duke time to fortify himself," Ralph answered; and there the conversation dropped again.

About an hour after that, Ralph said, "Hark! do you not hear the sound of a horse's hoofs beating upon a hard road or causeway? I dare say it is Stilling coming back."

"It must be on Zoyland causeway," said the old woman, "for all the roads are mere pease-pudding. You would not hear the galloping of a whole regiment of horses. That horse is six miles off, at the least; but the night is still, you see."

A short time then elapsed without any further observation; but suddenly Hortensia started and uttered a low exclamation. A bright flash of fire was seen to blaze through the fog toward the center of the moor, and some seconds after, a loud, ringing report of musketry; then, immediately after, flash after flash ran along in a straight line across the moor, extending some three or four hundred yards, and the peal of the shot was mingled with other sounds, probably shouts of command, or the cheer of troops in the charge.

It was clear a battle was going on--that a night attack had been made by Monmouth on the king's troops, and that mighty destinies hung upon the events which were taking place on one spot in the midst of that wild moor.

Some five or ten minutes after, a light broke out about two miles to the right, steady and persisted, as if a bonfire had been lighted there; but a number of flashes also poured down from that quarter, and then came the sound of many horses' feet beating the hard causeway.

The farmer and many of the people of the house came up, warned by the sounds which reached the house, to look out upon the distant battle. All were silent--all were pale with the strong emotions of the moment; and it is not at all improbable that from among the farming men, at least, many an aspiration went up for the success of Monmouth.

Again, at the end of a quarter of an hour, firing commenced upon the left; but it was faint and scattered; and still the heat of the strife was evidently toward the center of Feversham's position. There the firing was kept up incessantly, rising and falling, sometimes less fiercely than at others, but never discontinued altogether. At length a dull, heavy roar was heard, and brighter, broader flashes were seen.

"Those are cannon brought into play," said Ralph.

"Ay, that will soon settle it," observed the farmer. "The daylight is coming, too. See how gray it is out there."

"Heaven have mercy upon those poor men!" said Hortensia, with a sigh. "Do you not think you hear cries and shrieks, Ralph?"

"No, indeed, dear lady," replied her companion; "it is your own bright imagination hears them."

"They are heard by the ear of Heaven," replied Hortensia; and, bending down her eyes, she fell into a fit of deep thought.

The farmer's voice roused her. "And now, my lady," he said, "if you will take my advice, you will lie down and take an hour or two's rest--say till five o'clock. By that time we shall know how matters have gone, though I myself don't doubt. By that time, too, the chase will be over, and you can get some breakfast, mount your horse with this young gentleman, and ride away quietly, keeping to the rear of the army."

"But suppose we should be met by stragglers, and stopped?" said Lady Danvers; "I have a great dread of those troops of Colonel Kirke's; and there being no one with us to protect us, we should be quite at their mercy if they met with us."

"Well," said the old farmer, scratching his head, "I will ride with you till you're out of harm's way, and will take two of the lads with us; not that I should be any great protection, or they either, for that matter; but I think I've got a secret to keep them quiet. I don't believe they'll venture to hurt me, any how. So now go and lie down and rest quietly, there's a dear, pretty lady."

"I do not think I can sleep at all after what I have seen," answered Hortensia.

"Never mind that, my lady," said the farmer's wife; "it will rest you, at any rate, to lie down. Come with me, and I will show you the way."

Hortensia followed, and Ralph remained debating with himself whether it might not be better for him to place his fair companion under the charge and safe guidance of these honest people, and entreat them to see her unmolested to the house of some relation, than to persist in accompanying her, when his presence seemed but to bring mishap and inconvenience with it. He determined, in the end, to see her, at all events, safely beyond the immediate neighborhood of the field of battle, and then to propose his plan to her, and leave her to decide.

CHAPTER XXXIV

A small party on horseback rode quietly along upon the very verge of Sedgemoor, where the land begins to slope upward. They were still upon the moor, however, which was in those days a moor in reality; for few spots on the eastern side of the Atlantic have undergone a more complete change in the short space of two hundred years. A slight elevation of the ground--one of the waves, as it were, of that earth-sea, concealed the travelers in a degree from the field on which the battle had lately been fought; but this shelter was not complete, for the little ridge was irregular, and in some places sunk to the level of the rest of the marsh. Nevertheless, the party pursued their way unmolested for more than three miles, not hurrying their horses, nor putting on any appearance of haste or dismay. Lady Danvers was in the front, with Ralph on one side, and the good old farmer on the other; and their spirits and hopes were beginning to rise, from the impunity with which they had proceeded on their last half hour's ride. They were taking a slanting course somewhat away from the field of battle, and Hortensia fondly trusted that every forward step put her and Ralph further from danger. The old man upon her left, too, was cheerful and light-hearted, and seemed to anticipate no peril or obstruction. Suddenly, however, as they turned a little angle of the ground, they saw two mounted men with carbines on their knees, fixed motionless right in the middle of the way, evidently posted there to cut off any fugitives who, after having made their way round the flanks of the enemy's position, might now be seeking to escape by favor of the hollow way.

A little confusion occurred in Hortensia's party as soon as the soldiers were perceived; and one of the farm-servants, who was riding behind, exclaimed, "Let us gallop away across the hill."

"Stay!" said Ralph, whose presence of mind generally came to his aid in moments of danger, "every thing now depends upon coolness and propriety of conduct. These men can not be avoided. We must meet them, and then act according to circumstances."

Thus saying, he begged Hortensia to halt for a moment, and then rode on alone, waving his hand to the man who was nearest. He was speedily challenged, and replied at once, "The king--King James."

"Ay, ay," said the soldier, "every one calls out King James this morning, though many a one hallooed out King Monmouth last night."

"We, at least, hallooed nothing of the kind," said Ralph, "for I was prevented from going to Bridgewater by hearing that the duke was there. At all events, you can not suspect that a lady took any part in such things, and I trust you will let her pass quietly, as every good soldier ought in a woman's case."

"I can't let any body pass, man or woman," replied the soldier, gruffly; "my orders are strict to stop every one, and have him examined by one of the superior officers. You must stay where you are, and so must every one of your party, till we make the signal from that bit of a mound. Take care that you stay quite still, and do not attempt to move away, or my companion will fire in front, and I will fire upon you in flank."

"We will remain in perfect quiet where we are," answered Ralph, in an indifferent tone; "but one thing let me add, that we would greatly prefer to speak with one of the generals, who probably might know us, than with any inferior officer."

"That's as it may be," answered the man. "I saw the general Himself there just now. Perhaps he may look back, if he's not gone too far. Well, you go back and stay with the rest."

Ralph returned to his party, and communicated what had taken place, evidently greatly to the alarm of Hortensia.

"Don't be afraid--don't be afraid," said the old farmer, in a cheerful tone. "I've got a secret that will tame them, especially if they bring us one of the colonels or generals."

But Hortensia's fears were roused for Ralph. "I am not in the least alarmed for myself," she said, in a low voice; "but indeed, Ralph, you are in a situation of great peril. Will it not be better for you to turn your horse, and try to make your escape the other way."

"No, no," he said, "I should only bring suspicion on you, and probably be taken before I had ridden a couple of miles. Besides, dear lady, I am wearied with this continual uncertainty; and, in truth, I think I have fully as good a chance of passing unobstructed in this direction as in any other."

Hortensia hung her head, and his answer did not seem fully to satisfy her. But no great time was allowed for thought or consultation. In less than five minutes the head of a considerable party of military men appeared over the hill; and, riding at a quick pace, they were soon in the little ravine leading to the spot where Hortensia and the rest were waiting. Preceding them by a step or two came a man, somewhat above the middle height, of distinguished aspect, and a countenance which, though not absolutely handsome, was expressive of high mental qualities, if there be any truth in physiognomy or phrenology. The panoply of war had evidently been thrown aside since the battle, and he was now dressed in the ordinary costume of a gentleman of the court, with the exception of the large jack boots and long heavy sword, with which no mere courtier would have liked to encumber himself. He gazed with a keen, shrewd, penetrating look upon the party as he rode up; but when, within about five paces, he seemed suddenly to recognize one of their number, and, doffing his hat, he spurred on up to Hortensia's horse, saying, "Dear Lady Danvers, can I believe my eyes?"

"Yes, indeed, Lord Churchill," she answered, with a well-pleased smile, for she well knew the courtesy of that great but heartless man; "and, to tell you the truth, I have some cause to be very angry with you, for you have been art and part in the offense, I fear, of forcing me many a mile out of my way, breaking my carriage to pieces, and very nearly getting me into the midst of a battle."

"Serious offenses, indeed," said Churchill, with a laugh; "but how have I had any share in these terrible acts?"

"Why, the simple fact is, I have been trying to pass toward Wells with this gentleman who is escorting me," said Lady Danvers--Churchill pulled off his hat with a low bow toward Ralph, and a keen look at his person, and Hortensia proceeded: "I could not effect my object, however, for I always found some of your troops in the way, and I was not a little afraid of them."

"Nay, nay, what a satire," exclaimed Churchill; "we should have treated you with all courtesy, as if we had been knights of old."

"No satire, but homely truth, general," replied Lady Danvers, pointedly. "The first we met with was Colonel Kirke's Tangier regiment; and his men, we heard from every tongue, were plundering the whole country, and abusing every one who fell into their hands."

Churchill's brow contracted, and he muttered, "This is too bad. That man ought to be punished. I hope you did not suffer insult or injury At his hands?"

"No; but I escaped only by turning down a narrow lane," answered Hortensia; "there my carriage was broken to pieces, as I have said, and I was obliged to mount a horse, and get away as fast as I could. What has become of the carriage and its contents, my maid, and my servants, remains yet to be seen."

"I grieve exceedingly that you have suffered such inconvenience," replied the officer; "and I can only compensate for it by insuring that you shall be safely and immediately escorted to Wells, or any where else that you think fit to go within reasonable distance. But who are these three gentlemen behind," he continued, in a louder tone, "in such exceedingly country attire?"

"Why, general, don't you know me?" said the good farmer, riding up; "I saw you at my lord's head-quarters yesterday morning. There it is, all about it. I am Josiah Bacon; and I think that ought to pass me and every one with me;" and he held forth a scrap of paper which he had produced from his pocket.

"I think I do remember your face," said Churchill, taking the paper, on which were written the following words:

"These are to certify that Josiah Bacon, a true and loyal subject of our sovereign lord, King James the Second, has voluntarily furnished eighteen horses for the service of the royal artillery, and to require all faithful lieges of his said majesty, and officers in the army under my command, to suffer the said Josiah Bacon to pass and repass the several posts and stations upon his lawful business or the king's good service. Feversham."

Below was written, "I hereby prohibit any soldiers or officers being quartered in the house or on the premises of the above-named Josiah Bacon, and require all men in the king's name to give him aid and assistance on every lawful occasion."

"Good," said Churchill, when he had read; "but who are these two men behind?"

"They are only two of my lads," replied the farmer; "you see the way of it was this, general--her ladyship there and this young gentleman came to my house yesterday afternoon, wanting to make their way to Bristol, or Bath, or Wells, or any of those places, but in a great fright about your soldiers, for Kirke's lambs had scared them. They had a servant with them then, and while we took them in and did the best for them, they sent the man on--Stilling I think they called him--to see which way they could get on in safety. I heard them with my own ears; so this morning, you see, after watching the battle last night from the windows--and heartily did we all pray for the king's success--they determined to go on when they heard you had won the victory; but, being still a little bit frightened about stragglers from the army and such like, they got me and these two fellows to come with them and show them the way, and take care of them."

Hortensia bad seldom, if ever, so much wished a long speech at an end; but Churchill listened with exemplary patience, and when the farmer had done, inquired, "Do you assure me, upon your loyalty, Master Bacon, that these two men are actually your farm-servants, and that they took no part in the battle last night?"

"Upon my soul and conscience they never were out of the house, and have been with me for the last two years," replied the farmer.

"Well, then, you can pass," said Churchill. "Will you ride on with them, Lady Danvers?"

"Come, Ralph," said Hortensia, joyfully.

But Churchill interposed with a grave look. "I beg your pardon," he said, "but I must ask this young gentleman a few questions before he proceeds with you."

He paused, as if he expected her to go forward; but Hortensia kept her hand tight upon her bridle rein, and the general then proceeded, saying, "May I inquire who you are, sir?"

"A very unimportant personage, my lord," replied Ralph.

"Not so, I should suppose from your bearing, sir," interrupted Churchill, in a courteous tone, "though not so important as I at first believed. You are about the same height as the Duke of Monmouth; and I fancied, when first I saw you, that I had caught the bird for which we had been beating the bushes all the morning. I perceive my mistake; but may I ask your name? You must be of the court, I think; but I have not the honor of recollecting you."

"My name, sir, is Woodhall," replied Ralph, at once.

"Your Christian name?" asked Churchill.

"Ralph Woodhall," answered the young gentleman, calmly.

"Then I fear, sir," rejoined the general, "that I must request you to accompany me to my quarters, and deprive Lady Danvers for a time of the advantage of your escort. I will take care, however, that your place is properly supplied, and that she shall suffer no inconvenience."

"That is all I could desire," replied Ralph; but Hortensia demanded, fixing her beautiful eyes upon Churchill's face with a look earnest and intense, "Does he go as a prisoner, my Lord Churchill?"

"Not exactly as a prisoner, dear Lady Danvers," replied Churchill, "but as my guest for the time;" then, seeing a look of doubt and grief on Hortensia's face, he added, "The truth is, then, and I must not conceal it from you, that I have heard at the quarters of Lord Feversham, the commander-in-chief, that orders have been given for the apprehension of a gentleman of the name of Ralph Woodhall on some charge, I know not well what. I do not apprehend him myself, because I am not a constable or a messenger; but I feel it my duty to stop him, in obedience to the intimation I have received."

"Then the offense with which he is charged is not a military offense," said Lady Danvers; "and, if so, there can be no need for Lord Churchill to make himself a constable for the occasion. I beseech you, my lord, as you must well know that this gentleman has had no share in this most unfortunate rebellion, to suffer him to pass on with me, for I feel that I have been greatly the cause of his having been placed in this situation. Had he not undertaken to see me safely to Wells, he would have been many miles from this spot at the present moment."

"Dear Lady Danvers," said Churchill, with that captivating grace which so peculiarly distinguished him, "you have been now at the court of England nearly three years, I think. Where few pass unassailed, you have retained an unblemished reputation--and your honor is too high and pure for envy even to attempt to cloud it--"

The color rose in Hortensia's cheek; for she thought he was about to censure her traveling with Ralph, and point to the effect it might have upon her fair fame; but Churchill turned his speech quite in a different manner, saying, after a momentary pause, "You esteem this reputation highly, dear Lady Danvers; not the softest or tenderest persuasions would induce you to swerve from the line of duty, or do one act that could tarnish your fair fame. The honor of a soldier must be kept equally unsullied; he must be as well prepared to resist entreaties as any beautiful lady in the land, and, be the temptation what it will, keep his conduct beyond all imputation. Was not this so, I fear I should yield to you at once."

Hortensia seemed still about to remonstrate, but Ralph besought her not to do so, and then spoke a few words in a low tone to the general himself.

Churchill made a sign to the escort which had accompanied him, spoke with an old officer who rode forward, and then some changes took place in the disposition of his little force. It was all done very rapidly, and while the troopers were cantering in different directions, the general once more advanced close to Lady Danvers, saying, in a low tone, "Do not be apprehensive about this gentleman, dear Lady Danvers. Doubtless no harm will happen to him. I believe the charge against him is something concerning a duel not quite regular in its forms; but in these days such events are never treated severely when the first effect of them upon the public mind is passed. We will endeavor to keep the matter back as long as possible, and there can be no doubt of the result."

"Will you promise me, Lord Churchill, to do the very best you can for him, and on no account to give him up to Colonel Kirke?" asked Lady Danvers, in a voice trembling with emotion.

"I give you my honor of both," replied Churchill, "and I think you need be under no alarm."

At the same moment Ralph approached, and, taking Hortensia's hand, he bent his head over it, saying, "Farewell, dearest lady; may God bless and protect you ever;" and, without waiting for a reply, he turned his horse and cantered away.

Hortensia saw that, as he rode, two of Lord Churchill's soldiers joined him, the one placing himself on the right, and the other on the left. Without a word to Lord Churchill--for her heart was too full to speak--she urged her horse forward on the road she had been previously pursuing. The moment after, the old officer who had spoken with Churchill, accompanied by two or three troopers, followed and took his place by her side, saying, "Lord Churchill has commanded me, my lady, to see you ten miles on the way--or further, should you require it."

Hortensia merely bowed her head in reply; and at that moment she would have given much for a vail or a mask, for the tears were streaming rapidly down her cheeks.

CHAPTER XXXV

The insurrectionary war was over; but far the most bloody part of the whole tragedy was about to begin. There is certainly a degree of madness in the vices and crimes of the human race--a something beyond a mere spirit of evil--a something that hurries us out of the pale of reason, and teaches mankind to commit, even deliberately, acts which the right use of intellect would utterly forbid. We are all fond of the idea of glory. We feel our hearts glow at the recital of gallant actions. The splendor of great victories the sounds of triumph, and the shouts of military success excite our imagination, and warm the hellish part of the blood in our veins. But what becomes of reason?

No one has been fonder of such illusions than myself. No one has felt a deeper thrill in reading of feats of chivalrous daring, or listening to tales of great renown. But let the reader put such achievements to the same test to which I put them a few days ago. Let him take a picture of a great battle, where the fancy and skill of an accomplished painter have done the best that could be done to heighten the interest, and conceal the horrible details of the scene--where the dust, and the grime, and the convulsions are omitted altogether--where the languor of the dying and the prostration of the dead are made to group in fair, flowing lines around the feet of the trampling horses and the charging corps--where the blood is used sparingly in contrast with the pallor of the faces, to produce an harmonious effect of coloring, and the fiery bursting of a shell is kept in tone by a stream of gore lighted by the flash. Let him not strip it of any of the painter's adjuncts; let him leave it embellished as far as the pencil could embellish; but let him strip it of all that his own fancy has added, and let him take it and dissect it under the microscope-glass of reason. Let him look at the combatants, one by one, and ask what they are fighting for. The one for a name in history, which very likely he may never attain, and which, if he does, will benefit him in nothing. Another, because he is commanded to fight by some king or some leader, spilling his life's blood and taking the life of others at the nod of a man in whose face he would spit if he told him to black his shoes. Another is fighting for pure principles of patriotism, without ever asking himself if the same, or even higher ends, could not be obtained by any other than the butchering means with which he soils his hands. Others, and by far the greater part, are fighting for--from four-pence to a shilling a day; and they fight just as bravely, just as gallantly as the others! The whole, each and every one, are engaged in debasing God's image, breaking God's law, and taking from others the etherial essence they can never restore--the great, the mighty, the inestimable boon of life--for objects and purposes which two hundred years after, if not utterly forgotten, will be found to have changed but very little the course of events, or influenced the world's history. But take each of those figures separately--those dark, livid things lying on the ground, and think what has befallen him by this great achievement. That fair-haired youth, lying there, was the hope of a mother's heart, the only one dear to a widowed bosom, the support of her age and of her sickness. His last thought, as he felt the life-blood welling away from his side, was his "Poor mother!" and he saw before her, with the prophetic eye of death, years of wasting grief, neglect, and gnawing penury; and then, the workhouse. Then, again, that stout fellow, somewhat older, with the broad-sword still grasped in his dead hand; his fine open brow, his powerful limbs, all show a man who might have served his country, and the best interests of humanity, well in other fields than this--ay, in better, nobler fields. The last thought of his heart, when he felt the shot, was of his calm cottage in the country, and of the wife and babes he never shall see again. He thought of their future fate--of all the hard chances of life for them, deprived of a husband and a father; and a cloud of doubt came between his parting spirit and his God. Close beside him, slain probably at the same moment, lies the hardened reprobate, unchastised and unreclaimed, loaded with wickedness, and sent, without a moment's warning or a moment's thought, into the presence of offended Deity; and there, hard by, the young and unconfirmed waverer, with much matter for self-reproach in his heart--with a sense of wrong doing--with aspirations for better things--with resolutions for amendment not yet commenced; and he, too, is sent to his account, without real penitence or heart-breathed prayer, before purpose can become act.

There is a burning village in the back-ground, and doubtless there are many others round--homes destroyed--families left destitute--sons, fathers, husbands, brothers slain--weeping in all eyes--agony in all hearts. But this is only one circle beyond the immediate spot; for from that point of glory flow far away on every side deep streams of misery, and sorrow, and calamity, to which the transient joy and evanescent brightness of a great victory is but as a falling star in a dark night.

It may be said--nay, it has been said--that we must not look at these things too closely. Believe me, reader, that the act or the passion, which we dare not look at too closely, is evil. It needs no such close examination; for the judgment of the reason is pronounced upon it as it vails itself from inspection.

If such, however, be any true picture of the insane sin of war, what must we think of laws, and customs, and acts, and of the men who committed or made them, by which oceans of blood, shed deliberately on the scaffold, after fierce passion had subsided, have flowed over the page of history, making it little else than one scarlet crime? If it be doubtful--nay, more than doubtful--whether it be a less crime than murder to shed the blood of man for any thing but murder, what must we think of death, ay, and torture, being inflicted by one human being upon another, not only for acts, but for words, and even thoughts? Society must be a bad thing, and a weak one, if it requires to be defended by such crimes as these.

Of all periods known in English history, the time of which I write was perhaps the one most foully stained by such abominations. The scene was just opening--the tragedy had merely begun when the battle of Sedgemoor ended; law, and all its forms, were set at naught; prisoners were slaughtered without trial, as without mercy; the suspected had imposed upon them tasks more terrible than death; and the simple well-wishers of an unsuccessful cause were forced to quarter the victims of tyranny, and imbrue their hands in the warm blood of friends, companions, and, we are assured, even relations. The fiend Kirke was busy in his brutal office all day long, and his ferocious soldiery drank deep of blood, and reveled amid the carnage in unbridled licentiousness. None escaped him or them upon whom the jealous eye of power fell, who could not pay enormously for life from some store unattainable by his death; for where there was a choice, Kirke always preferred blood.

Had Ralph Woodhall been given up at once by Churchill to any inferior officer, or even to Lord Feversham himself, it is more than probable his fate would have been instantly sealed. His presence on the field after the battle might have been judged enough. No investigation--no examination of witnesses would have been deemed necessary; and he might have been condemned and died ere he quitted the verge of Sedgemoor. But Churchill remembered his promise to Hortensia, and fulfilled it honorably. There was also something in Ralph's demeanor which he liked; for--gold and ambition apart--that great general was not insensible to high qualities in others. He was a keen judge of human nature too; and there was a straightforward frankness in Ralph's dealings with him, from which he argued so favorably that he stretched lenity toward him to the utmost. He conversed with him on his return to his quarters for some time, treated him with every sort of polite attention, and said to him in the end, "It may be some days before I see Lord Feversham, or have an opportunity of delivering you into the hands of those who will insure you a fair and impartial trial. You have answered me straightforwardly in every thing, Mr. Woodhall, and I have not the slightest doubt you are a man of your word. If, therefore, you will give me your parole of honor to consider yourself a prisoner, and not to absent yourself more than half a mile from my quarters, I will free you from the unpleasant attendance of a guard."

Ralph's parole was, of course, immediately given, and Churchill continued this liberal course of conduct as far as possible, from the knowledge that, the longer a trial is delayed, the more likely is a just if not a more lenient one to be obtained. He little knew at the time that the arch-fiend--compared with whom Kirke was indeed a lamb--was coming down with all speed to crush those whom military vengeance could not reach. Rumor, indeed, said that the well-known Jeffries would be sent into the West; but Churchill fancied wrongly that common decency would impel the court to withhold or restrain this unscrupulous perverter of the law.

The general's head-quarters had been moved to a considerable distance from East Zoyland; and he had invited Ralph and some of his own officers to a very plain and homely dinner, when, toward the close of the meal, a paper was presented to him, which he read attentively. No change of countenance took place; and he merely said to his trooper who brought in the paper, "Tell them to wait without."

When the dinner was over, however, and the guests were retiring, he beckoned Ralph to a window, and put the paper he had received into the young gentleman's hand. It was an order to deliver him up to a messenger who was charged to lodge him, without delay, in Dorchester jail.

"I fear I must obey it," said Churchill; "and now I will only add as a hint, that as soon as I have given you up, your parole to me is at an end. More than one man," he added, with a meaning smile, and no very unpleasant recollection, "has found safety and fortune by jumping out of window."

Ralph thanked him gravely; and the messenger and his two followers having been called in, the young gentleman was delivered into their hands.

I will not pretend that, had opportunity presented itself, Ralph would have neglected the hint which Lord Churchill had given him; but the messenger was shrewd and keen, the two officers watchful and severe, and, at the end of three days, Ralph Woodhall was lodged in Dorchester jail, and experienced for the first time the taste of real imprisonment. A low, miserable, damp cell was assigned to him; no food but bread and water, except what he paid for at enormous prices, was afforded to him by the jailer, and a light was refused him when night fell. It was not, indeed, intended that this course of treatment should be continued, as he had the means of paying for better accommodations; but it was what a jailer technically termed in those days "the taming of a bird," or, in other words, the preparation necessary to make him submit quietly to every imposition, however gross. Thus, in darkness, discomfort, and gloom, with memories and expectations equally painful, he passed his first night in the prison at Dorchester, where, for the present, we must leave him.

CHAPTER XXXVI

It was still in the midst of summer, but London was yet crowded, although the Parliament had risen. The city was in great agitation, too; for news of a battle, and the defeat of Monmouth--the great Protestant leader, whom the Protestant Church had failed to support--the idol of the people, whom the people, or, at least, all those who were influential among them, had left to perish--had reached London on the preceding night by rapid post from the West. A general gloom hung over the metropolis in despite of the rejoicing of the court; and many a man began to regret, too late, that he had not mounted horse and buckled on his sword when every arm was needful, and every purse should have been opened to support the cause which fully one half of the nation had affected, at least, to advocate for many a long year. But a multitude of those whom timidity, doubts of his right, suspicion of his character, or disapproval of his conduct, had kept from joining the standard of the great insurgent, although truly attached to the cause of religious liberty, very soon had personal motives furnished to them for bitterly repenting that they had not thrown their weight into the scale, while there was a possibility of the balance being turned. The slightest suspicion of having held communication with Monmouth, or the smallest possible evidence of dissenting from the Episcopal Church on any side but popery, was treated as a high offense: rights, guarantees, statutes, were set at naught, and many hundreds were snatched from their homes and cast into prison without having committed any other crime than that of entertaining a conscientious objection to the government and the forms of the English Church.

Thus the gloom was increased through the city; nor was it diminished when men found that a sort of trade in accusations was once more about to commence; that the royal bounty was prepared to reward the informer; and that a multitude of harpies round the court were all ready to make a merchandise of clemency, as far as it could be wrung from the hard, cold heart of James the Second.

All was gloom, then, although bells were ringing, flags flying, and bonfires prepared, when a young gentleman, attended by two or three horsemen, rode quickly along what was then known as the Reading road, and entered the town without slackening his pace. He was impelled by even stronger motives than the reward which had hurried forth the earlier posts; and, though he took his way toward Whitehall, it was not at the gates of the royal palace he dismounted. In one of the streets in the vicinity of the court there was a large house, to which I have before led the reader; and in one of the rooms on the ground floor, at the moment the young stranger arrived before the door, sat old Lord Woodhall, reading a broad sheet which gave an account of the battle. He had been very much changed by the events of the last few weeks. He was no longer the stout, hale, robust country gentleman which he had previously appeared. He was shrunk and exceedingly thin, and old age was marked upon every feature of his face. He was tall and upright still, for the very fierce and angry feelings which consumed his corporeal frame served to give him an energy and a fire which sustained him with unnatural strength.

The middle of a paragraph had been reached, detailing with many blunders and exaggerations the closing scene of the battle, the flight of Monmouth from the field, and the direction which he was positively asserted to have taken, when the door was flung open at once, and Robert Woodhall entered, booted and spurred, and muddy from the road.

"News! news! my noble lord," he exclaimed, with a triumphant air.

"I have it here, boy," answered Lord Woodhall, rapping the paper with his finger.

"Ay, but better news than that, noble kinsman," said the young man, with a laugh; and then, keeping up a tone partly jesting, partly serious, he asked, "What did you promise me, my lord, if I put Ralph Woodhall, the murderer of your son, into the hands of justice?"

"Why," said Lord Woodhall, with a good deal of hesitation, "I promised I would give you Margaret, as your mother wishes; but I find she does not love you--can not love you, she says."

"Perhaps because she loves her brother's murderer," replied the young man, bitterly.

The old nobleman started as if a serpent had bit him, and exclaimed, "Robert, Robert, do not set my whole blood on fire at such a thought! Beware what you do, sir--beware what you insinuate! Is the man taken? is he in prison?"

"Oh no, he is not," replied Robert Woodhall, in a cool, indifferent tone; "I know where he is; I can put him in the hands of justice in eight-and-forty hours. In double that time he may escape, for he goes whither he will, and disports himself as a gentleman at large. But what is that to me, if Margaret loves him better than me--if your promise is to be unavailing, and your commands to be set at naught?"

The old man advanced sternly toward him, took his hand and wrung it hard, murmuring in a low, fierce, emphatic tone, "Robert, you shall have her! But put him in my power--but give him to the arm of the law, and you shall have her, with all my estates, at my death. I say not how soon she shall be yours; she must have time--I must have time; but she shall be yours, I pledge you my honor, and my conscience, and my soul. May God curse me and spare the murderer if I break my vow."

"That is all I can desire," answered Robert. "We will not hurry the fair lady; and I think, my dear lord, that I can soon contrive to clear her mind of any love for Master Ralph, if such a fancy has ever crossed it. There are certain tales down there, which, even without all that poor Henry knew--and told her, I believe--of this very honest, religious young man's fidelity to her, must soon banish from her heart every trace of affection toward him."

"It is false!" cried Lord Woodhall, vehemently. "She has no affection toward him. She dislikes you, because she knows you to be a libertine and a profligate."

"Better that, my lord, than libertine, profligate, and hypocrite too," answered Robert Woodhall, somewhat nettled.

"That is true, indeed," replied the old nobleman; "but no more of that; my word is given, and it shall be kept. Now, where is this man--this murderer?"

"Down in the West, there, my lord," replied Robert Woodhall; "but, saving your good pleasure, I must have the management of all this. None but myself must place him in the hands of the officer. I would not share that task with any one for half a kingdom."

"Thou art a fine lad, and shall have your way," answered old Lord Woodhall, attributing to regard for his dead son the zeal which proceeded in truth from mere personal hatred. "What is it you want now? How is it you intend to proceed?"

"I ask but a letter from you to the secretary of state," replied Robert, "desiring him to give me a messenger for the apprehension of Ralph

Woodhall, and for his safe transmission to Dorchester jail, and you shall have information that he is there lodged by the very next post from the West.

"The letter you shall have," replied the old man; "and I will keep my word, let come what may. Seek me pen and ink."

The letter to the secretary of state was accordingly written, and, without even asking to see Margaret, Robert Woodhall went on his way rejoicing. At the office of the secretary of state he was detained some time, for much important business was going on in consequence of the late important events in the West. An intimation given, however, to one of the clerks, that he was the brother of Lord Culdenham, and fresh from Sedgemoor, at length obtained admission for him, and the secretary received him with much courtesy.

"Your brother's regiment did good service, Mr. Woodhall," he said; "you were with it, I suppose."

"I command a company in that regiment, my lord," answered Robert, with the color coming somewhat warmly into his cheek from a knowledge that in reality he had not been in the battle at all--and that by his own fault; "but your lordship's time is precious, I know, and the business I come upon is very urgent."

Sunderland fixed his eyes upon him for one instant very steadfastly, and the slightest possible smile curled his acute lip, while he said, "What is the business, Mr. Woodhall? I shall be most happy to serve you."

"If you will read that letter, my lord, you will see," replied Robert; and the secretary took and perused it rapidly. He made some difficulties, however. It was not customary, he remarked, to send a secretary of state's messenger to apprehend any one accused of any thing but state offenses. Common constables, or any ordinary officer of police, might be employed.

"It is not improbable, my lord," replied Robert, who had a vigorous perseverance in his nature which was not easily baffled--a touch of his mother's strong determination--"it is not improbable, my lord, that affairs of state may be complicated with other offenses in this instance. This man was certainly upon the field at Sedgemoor. He is also accused of harboring, comforting, and defending, against the officers of the law, a noted Dissenting preacher named Calloway."

Sunderland still seemed to hesitate, and Robert immediately added, "If your lordship has any scruple, however, it can easily be removed, I think, by an application to the king, who I know is extremely anxious that this notorious offender should be brought to justice. I can go to his majesty with Lord Woodhall, and return in a few minutes;" and he raised his hat slightly, as if about to depart.

"That is not necessary," said Sunderland, quickly; "I think you have made out a case; but recollect that the office can not be charged with the expenses, unless the young man be taken. Are you prepared to pay them, should you fail?"

"Perfectly," replied Robert Woodhall; "for I am certain of his apprehension, if we proceed quickly. I only trust your lordship will impress upon the messenger the necessity of dispatch."

All was soon arranged to his satisfaction, and Robert Woodhall set off with the messenger in two hours from that time.

A change, which may at first sight appear strange, came upon him as he journeyed. Courage, like all other qualities, is very variously modified in different men; and, besides the two great divisions of moral and physical, it has an infinite number of subdivisions. Some men--especially those of great imagination and hypochondriac temperament--are hesitating and even timid in the contemplation of distant danger, but become bold as lions, and perfectly self-possessed, in the moment of action. Others--and of these Robert Woodhall was one--are exceedingly brave in determination, but somewhat fearful in execution. He had, when he set out for London from Somersetshire, regarded the apprehension of his cousin Ralph with a malevolent pleasure, which made him resolve to see the work done himself, and to have the satisfaction of witnessing with his own eyes Ralph's consignment to a dungeon. He pictured to himself, with great delight, the anguish of the man he hated, and his removal out of the soft guardianship of Churchill--from which Robert sincerely believed he could and would escape as soon as the hot pursuit after Monmouth was over--to all the horrors and inconveniences of a county prison of those days. All along the road to London he had amused himself with such contemplations; he had gloated over Ralph's anticipated sufferings, and he had pictured each particular scene as it arose. But when he had obtained what he wanted, and was riding back with the messenger and his followers toward Somersetshire, he began to doubt and hesitate. Ralph was fiery, and Robert thought him more so than he really was. There was no certainty that he might not resist; and if he did, his resistance was likely to be dangerous. Robert feared, too, that his cousin might speak unpleasant truths regarding him, and he went on in his own mind swelling up objections to any further personal interference, till in the end he determined to put the messenger and his followers so far upon the track that there was no possibility of their missing the game, and then leave them to hunt it down themselves, taking all the credit to himself, and avoiding every risk.

When the small party arrived at Taunton, Robert was anxious that they should proceed some way further that night; but the messenger, though a resolute and active officer, was a man who loved his comforts, and he would only consent to go on after having remained a couple of hours to rest and dine.

Robert had no stomach for his meat; for he had heard of the removal of Churchill's quarters, and he was anxious lest the prey should escape him. He wandered out, then, from the little inn at which he and his companions had alighted, and walked through the principal street of the town, where nothing but signs of gloom and dismay met him on every side, till, standing at the door of a larger inn, he beheld a good portly man in the livery of his family.

On inquiry, he found, much to his surprise, that his mother was in the house, and that a messenger from her had been dispatched that very evening to Lord Coldenham. In a few moments he was in Lady Coldenham's presence, and she showed as much gladness at the sight of her favorite son as she ever displayed on any occasion. She seemed much surprised to hear that he had been in London, but interrupted him in the course of his narrative to say, "You should not have been absent, Robert, when you knew that Ralph Woodhall was in the neighborhood. He has escaped the hands of Colonel Kirke, I find, but he must not escape us. There is much depends upon it."

She paused, and gazed upon him with a fixed, glassy sort of stare, and then added, "He must be taken--he must be tried--he must die! If he escapes you, you will repent your negligence long and bitterly. He is a viper in the path which must be crushed, and you should not have quitted the place till he was in prison."

"If your ladyship knew what I went for," replied Robert, "you would approve of my going. You know, of course, that the murderer was concealed at the house of Lady Danvers--"

"Give him no hard names, Robert," replied the old lady, with a bitter smile; "it signifies not to us whether he be a murderer or not. As to that pretty little bright-eyed doll, Hortensia Danvers, she must not stand in my way. She will find herself overmatched, with all her wit. But what were you going to say? Kirke searched her house; but the bird was flown. I know all that."

"But you do not know, my dear lady and mother," replied Robert, "that since then, Ralph Woodhall has fallen into the hands of Lord Churchill, who allows him to be what he calls a prisoner on parole--that is, gives him every opportunity of flying when he likes. Churchill would certainly not give him up to a common constable; and I went to London, first, to get a messenger to see our admirable cousin--as you object to the term murderer--lodged safely in prison, and, secondly, to secure for myself the fruits of my discoveries in pretty Margaret's hand and Lord Woodhall's estates."

Old Lady Coldenham shook her head gravely. "There will be difficulties there, I fear," she said; "the old lord's last letter on the subject was as cold as ice."

"The difficulties on his part are all removed," replied Robert. "I have his promise, sealed by every sort of vow and imprecation, that if I lodge Ralph in prison, I shall have Margaret's hand. Any difficulty will lie with her; but they must be overborne."

"What has she to do with it?" exclaimed Lady Coldenham; "she must, of course, marry whom her father tells her. His promise is quite enough, and he will not break it."

"It is to fulfill my part of the bond that I am now hurrying back," replied Robert; "and as Churchill has no knowledge whatever that I have made any discovery, we shall take him by surprise before he can afford Master Ralph the means of escape. The messenger is here in the town with me: a greedy beast, who spends half his time in eating. I trust he has done his supper by this time, and therefore, with your leave, will go and see if he be ready to ride forward. Where shall I find your ladyship when I have fulfilled my task?"

"The moment all is safe, send me a messenger," said the old lady; "and if I have the news that he is lodged in the clutches of the law, you will find me at Ormebar Castle the day after to-morrow. But mind he escapes you not. There is more hangs upon his life than you know of, Robert."

"He shall not escape," answered her son, confidently; "but there is one other man I would fain catch hold of too, if I could do so without burning my fingers--one who has insulted me, and been the chosen companion-- servant, as he calls him--of this serpent Ralph: I mean old Stilling's son."

The color rose in the old woman's cheek; and she answered sternly, "Let him alone! You have behaved very ill, boy, and your folly will cost me five thousand pounds. How dared you meddle with the old man's daughter? You might have made concubines of all the girls in the village but her, without my caring; but you know not what you have done. Touch not the young man, however--do no one act against him, as you value all that you possess on earth. And now away. See that Ralph escapes you not; that is your business for the present. We may have more to settle hereafter."

Robert took his departure gladly, for there was a look upon his mother's face which he knew too well to remain exposed to her anger willingly; and the result of his further proceedings is already known to the reader.

CHAPTER XXXVII

Once more back to London, dear reader, and to the house of Lord Woodhall, near the court. There were two rooms occupied in that house, and a little episode going on in each, about an hour after Ralph Woodhall's departure. Into each of these I should like to give my reader an insight, but know not well which to proceed with first. Perhaps the one the most completely detached from the story, and having the least influence upon the result, had better be chosen. We will walk up stairs, then, and into Margaret's room, where she sits with her door bolted to guard against interruption, and two letters before her. She has read one, in the hand of Ralph Woodhall, and it has clouded many hopes, and cast a deep shadow back upon her mind It has told her that he whom she loves is a prisoner, and that all chance of escape is at an end; that he must abide a prejudiced trial, and encounter all that the wrath of her own relations can do to destroy him. But as there are drops of bitter in every cup, so are there drops of sweetness in the bitterest chalice; and Ralph's letter has given her the most solemn assurances that he had no share whatever in her brother's death, and that he has loved her ever, and will love her ever to the last hour of life. He has spoken, too, of Hortensia--freely--frankly--easily, telling all that she has done for him, and showing the painful situation in which she has been placed by the result of her generous kindness to the son of her mother's friend.

That was a great satisfaction to her; for Margaret was a woman; but yet, perhaps, for the same reason, she was not quite satisfied. She would certainly have been better pleased had it been a man who thus befriended her lover. Nevertheless, she felt very grateful, and tried to persuade herself that there was not a vestige of such a thing as jealousy in her mind.

The other letter was written in a small, woman's hand, more beautiful than was common in those days, and though it was open. Margaret had kept it unread till she had perused every word in Ralph's handwriting twice. She had only seen the first words, and those were so familiar and affectionate that she thought they must come from some well-known friend, though she could not remember the writing. She now turned to it with some interest, and read:

"Dearest Margaret,

"If to have learned to love you like a sister can give me a claim to call you so, I have a right to use these words. I write to you in great sadness, but yet I will not be deterred from writing; for there are many causes which induce me to seek personal communication with yourself, and among the chief of these is the hope of serving you in times of difficulty, and supporting you in hours of trial. One very dear to you, and deservedly so both as a man and a relation, has read me a part of your letter to him, warning him that his residence at my house had been discovered, and that danger menaced him there. Do not think that this was a breach of confidence on his part, for it was absolutely necessary in the circumstances in which he was placed. That letter only served to heighten my affection for you both, and increase my anxiety to serve you. You spoke of gratitude toward me for what I did to shelter and save him. I deserve no such gratitude, for I acted entirely from personal feelings. He is the son of one whom my mother loved as few have ever loved a sister; and, therefore, I felt that he had as much claim upon me as a near relation. I served him, also, because I have a deep regard for him, and because I look upon him as injured and persecuted. After I had heard your letter, believe me, I only redoubled my exertions, periled myself, my fortune, and perhaps my fair fame to save him; but my own heart is satisfied that I did right, and I do not think that you will judge otherwise. We set out to seek for some port where he could embark, traveling in my carriage, and well attended; but we were met and turned by various parties of contending troops, till, in the end, my carriage broke down, and I was obliged to fly with him on horseback, traveling with a single servant only. At length, most unfortunately, we were suddenly stopped by a party of Lord Churchill's horse, and he was immediately made a prisoner.

"I give you all these details, because I know there are some about you who may seek to give a false impression of my conduct and his. The inconveniences I suffered I care not for at all; the opinion of the world I care for little; but your good opinion, dear Margaret, I care for much, as it must greatly depend upon that how much you trust me, and how far we can act together to frustrate the designs of those who wish no good to you, and all evil to him who loves you. Believe not a word that they say, Margaret; believe only that I have acted toward him as a sister to a brother, and that I have done that, ever thinking of you, and of his love for you, and seeking as one object to promote your happiness. I will own that when I saw him arrested, I wept for him as bitter tears as I ever shed, and probably exposed myself to imputations which I did not deserve; but be assured that there is no act of my life that I could have wished you not to see; no word that I have ever uttered to him that I could not desire you to hear.

"And now, dear Margaret--believing this, as I know you will believe it--listen to a few words of counsel from one more world-learned than yourself. Remember that you are surrounded by his enemies--by those who, either from malice or mistake, seek to destroy him, and if they can not succeed in that, to deprive him of you. Trust them not, Margaret. Receive every thing they tell you with doubt. Be firm, constant, and true to the last; for be sure it is the only road to--the only chance of happiness. Let them not persuade you to any thing that can ever put a bar against your union with him. Let them never induce you to give up faith in despair. Far be it from me to urge any child to disobey a parent; but there is a limit to obedience beyond which no parent has a right to exact it, and the less when any command is founded on passion, prejudice, or error. I see before you many a difficulty and many a trial; but still, be firm under them all, and if any service can be rendered to you, or any support afforded, fear not to apply to me.

"Hortensia Danvers."

Why, I will not stop to inquire, but Margaret wept when she read those lines.

It is now time that we should descend to the room below, in which Lord Woodhall still sat after his young relation Robert had left him. He had read over twice the news from Sedgemoor, and was reading it again, when first there was a tap at the door, and then a portly and jovial figure entered, in very neat and bright attire. The black silk stockings fitted the sturdy calves of the legs and the neat ankle to the utmost nicety. Nothing could be brighter than the shoe. The cassock glistened like a raven's wing; and the round, smooth, well-shaven face, beaming with good nature and a kindly heart, was almost as lustrous as the gown.

"Well, my dear lord, well," cried Doctor M'Feely, "I have won my bet, I think. Monmouth has been beaten before the seventh of July, and I have won the living that your lordship promised."

"You shall have it--you shall have it, parson," said the old lord, whose spirits Robert's news had somewhat cheered, "though you have had as narrow a squeak of it as ever ninth pig had, just escaped the tithe. You should have had it, indeed," he added, in a good-humored tone, "even if you hadn't won the bet. You have waited a long time, but you have got a good one now. The presentation was made out the day before yesterday, and you have nothing to do but go down and ring yourself in. The dedimus, too, is made out, and sent down to Giles somebody or other, who will receive your oaths; for, as I told you, you must act as justice too in those wild parts. We know better than to put many parsons in the commission in Lincolnshire."

"Ay, that's the worst part of the bargain," said good Doctor M'Feely. "I wish I could get over that. I never could bear to send a poor creature to prison, I'm sure."

"Pooh! pooh!" said the old peer; "go and take the oaths directly, the first thing you do, and my word for it you will be as hard as a flint-stone before a twelvemonth is over, committing any lad who steals a cabbage or nooses a hare as readily as you will give a text on a Sunday. If you look in that drawer, you will find all the papers."

Doctor M'Feely got them out, with great reverence for the papers, and great joy at his new situation. He was a man destitute by no means of imagination, and it is inconceivable what apple-trees he planted in the orchard, and how he plowed the glebe. When he had got the precious documents in his pocket, however, which made him, with the consent of the bishop--no very difficult thing in those days--rector of the united parish of Bridlington cum Saddletree, and justice of the peace in the county of Dorset, he did not forget another errand he had in hand, though it was rather a delicate one.

"I thought I saw Master Robert Woodhall pass by me in the street," he said, after having thanked Lord Woodhall again and again; "has he been here? I thought he was in Somerset."

"Ay, he has been here, and brought me good news, doctor. He has tracked out that villain Ralph; and, before the month is out, I hope he will be hanging as high as Haman."

"Ay, now," said Doctor M'Feely, with some hesitation, "that's just what I wanted to talk about. I can't help thinking, my lord, that your lordship is mistaken about Master Ralph; I don't think any thing on earth would have made that young man draw a sword upon your son. Besides, I have letters from his father, and from the good Doctor ----, the vicar of the parish. They both say that they are sure he did not do it--nay, more, that it was impossible; and, moreover--"

"Is the man mad?" exclaimed Lord Woodhall, starting up from his seat with a look of indescribable fury in his countenance, "or would he drive me mad? Was not the challenge sent, man? Did he not say that he would come? Was not the hour appointed? Was not my son killed? Will you persuade me that my poor boy is still alive, when I saw him cold, and stiff, and white, in his bloody coffin? Of what would you persuade me? Henry was killed--at night I--without witnesses--Ralph Woodhall killed him; and I will have vengeance."

The last words were uttered with a shout, and the old man's face was contorted with passion; but Doctor M'Feely, though not very clerical in all his habits, was roused, and felt himself at that moment the minister of the Gospel; and he replied, in a solemn and warning tone, "Vengeance is mine: I will repay, saith the Lord."

The next moment he stood in the hall; and then, taking up his hat and cane, he quitted the house.

A little more than a week after the period of which I have just been speaking, Doctor M'Feely stood in his small rectory-house, a few miles from the town of Dorchester, and looked about him with evident complacence. There was a boy in deep mourning, about fifteen years of age, standing by his side; and the house was completely furnished, plainly, but very neatly. The doctor was in high good humor; every thing was somewhat better than he expected; the glebe good, and largely measured; the house solid, and wanting no repair; the small tithes as well as the large were his, and some of them had come in, so that he was not likely to want butter and eggs in a hurry. There was a prospect, in short, of pleasant abundance before him, and, what is still better, blessed independence. At that moment he did not care a rush for the whole world.

"Well, my dear," he said to the boy, "and what does your mother ask for the whole of this?"

"She says she thinks, sir, two hundred pounds," replied the boy, modestly.

"Pooh! pooh!" cried Doctor M'Feely, with some little acquired feelings of parsimony hanging about him, "a hundred and fifty is quite enough."

"The furniture, the cart, and the garden things cost my poor father four hundred not eighteen months ago," replied the boy, with a sigh.

"Ay, but they have been used a good deal since," replied Doctor M'Feely, without looking at the lad.

"Well, sir, you must have them for what you will give," said the late rector's son; "my mother is very poor, and there are eight of us; but she says she could not bear to have the things sold by auction--it would break her heart."

"Eight of you? God bless the poor woman!" exclaimed the good doctor, turning and looking him full in the face, down which was rolling a large tear; "she shall have the two hundred. I didn't think there were eight of you!"

"Not if you think it above the value, sir," said the boy.

"I dare say not--I dare say not," said the doctor, hurriedly, with a gush of warm blood coming into his smooth face; "besides, I can spare it very well, my man. I have been a great economist, do you see, and when I made two pennies I always put by one. That's the way to thrive, young man, and to keep yourself from getting out at elbows. I have never wanted a whole cassock or a clean shirt since I came across the herring pond--I won't say much for what was between the two, but that was neither seen nor felt--I can spare it quite well, I tell you, so not a word more about it; the bargain's struck; and tell your mother, my dear, that I will come down and see her to-night, and if I can help you on with your Latin and Greek, I'll do it, and perhaps communicate a touch of the genuine dialect into the bargain."

The boy went away well satisfied with his father's successor; and Doctor M'Feely sat down and took some dinner, prepared by a clean country servant, regretting that he had got no wine in the house to drink his own health on the first day of his residence. He then leaned back in his chair to indulge in an afternoon's nap, a habit which he had lately cultivated a good deal. His eyes were just closed, and two or three deep inspirations showed that his efforts had not been unsuccessful, when the door of the room shook by the opening of the outer door, and the next moment a stranger stood before him.

Doctor M'Feely started, rubbed his eyes, and gazed at the stranger, who was a young man of powerful frame, but somewhat gaunt and haggard in appearance, with a wild, somewhat wandering eye, and a broad but knitted brow.

"What do you want?" asked the doctor, without rising.

"Are you a magistrate?" asked the stranger.

"Yes; by God's blessing, I am justice of the peace," replied the good doctor. "What do you want with me in that capacity? I thought you wanted to be married, or buried, or christened; for you look in a perilous state of mind, young man, and I don't know which would be most appropriate to your case."

"The second," answered the stranger, sternly. "Christened I have been, by better hands than yours. Married I shall never be. Buried I shall soon be. But where have I seen your face before?"

"'Pon my soul and conscience I can't tell," replied the doctor, with a sly twinkle of the eye, "in no place, I hope, where I should not have been. It's Ireland perhaps you're thinking of."

"Not I," cried the stranger. "Lincolnshire, if any where; but that must be a mistake."

"Devil a bit of that," answered Doctor M'Feely, "for if you ever saw me any where in the whole world--barring Ireland--it's just as likely it was in Lincolnshire as any where else, for I never lived there a bit longer than I could help, and that was three quarters of my whole time, seeing that the old lord was so mighty fond of the hall, and the fox-hounds, and all that, to say nothing of the good wine, which was a sore temptation to his carnal nature, and to me too, it must be acknowledged. The Lord have mercy on us both, and send us more of it."

"I have it now," replied the stranger, "you are the fat chaplain who came over with him, and passed a week at Coldenham."

"I never tasted worse stuff in my life," said Doctor M'Feely, with a bitter remembrance of Lady Coldenham's wine; "and as to fat, there's a leg, boy! Where will you match that?" and he stuck it out from under his cassock, adding, in the same breath, "I can tell you what, that visit to Coldenham-- what between the sour wine and the sour woman--took two as good pounds of beef off that same identical leg as ever were cut out of an ox's rump. I thought he'd never plump out again."

"You were reckoned a good man, I think," said the stranger, in the same wild, grave tone.

"Good! to be sure I was. Did you ever see any body who was not good bloom and blossom like a rose? I always loved every thing that was good all my life--a good bottle above all. I wish I had one now," he added, in an under tone; "though I don't object to punch, when nothing else is to be had; but the devil a drop of rum is there in the house."

"Well, then," said the other, taking a paper from his pocket, "I want you to swear me to this deposition."

"Let me see--let me see," cried Doctor M'Feely, stretching out his hand.

"Not one word," replied the stranger, sternly. "It is all written in my own hand, properly drawn up, for I was bred to be that beastly thing, an attorney, and all I wish you to do is to swear me to the truth of what is contained in this paper, and to attest my signature of it."

"Lord bless you, I'll swear you fast enough," cried Doctor M'Feely. "I've seen a good deal of that done in my day on both sides of the water. Heaven help us! where's the Bible? Sally, Sally!--There's a pretty forget! Sally, is there such a thing as a Bible in the house? The old parson must have had a Bible--if not, there must be one in the village."

"Oh, I've got one, your reverence, up in my box," replied the servant.

"Reverence!" muttered the doctor. "Bring it me, there's a good girl. Here's a gentleman wants to swear a little."

"Bring a light also," said the stranger.

"A light at noon day!" exclaimed the worthy divine; "what does the man want with a light?"

"To seal this up when I have done," answered the other, with an imperturbable countenance.

"Then you may just as well blow the candle out," said the worthy doctor, "for there isn't a bit of sealing-wax in the whole house so big as a boy's marble."

The servant had in the mean time disappeared, but soon returned with a light and the Bible. Her reverend master then sent her for pen and ink, and, when all the preparations were completed, and she had quitted the room again, he once more held out his hand, saying, "Come, don't be nonsensical; give me the paper. I don't want to read a word of it--to tell the truth, I wouldn't for any thing less than half a bottle; but I must write at the top, 'Personally appeared before me, Peter M'Feely, Justice of Peace, et cetera.'"

"I have done all that for you except the name," replied the other; "put it in there;" and he held the paper before the parson while he wrote his name.

"Now, then, get over the swearing," said Doctor M'Feely. "Take the book in your right hand, and the paper in your left--mind your thumb, boy, when you kiss the book--the cover's not over clean, but it's as good as your own, I fancy. Now we'll be serious--if possible. It's an awful job, swearing. You know the nature of an oath, I suppose?"

"Better than you do," answered the stranger fiercely, "for you have taken many an oath that you have broken to God, if not to man;" and then, in a clear and audible voice, and without any prompting, he proceeded to swear to the truth of every word that paper contained, and then signed his name to it in a bold, free hand.

Doctor M'Feely then attested the signature, exclaiming, as he did so, "Gaunt Stilling! Now I recollect. Stilling was the old clerk and sexton at Coldenham; many a chat we've had together. Gaunt was his son, who had been in the Tangier regiment--you are gaunt enough now--why, what in the name of Misfortune has changed you so, lad? Why, I do recollect you, only you look ten years older. Come, take a cup of ale; there's that in the house, at all events."

Gaunt Stilling waved his hand. "You shall have this within three days," he said. "It will not be wanted before then."

"Three days? I shall be at the assizes in three days," said the parson.

"You must wait till you receive this," replied Gaunt Stilling, "and then act with it as I shall direct you. The assizes will not be at Dorchester for four days at least. The commission was only opened at Winchester on Monday; and now good-by. You are not a bad man at heart, I believe. I recollect the sermon you preached in Coldenham Church, and you spoke bold words upon the vices of the great, which did you honor. Do not forget your master's service in seeing justice done to the innocent. Be bold, and true to the right, and that may cover a multitude of little sins like yours."

"Whew!" whistled Doctor M'Feely, "as if a man were a bit the worse for liking a good bottle and a slice out of the haunch, to say nothing of the fat! I can prove that it's a crying sin to neglect such mercies. All the fathers held it so, and when I write their *lives* I'll make it appear, whatever their *doctrines* might be;" but Gaunt Stilling had waited for no such proofs; and, after rubbing his good broad forehead for a moment, Doctor M'Feely sank back in his chair again and took a nap.

CHAPTER XXXVIII

The very name of Jeffries spread terror and despair through the various prisons in the west of England in which the unfortunate participators in Monmouth's rebellion were confined. He was known to be the unscrupulous tool of arbitrary power. He was known to love blood, and to revel in misery. He was probably the only judge who ever disgraced the English bench by openly rejoicing in the power to torture or to slay. He was the terror of the bar, the brow-beater of witnesses, the bully of a jury. With a sufficient knowledge of the law to twist it to his own purposes, and make it serve the ends that were dictated to him; with a sufficient contempt for it to set it at naught when it interfered with his designs; with a sagacity and clearness of judgment that were applied only to derive from any case all the arguments it could afford in favor of a prejudiced judgment; with an impudent daring befitting only the brothel or the gambling-house, he feared no consequences so long as his savage instincts could be gratified, he shrunk from no opprobrium so long as it was a means to wealth and power.

The news soon spread far and wide that Jeffries was coming down to judge the prisoners in the West. It was soon followed by intelligence of his having opened the commission at Winchester, of his having tried the Lady Alice Lisle for harboring two unfortunate rebels, of his having violated the first principles of justice and the strict letter of the law, of his having brow-beat, insulted, and abused the witnesses, and wrung by threats and violence a verdict of guilty from a reluctant jury. Then came the sentence that she should be burned alive in the public market-place, and then the mockery of mercy in the commutation of the sentence to another kind of death. Dismay spread through all hearts; for no man found himself safe, however conscious he might be of innocence. The safeguards of law and justice were gone. Party prejudices, private malice, cupidity, revenge, caprice, could at any time strike its victim from the judgment seat; and men learned to fear enemies whom they had contemned and scorned before.

If such was the feeling produced throughout the public, what must have been the sensations with which prisoners already accused heard the fatal tidings that Jeffries was coming on into the West? The savage jailers of the prison in which Ralph Woodhall was confined--men of the basest minds and lowest habits--took care that he should have the whole intelligence piece by piece. As far as personal comfort was concerned, they had consented, for high considerations, to improve his condition: he had a comfortable room in the governor's house; his food was no longer bread and water; he had pen and ink allowed him; and a good and honest lawyer was admitted to him; but the jailers, who loved misery next to money, took part payment for the conveniences they were bribed to allow, in torturing the prisoner with continual thoughts of his coming fate.

To say that Ralph gave himself up to despair would give no proper idea of the condition of his mind. He gave himself up for lost, indeed, and prepared to meet the worst with firmness, and in this respect, perhaps, a knowledge of the character of his judge was serviceable to him. There was very little uncertainty to be struggled with, the most unnerving of all agonies. He had not to think of chances, and calculate probabilities, and vacillate between hope and fear. He had only to prepare. Had any just judge been the person to try him, he would have entertained no doubt, no apprehension; for his full consciousness of innocence made him imagine that his innocence must be clearly established. But with a Jeffries on the bench, with his known corruptibility, with all the strong influence and great wealth of Lord Woodhall arrayed against the prisoner, there was little--there was no chance of an acquittal, and he felt that there was nothing remaining but by an honest and firm defense to keep his name pure for after time, and to make ready to die with manly fortitude.

That was a bitter task enough. He was in the bloom of youth, full of the fresh vigor of early manhood, with every capability of enjoyment unimpaired, with the bright, cheerful world unclouded by disappointments, unsullied by vice. All that he had seen of life, up to a few months before, had been calm, cheerful happiness; and he had now to part with all. Hope, too, had opened her garden gates before him, and but a short time previously he had been breathing her odors and reveling among her flowers. All this was to be parted with--the bright expectations of love, the long vista of happy hours ever open to the eye of youth, the high aspirations, the brilliantly-painted pictures of fancy, were all to be given up together, and buried with him in the dark, cold grave. The strong energies; the warm, chivalrous courage; the firm, enduring resolution; the activity of thought, the might of a strong mind, which he had expected, exercised with honor and with faith, would lead him to distinction, were all to come to an end upon a public scaffold; and a death of dishonor was to close a brief, bright life of honest effort and unstained integrity.

For all this he had to prepare; but he did so, and did it well.

He wrote to his father, to Margaret, to Lady Danvers, and to Lord Woodhall, and on each letter he put the words, "To be delivered after my death." To all he gave the most solemn assurances, as a dying man, that he had no share whatsoever in the death of his cousin Henry, adding that he trusted to make the facts so clearly appear at his trial, that when prejudice and passion should have subsided, there would not be one man who would deny his innocence. At the same time, he declared the conviction that he should be condemned, alluding only generally to the circumstances which rendered that conviction reconcilable with the full consciousness of innocence.

His lawyer was active and eager; there was something in the young man's demeanor, in his calmness, in his firmness, in a certain cheerful tone with which he spoke of his coming fate, that touched the good man much, and he took more than a mere mercenary or a mere professional interest in the case. Ralph let him do what he would; but he showed considerable indifference to all the legal and technical points connected with his situation. He answered all the questions that were put to him frankly and sincerely, and gave a full and clear account of all the events affecting the case, as far as he knew them, mentioning the names of every one who had taken more or less part in the transactions which I have recorded.

The man of law rubbed his hands, and declared that if the evidence of the persons mentioned could be procured, there was no doubt about obtaining a verdict. There was one point, he said, that required some consideration. The trial ought to take place in the county where the alleged offense had been committed. "Doubtless," he added, "the crown is prepared to change the venue, and that is done so easily nowadays that any motive will suffice where the crown is concerned. I should not wonder to find in this instance the pretext is, the difficulty and inconvenience of moving you to Norfolk without the slightest consideration of the difficulty and expense to you of moving your witnesses hither. Perhaps, indeed, the trial may not come on, and you may still be sent to Norwich; but even in that case my labors will not have been in vain, for your defense will be fully prepared."

Ralph smiled faintly. "You have furnished me with the first ground of hope," he said, "and I am almost sorry for it. In Norfolk I should be certainly acquitted. Here I should be as certainly condemned; but I will not give way to any expectations. Those who have determined to condemn me have taken their precautions, depend upon it, and be you sure the venue will be changed."

"Well, well, it gives us a chance," said the lawyer; "great men sometimes make great mistakes, and an oversight may have been committed in this instance."

At this time he had stayed with Ralph, as was sometimes his custom, for several hours, and day had declined into night when he took his departure.

The old town of Dorchester was, I believe, not very much less in size at that time than at present. It was always a very prosperous and quiet town, not very much celebrated for any manufacture but that of ale. The streets were then very narrow and tortuous, and the houses opposite to the prison itself were only separated from the outer wall surrounding the old building by a road not four yards broad. They were low, mean houses, inhabited by the poorer classes, which have long since been swept away. Under the eaves of one of these houses, when the attorney came forth from the prison gates, he perceived a man standing with his figure clearly displayed by a light in one of the windows, for there were no lamps in the town at that period. It was a rainy night, however, and as the roof projected far, it afforded a shelter. The moment the attorney moved on, however, the man followed him, and at the end of the street overtook and tapped him on the shoulder.

"I want to speak with you," he said, in a civil tone. "Is your name Danes? Are you a lawyer?"

"Right in both," replied the attorney. "What do you want with me?"

"I want nothing," replied the man, "but a lady does. She wants to see you directly--a great lady, too, whom you must have heard of, if not seen."

"Who is she?" asked the attorney.

"Come with me, and you will see," replied the man; and Mr. Danes followed him with the full determination of taking to his heels if his guide conducted him to any place of suspicious appearance.

Far from so doing, however, the man led him to one of the most frequented parts of the town, and to the house of one of the most respectable inhabitants--a gentleman well affected also to the reigning family, and in some favor with the powers that were:

"Why, this is Mr. Winkworth's house," said the attorney.

"Very true," replied the man, laconically, and opened the door, for doors in Dorchester at that time usually remained unlocked till the family retired to rest. "Come up," said the man; and, passing several doors in the great hall, through which the sounds of conversation found their way, he led his companion up a broad, venerable stair-case of carved oak, and opened a door, saying, "Master Danes, my lady."

The attorney entered the room, and though it contained only two persons, he felt dazzled, as it were, not so much by the bright light which succeeded suddenly to darkness, as by the blaze of beauty before him. He paused a moment in his advance, thinking he had never before beheld two such beautiful creatures as those which were seated near the table with hand clasped in hand. One was dressed in deep mourning; and on the table near her lay one of those black half masks very commonly worn by ladies of that day, and known in France by the name of loup. The other was richly dressed in the style of the court; but even the costume of the day, which by that time was becoming stiff and rigid, could not conceal the beauty of her form. About the one there was a certain wild freshness and youthful grace that was very captivating; while the other, though evidently but a very little older, had a sort of quiet dignity and self-possession in her carriage which spoke the long-accustomed guest of courts.

The lawyer had not much time to observe, however, before the voice of the elder lady said, "Come in, Mr. Danes, and take a seat, if you please."

He thought he never heard such music in his life as the tones which proceeded from those sweet lips, and, advancing to the table, he remained standing, with his wet hat in his hand.

"You have seen me before, Mr. Danes," said the lady who had spoken, "but perhaps you do not recollect me."

"I can not say I do, my lady," replied the lawyer, "and yet I do not think I could forget you, if ever it had been my good fortune to see you."

"I was a little girl," she answered, with a faint smile; "you may perhaps, recollect Hortensia Danvers."

"Oh, God bless me, my lady!" said the lawyer, with a look of delight, "I remember you quite well, and your noble father, and your excellent lady mother. I owed my first success in life to them. What can I do to serve you? Nothing can give me greater pleasure, if it be in my power."

Hortensia made him take a seat, and then informed him that, having heard he had been engaged to prepare the defense of Mr. Ralph Woodhall, she had sent for him to inquire his opinion of the case, and to offer whatever assistance might be wanted, and she could give.

"The case would be very clear, my lady," replied the lawyer, "if we could count upon a fair jury and an unprejudiced judge--I must speak plainly, for the matter requires it--we know that his lordship, who is coming down here, is subject to all sorts of influences, and, to tell you the truth, I discover, what I have kept from the young gentleman himself, that no means, however unscrupulous or iniquitous, are neglected by the relations of the dead man to get a verdict against the living one."

"Hush!" said Hortensia, with a glance toward her fair companion, "hush, Mr. Danes! Do not impute such great blame to persons only moved by deep love for one whom they have lost."

"Let him speak, dear Hortensia," said Margaret, "let him speak plainly. It is necessary for you and for me to hear the truth, however bitter it may be."

"Indeed, my lady," said the lawyer, "in a matter of this kind, where life and death are concerned, one can not stop to pick words. If Mr. Woodhall should be tried here, a verdict is very likely to go against him, for the most violent influence is being used to prejudice the minds of juries, and the same influence will undoubtedly be exerted upon the judge."

"But can he not be tried somewhere else?" asked Hortensia.

"He ought to be tried in Norfolk," replied Mr. Danes; "but the crown can change the venue, and there is but the remotest possible chance of their neglecting to do so till too late for these assizes. They won't stand upon any forms of law, depend upon it, and perhaps may break through all recognized principles of justice; but nevertheless we may thwart them if they do make any mistakes, though there are few men at the bar who dare to face Jeffries."

"The boldest, the most skillful, the most learned, must be retained, at whatever cost," said Hortensia, eagerly. "I make myself responsible for the amount, Mr. Danes, whatever it may be. Hesitate at no expense whatever; use all the means that may suggest themselves; for, in proportion to the vigor of the efforts made to oppress, so must be the vigor of our efforts to defend."

As she spoke, she laid her hand upon Margaret's, and pressed it gently; and, if there was ever abnegation of self in a woman's heart, it was in Hortensia's at that moment.

"This is very necessary kindness, my lady," said the attorney, "for witnesses have to be brought from a great distance, and the little means we have will be consumed in that part of the affair. The fees of eminent lawyers are very great; and my only hope was that old Mr. Woodhall might arrive and bring a further supply; but he has not come."

"Let not that stand in the way for a moment," replied Hortensia; "I am responsible to you for any amount employed in this case."

"If so," said the lawyer, gazing at her with an inquiring look, "we might try what can be done with his lordship himself. I think it would answer if the sum were large enough."

The blood rushed into Hortensia's face, and there was an evident struggle.

"I can not say that," said she, "I can not tell you to do any thing that is wrong; but this I will say, Mr. Danes, do all that is necessary to insure that real justice is arrived at, and I will shrink from no engagement that you may make for me. Now, can you explain to me some circumstances that I do not understand. It appears even to my eyes, unlearned in the law as I am, that it may be necessary and right to summon myself and all the servants who were with me at the Duke of Norfolk's when the supposed quarrel took place, to give our evidence at the trial. But I find that several other persons attached to my household, who were not near the spot, but resided at Danvers's New Church at the time, have likewise received notice to appear--what can be the cause of this, Mr. Danes?"

"Rather strange, certainly, my lady," said the lawyer. "But was not the young gentleman at your house for some time after the event?"

"He was," replied Lady Danvers; "but I see not how that can affect the question whether he did or did not kill his cousin in a duel, and whether the circumstances attending that duel were fair."

"They may think they can prove admissions of some kind," said the lawyer; "but still, I will acknowledge it strikes me as strange; and where it is evident that there is an intention to persecute rather than prosecute, one does become suspicious of every move in the game. I will tell you what I will do, my lady. I know something of most of the men engaged in the courts here. Some of them have already given information as to the unfair means which are being employed to obtain a condemnation. I will go and see if I can discover any motive for the proceeding you mention. Can you give me the names of your people who have been subpœnaed?"

Lady Danvers wrote down five or six names on a piece of paper, and at the head of them appeared that of the steward, Mr. Drayton. Furnished with these, the attorney went upon his way; and, in the mean time, Margaret and Hortensia remained for some time alone, conversing sadly on the topic which occupied the thoughts of both. Other subjects connected with Margaret's own fate and circumstances mingled from time to time with their discourse; and when, at length, she rose to go, Hortensia repeated twice the injunction to be firm.

"While there is life there is hope, dear Margaret," she said; "and, though your fate may never be united to that of the man you love, you owe it to him, methinks, never to wed one whom you so justly abhor. What I have told you this night of the character of that man is more than mere hearsay, and I should as soon expect oil and water to mingle as you to give your hand to him. I must not go with you back, for doubtless your father has returned by this time, and I should be no very welcome guest, I suspect; but two of my men shall accompany you, although, in this good town of Dorchester, one might walk alone, I believe, without much risk."

"I hope my father has not returned," said Margaret, timidly. "I fear he might be angry at my absence. He has become exceedingly irascible since I refused to listen to Robert Woodhall's suit;" and the tears rose in her eyes while she added, "He never showed me such unkindness before. Where shall I find my maid?"

"We will call her in," replied Lady Danvers; and, after having summoned the good woman from another room, she kissed Margaret tenderly, saying, "Hope still, dear girl, hope still."

"Ay, hope still!" repeated Lady Dangers to herself when Margaret had left her. "*You* may hope, poor Margaret. One of the strange turns of Fate may open before you long vistas of happiness. For me, the view is closed all round. Well, I can be an anchorite even here."

A few minutes after Mr. Danes returned, but it was only to bring the intelligence that he could obtain no information. He seemed even more doubtful and suspicious regarding the circumstances to which Lady Danvers had called his attention than before. "Either the people themselves, who are immediately employed, do not know the motives," he said, "or they will not tell them; and, in either case, the matter does not look well. There must be motives of secrecy somewhere; and in such a case as this, where simple justice is concerned, that is in itself suspicious. However, my lady, all that we can do is to prepare the defense as carefully as possible. I must send off fresh messengers eastward this very night to hurry our witnesses; for I hear that his lordship is making speedy work of it on the way, and it would not surprise me if he were to refuse even a postponement of the trial, although our defense was necessarily incomplete." He then went on to ask Lady Danvers some questions as to what she could testify concerning the events of that night on which Henry Woodhall's death had taken place, and then left her with a mind but the more depressed from inquiries, the object of which she did not altogether see. She expressed her perfect readiness and willingness, however, to be called as a witness for the defense; and Mr. Danes went away, convinced that she would give her evidence well and firmly.

CHAPTER XXXIX

Those who have remained any time in Dorchester or its neighborhood will know that within a circle of not many miles' diameter around that town, there are many spots to be found as wild and solitary as in any part of the island of Great Britain; on the side of Weymouth especially, there are some scenes in the midst of which one might fancy one's self very far removed, indeed, from the high cultivation which closely surrounds them. In the days of James the Second, when agriculture, as a science, had made very little advance upon the knowledge possessed by the Anglo-Saxons, and when cultivation had spread but slowly under the influence of a great many deterring causes, these solitary spots were, of course, more numerous in all counties of England; and it was upon one of these in Dorsetshire, not very many miles distant from the capital of the county, that was built an ancient, fortified house, dating probably from two centuries before. It was placed upon an eminence overhanging a river, brief in its course, and utterly unimportant till it reached a point about five miles from its mouth, where it widened out into a creek or narrow bay of salt water, which afforded a convenient refuge for fishing-boats. Near a spot where the first considerable extension of the banks of the stream took place, a sort of sandy bar had formed itself, marking the navigable from the unnavigable water, and it was just at this point that the house, or castle as it was called, had been built. I will name the river the Orme; and from it and the sandy bar I have mentioned, the house had derived the name of Orme-bar Castle.

The ground around was covered with smooth, green turf, or short, but rich grass, disposed in easy undulations, and watered by many a clear and beautiful stream, and such a thing as a hedgerow or a wall was not to be seen for some miles round the inclosure of the park. It was a gloomy-looking building too, consisting of tall, wide, irregular masses of masonry, put together any how; and one could easily see from the outside, from the numerous and very much varied windows, and from the irregular distribution of the chimneys about the house, that in searching for any room within, one might have a real journey to go, in order to reach a door hard by.

It was in this curious old building, and amid the solitary scene around, that a little party had met together on the night of Margaret's visit to Hortensia. The kitchen and the hall were well tenanted--better, indeed, than they had been for many a year--for a large household had been transported there from a distant part of the country, and two or three old servants, who had remained for years in the place, were added to those who had freshly arrived. But in a large, curious, old-fashioned hall above, only three persons were seated at the hour of sunset. They were a mother and her two sons, and they grouped themselves together near the window, not to watch the passing away of the western light, but upon business which two of them, at least, considered of no light importance. In the midst, on a tall, high-backed, velvet-covered chair, with a foot-stool under her feet, sat old Lady Coldenham. Her eldest son was on her right hand, looking somewhat listlessly out toward the sea, in a direction where the tower of a little church was just visible over the slope of the ground. His arm was thrown over the back of the chair, his head leaning somewhat on one side, and his whole figure disposed in an attitude of graceful idleness. On the other side appeared his brother Robert, with a very different air. He leaned rather forward than otherwise, with his right hand resting on his knee, and his eyes fixed on his mother, as if watching for some oracular word from her lips.

At length, as the day began to grow dim, Robert inquired, "Shall I call for lights, madam?"

"No," replied Lady Coldenham; "I love this sort of light--ay, and enjoy seeing the stars come out one by one, when darkness resumes her sway over the earth like a powerful monarch triumphing in stern, proud serenity over some weak and glittering pretender who had disputed his sway. Besides, Robert, it is full as well to talk of all we have to notice under the shadow."

She paused, and relapsed into silence again; and then, when the sky was nearly dark, she said, "You have done your part well, Robert; and now we must make sure that the blow goes home. You have lodged him in prison as you promised--but he must die."

"I think you may leave that to the care of the good old lord," replied Robert. "He is as eager for his blood as a hound for the blood of a deer."

"I will leave it to no one with entire trust," replied Lady Coldenham; "too much depends upon him to have any thing risked upon the conduct of a blundering old man, or a heedless, inattentive lawyer."

"I wonder what poor Ralph has done," said Lord Coldenham, breaking silence for the first time during a quarter of an hour, "to make you two so bitterly his enemies. One pursues him like a blood-hound, and the other says he must die."

Lady Coldenham fixed her large dark eyes upon him with a look of angry astonishment; but the young lord had long been growing somewhat restive, and he repeated, "I wonder what he has done, I say--what is his fault, I should like to know?"

"He is his father's son," said Lady Coldenham, with stern emphasis.

"I did not know that that was any greater crime than being one's mother's son, but rather thought it a virtue," said Lord Coldenham, with a light laugh; "as to the father, I don't see much harm in him any more than in Ralph. He is a very good sort of old gentleman--rather pedantic, it is true, but not much the worse for that. Shrews, pedants, and libertines are, I suppose, necessary evils in our state of society; and as I don't approve of persecuting them, I think I had better leave this somewhat intolerant council, and amuse myself elsewhere."

As he spoke, he rose; but Lady Coldenham exclaimed, in a fierce, stern voice, "Sit down, Lord Coldenham!"

"No, indeed, dear mother," replied the young lord, "I can employ myself better. There is Robert, who is peculiarly fond of either sitting or running--which was it you did at Sedgemoor, Bob! I am too active for the one, and too idle for the other; and so, with your blessing, I will walk."

Lady Coldenham eyed him with an expression of anger, surprise, and contempt, which could hardly be described; but the young lord had chosen his part, and, though idle enough in his habits, he was resolute. His mother's look nettled him a little too, and he said, in a cool but determined tone, "In a word, dear lady and mother, I am of age, I think, and master, at least, of my own actions. I do not desire particularly to be master even of my own house, as long as it has got so much better a master in it; but I will not be here consenting to things that I disapprove and dislike, let it cost what it may."

"Hark, you, Coldenham!" cried his mother, as he moved toward the door; "a word in your ear, if you please."

He bent down his head, listening gravely; and the lady whispered something to him, gradually raising her voice till the last words became distinct and audible enough. They were, "And leave you a beggar and an outcast at a word."

"Do it!" said Lord Coldenham, with the most indifferent tone in the world, and quietly sauntered out of the room. Lady Coldenham shut her teeth tight together, and the violent emotion that was going on within might be seen by the close clinching of her beautiful white hands as they lay upon her knee; but she made no comment, and, perhaps, was sorry for the words she uttered. They had not escaped the ears of Robert Woodhall; and he might build upon them some strange expectations. But he was wisely silent; and, after a very long pause, Lady Coldenham resumed the conversation, saying, "Let us think no more of that foolish boy's caprices. You are a rational being, Robert. Tell me what you think of this case. Are we certain of getting a condemnation?"

"Really, I do not know, dear lady," he answered, and then added, with some emphasis, "that must depend upon the judge and the jury."

"They must both be taken care of," said Lady Coldenham, slowly nodding her head. "I will crave an audience of his lordship when he first arrives. He will not refuse me. You must see to the jury, Robert; and if the youth be really guilty, there surely can be no great difficulty in proving him so. Tell me, upon your honor and soul, do you really think he committed the deed?"

"Upon my honor and soul I do," replied Robert Woodhall; and for once in his life he spoke the truth. Nay, more, he carried his frankness further, adding, "But I do not doubt that it was all done fairly. Ralph, I have heard, was reputed the best fencer in his college, and the best quarter-staff man in all Lincolnshire. Three or four passes would soon settle the matter with Henry, without any foul play. That letter of Henry's, too, written with his absurd generosity, clears away all suspicious circumstance. That is the worst point of the case against us for juries are not fond of condemning men for duels where no unfairness is proved."

"Can not the letter be suppressed?" inquired his mother.

Her son shook his head; and she went on to ask, "Is it in Lord Woodhall's hands?"

"No, in the Duke of Norfolk's," answered her son; "he gave the old lord a copy, but he kept the original."

"This is frightful!" said the old lady, in an under tone. "He will escape us yet: the only chance is with the jury, Robert. There must be two or three sturdy men found among them who will starve the others out and get us a verdict--Hark! there are horses' feet! that must be the old lord himself.

He promised to bring a great lawyer with him, who will enter into our views. But mind, be not too rash--speak not too plainly, boy; for these men sometimes take fire when their own image is shown them in too perfect a glass, and they assume a fresh honesty but to show us that our thoughts of them were calumnious."

"No fear of my being too rash," replied Robert Woodhall. "Besides, I shall apply myself principally to this business with Margaret. It seemed to me the old lord wavered before her steadiness; but I will not be kept in suspense. I will know at once whether he intends to keep his oath or not."

"There is business on hand," said Lady Coldenham, very gravely, "more serious than any pretty painted puppet in the world.

"Ay; but the estates, mother!" said her son.

"True," she answered, "true--the estates;" and, at the same moment, Lord Woodhall entered the room, followed by a man in dark clothing, whom he presented to Lady Coldenham as Counselor Armitage.

The conversation was led at once to the predominant subject in the thoughts of all; and was discussed for some time, principally by Lord Woodhall, Robert, and Lady Coldenham, who stated briefly but distinctly the new-born fears of failure which her son's previous words had suggested.

The lawyer, who had listened attentively, but had spoken little, now interposed, saying, "Do not be afraid, Lady Coldenham; we will take care that justice shall be done; and if, through the weakness of a jury, it could not be done in one way, it would be done in another. It matters little for the true cause of justice what are the means employed so that the end be favorable to herself. We will reach him, depend upon it. Let him attempt to conceal the facts if he will and if he can. The case of the slaughter once clearly proved against him, we must overcome the scruples of the jury--and, if not, it does not much matter."

"Does not much matter?" said Lady Coldenham, with a stare; "I do not understand you, sir."

"I am instructed for the crown, Lady Coldenham, and that is the reason why a great number do not understand me," replied Mr. Armitage, with a slight smile at what he imagined to be a jest; "all I can say is, you shall be satisfied, and this good lord too. The young man has evidently committed a great crime, and it shall not be the foolish lenity of a jury that shall save him."

"No, I trust there is no chance of that," said old Lord Woodhall. "He killed my son, and I will have justice. Now I have found him, I will never leave him till I have justice. I am an old man to take such a journey as this from London to Dorchester in three days; but the spirit that brought me down here will support me to follow him all over the world till I have justice upon his head."

"There will be plenty to second you, my noble lord," said Robert Woodhall. "I, for one, can not rest satisfied so long as this man is with me on the earth; for it is very clear to me, now, that I never shall have the love of my promised bride so long as he lives."

Lord Woodhall was silent; and Robert Woodhall, finding that his indirect mode of proceeding produced no reply, asked boldly, "If she persists in her refusal, what do you intend to do, my lord?"

"Keep my word, young man," replied the old lord, dryly; and then turning to Lady Coldenham, he inquired, "Where is your eldest son, madam? I thought to find him here."

"Oh, never mind him," replied Lady Coldenham. "He is in the house; but can see, with his idle whims, he is more likely to spoil all than to help in any thing. He is better out of the way. As to Margaret," she continued, "you must let me see her, my good lord. Women can often find means of persuasion when men fail."

"See her if you like, Lady Coldenham," replied the old lord, "but it will make little difference. I have pledged my word, and it shall be kept. She must obey. But as to your son, I am sorry he goes not with us in this business. What is the reason?"

"Oh, none," replied Lady Coldenham; "old affection for this young man, I believe. Depend upon it, he is better out of our councils; and now, sir," she continued, turning to Mr. Armitage, "will you explain to me clearly how the case stands, what are its chances, and what remains to be done to make chances secure? Remember, I am accustomed to deal with lawyers, and will not be put off with ambiguities."

She had hardly uttered these words in a stern, masculine tone, when a loud voice--rich, and deep, and full--was heard, saying, "Beware! Once more I tell you, Catharine, beware!"

The three gentlemen looked round, for the speaker seemed to be in the room but no one was to be seen; and Robert's voice; soon called attention another way, as he exclaimed, "Good God! my mother has fainted."

It was long before Lady Coldenham could be brought to herself; and for a time those who surrounded her thought she was dead, so still and breathless did she lie, and so cold did her hands become. Lord Coldenham was sent for in haste; but he could not be found; and the only intelligence that could be obtained regarding him was, that he had been seen speaking to a tall old gentleman in the gate-way, and that shortly after he had ordered his horse and ridden away.

The attempts to recall Lady Coldenham to life at length proved successful; but she was in no state to continue the conversation, and the party separated, Robert Woodhall promising to visit his noble relation on the following day

CHAPTER XL

The court assembled in the town of Dorchester, and the notorious Jeffries, with his gross, ferocious face, took his place upon the bench. Several trials for treason were entered into in the morning, and dispatched with terrible rapidity. Death! Death! Death was the news brought to the prison every hour; and each man awaited his doom as his character permitted.

The court was crowded to suffocation; and most of the magistrates of the county were assembled near the bench. There were several clergymen among them; but one, in particular, seemed much interested in the course of the proceedings. He was a stout, tall, portly man, of the middle age, with bright, twinkling eyes, and a smooth, rosy countenance. He moved frequently on his seat; often looked toward the dock and the jury, and sometimes cast his eyes with an inquisitive glance at the paper of notes which lay before the judge, from whom he was not very far distant.

At length the case of Ralph Woodhall was called on; and, before the prisoner was brought into the dock, the good clergyman I have mentioned approached the judge, and was seen to whisper to him with a paper in his hand. Jeffries turned round, bent his beetle brows upon him, and surveyed him from head to foot.

"I thought it was some Presbyterian knave," he said, aloud, "and not a clergyman of the establishment. What do you come here for, sirrah? Like a straw witness, to bring off the guilty?"

"No, faith, my lord," replied Doctor M'Feely, with a laugh, and perfectly undismayed by the menacing aspect of the judge, "I came according to my duty, as a magistrate, and, moreover, to get your advice about this little bit of a paper; and perhaps to drink a bottle with you--or maybe two--after you have done the hanging and quartering, if you should be good-humored enough to ask me to dinner. We have drank a bottle together before now at the Miter, when you were a little man and I not much bigger: I paid for it, too, by the same token--But what am I to do with this paper?"

"It's not evidence, knave," thundered Jeffries, unable to restrain himself under the half-suppressed merriment of the court. "Is the witness forthcoming? Is he dead? Is he buried? Is he gone to the devil by your ghostly counsels? It is not evidence, sir. Take it away, and yourself too, for fear I have the gown stripped off your back. You shall not long disgrace the bench."

"Faith, my lord, if I do, I am not the only one," replied Doctor M'Feely, walking away; but, ere he had taken many steps, pushing a path through his fellow-magistrates, Jeffries recollected himself a little, and called out aloud, "Here, fellow--you parson!--give me the paper. Let me look at it."

Doctor M'Feely seemed to be suddenly stricken with a fit of deafness, and walked on deliberately; but those whom he was passing at the moment heard him say, as it to himself, "Don't I know better? He's just in a humor to tear every thing to pieces--why not this? No, no, I know what I will do;" and, getting into the court below, he forced his way to a spot just behind Mr. Danes, and spoke to him in a whisper over his shoulder. Mr. Danes in turn whispered to an elderly counselor before him, who turned round his grave, hard-lined face, and said, "Good! We will use it in some way, if need be. The very tendency will have its effect upon the jury."

Doctor M'Feely remained standing where he was during the whole of the events which succeeded, although his fat sides suffered severely from the pressure of the crowd.

The little incident of the sparring between the parson and the judge had withdrawn the attention of the spectators from the dock, and when heads were turned round and eyes bent in that direction, Ralph Woodhall was seen standing between two jailers. Every one knows the impression produced by a fine person and dignified bearing, even upon a court of justice; and, as the young gentleman stood there, his handsome face, athletic form, and calm, resolute demeanor, had no slight influence in his favor. He fixed his eyes for a moment or two upon the judge, and then let them run round the court. There was no loved face to greet him--no look of encouragement for his support--nothing but a sea of unknown, indifferent faces gazing at him as an object of curiosity.

Some forms were gone through, and then at once the counsel for the prisoner rose. Jeffries would fain have refused to listen to him at that stage of the proceedings; but he insisted, and the harsh judge knew his man too well--his firmness, his quiet, persevering courage, and his profound knowledge of law to resist too far. He was permitted to speak, and at once took an objection to the competence of the court. He pointed out that the venue had not been changed, and that the case ought to be tried in Norfolk.

It required but little argument to show that the law of the land was entirely on his side; and that argument was placed in the plainest and briefest form.

Jeffries was furious. He looked over his desk to a little man sitting near his feet, and asked him a question. The reply was in a very low and humble tone; but it stirred up the wrath of the judge still higher. His face became actually purple, and he poured forth upon the poor man's head a torrent of invective, of which the words "knave, villain, and pitiful impostor" were the lightest ornaments. A vast string of very blasphemous oaths was added; and then, having thus vented his first fury, he consulted for a few moments with the counsel for the crown, whom he beckoned up; and then, raising his great coarse voice as if addressing the whole court, he said, "Look you here now! See what law is, and how carefully it protects the subject! There stands a murderer--a man who should not be suffered to cumber the face of earth one hour longer than needful--a bad fellow--always a bad fellow from his cradle--and yet some of the officers of the crown--drunken knaves, I warrant--having neglected, or, perhaps, been bribed--to neglect their duty in a matter of mere form--a thing of no moment--this fellow thinks that he will protract his life for some miserable months to come. He must be a cowardly villain, to wish to live on in a prison--"

"I wish a fair trial, by a just judge," said Ralph, in a firm, loud tone, which startled even Jeffries.

"Hold your tongue, knave!" cried the judge; "we will fit you. You shall be disappointed of your fine project. You may gain a few hours, but no more. You shall be hanged before I quit Dorchester, if I live. See here, now, what a fellow this is! There are no less than three charges against this man. One for murder--cold-blooded, premeditated murder--one under the statute regarding conformity--and one for high treason. The indictment is ready; but he must have a copy, and time to read it. Oh, yes, he shall have a copy--but we will fit him." Then, leaning forward a little, he looked full at Ralph's counsel, and said bitterly, "You have gained so much for your man, sir, and you shall not say I overstepped the law. Oh no, sir! You strive to withdraw him from justice, but you sha'n't succeed."

"You mistake, my lord," replied the counsel, "I have no intention of charging you with overstepping the law; and still more do you mistake in supposing that I wished to withdraw this honorable and noble-minded young man from fair trial and justice. Had I done so, I should have taken another course. As the venue is laid in Dorsetshire, and the indictment, on its very face, alleges the crime charged to have been committed in Norfolk, I should have suffered the trial to proceed to a verdict, and then pointed out the flaw in the indictment; but, in consultation with this honorable and very high-spirited gentleman last night, I agreed, at his suggestion, to raise the objection at once, in order to show that he shrunk not from a fair trial, but only claimed the same rights as other British subjects."

"Silence, sir, silence! Sit down this instant!" exclaimed Jeffries. "Jailer, remove the prisoner, and keep him in safe custody. Call on another."

Several persons left the court from the outskirts of the crowd, and Doctor M'Feely elbowed his way out with difficulty, taking the paper he had brought in his pocket. Tidings of what had occurred spread to various houses in the vicinity--to the great inn, and to the temporary dwelling of Hortensia Danvers; and various were the feelings which the intelligence that Ralph Woodhall's trial for murder had been put off, on account of an error in the indictment, excited in the bosoms of the many persons interested.

Lord Woodhall received the news with stern bitterness, and said little, but remained gloomy, dark, and silent till Robert Woodhall joined him with a very cheerful face.

"Well, what think you of this?" said the old lord; "you seem gay, young man."

"Because every thing is going well, my lord," replied Robert Woodhall; "we have ten times the chances of getting a verdict against him, as things stand at present, on the charge of high treason, than we should have upon the charge of murder. Armitage says that he would most certainly have been acquitted--that poor Henry's letter would be quite sufficient. I told you how refractory the jury were last night, and those who know them say that at least five of them would have held out for acquittal, even if they had died of starvation. It not being a state case, the jury was badly struck; but upon the charge of treason Armitage declares he is perfectly certain. Armitage says they are condemning every body, and when once they have got a taste of blood, they will go on."

"It vexes me," said the old lord, with a dissatisfied look. "He should be hanged for Henry's death, and nothing else. A gross and culpable act of negligence has been committed; and the clerk, or whoever he is, should be discharged and punished."

"Counselor Armitage declares it is very well as it is," says Robert; adding, with a laugh, "He vows that he saw the flaw, and would not notice it, because he knew we should fail of conviction; but I don't believe he did see it, or even looked at the indictment. The charge of treason, however, will succeed, depend upon it; and if it should not, by any chance, we have still another left to go upon with a better chance of success."

Lord Woodhall, however, was still dissatisfied, and would not be convinced that it made no difference whether Ralph Woodhall was condemned for another offense or for the murder of his son. He drew a distinction, which Robert Woodhall, only anxious to destroy an enemy, could not at all perceive. Knowing how impossible it was to move him in any opinion which he had once taken up, he at length left him, but did not even ask to see Margaret, for he knew there was little to be hoped from an interview at that moment.

CHAPTER XLI

It was night, when, in a large, airy chamber of the great inn, where Lord Woodhall had taken up his abode on his arrival in Dorchester, Margaret sat, side by side with Hortensia, who had quietly entered the room a moment before. The faces of both were pale from anxiety, and from thought fixed intensely upon one subject. It was the day of Ralph's trial for high treason; and both were well aware, Hortensia more especially, that Ralph had never had any share whatever in Monmouth's rebellion. They had not met till then, during the whole day, and each had looked upon the charge somewhat lightly, and entertained but small doubts that upon that, at least, Ralph would be acquitted.

As the day had passed on, however, and messenger after messenger brought tidings from the court to each, their feelings had become very different; and they were startled and astounded by the evidence which was produced. It was proved by Hortensia's own servants that Ralph had come to Danvers's New Church during her absence; that he had been found in her park in close communication with a notorious rebel, then actually levying war against the crown, one Thomas Dare; that, very shortly after this, Dare appeared in Taunton, and raised the people of that town in favor of Monmouth, and that he boasted publicly there that he had assurances of Lady Danvers's tenantry joining the duke. This was enough to shake Hortensia's confidence--to agitate--to terrify her. But another messenger had followed soon after, bringing her the news that two of her servants had sworn to the fact of Ralph having had a long private interview with Monmouth in her house during her absence, and that Mr. Drayton himself had sworn to the same. Then she heard that two more of her people had deposed, that, on leaving Ralph at the door of her house, the duke had turned to him, saying, "Remember my commission. I trust to you;" and that Ralph replied, "I will not fail your grace."

Hortensia herself, though she easily conceived the words to be innocent, did not understand to what they could apply; and she evidently saw the chain, which bound the victim, being drawn tighter and tighter around him. Then came the evidence of his having been on the road to Axminster when Monmouth was actually in combat with the royal troops; and then of his having been taken on the very field of Sedgemoor. She knew that many a one had already been condemned upon evidence slighter than this, and her heart failed her. The summing up, too, of the judge, had been brought to her with tolerable accuracy; and she perceived how skillfully he had pieced out the evidence against the unfortunate prisoner, not only indulging in violent abuse of him, but attributing to him much to which none of the witnesses testified.

Ralph's defense had been simple and straight forward. He told the facts just as they had occurred, plainly and straightforwardly. He pointed out that the Duke of Monmouth had come to Danvers's New Church with a considerable body of men, whom he had no power of opposing, even if he had been personally cognizant of then being in rebellion; that the duke had left with him a sealed letter for Lady Danvers, which, he believed, had come from the young Baroness Wentworth, charging him to deliver it as soon as possible, and that the words which had passed between them at the door referred solely to that. At all this Jeffries scoffed in his summing up, declaring it to be a trumped up story which would not deceive an oyster wench, it was clear, he contended--as clear as any thing under the sun, that Ralph had held friendly communication with the rebel and his agents, had agreed to assist him, and had endeavored to induce Lady Danvers to take part in the same criminal proceeding. "Doubtless," he said, "the young knave entrapped her to go into Axminster, for the purpose of entangling her with the insurrection, so that she could not draw back."

"Either her ladyship's good sense or her good fortune," said Jeffries, "kept her out of the scrape; but with that we have nothing to do at present. The case is against this young felon--felon in all senses of the word--guilty, beyond a doubt, of a thousand different crimes."

He then hypocritically declared he left the case entirely in the hands of the jury, though he could not have any doubt as to the verdict they would bring in.

Poor Hortensia--despair took possession of her when these tidings were brought to her solitary room. She did not fail to perceive how the evidence might be made to bear against herself; but she gave that hardly a moment's thought. Her whole mind was fixed upon the fate of Ralph; and, after pondering gloomily for a few minutes, she started up suddenly, saying, "I will go and see her, let the old man behave as he will;" and, calling her maid, she hastened away to the inn, where she now sits with poor Margaret, not exactly alone, for the two maids are there, standing at a little distance, and entering partially into the feelings of those whom they served.

Old Lord Woodhall had gone forth several hours before to the court; for his disappointment at the result of the first charge against Ralph had but stimulated his eagerness, and he could not rest satisfied without watching the progress of events. When once there, the interest increased upon him. He was torn, it is true, by various contending feelings. He could not see the gallant young man, whom he had loved only less than his own children in former years, stand there in the dock, defending his life with calm dignity and firmness, without feeling emotions he strove hard to crush. But when he thought of his own brave, high-spirited boy, and persuaded himself that Ralph's hand had killed him, returning affection was changed again to gall and bitterness. The interest was but the deeper, however, from this contention. He stayed out the examination of all the witnesses--he stayed out the prisoner's defense and the judge's summing up; and now, with the greater part of the auditory, he was lingering still in the court to hear the verdict of the jury, who had retired to deliberate.

The time was one of anxious suspense to all, but to none more terrible than to Margaret and Hortensia. From time to time they would send out a maid to inquire, or one of Lady Danvers's servants would put his head in and say, "No verdict yet, my lady." Hortensia bore it all firmly, and apparently calmly, though her anxious eye and pale cheek belied the tranquillity of her manner. Poor Margaret could hardly bear up at all: often the tears would not be restrained, and the long-protracted suspense kept her only under increasing agony.

At length there was a noise of bustle and confusion in the street and a hasty step was heard running up the stairs. The moment after the door opened quickly, and Mr. Drayton himself appeared. His face was sufficient answer to all inquiries. It was pale, haggard, ghastly and full of deep grief.

"Speak!" cried Hortensia, "speak!"

"Condemned, madam," replied the steward, solemnly, "and partly upon my testimony. But, indeed, I could not help it. I only told the truth."

The words had hardly passed his lips, and Margaret's head had fallen forward on the table, with her eyes deluging her fair hands with tears, when Lord Woodhall entered the room with a slow and somewhat feeble step. He was a very much altered man. His eyes were fixed upon the floor, his look grave and sad, his whole aspect downcast and sorrowful. Oh, how often does fruition bring to strong passion ashes and bitterness. He was sated; the fierce desire of his heart was gratified; the man upon whom he sought vengeance was condemned to a terrible death. The awful words rang in his ear; he saw the gallant youth stand firm and unshaken while they were uttered; he saw him wave his hand as he left the dock, and say as calmly as if he had been going to his rest, "Farewell all! Remember, I die innocent!--Remember!"

Remorse and pity had touched the old man's heart. For the first time he doubted the guilt of the man he had persecuted; and, as he sank into a chair, his first words were, "Poor Ralph!"

Margaret's ear caught those friendly sounds; and, springing up, with a wild gesture of entreaty, she cast herself at her father's feet, exclaiming, "Oh save him! save him!" The old man shook his head sorrowfully, and replied, in a very low tone, "It is in vain, my child; I can not even interfere to save the slayer of my son."

"Oh! he did not--he did not!" cried Margaret, vehemently; "it is all false--a device of that traitor's. Ralph would have died ere he injured Henry."

"You have been deluded, Lord Woodhall," said Lady Danvers, wiping the tears from her eyes; "and if the trial for murder had taken place, you would have seen that your poor young kinsman is innocent. I can give testimony as to the impossibility of his ever having drawn his sword against your son; for I know where he was, and can account for every moment of his time, from nine o'clock of that fatal morning till after the deed was done. Lord Woodhall, if you had any share in bringing about this condemnation, now exert yourself to the utmost to save this young man's life, or I will, ere two days are over, lay before you such evidence of his innocence as shall fill you with horror and remorse until the last day of your existence."

"Can you so?" asked the old man, gazing at her. "Is it so doubtful as that?"

"It is not doubtful in the least," replied Hortensia, almost sternly. "He did not do it--it was impossible for him to do it. Stay with him, Margaret! Cease not to plead until you have wrung it from him! I have heard some of the doings in this case, and know how much influence he has exerted and can exert. I will away at once to another quarter, and see what can be done there. When I return, I will bring with me those who can show your father where Ralph Woodhall spent every moment of his time, on the day of your brother's death, which he did not pass with me. They are now in the town, though they would have come too late had he been tried three days ago."

Thus saying, she hurried away, followed by her maid, and on the stairs passed Robert Woodhall with a look of contempt and horror which she could not hide.

The young man doffed his hat, and smiled, with one of those meaning serpent looks which often accompanied with him a sense of triumphant cunning. He walked on to the room in which Margaret and her father had been left together, but merely opened the door and looked in. Then, seeing her at her father's feet, he bowed his head slowly to Lord Woodhall, and retired.

The sight of him made the old man start; and he gazed round vacantly for a moment, as if looking for something. It was some resource he looked for, for his mind was greatly troubled. At length some sudden scheme seemed to strike him, and he grasped his child's hands in his. "Margaret, my child, Margaret," he cried, "you can save all--him--me--all of us, if you will. I have promised your hand to your cousin Robert. I have pledged him my honor and my faith. I have imprecated the curse of Heaven upon my head if I do not keep my word. Now, Margaret--now give your consent; promise to be Robert's, and I will do my best to save this young man."

Margaret started up and gazed upon her father silently with a look of icy horror. "Oh God!" she exclaimed, at length, "what is it my father imposes on me!" Then she raised her hand to her brow and pressed it tight, as if to still the throbbing of her brain.

"You will do your best to save him?" she said, gazing wildly in the old man's face.

"I *will* save him--he *shall* be saved!" exclaimed Lord Woodhall, vehemently. "If not, your promise shall be void. Do you consent, Margaret?--Consent, my child, consent! Your old father beseeches and entreats his child to save him from dishonor and from remorse, and this young man from death."

Margaret clasped her hands together, and raised her eyes on high, as if praying to Heaven for help. But then she placed her right hand in her father's, and said in a low, sad, solemn tone, but with every word marked and distinct, "On that condition I do consent. But give me time--you must give me time;" and she added, in a lower tone, "to die."

"You shall have time--ample time. Thanks--thanks, my dear child," said Lord Woodhall, kissing her. But when he withdrew his arms again, Margaret fell senseless on the floor.

The maid, who had been in the room during the whole scene, ran hastily to her mistress's aid; and poor Margaret was removed to her own chamber still in a state from which it was cruelty to rouse her.

"Send for a doctor--bring her to herself!" said the old lord. "I will away as speedily as possible, and see the judge; he has blank pardons in his pocket, they say, ready signed, which he tosses about among boon companions in a drinking bout. I must find him forthwith, though doubtless he is now at his revels. Tell her where I am gone--that will please her."

Thus saying, he sped away; and when Lady Danvers returned, about three quarters of an hour after, with a young man and an elderly woman, she found the room vacant. Inquiring further, and leaving her two companions behind her, she sought out Margaret's chamber. The fair, beautiful girl was lying on the bed, as pale as death, and with her eyes still closed; but Hortensia could see by a tear which trickled through the lids, and gemmed the long, dark lashes, that she had been recalled to sense and suffering.

Her maid was now with her alone, and making a sign to Lady Danvers not to speak aloud, she advanced, and said in a whisper that her poor mistress was better, but that the least effort made her fall into a fainting fit again. In the same tone she communicated to Hortensia all that had occurred.

"Poor girl!" said Hortensia, clasping her hands together, "what hast thou done? They have been very cruel to thee. Thou hast done all to save him thou lovest, but at the expense of peace and happiness, and perhaps life."

It is probable Margaret heard the murmur of her voice; but she stirred not in the least, and Hortensia quitted the room in deep sadness.

CHAPTER XLII

A large table was set in a rich and costly room, and round it were seated a number of persons very dignified in station, but certainly not at that moment very dignified in demeanor. At the head of the table was an elderly gentleman, well fattened and of rubicund face, which had evidently lost none of its roses by the accessories of the meal. This was Mr. Mayor, entertaining the judges at supper. On his right hand sat Lord Chief-justice Jeffries, with his wig a good deal on one side, a curious sort of tightness about one corner of his mouth and a depression of the other corner, as if he had been slightly affected by palsy. There was a merry leer in his eyes, however, and a robustious jollity about his whole appearance, which contrasted strangely with his savage and ferocious look upon the bench. Yes, it did afford a strange contrast; but yet it was nothing, compared with the harsh, jarring discord of his light, licentious levity at the table, when closely opposed to the savage cruelty which occupied the morning. There he was, laughing, and drinking, and jesting, and singing, immediately after having condemned half a score of innocent men to death.

Judges, like undertakers, I believe, get hardened to the idea of death.

"How many are you going to pardon, my lord?" asked the worthy mayor, with a half-suppressed hiccough.

"That depends upon their circumstances, Master Mayor," replied Jeffries, with a broad laugh.

"That young man, I hope," said the good-natured magistrate; "I mean the Mr. Woodhall who was convicted of seeing Monmouth before the rebellion broke out. His case was not half as bad as the rest, and he seemed a fine young fellow."

"His case will be worse before Saturday night," said Jeffries. "A knave--an arrant knave, sir! Why, they tell me his father is not worth five hundred a year. Was there ever such a knave? By God's wounds! the son of such a knave ought to hang for having such a father, and the father ought to hang for having such a son. Ha! what is this? Say I am supping; I will not be disturbed. I have done work enough for one day, and cut out work enough for a few others."

"The lady says she must and will see you, my lord," replied the servant to whom his last words were addressed, and who the moment before had slipped a note into his hand.

"Ha, ha! a lady!" cried Jeffries, with a leer round the table; "we must see the lady. Is she young, fellow? Is she pretty?"

"Quite beautiful, sir," replied the man; "and such a dress!"

"'Twill do--'twill do!" cried the judge; "show her into a private room--quite private, and I will come to her anon. I must steady myself, gentlemen--I must steady myself. I'll even drink a cup of water--that is the most steadying thing I know;" and, after a moment's thought, Jeffries rose and walked out of the room coolly and straightly enough, for it required an infinite quantity of strong drink to produce any thing more in him than a sort of boisterous merriment, in which he strangely forgot all dignity and propriety.

As the reader has probably by this time supposed, the person whom he found waiting for him was Lady Danvers. She was accompanied by her maid, however, and two of her men were stationed at the door of the room.

"My lord," she said, as soon as she entered, "I am glad to see you. You have condemned my young friend, Ralph Woodhall, this day: I come to intercede for him."

"All in vain, my lady--all in vain!" said Jeffries, glancing his eye at the maid-servant. "Found guilty by a jury, he can expect no mercy."

Hortensia had spoken very calmly, and she knew the man too well to let him see any agitation. "Why not?" she asked, in the same quiet tone. "If his guilt were proved, which you, my lord, know quite well it is not, and which I deny, still he would be very much less culpable than any of the others whom you have condemned. You must, and of course will, pardon some, in mere compassion to the executioner. Is it not right, then, to choose the least guilty? Alice, go to the door and stay with the two men; shut the door, remember."

Jeffries grinned; for he saw that Lady Danvers was now coming to the point.

"I do not mean to say," he answered, "that this young man's guilt is quite as atrocious as that of some others, but--"

"The levying of a severe fine," replied Hortensia, "will meet the justice of the case better than execution."

"That may be, ma'am," said Jeffries; "but the law says death."

"One is bound and justified to evade the law in the cause of mercy where law is too severe," replied Hortensia. "You have, my lord, I understand, received from the king, with a view to such very cases as these, a number of pardons signed in blank, in order to prevent a waste of time in referring to him. Now I can see, by what you admit, that you judge this young man is worthy of one of these pardons, and the only question is, what is the fine you think sufficient? If the strict letter of the law prevents you from commuting the sentence openly to a fine, the money can be paid quite privately, justice be satisfied, and yet no deviation from the law appear."

"Madam, they should send you ambassador to the hardest-headed court in Europe," said Jeffries, with a laugh. "The worst feature, however, of this case is, the young man is too poor to pay a fine. There is nothing to levy upon."

"Oh, I beg your pardon," replied Hortensia, "there are the purses of his friends; and let me tell you, my lord, he has many not only rich, but powerful friends. The Duke of Norfolk crossed the whole country four days ago, to give evidence on the trial for murder, and remained in Dorchester till that part of the matter was settled."

"Ay, that's the worst of the whole business," said Jeffries. "Were it not for that, we might content ourselves with levying a fine of ten or twenty thousand pounds--"

"Nay, nay!" exclaimed Hortensia, "say five."

"Ten at the least," said the judge, "ten at the least;" and he shook his head decidedly.

"Well, ten be it," replied the lady. "Do we understand each other?"

"Not quite," replied Jeffries; "for what's the use of saving his head from treason if it is to be touched for murder? Besides, it's only fair to tell you, putting all roundabouts aside, that the king will have Lord Woodhall satisfied in this matter. His son has been killed in a duel of a very irregular kind, and the old man is furious."

"Not so furious as he was," answered Hortensia. "His son has been killed, but not by Ralph Woodhall. The case would have failed against him, my lord, for there is evidence in this town to show that it was impossible he could have been on the spot where the duel took place for at least two hours after the occurrence."

"Ay, I thought there was something of that sort at the bottom of it," said Jeffries; "but what then? He will have to be tried for that, and these things are uncertain, my lady."

"If such evidence is laid before Lord Woodhall as to make him see clearly that the young gentleman is innocent, and he desires to desist from the prosecution, and even joins in our application for pardon in this other case, and if the same evidence convinces the attorney general that there is really no case to go to the jury, is there no means--"

"Oh yes," replied Jeffries, "Mr. Attorney can enter a nolle prosequi at any stage of the proceedings; but do you think that the old lord will really sue for his pardon? I saw him last night, and he was as fierce as ever."

"He did not know any thing of what he now knows, or will know in a few hours," replied Hortensia. "His heart is already melted, and if it is clearly proved to him that Ralph is in truth innocent, he will be the first to apply to the crown himself for a pardon."

A change came over Jeffries's face, and he muttered between his teeth, "We must stop that--that would never do."

Hortensia saw how her words affected him, and she hastened to take advantage of the impression. Leaning a little forward, she spoke a few words to Jeffries in a whisper, to which he replied in the same tone. Then she put some question to him again, and he answered aloud, "Oh, to my man Silas Jones. He was once a Presbyterian knave, but I have converted him into an honest Churchman. He dare not finger any thing that belongs to me; so pay it to him."

"And he will have the pardon ready?" said Hortensia.

"Ay, ay," answered the judge, "by half past nine of the morning; but remember, my lady, I must have Lord Woodhall's approval."

"That shall be done," answered Hortensia; for she had good hope that, even if the old lord remained obdurate, the judge, having been brought thus far, might, by the same means, be brought one step further. "Farewell, my good lord," she added, when about to retire; but Jeffries extended his hand, saying, "Let me kiss that lovely hand, divine Lady Danvers."

She repressed the inclination to shudder, and gave him her hand, over which he bent his head with a look of maudlin admiration.

"That is a lovely ring," said Jeffries, pointing to a remarkably large diamond which she wore upon her middle finger. Hortensia immediately took it off and presented it to him, saying, "Take it, my lord, and wear it in remembrance of this interview, in which you have been induced to show mercy; and whenever you look upon it, let the remembrance produce the same result."

Jeffries took it reverently, and placed it on his fat little finger; but I very much fear that it never reminded him of mercy with any result.

When Hortensia was gone, he returned to the table, and, sitting down by the mayor, soon turned the conversation with the good-natured magistrate to the subject of Ralph Woodhall; for I must pass over all the jests that took place with regard to his interview with a lady, and the allusions to the diamond ring upon his finger, which he rather encouraged than otherwise. Mr. Mayor again urged his remonstrances in regard to Ralph Woodhall, saying, "I do really, my lord, wish you would think of that case."

"Well, well, I will," replied Jeffries, "at your request, Mr. Mayor; but, if you get me to take compassion upon him, your worship will be the first mayor that ever moved George Jeffries."

"Had you not better respite him, my lord?" said the mayor.

"Ay, that can be done to-morrow," said Jeffries, "according as I determine. It won't do him any harm to have one day of hanging, drawing, and quartering. My life for it, he'll be seeing his bowels in the hands of the hangman all night long. But I'll think of it--I'll think of it, Mr. Mayor, for your sake. Now another glass, if you please, and that shall be the last, upon my honor--the last but four. Armitage, you dog, you are as dull as a swine to-night; there's a pardon for you, for that fat Presbyterian knave whom you convicted this morning of buying arms to supply the rebels. The fellow is an armorer by trade; but that makes no difference: he had no business to buy arms when there was rebellion in the land. He's rich, man, he's rich; and, if you understand coining, you may know him into five hundred or a thousand gold pieces, with the effigy of his blessed majesty upon them."

The servant again came in, and whispered something over the back of the lord chief justice's chair. "Who? who?" exclaimed Jeffries, with a scowl.

"Lord Woodhall, my lord," replied the servant, aloud.

"Oh, ask him in, by all means," said the mayor.

"On no account whatever," said Jeffries, rising at once; "this is private business; and I fear me much that it is to move me against your request concerning that young man Ralph. God help me! how we poor sinners are torn to pieces by opposite applications!"

"Attend to mercy, my lord, attend to mercy," said the mayor; but the judge was half way down the room by this time.

Jeffries was learned in the art, in which statesmen of our own day are not unlearned, of making one favor serve three or four applicants. When Lord Woodhall, therefore, urged his request that Ralph might be pardoned,

Jeffries made innumerable difficulties, and seemed, at length, to yield only at the old nobleman's most pressing entreaties. He insisted, at the same time, that Lord Woodhall should undertake to express to the attorney general his full conviction that Ralph had no share in causing the death of his son, and request that he would enter a nolle prosequi when the case came again for trial. "There would be no pretense for pardoning him in this case," said Jeffries, "if we were to have another trial next day, and hang him for murder--waste of parchment, my lord, waste of parchment."

Lord Woodhall agreed to all that he demanded, and obtained, in return, a respite for Ralph before he left this admirable lord chief justice. He went away with a heart wonderfully eased. Four-and-twenty hours before, he could not have imagined that he should have felt any thing like satisfaction at saving the life of Ralph Woodhall; but now his feelings had taken a very different turn. "Every body says he did not do it," he thought; "the Duke of Norfolk says it was impossible. This Lady Danvers too--and the parson--all of them. I do not want to wrong an innocent man; but I will find out the murderer yet, and have vengeance upon him. Well, well, if Ralph is innocent--and I begin to fancy it may be so--he'll marry Lady Danvers, and Margaret will marry Robert, and we might all be happy again--but for the want of poor Henry!"

Poor old man, how completely he had forgotten, or how little must he have ever known of the feelings and passions of youth! The indifference of old age to those things of the heart which make the brightness of active existence, is one of age's greatest evils, considered as a stage of mere mortal life, but is, perhaps, a good preparation for parting with mortal things to enter upon life eternal.

Thus musing, as I have shown, Lord Woodhall approached the door of the inn, over which a great lantern was burning. When his foot was upon the step, a man came out and was passing; but he suddenly stopped, gazed at the old lord, and exclaimed, "Ah, persecutor of my unhappy boy, is that you?"

"Hush, man, hush!" cried Lord Woodhall, grasping old Mr. Woodhall's hand; "I have been in error--you are in error now. I am not persecuting your son--I have a respite for him in my pocket now, and the promise of a pardon."

Old Mr. Woodhall staggered back and would have fallen; but one of Lord Woodhall's servants caught him, and took him into the inn. An agitating scene followed, and Lord Woodhall, who was by nature a good-hearted and kindly man, rejoiced greatly that the life of his own cousin's son was not to be sacrificed. A short time passed in loose and rambling questions and answers; and at length Mr. Woodhall rose to go, saying, "I must see him, my lord, I must see him at once; for he must think that his father has forgotten him, and left him to his fate. I was detained upon the road by accident. But now, my lord, I may carry him good news. Is it not so?"

"You may assure him that he is safe," said the old nobleman. "Here, take the respite with you, man. That will be the best comfort you can give the boy;" and, taking it from his pocket, he put it in Mr. Woodhall's hands.

Engaging one of the horse-boys of the inn to guide him through the streets of a strange town, Ralph Woodhall's father found his way to the jail, and rang the great bell which hung at the gate. A moment after, a little panel, just large enough to frame a man's head, was drawn back, and the face of a jailer appeared behind an iron grating.

"What do you want?" said the man.

Mr. Woodhall explained his business, and demanded to see his son. A rude and abrupt refusal was his only answer. He insisted, and demanded, at all events, to see the governor of the prison. The jailer, however, said sullenly that the governor was absent, that the visiter was behind the hours, and that he should not have admission.

Mr. Woodhall then tried money; but, strange to say, even this proved in vain. The man refused it with real or affected indignation, and seemed about to close the wicket, when Ralph's father announced that he had a respite with him for the prisoner.

"Then hand it in here," said the jailer; "I suppose this means that he will be pardoned."

"Undoubtedly," returned Mr. Woodhall; "therefore there can be no objection to my seeing him."

"I won't break through the rules for any one," said the jailer, doggedly. "The jail is crammed full, and our orders are strict."

Sad and disappointed, Mr. Woodhall handed in the respite, calling up the boy who had accompanied him to witness its delivery, and desiring the jailer to announce the good tidings he bore at once to his son.

The man promised to do so; but, the moment he had retired into his lodge near the gate, he threw the paper upon a shelf with a laugh, saying, "Well, lay thou there. Thou sha'n't stop me getting my fifty pounds. Devil take the judges, they won't let a poor man earn any thing; they pocket it all themselves! I wonder how much this cost. A great deal more than I get, I dare say."

His words may seem somewhat mysterious without explanation, which only can be given by entering one of the prison cells, and displaying what had been passing within about half an hour before.

Ralph Woodhall was sitting alone, about an hour after the judge had passed sentence upon him, with his limbs heavily fettered, and a still heavier weight upon his heart. Strong resolution had borne him up through the terrible scenes which had lately passed; but all the bitterness of parting with life, at the very period of early joy, had been tasted in that last solitary hour. Suddenly the door opened, and a turnkey came in. He carried in his hand a small instrument; and closing the door carefully behind him, he put it in Ralph's hands, saying, in a low tone, and pointing to the fetters, "Work away and get them off. Leave them and the saw behind you."

Ralph gazed at him with astonishment, saying, "What do you mean?"

"Haven't I told you?" said the turnkey. "Hark ye! at one in the morning, be dressed and ready. However hard I lock that door just now, you will find it open then. Walk out. Turn to the right along the passage. You will come to a door; it will be open too. You will find a man beyond it who won't see you. Don't you see him. Walk straight on till you find another man, who'll go on before you. Follow him as far as he goes. There you'll find a horse and your people, and when they've paid the other two hundred, you can ride away."

He waited for no reply, but, turning away from the prisoner, quitted the cell, taking more than ordinary care in locking the door behind him, and making a good deal of noise about it.

On the following day, at about ten minutes before ten o'clock--when a good deal of bustle and excitement was visible in the prison, in consequence of the preparations for bringing the prisoners for trial rapidly into the court--the deputy sheriff presented himself at the gate and demanded to see Mr. Ralph Woodhall, announcing, with an important air, that a free pardon under the broad seal had been received by the high sheriff, and was then in his possession.

"Quick work, Master Deputy," said the turnkey, who was standing beside the porter; "condemned yesterday at seven, sentenced at nine, and pardoned this morning before ten. But come along; you'll like to give him the news yourself, I dare say, for you may get something for your pains. He doesn't want the stuff, and has paid well enough considering. We haven't been in this morning yet, for he said he'd like to sleep till twelve, seeing he'd a hard day's work of it yesterday."

Thus saying, he led him away along the passages of the prison to one of the condemned cells. When he put the key in the door, however, it would not turn, and he exclaimed, with a great oath, "Why, it's unlocked!"

So it proved, and the cell empty.

Nothing could exceed the horror and consternation expressed by the turnkey. He called the watchman who sat in the passage, and insinuated that he had unlocked the door and let the prisoner escape. The watchman repelled the charge with every appearance of indignation, asked how he could unlock the door when he hadn't the keys, and vowed he hadn't left the passage a minute except when he went to call the doctor for John Philips, who had fallen into a fit, and was screaming like a madman.

"Ay, he must have got out just then," said the turnkey. "How he picked the lock I don't know. I locked it fast enough last night, I'm sure."

"I saw and heard you," said the watchman.

"Ay, he's been well supplied from outside," said the turnkey, pointing to the fetters which lay upon the floor of the cell; "you see he has filed the irons right through."

The sheriff's deputy was not altogether satisfied, however. The governor was called; a search was instituted, and a rope-ladder was found thrown over the wall of the prison yard. As a pardon, however, had been received, the governor wisely thought that the less said about the matter the better; and the sheriff's deputy, who was his friend, agreed to take the same view of the case. Their plans were somewhat deranged, indeed, by the arrival of old Mr. Woodhall in the midst of their consultations; but, with great presence of mind, the deputy sheriff asserted boldly that the prisoner he inquired for had been set free upon pardon, and had departed more than an hour ago.

CHAPTER XLIII

Oh the night after Ralph Woodhall's trial for treason, at the end of a lane, which at that time ran at the back of Dorchester jail, stood a man holding the bridles of two horses over his arm. From time to time he looked forward toward the prison, but more frequently kept his eyes fixed upon the ground. At length his sharp ear caught the sound of steps; and shortly after, the figures of two men appeared advancing at a quick pace. The watcher did not move from the spot, but put his hand on the hilt of his sword, and ascertained that it moved easily in the scabbard. The two men he had seen came forward rapidly, and when quite close, one of them said, "Stilling?" in an inquiring tone.

"The same, sir," said the man. "Here, fellow--here are the other two hundred pounds for you; look at it, and count it, if you will."

The third man took a bag which was held out to him, withdrew the shade of a dark lantern, and by its light examined what he had received. He soon saw that the contents of the bag were gold, and, after weighing it in his hand, seemed to be satisfied that the count must be about right.

"I dare say it's all fair," he said, "but I can not stop to count it. Good-night, sir, and good speed to you. You will be far enough by this time to-morrow, I hope."

"That he will," answered Stilling; and, drawing one of the horses forward, while the jailer closed his dark lantern and hurried rapidly away, he continued, "Let us mount and be gone, sir; we ought to be ten leagues at sea before daybreak."

Ralph sprang upon the horse's back, and in a few moments he and Gaunt Stilling were riding away from Dorchester at full speed.

The latter led the way; and very little was said by either for somewhat more than an hour end a half, when Stilling turned to his young master, saying, "We are beyond pursuit, I think, sir. Twenty minutes more will bring us to the boat's side. All is ready and arranged; and they but wait for us, to put off."

"I have much to thank you for, Stilling," replied his master; "but you must have had some assistance from others. Who has furnished you with the means to bribe these men?"

"Faith, no one furnished me with any thing for that purpose," replied Stilling; "but Lady Danvers's steward gave me five hundred pounds, to make all smooth at Bridgewater, when we were going there. I had no scruple in using it now, as I knew she would wish it used; so I paid these knaves three hundred and fifty pounds to let you out, and hired a good lugger for another hundred."

New questions and answers succeeded; and Ralph found that the cause of Stilling's never having returned to the farmhouse at the edge of Sedgemoor, when sent to obtain information, was very simple. He had fallen in with some men of the Tangier regiment, and had been carried to the quarters of Colonel Kirke. That worthy officer had thought fit to detain him, strongly suspecting that he had some design of joining the forces of Monmouth.

"I do not mean to say," continued Stilling, "that I had not a strong inclination to do so; for there was one good stroke I would fain have given in that battle. However, Kirke could prove nothing against me, except that I had made my way straight to the quarters of the king's army, which didn't suit his purpose, otherwise he would have had as much pleasure in hanging his old comrade as any of the poor rebels whom he butchered. He was forced, in the end, to let me go; and the first thing I heard was that you were in Dorchester jail. I took what measures I thought necessary, regarding the first charge against you; but I was quite unprepared for the second--and marvelous well they got it up; so I had nothing for it but to do my best to get you out after condemnation, which, knowing well all the people here in Dorchester, was no very difficult matter."

Less than half an hour more bought the two horsemen to the sea-shore at a spot where the coast was low and sandy; and after riding along for some way, they came upon a small group of fishermen's houses, where lights were still to be seen, and several persons moving about. At some little distance from the shore was a large lug sail-boat of some forty or fifty tons burden, and Ralph and his companion were instantly accosted by one or two of the fishermen, who urged them to hurry their movements, as the tide was going out.

Neither was inclined to make any long delay. Ralph sprang to the ground at once. Stilling gave the horses to one of the men, with injunctions to do with them as they had been directed before, and both entering a little row-boat which lay at the beach, were pushed off by two of the fishermen who accompanied them, and were soon safely on board the lugger. A favorable breeze was blowing, the large, heavy sails were speedily filled, and away the boat went, bounding over the waves, directing her course right toward the coast of France.

It might render the narrative more interesting, perhaps, if I could recall any hair-breadth escapes or marvelous passages in the voyage; but, alas! there were none such to chronicle. The wind was perfectly fair; the water slightly agitated, but not stormy; no king's vessels appeared, to give chase to the little craft; and the only objects they saw, except sea and sky, until they reached the French coast, were several other large fishing-boats like their own, and, just about daybreak, one man-of-war, in the far distance, with all sails set, but steering away from them. She looked like a phantom upon the waters, with her hull below the line of vision, and her sails figured faintly on the distant sky.

Toward the close of the day they reached a little French port; and doubtless it would not be very interesting to the reader to hear all the little difficulties that beset them in making their way to Holland, or how they overcame them. Suffice that they were overcome, and that Ralph and his companion crossed the frontier line in about a fortnight after they had quitted England. They made their way as rapidly as possible to Amsterdam--the Hague not being a place quite safe at that time for refugees from England. Having passed all his early life at college or in the country, Ralph Woodhall only found one person in the city with whom he had any acquaintance. This was a dry, melancholy young man, who had been at Cambridge with him for some time, but had abandoned the Church of England, and adopted the views of the most extreme Calvinists. He was kind in his own way, and Ralph was in need of kindness; but the views of this fellow-collegian were so different from his own that there could be no great companionship between them; and certainly the young Dissenter's conversation was not at all likely to lighten the load of care for any man.

Gaunt Stilling, on the contrary, found numerous acquaintances among the English who had taken refuge at Amsterdam. But both Gaunt Stilling and his master had too many dark and gloomy chambers in the palace of the breast to be willing to admit many to their intimacy. Ralph Woodhall, on his arrival at the Dutch capital, it must be recollected, was in no degree aware that a pardon had been obtained for him in regard to the crime of high treason with which he had been charged; nor did he know that Lord Woodhall, satisfied with his innocence, had ceased to pursue him for the murder of his son. Condemned for one offense which he had never committed; liable to be tried the moment he returned for another of which he was equally innocent; and, moreover, charged with a third, which was little less heinous in the eyes of the court than murder or treason, he saw nothing before him but a long and hopeless exile, the loss of all bright prospects, and the vanishing of all his dreams of love. At the same time, gnawing care preyed upon him. It may easily be supposed that he carried no great sum of money with him. Almost all he possessed had been expended in the prison; the fifty pounds which remained in Gaunt Stilling's hands from the money given by Lady Danvers was nearly exhausted, and coming want stared him in the face. Many an anxious consultation did he hold with Gaunt Stilling as to what was to be done in the circumstances in which they were placed; and but little comfort did he get from the servant, of a kind that could be at all available. Stilling's reply always was, "Oh, you will have money soon, sir, from England, and so shall I. I have taken care to let the people know where we are, and they won't leave us destitute. Your father will take care of you, and I have friends who will look out for me."

"But I can not and will not bear to be a burden upon my father," replied Ralph; "I must seek out some employment here, in the service of the state as a soldier, or in any other capacity for which I may be suited. Methinks I will go to the Hague and see the Prince of Orange. I can show him that I have had no share in this mad insurrection of Monmouth's, and prove my innocence pretty well of all other crime. I have letters, also, for several gentlemen at the Hague from the Duke of Norfolk, and doubtless they will use their influence to obtain for me some employment."

"Wait a little, sir--wait a little," was Gaunt Stilling's reply; "we shall hear something from England soon. There is news that must be sent to me, and that speedily. In the letter that brings them, we shall most likely hear more of those in whom you take an interest."

He was not wrong in his anticipations. Ten days had hardly passed when several letters reached Amsterdam for Ralph, and two for Gaunt Stilling. Ralph's intelligence was joyful on all points but one. The letters conveyed to him information that a full pardon had been obtained for him on the charge of treason; that a nolle prosequi had been entered by the attorney general in regard to the charge for murder; and that Lord Woodhall was fully convinced, from evidence that had been laid before him, of his innocence of the death of Henry Woodhall. But it seemed, from the tenor of all the letters, that a charge still hung over his head of having comforted and assisted a Nonconformist clergyman, and attended a Dissenting conventicle, which might subject him, if he returned unadvisedly, to lengthened imprisonment. Several passages in these letters were somewhat obscure; for his father, by whom one was written, did not seem to be aware that he had made his escape without any knowledge of the pardon, and Hortensia, who wrote to him likewise, though she appeared to have comprehended at once how his flight to Holland had been effected, alluded to the painful and unhappy circumstances in which he was placed in terms which he thought hardly applicable to the mere chance of his being tried for a very inferior offense.

A third letter, which surprised him much, was from his cousin, Lord Coldenham. It was written in a frank, but not cheerful vein, congratulating him on his escape from death, but urging him strongly to return to England immediately. It assigned no motives on the part of the young lord himself for pressing this point so strongly; but the concluding words of the letter were, "For the sake of your own best interests, Ralph--for the sake of your dearest hopes--come, and come directly."

The effect of the intelligence he received upon his mind was to render him thoughtful, but not sad; and he was still hesitating in some degree how he should act, for his father's letter contained a remittance which enabled him to act freely, when Gaunt Stilling joined him with an expression of countenance which puzzled the young gentleman a good deal. His brow was contracted with a heavy frown, but his eyes were bright and sparkling, and there was a quivering sort of eagerness about his lip at every word he spoke, which betrayed no inconsiderable agitation within.

"Well, sir, what news?" he said, abruptly.

Ralph gave him a summary of the intelligence he had received, and the man laughed rather wildly, saying, "Ay--is that all? better news than mine."

"I am sorry to hear that you have had bad tidings," replied Ralph; "I hope they are not of a very serious character."

"Family matters--family matters," answered Gaunt Stilling, walking twice up and down the room. "The old man is ill, and well he may be--a bad complaint, sir--a broken heart."

"I have just been pondering, Stilling," said Ralph, "whether it would be better or not for me to return to England at once. My cousin, Lord Coldenham, urges me strongly to do so, and if I do, we can go together."

"Let me go first, sir," said Gaunt Stilling, quickly and eagerly. "You shall soon hear more from me or of me--more than all the rest have told you, I'll answer for it. As for myself, I must go, and this very day. See what there is written to me;" and he put in Ralph's hand a letter containing the following few words:

"Come back instantly. You are wanted here at once, for the great work which must be done at length. I have refrained too long. I will hesitate no longer. Moraber."

"This is strange," said Ralph, returning the letter.

"Not so strange as some tidings in this letter, sir," said Gaunt Stilling, striking lightly the other he held in his hand. "However, before I go, let me ask you one question, sir, which is of more importance than you may think. I am very bold; but you will pardon me. Are you to be married, as men say, to Lady Danvers?"

"Not the most remote chance of it," replied Ralph. "Have you too, Stilling, been deceived by appearances, the deceitfulness of which none could judge better? Neither Lady Danvers nor myself ever dreamed of such a thing. She knows my heart too well, Stilling."

"Thank you, sir--thank you," said Gaunt Stilling, warmly; "and now good-by."

"But is there such great haste?" said Ralph; "I would fain have an hour or two's time for consideration as to whether I had better accompany you or not."

"Better stay where you are, sir," replied Stilling, "for the present, at least. I would not stop one hour after having received this letter for more than King James could give. I owe this man, sir, a deep debt of gratitude, which must be paid in whatever way he chooses."

"Besides," added Ralph, "I am deeply your debtor, Stilling, and I would fain do something, however little is in my power."

"Never mind that, sir," said Stilling, slowly inclining his head with a very significant gesture; "all debts, to me and from me, will soon be paid. Fare you well, sir; may God speed you better when I have gone from you than you have sped while I have been with you;" and, without further leave-taking, he turned and quitted the room.

There was something very remarkable in his manner, a sort of sharp, wild abruptness, which, in all the variations of his mood, and they had been many, Ralph had never remarked before. He mused over the matter for a moment or two, but we are too apt to look upon the signs of suppressed passion in others as matters of no moment, not seeming to comprehend that where emotion is so strong as to carry with it a sense of the necessity of concealing it, the very temporary resistance with which it meets only seems to concentrate its power, and it bursts forth at length in act because it was denied expression in words.

After thinking over the character and conduct of Gaunt Stilling for a few minutes in silence, Ralph dismissed the subject from his mind, and returned to other thoughts. He wrote to his father, to Hortensia, and to Margaret, without much hope, indeed, of finding an opportunity to forward the letter to her in safety and with secrecy. He wrote, too, to Lord Woodhall, repeating his assurance that he had never drawn his sword against his cousin Henry, and buoying himself up with false and flattering hopes that Margaret might still be his. To Hortensia and his father, he judged it necessary, from the ambiguous expression in their letters, to give a detailed account of his escape, as far as it could be done without committing any of the persons engaged in it, and assuring them both that he had never heard of the pardon till the morning on which he wrote. Lord Coldenham's letter he reserved for further consideration; and a gleam of peaceful hope seemed to break upon him once more, after so many had passed away, overshadowed as soon as seen.

CHAPTER XLIV

Ormebar Castle presented a gay and festive scene--such as had not been beheld within its walls since the time of the first Charles. A number of the neighboring nobility and gentry had been invited to pass a few days there, in a sport already beginning to fall into disuse, although it had been revived for a short time by the favor of Charles the Second. A mew had long been attached to the castle; and the hawks of Ormebar were famous throughout the country. The merry monarch himself had even considered the present of a couple of pair of well-reclaimed birds of that breed as a great gift; and a grand hawking party at Ormebar was sure to attract all that was gay and graceful in the county. Two facts were remarked as strange by the guests: that the young Lord Coldenham was not present at the castle, for which various unsatisfactory reasons were assigned; and that Margaret Woodhall, publicly announced as the affianced bride of her cousin Robert--though in the castle with her father, and appearing occasionally at meal-time in the hall--shared not in any of the sports or amusements which were going on, and when seen, came with a pale cheek and sorrowful brow, self-involved in her own thoughts, and smiling not at the gayest jests or most pleasant amusements. She seemed to take no interest in any thing. She hardly appeared to notice aught around her. She looked like a person walking in a dream, and that a sad one; and vain was every effort to call her attention, or to awaken her interest. Lady Coldenham for several days seemed to take no heed of this conduct--let it pass as if it were undeserving a thought; but at length, one day, as Margaret sat alone in her room, the imperious woman entered, and seated herself with an air of proud disdain.

"I come," she said, "to inquire what you mean, my pretty cousin, by your treatment of my son."

"Me, madam," said Margaret, gazing at her with a look of abhorrence; "I have no particular meaning in my conduct."

"Then I wish you would have," replied Lady Coldenham, bitterly; "and a very different meaning from that which every one puts upon your demeanor. I wish you would mean to please your promised husband--to show him some sort of courtesy, if not respect."

Margaret was roused. "Respect!" she said; "what should I respect in Robert Woodhall?"

"You should respect him whom you have promised to marry," said Lady Coldenham; "you should respect the house from which he springs."

"My promise to marry him," replied Margaret, with cold calmness, "was cruelly wrung from me in a moment of the greatest agony. It is sufficient that I keep it, without exacting more. He can not make me more than his slave. Knowing that I abhorred him, he persisted in a suit which he ought to have felt could only make me abhor him more--obtained from my poor father, by what means I know not, a solemn promise that I should be his--instigated my father to take advantage of the most terrible circumstances to obtain a pledge from me. And now, Lady Coldenham, my father will redeem his vow. I will redeem my pledge. My hand shall be his; the estates, which he covets more than my hand, will be his likewise; but ask nothing further. My heart never can be his--my esteem, my respect, my love, he can never obtain."

"Impudent girl!" exclaimed Lady Coldenham; "this to his mother?"

"Ay, to any one, to every one, to all who question me on the subject," answered Margaret. "I am no longer the timid child whom you once knew, to quail at your presence, and to shrink from your proud eye. You and yours have taken from me all hope and all fear. You have strengthened me by misery. You have made life valueless--death a blessing to be coveted, and not far off, I trust. My father has brought me here, Lady Coldenham, against my will; but I trust at least that the privacy of my own chamber will be allowed to me."

"Good! mighty good!" cried Lady Coldenham, with a scornful laugh. "Now mark me, Mistress Margaret Woodhall, we will tame you a little. You seek, I know, to put off this marriage till the latest possible hour; but as we find that kindness has no effect upon you, we will try sterner measures. We will not allow you to trifle with us; the marriage shall take place soon--immediately."

"That will be as my father shall decide," replied Margaret, in as calm a tone as before. "I have always held that a man, doomed to die, shows himself a coward if he attempts to put off his execution for a moment. You have made me brave, Lady Coldenham; you can not frighten me."

"Ha, ha!" said the old lady, rising with an air of triumph; "lucky that no compulsion will be needed;" and she passed majestically out of the room.

Well might she triumph, for the object of her visit to Margaret was attained with less difficulty than she had expected. No opposition had been shown to a speedy marriage, and she hastened to Lord Woodhall to tell him that his daughter consented.

The old man could hardly believe his ears; but the assurance of Lady Coldenham was strong, and she told him, with a slight gloss, what had passed between her and Margaret.

Robert Woodhall came to her aid, seeming to understand his mother's schemes almost by intuition. Between them both, they soon obtained Lord Woodhall's consent that a very early day should be fixed, and preparations were immediately begun.

Margaret bore up well when the public eye was upon her. She quailed not, she wavered not; no tear was seen to dim her eyelids; not a word of opposition did she utter. Her character seemed to be entirely changed. The frank, simple, timid girl, blooming in rich health, and agitated by manifold emotions, was now the cold, grave, firm, decided woman--pale as monumental marble, and unmoved by any of the passing things of life. A petrifying hand had touched her--that of despair, and she was indeed no longer the same.

Robert Woodhall saw it all--understood it all. But he had no pity: he rejoiced.

Margaret was more alone than ever. She seldom, when she could avoid it, quitted her own room. She left to others all preparations, and only stipulated that the marriage should be performed by the good Irish clergyman who had been for so many years her father's chaplain--who had known her mother, and been the friend of her childhood. She knew that he had many faults; but she knew that he had many virtues too, and she thought that his familiar face would be a comfort and a support to her.

She was sitting alone one day in a little chamber communicating with her bed-room, while all the family and guests were absent on some gay occasion at Dorchester, when her maid announced to her that Doctor M'Feely had come to visit her.

"Bring him hither--bring him hither," cried Margaret, with the first appearance of eagerness she had displayed for many a day. "Here we shall not be interrupted, and I want much to speak with him."

In two minutes more, Doctor M'Feely, with his portly person and buoyant step, swung into the room, and, taking her hands in his, exclaimed, "Ah, my dear child--my dear young lady, that is--I am glad to see you again, but not to see you looking so. Bother it, Mistress Margaret, they have worried all the color out of your cheeks. They used to bloom like a couple of roses in a summer's day, but now they are like lilies in the shade. Well, man's a curious beast! I would not have had a hand in withering those roses to be Archbishop of Canterbury."

"The stem on which they grew will soon wither too," said Margaret, sadly. "The tree is dead at the heart, doctor, and can never bloom again."

"Don't say that, Mistress Margaret--don't say that, my dear child," cried the good parson; "that's just what I came to see you about, with just the least possible hope that one way or another--what between representations and denunciations--oh, that I were but a Roman Catholic, and believed in transubstantiation; wouldn't I curse them from the altar, and put a great seal upon them!--but, as I was saying, I do think something might be done; though what the foul fiend, the man intends to do, I don't know; for your father seems to me like a rock; and as to Robert Woodhall, he is mischief itself, and the more he thinks he vexes you, the more he'll do it. Couldn't you get up early one moonlight morning, my darling, and just make a run of it? There's a young man on the other side of the water who would be glad enough to hold you to his heart, and I'd go over and marry you to prevent mischief."

"Hush, hush, hush!" cried Margaret, clasping her hands wildly. "Oh forbear, forbear, my good friend! No," she continued, "my father has called down the curse of God upon his head if he does not give me to Robert Woodhall. I have consented, in order to save poor Ralph's life; and I will be honest. I will keep my word, though it kill me."

"Ay, but wasn't that word cheated out of you, my darling?" asked the parson, earnestly. "Did they not persuade you that poor Ralph had killed your brother Harry? If they did, I can show you in this paper here that it was one of the biggest lies that ever was told. I may show you the paper, dear Mistress Margaret; for, though it was given to me in confidence--sub sigillo confessionis, as I should say if I were a Romanist--God help the benighted people, and the king at the back of them--I was permitted by the letter to bring it forward, if they tried Ralph for the murder, and to show it to you if need be. Now I say I can prove from this--"

"No need--no need," replied Margaret, laying her hand upon his arm. "There is only one thing you can do for me, and that I wish you much to do. I have never been deceived in regard to Ralph's innocence of my brother's death--I have always done him justice; but I want you to tell him, Doctor M'Feely--I want you to tell him hereafter" (and the tears rolled plentifully down her face) "that Margaret loved him to the last hour she was permitted to love any one on earth. At the altar I renounce all earthly love. The ceremony might as well be my funeral as my marriage, for it consigns my heart to the tomb, and leaves my spirit only to seek its Maker. Thank God, I have wept again! I believe these tears will save my reason."

The good clergyman wept too--wept like a child; but in the midst of his tears, he kept feeling in his pocket till he brought forth an unsealed letter, from the midst of which he took out another paper. "But what answer do you mean to give to this man?" he asked, totally forgetting that poor Margaret knew not who the man was. "He's a strange creature, and deals with the devil, I've little doubt. I spent a couple of hours with him one day, and he told me all manner of things--a learned man, too. I was his match in Latin, but he beat me to mud in Greek; and as to Hebrew and Arabic, Lord ha' mercy upon us!"

"Who--who?" cried Margaret; "do you mean Moraber?"

"Oh, ay, just Moraber," answered the parson; "Moraber's his surname, and Devil, I suppose, is his Christian name, though not a very Christian name either. But here--see what he writes to you here; for I take it for granted it's intended for you, because he told me to give it you;" and he spread out the inner paper before Margaret's eyes.

"Misguided girl!" the paper ran, "you have nearly destroyed your own happiness forever, for want of truth and confidence. Did I not tell you to be true and faithful to the last, and your happiness would be secure? Write me down an answer to these questions:

"Do you still love him whom you loved first?

"Has your heart never swerved from him through vanity, lightness, or caprice?

"Was it solely to save his life that you consented to wed a man whom, if there be any honesty in the heart of woman, you are bound to hate?

"Answer at once, and answer truly."

"Here's a pen and ink, darling," said Doctor M'Feely, bringing the implements for writing from a distant table. "I'll take it upon me that you can answer all the questions handsomely enough; and the man says something about a hope, in his letter to me--though how the devil he found me out, or his little spalpeen of a boy in blue and silver either, I can't tell. He can't have an optic glass that will look all the way from Lincolnshire to Cerne Abbas--to say nothing of the corners it would have to look round."

"I will answer truly at all events," replied Margaret, "be there hope or no hope;" and, taking the pen, she wrote rapidly, "I love him ever. No feeling of my heart has ever swerved from him. It was solely to save his life that I consented to wed a man whom I do hate. This is all true, so help me Heaven at my utmost need."

"There, Doctor M'Feely," she said, "give him that. But it is all in vain. You know the marriage is appointed for Friday next."

"Friday!" said the doctor; "that's an unlucky day, my dear; I never knew any one married on Friday in all my life."

"There never before was such a bridal," said Margaret. "Unlucky! Oh, Doctor M'Feely, if they chose the most unlucky day in all the calendar, they had hardly found one black enough to fit my wedding. I will not be married in mourning," she said, "for it would grieve my father; but I will have no bridal finery; I will not affect to rejoice while my heart is dying."

"Well, I think it would have been but civil," said the doctor, "to have let me know about the Friday."

"Doubtless you will hear of it to-day," replied Margaret. "Originally the day was fixed for the Monday after, but something seems to have affected Lady Coldenham strangely, and she has urged my father to curtail even the short space allowed. To me it is indifferent what is the day of execution. Doubtless Jane Grey shrunk from the block and ax, as I shrink from the altar and the ring; but she met her fate firmly, and so will I. Hark! there is a halloo in the fields; they are coming back. Take the paper, but say I have no hope; that my fate is sealed. Remember to tell Ralph what I have said; and bid him think of me as one dead; for to every thing that makes existence life, I must be dead from the moment the ring is upon my finger."

After a few words more, Doctor M'Feely left her; and in less than a quarter of an hour, the house, so lately silent and solitary, was full of gay sounds and heedless laughter, jarring painfully with the thoughts of the melancholy tenant of that solitary room. Indeed, it seemed as if the whole party, with the exception of Lord Woodhall, had determined to leave the poor girl to her own imaginations. No one came to console or support her; no one even attempted to cheer her by conversation, or to withdraw her from her sad and lonely state. Her father did come to see her, and strove to speak cheerfully; but there was a silent reproach in his daughter's deep gloom which sent him ever away with a heart depressed, and a consciousness that he had destroyed the peace of his only remaining child.

CHAPTER XLV

There were horses and carriages at the door of Ormebar Castle. The court-yard was crowded with servants in all kinds of livery. Lady Coldenham had resolved that the marriage should not want witnesses; and every one of noble blood in the county had been invited. One or two, who had been there the preceding week, asked, as they arrived, whether Lord Coldenham had returned; and though the answer was no, they did not much marvel, for Lady Coldenham was so completely monarch in her own family, that no one could expect she would make any alteration in her arrangements for the pleasure or convenience of a son.

The great hall was thrown open on that inauspicious morning, and richly decorated with evergreens and the few flowers which still lingered after the year's brighter part had passed away. Not less than forty or fifty people were assembled in that hall; but none of the family yet appeared among them, with the exception of Robert Woodhall, who had entered the room, remained for a few minutes, and retired again, explaining that some deeds and other writings had to be signed in the small room hard by, where Lady Coldenham usually received her guests. It is to that room which we must, in the first place, turn our eyes, before we relate what occurred afterward in the hall when the party was setting out for the wedding.

It was a handsome and beautifully decorated chamber, nearly square, with a highly-ornamented ceiling of black oak. It was called in those days the little withdrawing-room, but was at least thirty feet in length, and seven or eight-and-twenty in width. A large table was placed in the middle of the room, and at it was seated old Lady Coldenham, in a large armchair. She was richly attired, and looked in her stern dignity like a queen upon her throne. She had become awfully pale, however, during the last few weeks. The delicate blending of color in her cheek was gone, and the flesh looked not like marble, but wax.

Old Lord Woodhall was seated near, with a nervous, anxious, apprehensive expression of countenance. Two or three lawyers were further down the table, with a number of parchments before them. Robert Woodhall and two of his gay friends, somewhat older than himself--loose, debauched men, with that weak, supercilious expression of countenance which almost always gathers upon the face after a life of promiscuous licentiousness--stood at a little distance from the table on Lord Woodhall's right, while Margaret appeared behind, near a window, leaning heavily on the arm of Hortensia Danvers--the only bridemaid she had chosen, and whom she had persisted in choosing, notwithstanding a cold sneer from Lady Coldenham, and some opposition on the part of the poor girl's father. Hortensia was in a blaze of beauty, and magnificently attired. Her bright eyes were flashing with light, her brow slightly contracted, her beautifully chiseled nostrils expanding like those of a proud horse, and her fine arching lip quivering with feelings of indignation that hardly could be repressed. Her arm passed across her waist, and her hand rested upon poor Margaret's, as she leaned upon her, with a fond and comforting pressure; but her eyes were turned forward toward Lord Woodhall and Lady Coldenham, and seemed to express wonder as well as disgust. Behind her and Margaret stood their two maids, and the faithful old attendant of the unhappy bride often put her handkerchief to her eyes, which bore marks of many tears.

Some conversation took place between the persons seated at the table regarding the contents of the documents before them. There were some points which Lord Woodhall seemed not to comprehend easily, and which the lawyers did not explain clearly.

At length, however, after some minutes had passed in question and answer, the old lord seemed to grow impatient. "Well, give me the pen," he cried; "it does not much matter. I dare say it is all right;" and in a bold, dashing manner, which hardly covered the trembling of his hand, he wrote the word "Woodhall."

"Now, my lady," said one of the lawyers, addressing Lady Coldenham, "you will have the goodness to sign this paper, and your son will sign below."

A slight shade of hesitation seemed to pass across Lady Coldenham's face; and though she took the pen and dipped it in the ink, she held it suspended for a moment ere she wrote her name. The noise, perhaps, of the opening door, which was a little behind her on the left, hurried the act, and the paper was signed.

Robert Woodhall had already advanced to write his name after his mother's, and had received the pen from Lady Coldenham's hand. But at that moment Lord Coldenham himself came forward, and put his brother aside, saying, "Stop a moment, sir."

His tone was so stern and decided that Robert drew back, and Lady Coldenham fixed her eyes upon her eldest son with an expression of fierce but yet apprehensive inquiry, as one may see a chained eagle, when menaced by a child's cane, gaze at him, ready to strike, yet watchful for the blow.

"Nonsense, Coldenham, no trash just now!" cried Robert Woodhall, with an affected laugh.

"Trash, sir!" said Lord Coldenham, in a stern and bitter tone, which he had never assumed in his life before; "do you suppose that I would jest even at a moment like this? I ask you, madam," he continued, turning to his mother, "is this to go on? There stands a poor girl, driven by hard usage to marry a man whom she detests. This marriage has been hurried rapidly forward for fear of the appearance of certain unpleasant impediments. Though I wrote from a distant part of the country, it would seem either that it was not understood how much I knew--or that it was believed I could not get here in time--or that I was supposed to be so base and mean as to conceal facts detrimental to myself which could be beneficial to others. I am here, madam. Those who have so judged me are mistaken. I ask you again, is this to go on?"

"Yes!" said Lady Coldenham, between her closed teeth, grasping tightly the arm of her chair. "Yes, serpent!"

"It shall go on, so help me Heaven!" cried Lord Woodhall; "I have pledged my honor and my word, and no power on earth can shake me. She shall be his, if I live three hours longer. I will not live perjured and forsworn."

"Yes, generous brother," said Robert Woodhall, "it shall go on. That I will maintain with my voice and with my sword."

"Your sword!" said Lord Coldenham, with a bitter sneer. "Those who rest upon that had better ask Sedgemoor of its glory--But tell me, sir, what name are you going to sign to that paper?"

"My own, of course," replied the young man.

"And what is your own?" asked his brother.

"Forbear! forbear!" shrieked Lady Coldenham.

"Forbear!--Have you forborne?" said her son, sternly; and then, turning to Margaret, he took her hand kindly, saying, "Margaret, my dear cousin, I ask you, shall this go on? I tell you, you are in no degree bound to that young man; that he is not what he seems; that he stands before you there, a lie. Speak one word, and I will end it all. I tell you, you are not bound to him."

"I am bound by my promise to my father," replied Margaret, in a low, still, solemn voice.

Lord Woodhall's face had been becoming redder and more red; and as his daughter answered, he exclaimed, "And I say she shall marry him, be he who or what he may;" and he added a fearful oath.

"Well, then, without there!" cried Lord Coldenham, raising his voice high, and the door was immediately partly opened.

"You can not go in there, sir," said a voice, in quick accents, without; "we are ordered to keep every one out but the family."

"Out of my way, knaves!" said a loud, rich, powerful voice, which echoed round and round the room. "Learn that I am master here!" and, at the same moment, the door flew wide open, and two of Lady Coldenham's servants were cast headlong into the room.

Following them, with a firm, calm step, and a brow stern and gloomy, came a man of some sixty years of age, above the ordinary height, powerful in frame, and dignified in carriage. He was richly though somewhat darkly attired, and in his hand he carried a large roll of paper.

All eyes turned in that direction, and Lady Coldenham's with the rest. She uttered no word--no scream; but a low groan escaped her, and her eyes closed.

A multitude of questions were asked, and sudden exclamations uttered.

"Why, that is the old man we saw in Lincolnshire," cried Robert Woodhall.

"God bless my life! why, I recollect you quite well, Sir Robert," said one of the old lawyers sitting at the table.

"Who are you, sir?" demanded old Lord Woodhall, almost fiercely.

"That woman's husband!" replied Moraber, pointing to Lady Coldenham, "otherwise Sir Robert Hardwicke, of Ormebar Castle. Take her away. She has fainted, as well she may, at the sight of one who has forborne too long."

"But you were supposed dead," said the lawyer who had before spoken; "she married under a false impression. She thought you had been killed by the Moors on the coast of Africa."

"She knew that I was a slave of the Moors," replied Sir Robert Hardwicke, "and she amused me with hopes of ransom for three long years after she had married Lord Coldenham, as these loving letters will testify. Then, indeed, she thought me dead; for I discovered the fraud, and suffered the tale of my death in captivity to go forth."

"Then I am Lord Coldenham," exclaimed Robert, with a disgusting laugh of exultation; "for I was born more than four years after my mother's marriage."

"Not so," replied Sir Robert Hardwicke, seating himself in the chair from which Lady Coldenham had just been removed; "your mother's marriage was a fraud, and, as such, invalid altogether."

"We will have proof of that," said Robert Woodhall.

"Were these letters not proof," answered the other, gravely, "the fact of her having a monument erected to a man whom she knew to be living, and having buried therein a wooden figure, pretending it to be a corpse brought from beyond sea, would, methinks, be sufficient. I tell you, sir, and I tell all, that you are simply Robert Ratcliffe--the natural son of Catharine Ratcliffe, Lady Hardwicke, by the Earl of Coldenham. Now let us see whether Lord Woodhall will marry his only child to you or not."

"He promised her to me without reservation," cried Robert, vehemently. "He did it for services I performed to him, unconnected with my birth. He took God to witness--he pledged his honor and his faith--"

"And I will keep them sacredly!" cried Lord Woodhall, after an instant's hesitation. "Margaret, there stands your husband: let us end this scene. The clergyman is waiting. The guests are all prepared. Shuffle those parchments to the dogs. My heiress can build up a new family. It was not his fault if his mother played the fool!"

Margaret pressed her hand upon her brow, for a momentary hope had risen up in her breast but to be extinguished. Lord Woodhall, however, grasped her arm, saying, "Come on."

"Leave her with me, my lord," said Hortensia, sadly; "you go on with him; we will follow."

"Come on, then, Robert," said the old lord, taking the young man's arm. "Sir Robert Hardwicke, we leave you and your wife's eldest son to finish as you please the fine scene you have arranged this day. This one, at least, I will take care of."

"So be it!" said Moraber. "But methinks, in courtesy, I must grace the wedding, seeing it is so joyful a one. Lead on, my lord; and, if the bride comes living from the altar, we will still feast the gay company here, in this place, where one happy marriage was celebrated some thirty years ago. Lead on, my lord, I say."

"I will so," replied Lord Woodhall, sharply. "Come, Margaret: follow close behind."

Thus saying, he walked on with Robert Woodhall, throwing wide the door which led into the great hall beyond.

Margaret followed with a faint step, and a hand which Hortensia felt trembling on her arm.

Lady Danvers whispered to her eagerly, and her last words were, "At the altar--at the very altar! He has no claim; your promise is not to him; you promised to wed Robert Woodhall, not this man."

But still Margaret moved on.

The gay company in the hall separated, making a sort of lane as the bridal party passed, and several voices said, "Health and happiness to the bride and bridegroom!"

But the cheek of Robert Woodhall, which had been flushed with excitement, turned deadly pale a moment or two after he had entered the hall. What was it produced the change? and why did his eyes stare so fixedly forward? There was nothing in the way to the hall door but an old man and a young one. But that young man was taking a step forward, and the old one tried to hold him back in vain.

"Robert Ratcliffe, you are a knave, a liar, a villain, a cheat, a traitor!" said Gaunt Stilling, approaching close to him and striking him a blow.

The ladies scattered back in terror; the gentlemen gazed in surprise without interfering; and Robert, after an instant's hesitation, laid his hand upon his sword and drew it. The moment it was done, Gaunt Stilling's sword was crossed with his blade.

Lord Woodhall and Robert's brother beat up the weapons ere two passes had been exchanged; but as they did so, Robert Woodhall fell back upon the pavement; and then Gaunt Stilling thrust his sword into the sheath, and dropped his hands by his side, for any one to take him who would.

The confusion that succeeded was indescribable. Some rushed round the fallen man and raised him up, gazing on his face, or striving to stanch the bleeding of a small wound on the right side, which would have seemed of no great importance, had not the torrent of gore which poured from it told how deep the avenging blade had gone. Those who gazed upon his face soon saw that the attempt to keep in the flood of life was vain. The unhappy young man's eyes rolled in his head; but they were meaningless--lifeless. Their motion was merely convulsive, as probably were also the gasping efforts he made as if to speak.

Others rushed upon his slayer and seized him roughly, while Stilling's father approached slowly and exclaimed, "Oh, my son, what have you done?"

To the latter he answered sternly, "Avenged my sister, old man--avenged her whom he deceived, and wronged, and killed by falsehood. The serpent, whom your weak compliance with his mother's fraud warmed into venomous power, stung your own child to the death, and your other child has crushed him."

Then turning sharply upon those who had laid hands upon him, he shook them off, saying, "What need to seize a man who seeks not to escape--who is neither ashamed of the deed he has done, nor afraid of its consequences? Stand back, and let me look upon the villain!" and, striding forward, he gazed upon the face of Robert Woodhall, while the dead man's brother supported the flaccid form partly on his knee, and Sir Robert Hardwicke held his hand upon the pulse.

"Ay, young rebel," said Gaunt Stilling, looking sternly in his face, "I warned thee; but thou wouldst not be warned: thou hadst timely notice to forbear--thou hadst timely notice to keep thy word with my poor Kate. But thou must wed a great lady, must thou? Thou must have the broad lands of Woodhall. Thou must leave Kate Stilling to die of grief and shame, after having poisoned her mind against father and brother. But I warned thee--I warned thee long ago; and thou didst contrive, too, to make me take the life of thy noble cousin--believing that one who bore the name of Woodhall was bold enough to fight his rival manfully, and not to put the peril upon another. That is the only thing I regret in life. You stare," he continued sharply, turning to one of the guests; "do you suppose that, standing here, and seeing him be there--a piece of carrion--with his soul fresh flown to another world, whither I must soon follow to stand before the same judgment seat, that I feel the least regret, remorse, or shame for having sent him thither? No, man, no. I am proud of the deed--Society is my debtor--God has taken vengeance by my hand; and only timely did it come. Look at that lady there," and he pointed to Margaret, who stood trembling like an aspen leaf hard by, "trapped to his snares by the most deceitful artifices--loathing him, yet bound to him by lie-obtained promises--on the point of sacrificing happiness, and life itself, rather than break her plighted word.

Look at that old man," and he pointed to Lord Woodhall, "whose heart would have been one everlasting curse--a core of fire in his bosom, if he had been suffered to drag his daughter to the altar to unite her fate to that reprobate. These have I saved by that one blow; but not only these. All you around me owe me much. From such a pitiful villain as this--from such a dark and secret plotter, who did his blackest deeds by other men's hands, no heart is safe, no home is sacred. Hark you, Robert Ratcliffe! I come after you very speedily. Prepare to meet me before the throne of the great Judge--the God who judges the heart, and knows whether mine has been upright and honest, even in this last deed. To Him I appeal my cause; let Him judge between me and thee."

He spoke so vehemently, with such a rapid flow of words and sternness of aspect, that no one even dreamed of interrupting him. All seemed horror-struck--paralyzed, as it is called, by the terrible event which had just taken place and the strong passion of the young man's demeanor.

At length, however, Sir Robert Hardwicke spoke, letting drop Robert Ratcliffe's hand lifeless from his own. "Thou speakest to the dead, unhappy young man," he said. "For many years thou didst my bidding well in every thing. Alas! why didst thou not obey unto the end? But it was thy fate: in vain I sent thee to a foreign land--the doom was to be fulfilled."

"It was my fate," answered Gaunt Stilling, "and I thank God for it! Now take me hence. Put me where you will. I know what I have to undergo, and I will meet it as a man. This heart may throb as if it would burst, but it shall never quail."

They laid hands upon him gently, and led him away unresisting. The corpse of Robert Ratcliffe was taken up by the servants, and removed quietly to another chamber. The guests gazed strangely upon each other; and those the least familiar with the family began to drop away one by one, begging to be excused to Lady Coldenham. These words of ceremony had been repeated once or twice to her eldest son, who had merely bowed coldly, till one flippant woman added, with an inquiring air, "though we have not had the honor of seeing her ladyship."

"There is no such person as Lady Coldenham," said the young man, impatiently; and the news was whispered round that Lady Coldenham was dead, but that this strange family had been going to celebrate the marriage even while she lay a corpse in the house.

There was more truth in the rumor than rumors usually have; for Lady Coldenham never woke completely from the terrible fit of fainting into which she had fallen. She once made an effort, as if to get up from the bed on which they had laid her; and one of the servants raised her suddenly; but she instantly fell back, and expired without a word. This event had already taken place when her son spoke, but he knew it not; and, turning his eyes from the departing guests, he looked round for one who had greatly moved his interest that day.

Margaret was seated by this time in a distant corner of the room, with her head leaning on Hortensia's shoulder, and her handkerchief pressed upon her eyes. The young man approached her kindly (while another and another of the guests took their departure in silence), and said, "Be comforted, Margaret be comforted, my dear cousin--for you are still my cousin Margaret. These are sad and terrible scenes for a young and gentle thing like you; but you have borne yourself nobly and well; and I trust a better Lord Coldenham will console and repay you for all you have suffered on his account."

Margaret started, and gazed in his face.

"Ay, Margaret!" he said. "In the common course of events, Ralph Woodhall will soon be Lord Coldenham, as his father now is. For myself, I am so no longer; and what will become of me I know not. My mother's small property will but be sufficient for herself; but I have my sword unstained, and my heart unburdened, and I too can carve a way for myself in the world."

"Young man," said a voice close to him, while a hand was laid upon his arm, "I have not put you to these bitter trials without motive. You are my son, if you will be so, and heir of all that I possess. Your mother I once loved well, till her imperious temper drove me forth to wander over the world. In her ambition she soon forgot and hated me. I became a captive, a slave, a favorite, a rich merchant, as is often the case in Eastern lands. The liberty which she would not seek for me, I repurchased by my own industry and skill. This estate of Ormebar, good as it is in these lands, is but small to what I possess. If you have lost rank and station, with me you may find affluence and peace; and I promise you, after all I have seen of your noble conduct in such trying circumstances, that you shall ever find the affection of a parent also."

The young man grasped his hand, but bent his head, and something like a tear stained his cheek.

Old Lord Woodhall had remained nearly alone in the middle of the room. Some of the guests had come up and spoken to him ere they departed;

but he seemed hardly to notice or to hear them, remaining with his eyes bent upon the ground and his arms crossed upon his chest. Suddenly something seemed to move him. He strode across the hall with a rapid step, and took Margaret's hands in his.

"Forgive me, my child, forgive me!" he said. "Henceforth your fate is at your own disposal. Your father will never seek to mar it again."

CHAPTER XLVI

In the same cell in Dorchester jail which had first received Ralph Woodhall after his capture, sat Gaunt Stilling on the evening succeeding the events which I have mentioned. He was heavily ironed; but he had a light--a lantern fixed upon the wall at a considerable distance above his head, and by its rays, feeble as they were, he was reading a small book very closely printed. One passage seemed to interest him much, for he read it over three or four times. It contained a curious and somewhat subtle argument, translated from the Italian, concerning the lawfulness of certain actions according to the circumstances in which men are placed, and it ended in a quotation in Latin of the well-known epitaph of Cardinal Brundusinus:

"Excessi è vitæ ærumnis facilisque lubensque

Ne perjora ipsa morte dehinc videam."

He was interrupted before he could go further by the entrance of the chief turnkey, who took especial care to look along the passages before he entered, and then closed the door securely behind him.

"Has the parson come?" asked Stilling, raising his head suddenly.

"No," replied the turnkey: "not yet, Gaunt; but I want to have a little talk with you; and I have brought the light irons, for these are too heavy."

"I care not for them," answered Stilling: "what matters it to me whether they are fight or heavy? Do you suppose I am going to try to escape?"

"No, no, Master Stilling," said the turnkey, "we must have no more escapes."

"Ay," said Gaunt Stilling; "yet I could frighten you into opening that door and letting me out in five minutes."

The turnkey shook his head.

"What! not if I could prove you received eighty pounds out of the three hundred and fifty?"

"You can't prove that," said the turnkey, with a grin.

"You are mistaken," replied Gaunt Stilling. "Every piece was marked in the presence of a witness, and five of them which you spent are easily to be found. There is not one of you--of all the five who shared the money--that is not just as much in my power as I am in yours. If it depended upon my word, that might be nothing; but remember, there are several others in the business, who are now free enough to bear testimony."

"But you are too honorable a man to 'peach," said the turnkey, a good deal frightened.

"Honorable!" said Gaunt Stilling, with a scoff; "but no matter. I don't want to escape, Master Blackstone. I can die one day as well as another, and I do not know any day this last twelvemonth in which I should not have been quite ready to go. Hanging is not unpleasant, they tell me; and, at all events, it must be a great deal better than lying for weeks in a sick-bed, and then going out like the end of a candle."

"I am glad you think so," said the jailer, dryly. "But come, Master Stilling, give me your word of honor that you will not 'peach of us. You know it was only at your request, and because you were an old friend, that we did what we did."

"You have forgotten the three hundred and fifty golden Jacobuses," said Gaunt Stilling, with a laugh. "Well, well, I must have a better room, and that to-night. I must have a better light, and that speedily. I must have a pen and ink, and paper, to write with. I must have a bottle of wine and cold chicken for the parson. It's a long time till the assizes, and I must make myself comfortable."

The turnkey rubbed his head and thought for a moment, for his predicament was somewhat unpleasant. "The best I can do for you to-night, Master Stilling," he said, "is to put you in the little room in the third ward. It has got a good planked floor, and a fire-place. You'll be out of my district, but I'll tell you who has got the keys. It is Jones Barstow--you'll recollect him, I dare say--a green hand, mighty fond of strong waters, which, when he gets enough of them, send him sound to sleep. The governor doesn't put many capitals there, for fear Barstow should let them out--he's such a soft one! But I'll speak with the governor, and get it done for you."

"Very well," answered Stilling; "set about it quick; and remember, I shall look to you, Master Blackstone, for every thing I want."

"In reason--in reason," said the turnkey, and went his way.

The governor made some objections; for, although Barstow, being a distant cousin of his wife's, enjoyed his favor, yet he had but little confidence in him, and Stilling had been represented to him as a resolute, desperate fellow, requiring the strictest watch. The head turnkey overcame his scruples, however, representing that the man had no thought of escape, and adding "that he seemed to think hanging rather pleasant than otherwise."

"Wait till he tries it," said the governor, laughing. "However, if you are sure of him, put him there. I don't mind."

In about half an hour Gaunt Stilling was in a more comfortable room, and in a few minutes after Doctor M'Feely was admitted to him.

"Ah, young man, young man," said the good doctor, "this is a sad pass you've brought yourself to. You go on your own way all your life, and then you send for the parson."

"Sit down, doctor," said Gaunt Stilling, with a look so much gayer than any which Doctor M'Feely had seen upon his countenance when last they met, that the worthy clergyman was both surprised and grieved. Nor was his mind much relieved when Gaunt Stilling went on to say, "I didn't send for you, doctor for the purposes you imagine. I dare say you think I am sorry for what I have done; but there you are mistaken--or that I'm afraid of being hanged; but there you're mistaken again."

"You'll be hanged as sure as a gun, and no help for it, my dear boy," said Doctor M'Feely; "I'll bet you a bottle of it, and let the longest liver drink it."

"I know I shall be hanged," answered Gaunt Stilling; "but what I sent for you for was, that you might take down the whole particulars of every thing that has happened, exactly as it did happen. I am determined to save judge, and jury, and lawyers all sorts of trouble, and I sha'n't give the hangman much either. You've got that paper I sent you. You behaved like an honest man about that, though I believe the law would have had you give it up."

"Well, well, perhaps it might," said the doctor; "but the paper didn't tell much, young man: it only said you killed poor Henry Woodhall in mistake, and that Master Ralph was never back in Norwich that night; but not a word did you say about how it all happened."

"Well, I'll tell you now," replied Gaunt Stilling; "so take your paper and write down my confession; then I will sign it, and you shall witness it."

Doctor M'Feely seated himself at the table, dipped the pen in the ink, and dated the paper, saying quietly, "Don't make it too long, lad--about the length of a sermon will do."

"You shall have a bottle of wine and a chicken when you've done," replied Gaunt Stilling.

"The wine I don't mind," answered the doctor, "but as for the chicken, I've no stomach. The sight of all the passages, and locks, and bolts, and you here in the middle of them, has taken away my appetite; so fire away, my boy, and make haste."

"Young Robert Ratcliffe," said Gaunt Stilling, leaning his head upon his hand, "who always passed for the lawful son of Lord Coldenham--"

"There's another pretty affair!" cried Doctor M'Feely. "Who would ever have thought that that proud old woman was a ---- whew!"

"Never mind her," said Gaunt Stilling; "bad the crow, bad the egg. Put that down. Young Robert Ratcliffe, who passed for Lord Coldenham's lawful son, was an insolent, profligate fellow. He had done much mischief in the village; and when I returned from Tangier, I found him often coming to our house, and seeing my sister Catharine--poor unhappy girl, I came too late! I warned him off--told him I would not have him there, and gave him fair notice I would beat him if he came--punish him if he wronged my sister. My father had been foolish enough to think he would marry her, because she was handsome and well taught, and he had a hold upon the old woman by knowing her secrets. The young man one day, too, said that he would marry her; and that was the poor girl's ruin. I knew better than to believe such nonsense, and opened my father's eyes at length, so that he was as eager to move her out of the way of temptation as I was, and we agreed to bring her here to our relations in Dorset. My uncle met her half way, and she was kept secure enough from that time. But her shame soon became apparent; and when I came over from Norwich to see her, there was no longer any concealment. I had promised revenge, and I resolved to take it. But it was needful to wait my time, when, as if good fortune would have it, chance seemed to throw the opportunity in my way. I heard that there had been a quarrel between young Ralph Woodhall, with whom I was, and Robert Ratcliffe, in the ball-room of the duke's house. I heard that Ralph had dragged him away by the neck from Mistress Margaret when she fainted, and that the villain quitted the room, and sent for his cousin Henry. I did not suspect, at that time, that he was altogether a coward, and naturally thought that a duel would follow. That did not please me; for I wanted to punish him myself; and I would have given a great deal to take Ralph's place; for, though he is a good swordsman, Robert was fencing all his life, and full of tricks. As I suspected, Robert Ratcliffe's servant Roger came twice seeking Ralph Woodhall. The last time he brought a sealed letter. I asked him if it was a challenge, and he said yes; so I naturally thought it came from the man with whom Ralph had quarreled. My master was then absent, gone with Lady Danvers to Thetford, but he was to be back long before night, and I managed to find out, one way or another, that the duel was to take place by moonlight, and without seconds. I got hold of the place too; and a quick thought passed through my mind, that if Ralph did not return, I would take the opportunity myself. I answered, therefore, boldly, that he would be at the place appointed, adding, below my breath, 'or somebody else in his place.' When the knave was gone, I had a strong inclination to look into the letter; but I had heard Ralph speak so highly about the shame of opening letters to other people, that I could not bring my mind to do it. I was uneasy, however, for fear he should come back in time; and I rode after him part of the way toward Thetford. He told me he should certainly be back before night; but they had made so little progress, it was not likely; and I found out from the Duke of Norfolk's servants that they did not intend to let him come back; for that the duke had sent him out of the way to prevent his receiving the challenge. I kept it snug in my pocket, therefore, and returned to Norwich, where I remained in a great fright lest he should come. Night fell again, and at ten o'clock I was upon the ground. Nobody was there; and, sitting down upon a bench, I fell into a doze, out of which a quick step awoke me at length. It was a foggy night, and though the moon gave some light, one could not see a man's face clearly. The man was of the same height, too, as Robert Ratcliffe, dressed much in the same way, and I was hardly awake. His sword was in his hand when first I saw him, and he said, 'Come, no words, sir; draw your sword. On my life, you take it coolly.' There was something in the voice that startled me, though I knew neither of their tongues well; but, as his sword was out, mine was soon out too. We made two or three passes, and he pressed me hard; for I had a doubt, and wanted to be sure. He beat me out from beneath the trees to a place by the side of the basin where there was more light, and then he seemed surprised, and lost his guard just as I was lunging quart over the arm. I had no notion I should hit him; but he did not parry, and the blade went through his body. He was killed in a fair fight, however; and, though it was a mistake, it was no murder. The knave Roger, Robert Ratcliffe's servant, can tell you more as to how his cowardly master got Henry Woodhall to take the burden off his own shoulders."

Doctor M'Feely shook his head: "Whoso sheddeth man's blood, by man shall his blood be shed," he replied. "If this isn't murder, Gaunt Stilling, I should like to know what the devil it is."

"Be that as it may," answered Gaunt Stilling, "I was only the more resolved to have vengeance upon that villain Robert. I went to seek him at Sedgemoor, when I heard he was there; but I was stopped and prevented, and I heard afterward that he had slunk away from the battle. After that," he continued, "I found that poor Master Ralph was in prison, and my heart was torn many ways; for my sister sent for me, and I found her dying. The villain had broken her heart by a letter he wrote her, mocking her claims, and making a scoff of her love. She never took heart again, and died a fortnight after the birth of her child. I was resolved, however, that Ralph should not suffer for my deed, if I could help it, and I wrote that paper and brought it to you. I kept myself out of the way, indeed, because I always thought the time for my vengeance would come; and when I heard in Holland that Robert Ratcliffe was going to marry Margaret Woodhall, to gain all his ends and objects, and, perhaps, in time to become Lord Woodhall, I made up my mind what I would do. I found out Sir Robert Hardwicke, who went so long by the name of Moraber--"

"What could make him take such a heathenish name?" asked Doctor M'Feely. "There is not a Christian letter in it."

"It is but Ormebar turned another way," replied Gaunt Stilling. "But write away, write away. I did not tell Sir Robert all I intended, though he has ever been kind and generous to me. But he seemed to divine a great deal, and cautioned me to beware. He told me that he intended to claim his own--to bring the adulteress to shame, and dispossess the son of Lord Coldenham, giving Ralph his place, because he had loved his mother when she was young. He said that would be punishment enough; and I hesitated a little. I resolved to make sure, however, for I knew him to be soft-hearted; and I went with my father this morning to Ormebar Castle, where Sir Robert had appointed him to come to bear witness. When I saw the villain, however, come out into the hall with Margaret Woodhall to go to the church, my blood seemed to boil up. I had no longer any command over myself, or any scruple; and I killed him. Now don't say a word, good man; there are some offenses that the law does not touch--there are some evils that no law will prevent; I have punished the one, and have stopped the other. That is my only offense, and I am ready to die for it."

"If I put those last words down, they'll twist a cord round your throat to a certainty, Gaunt," said Doctor M'Feely. "Lawyers won't have it that there is any thing law can't do; and they always hang a man who preaches the contrary."

"Put them down, put them down," said Gaunt Stilling; "they will make no difference in my fate. Now give me the paper, and I will sign it--you put your name there."

"We had better have in another witness," suggested Doctor M'Feely; and, calling the turnkey, he made Gaunt Stilling read over the whole paper in the man's presence, and acknowledge its accuracy before he signed his name.

The chicken and the bottle of wine were then brought in; but good Doctor M'Feely was in no mood for either eating or drinking; and after taking one glass to please the prisoner, he retired, promising to visit him again in a couple of days. Some weeks passed without any thing remarkable occurring in Dorchester jail, till an early fall of snow took place; on the morning after which, the room of Gaunt Stilling was found vacant. A plank had been taken up in the floor, and extended from the high window, the bars of which had been wrenched out, to a parapet of the doorkeeper's lodge; thence, for any one to make their escape, a wall some six feet high was to be surmounted, and then a leap of fourteen or fifteen feet into the lane was to be taken. That this had been accomplished was evident by the marks in the snow; and foot-prints, undoubtedly those of Gaunt Stilling, were traced for some way on the Weymouth road, till the marks of traffic effaced them. He was never actually heard of more; but in the fourth year of the reign of King William the Third, some portions of a skeleton, and a complete set of irons covered with rust, were taken out of a deep hole in the River Wey.

CHAPTER XLVII

Two brief scenes more and I have done. The outline of the one probably the imagination of the reader could fill up; the other, however, would require to be pictured more completely.

Let me premise that all applications to King James, for assurance that Ralph Woodhall would not be prosecuted for the events which had taken place at Thetford, were vain, and the king, rampant with his success over Monmouth, only showed a more and more strong determination to persecute all who showed any favors toward Dissenters. In vain Lord Woodhall petitioned. In vain the young man's father, now Lord Coldenham, urged that his son was a steadfast member of the Church, and had only acted from motives of pure humanity. They knew too well what would be the consequence of Ralph's return to England, and both of them at length went over to pass a few months with him in Holland.

When, at length, William of Orange landed on the shores of Great Britain, and marched toward London, one of the most favored officers of his army was the Honorable Colonel Woodhall; and when the crown was placed, by the voice of the people, upon that prince's head, and James himself became an exile, a beautiful and blooming bride sailed gayly over with Queen Mary from Holland, and joined her noble husband at Coldenham Castle. She was beautiful and blooming again; but a certain delicacy of complexion--a want of that high and somewhat rustic health which Margaret Woodhall had once enjoyed, gave her husband some uneasiness, especially as her strength did not seem to increase even in the air of her native land and county. She was very joyous, however, and very happy; and three beautiful babes came as blessings to the household. But no happiness can endure long unalloyed. Within the four years that followed Ralph's marriage, his father and Lord Woodhall both sunk quietly into the grave; and Margaret mourned much for her father. Her color became less vivid, except at night; and she often visited the old monuments in Coldenham church, and gazed at several vacant places, where there was space for a tomb or two more. When people inquired after her health, however, she always said she was very well; and her husband's eye never but once found a sad look upon her face, except when she was mourning for her father. She was at the moment gazing at her children; and when Ralph bent down his head and kissed her cheek, she put her arms round his neck, and whispered a word or two in his ear: "There is one whom I should greatly prefer," she said, in conclusion, "if that should happen--You know whom I mean."

"Hush! hush! dear Margaret," said Ralph; "you grow gloomy here. We must change this scene, and in the softer air and brighter landscapes of Devonshire, find health and spirits for you."

Margaret smiled, and said that was not needful; she only spoke of what might be.

But Ralph carried out his plan, and ere a week was over the whole family were moving gently toward Devonshire.

Suppose two more years over, reader; and you see once more Lord Coldenham, not yet quite nine-and-twenty years of age.

A lady--a very beautiful lady--is seated in a chair where Margaret used to sit. She is in a traveling dress; and one young child, of about eighteen months old, is pressed close to her breast, and playing among her rich brown hair with its little fingers. Three others, somewhat older, are clustering round her, and all their young forgetful faces are raised gladly toward her; but the tears are falling rapidly from her eyes; and even her husband turns away toward the window to conceal a drop that has gathered in his own. The next moment he returned, and clasped her hand in his without uttering a word; and the lady pointed to the children, saying, "These dear ones do not remember, Ralph; and, indeed, how should they; but neither you nor I, my dear husband, can ever forget there has been a Margaret. I will do all I can to supply her place, but that can never be completely."

"God bless you, my Hortensia!" said Ralph, and hurried away from the room.